PRAISE FOR WORKMAN'S COMPLICATION

Immensely entertaining! In the seven years I've been reading and reviewing books for SPR, I'd put Workman's Complication in the top five...It's funny, exciting, insightful, and inventive; the kind of book where you forget you're reading. Get this one!

— SPR

Fully, gloriously self-aware, which is why it works so well! Kate is a wonderfully appealing character. Readers won't be surprised to see that she comes out on top, but they'll rejoice in the humor of her journey.

— KIRKUS REVIEWS

PRAISE FOR WORKMAN'S COMPLICATION

One of those books that makes you cheer for the underdogs!

— BOOKS THAT HOOK

Fast-paced, with a sharpness and wit that all come together to create a thrilling plot. And that end twist... absolutely brilliant!

— REVIEWERS DIGEST

A must read murder mystery! Entertaining, fast-paced, and comical! From the first word to the last I was truly entertained! I immediately fell in love with Kate McCall. I can't wait to read author the sequel!

— EBOOK REVIEW GAL

PRAISE FOR WORKMAN'S COMPLICATION

Cleverly written and highly entertaining! At times raucous, Workman's Complication is shrewdly funny but is also an intriguing mystery, a romance, a family drama, and an addicting tale. I was already chuckling and snorting in merriment during the first chapter.

— BOOKS AND BINDINGS

I can't recollect the last time I laughed out loud this heartily reading a book! Leder's writing is captivating and brilliant. Be it humor or the page-turning suspense, he handles it all with splendid ease. A brilliant read!

— SIMPLIREAD

Witty and hilarious! Highly recommend!

— GEEK HEAVEN

WORKMAN'S COMPLICATION

THE FIRST KATE MCCALL CRIME CAPER

RICH LEDER

LAUGH
RIOT
PRESS

CONTENTS

1

WAY MO' SHEEP

It was harder to sing with the vampire teeth than I thought it would be. I was rehearsing the role of Farina LeBleu, a Cajun vampire trolling the desolate platforms of Grand Central Station by night and selling one-way tickets out of town on the main concourse by day. New Yorkers leaving the station at midnight—Farina had sold them their tickets—were her victims.

That there was a never-ending stream of New Yorkers purchasing one-way, midnight tickets out of town on a daily basis was a hole in the plot that had never been filled. That I was a vampire working in a train station ticket booth *in broad daylight* exclusively selling one-way tickets out of Manhattan was a leap of faith that Dennis, the writer-director, and Posey, the composer-producer, were certain the audience would take once they felt the power of Farina's internal conflict.

My victim was Roger Platt, whose name in the play was Orlando Bilzi. Roger was a twice-divorced, fifty-two-year-old, part-time janitor in a mid-town high-rise. He also sold cars in Queens and delivered frozen shrimp in Staten Island, stitching together enough income to keep acting, although if you asked him, he would say he was an actor and not anything else. At this moment, he was an actor on the verge of hysterics. His face was blown up like a red balloon about to burst. He'd heard me rehearsing the song at the piano earlier. He knew what was coming.

"I am Farina LeBleu," I said, though with the plastic teeth it sounded something like "Siam Hyena Baboon." I stalked Roger around the stage, preparing to pounce. All around us, the late-night lost souls of Grand Central skulked in the shadows, awaiting their cue to join in the closing number of the first act, a barn-burning ballad called "Railroad Street."

It was a lament, "Railroad Street." Farina was a reluctant drinker of blood. Deep in her cold vampire heart, she wanted to sing, dance, and live the life of a cabaret star, but when the sun went down and the ticket booth closed, her thirst overcame her, and she found herself once more on Railroad Street in search of a warm neck.

"You sold me my ticket," Roger said, laughter leaking through his nose. "You're the vampire of Grand Central Station."

"And do you know where we are?" I said, moving in for the kill as Posey played the first notes of the ballad.

Roger was ready to explode but knew his cue, even if what I'd asked had sounded like, "Ann voodoo no hair Eeyore?" His answer would propel us into the song and then all bets would be off. "Railroad Street," he said, already laughing.

"Yes," I sang. "Way Mo' Sheep, Way Mo' Sheep, I'll drink the blood of Way Mo' Sheep."

All the members of The Schmidt and Parker Players stopped acting and started laughing. Roger fell to his knees on the stage, the air gushing out of him. Everyone in the loft lost their minds and busted their guts—except for Dennis and Posey, who stopped playing the piano.

"Kate, when you sing, 'Way Mo' Sheep, Way Mo' Sheep, I'll

drink the blood of Way Mo' Sheep,' the audience is pulled out of the reality of the moment," Dennis said.

He was sixty-two years old, five feet three inches tall in his boots, and as thin and limber as Joel Grey, who he dressed like, looked like, acted like, and sounded like.

"They're with Farina, sweetheart," Dennis said. "They're feeling Farina's pain. They're rooting for Farina to give up her bloodsucking ways and become a nightclub singer, and then, at the first-act curtain, they're wondering, 'Way Mo' Sheep? What does that mean?' They're turning to people in the next seat, people they've never once seen in their entire lives, and asking them, 'Do you know what that means, Way Mo' Sheep, because now I'm confused. Are there sheep in Grand Central Station that I don't know about? Is she asking for more sheep? Why does she want more sheep? Maybe she should stay a vampire after all or become a shepherd. Maybe nightclubs aren't in Farina's future.'"

"It's the teeth, Dennis. I'm still getting used to them. They're on the big side."

"Would you like a moment to adjust them?"

"That would be nice."

"Ten minutes, people."

I stepped off the stage and walked to the bathroom at the far end of the loft, a large, open, industrial space with a rectangular floor plan, fourteen-foot ceilings, and ten-foot windows. There were two rows of steel columns running the length of the room; their dual purpose was to hold up the building and block audience sightlines. The heating and air-conditioning systems were exposed and commercial lighting hung down below the ductwork. Dennis and Posey had inherited a big chunk of change, bought the place, built a stage, and installed theatrical lights, and the D-Cup Musical Theater was born.

It was called the D-Cup because the loft was the third floor of what was once a three-story bra factory. Some of the exposed brick walls still had large, faded pictures of women's torsos wearing old-fashioned brassieres. An industrial elevator with sliding cage doors opened right into the space. A bell rang when it was on its way up, sometimes in the middle of a show. It rang as I walked by.

The former men's room for the bra factory workers (now a unisex facility) was tiled by European immigrants a half-century ago and had two urinals tall enough to stand in, two toilets, and two sinks. Dennis and Posey added a shower.

I shut and locked the door, moved to the sinks, looked in the mirror, adjusted the plastic teeth, put them back in my mouth, bared my fangs, and sang the first lines of the chorus. "Rainbow Seat, Rainbow Seat." *Better*, I thought.

I was in the seventh grade when I dedicated myself to acting. It was after my first musical, *Bye Bye Birdie*, in which I played the role of Kim MacAfee, the lucky girl from Sweet Apple, Ohio, who gets chosen to kiss Conrad Birdie on the Ed Sullivan Show before Birdie heads off to the army. We had sold-out performances with standing ovations every night. So what if it was our parents—I was hooked.

But the acting career path I was planning took a sharp left turn when I got pregnant at sixteen and gave birth to a boy, Matthew, exactly on my seventeenth birthday. The young man who assisted in getting me pregnant left immediately for San Francisco to be, among other things, gay.

I was a seventeen-year-old single mother in Manhattan with my sights set on the stage, which, I figured out fast, was one of the greatest moving targets of all time. Still, I kept aiming for it. I dropped out of high school and went to endless auditions for late-night local television commercials promoting shady used-car dealerships, ambulance-chasing lawyers, desperately empty eateries, and laundry detergent that could remove blood—good news if you were a hit man or a vampire, which, poetically, I now was.

I acted in mini-budget independent horror films and micro-budget experimental plays that included incomprehensible dramas with music, and inconceivable musicals with drama. There were comedies that weren't funny and tragedies that were laugh riots.

Some were paying gigs but not enough of them to keep Matthew and me housed and clothed and fed. So to keep the ship afloat, I went to work.

I worked as a waitress, a trade-show hostess, a secretary, a bartender, an acting coach, a line cook, a bank teller, a lingerie saleswoman, a tour guide, a house painter, a used-book seller, a dating service coordinator, a bagel-maker, a retirement home entertainer, a convenience store clerk, a grocery store checker, a law firm receptionist, a medical office receptionist, a dental office receptionist, a real estate office receptionist, a publishing company receptionist, a computer company receptionist, an advertising company receptionist, a construction company receptionist, an art gallery receptionist, a public relations company receptionist, a fashion company receptionist, an investment company receptionist, a museum security guard, and, for a short but memorable time, an exotic dancer.

I also worked—between gigs, when I had nothing else happening, usually kicking and screaming—for my father's New York City private investigations company, doing surveillance and other PI particulars for Jimmy, my father.

All of which left me, at age forty-five, adjusting plastic vampire teeth in the former men's room of a 1940s bra factory on the last Friday night in July. I put them in my mouth and sang, "Mailroom Pete, Mailroom Pete."

"Kate." It was Posey, knocking at the door.

"Yes, Posey."

She was fifty-five, the spitting image of Liza Minelli, who

she emulated in the same way that her husband channeled Joel Grey. Except for the fact that Posey was perfectly round, there was the constant feeling that we were in a never-ending loop of *Cabaret* as soon as we entered the D-Cup.

"From out here that sounded like Mailroom Pete."

I took the teeth out, reshaped them. "Are you spying on me?"

"Yes and no."

"It can't be both."

"Yes, I'm spying. And no, there's a man here to see you."

"Who is he?" I put the teeth in.

"His name is Barnes."

I sang the chorus. "Fat Toad Creep, Fat Toad Creep."

"That sounded like Fat Toad Creep," Posey said.

I took the teeth out. "Can he wait until after rehearsal?"

"I don't think so, Kate. I'm afraid it's bad news."

"About what?" I said, unlocking and opening the door.

Standing beside Posey was a fire hydrant in a gray suit.

"Your father," Posey said.

2

———

THE BEARER OF BAD NEWS

"Paul Barnes," the fire hydrant said.

He was probably sixty, but his shoulders sagged under the weight of a life much longer. His skin was nearly as gray as his suit, which looked lived-in, more like a second skin than clothing. It was possible he had slept in it. He had the unmistakable aura of unhappy tidings.

"Kate McCall," I said.

"Can we talk in private?" the fire hydrant said. "I think it'd be better."

"For who?" I said.

"All the way around," Barnes said.

"I'll be at the piano," Posey said, and she turned and walked away.

The fire hydrant gestured inside the bathroom. I stepped aside, and he walked in. I shut the door as he took out a pack of unfiltered Camel cigarettes.

"Smoke?" he said.

"No thank you. I'm in the middle of rehearsal. Would you mind making this fast?"

I moved to the mirror and put the fangs in. He walked to the sink and stood beside me, watching me open and close my mouth in various patterns and shapes.

"You might want to sit down. And maybe take the teeth out," he said, gesturing at the toilet directly across from the sink he was now leaning on.

I took the teeth out. "If Jimmy owes you money, you're barking up the wrong tree," I said.

"Your father's dead, Miss McCall. Got himself murdered."

I thought I might hear that sentence one day, but I was even less ready for it than I imagined I would be. I blinked a few times, then walked to one of the toilets, sat down, and gestured at his cigarettes. "I'll take one of those now." Some bad news is simply too big to process right away.

He gave me a Camel, lit it, and moved back to the sink. "I work for Mel Shavelson, your father's attorney. I'm the bearer of bad news. That's my job."

He talked about how my father got himself murdered—something about sticking his nose someplace it had no business being, something else about the police finding him late last night (actually, at three o'clock on Friday morning) tied to a chair in an elevator in an office building, two big fat bullet holes where his eyes used to be—but I wasn't listening.

Instead, I was thinking about the final curtain of the last performance of *Bye Bye Birdie*. My father had given me flowers, handing them to me on the stage while the audience applauded. They were roses from a Korean market and smelled like ginger.

"Shavelson's going to read the will, and you're supposed to be there," Barnes said. He put his cigarette out in the sink, tossed the butt in the trash, and crossed to the toilet, where I sat watching the Camel burn down to my fingers (I don't smoke). He handed me Mel Shavelson's business card and said, "Date and time's on the back. Monday morning, ten thirty."

I took the card, still smelling the ginger roses, grief growing inside me, building, building, getting ready to bust through the wall of shock that had been constructed in the same second the fire hydrant had delivered the bad news, which, as he said, was his job.

"I knew your old man," Barnes said. "He was a hell of a PI." And then he left.

There had been a voicemail for me from a Detective Harriman earlier in the day, but it was just a general "Please call me as soon as possible" sort of message. I had been busy, and usually the police only contacted me to verify something or other about Jimmy getting into trouble on the job. Jimmy always worked that kind of thing out for himself and had told me, "Never cozy up to the cops unless you're impersonating one." I deleted Harriman's message and didn't call him back. Maybe that's what he was going to tell me, that Jimmy had been murdered. Anyway, now Barnes had told me.

I dropped the Camel in the toilet, looked at the card, and wept like a seventh-grade girl.

3

YOU GET THE BOX

Shavelson was sitting at his desk, eating a pastrami sandwich and smoking two cigarettes—one Lucky Strike and one Winston, from different ashtrays—while washing it down with a cup of scalding black coffee and a glass of Johnnie Walker Black on the rocks. It was ten thirty on Monday morning. While he was chewing the pastrami, he took a drag from the Winston. With the food in his mouth. While he was chewing. I had never seen that before.

"You going to cry?" he said, food and coffee and cigarette smoke all mixed in his mouth at once.

"All cried out," I said, lying. I might cry for the rest of my life. Who could tell? It had been a terrible weekend. A trip to the city morgue, a visit to Jimmy's girlfriend's place to retrieve his things, a sad lunch with Matthew to tell him the news, a dozen weepy trips down Memory Lane.

Shavelson was overweight in a way that made it impossible for him to keep his shirt tucked in. His tie was loose at his neck, which was wider than his head, which was as big as the moon. He had dark, unruly hair and small eyes black as ink. He needed a shave. Or maybe he shaved an hour ago and always looked like this. I pegged him for fifty-five years old. Jimmy's will had pastrami stains around the edges.

"I'm going to charge you for this call. Client pays for long distance."

"I'm not your client."

I was sitting in the chair across from his desk. His office was near the corner of Broadway and 98th Street, above Epstein's Deli, a small, smelly storefront in the middle of a two-story building that stretched the length of the whole city block facing Broadway. It was an odd and charmless place for a law office, so it was perfect for him. The room was paneled in dark wood and decorated with framed black-and-white photographs of nude women (surprise!), old-time baseball players, and New York City skyscrapers. There was leather furniture, a big walnut desk and credenza, some file cabinets, a small conference table, a television, and a stuffed Kodiak bear. There were no law diplomas on the walls. No indication that he had ever gone to school anywhere.

"That's what Jimmy used to say." He polished off the last of his sandwich, took a swig of coffee, a gulp of Johnnie Walker, a hit off the Lucky Strike, and punched a button on the speakerphone.

"My name is Mel Shavelson. I'm Jimmy's lawyer. This is the reading of his will. On this conference call right now is his older daughter, Marilyn, in Cleveland, his brother Kevin, in Las Vegas, his Uncle Mike, in Tampa, and his cousin John in San Diego. Sitting in my office is Jimmy's younger daughter, Kate."

"Just because she stayed in New York doesn't mean she should get everything."

That was Marilyn. She was six years older than me, so gone by the time I was pregnant. She went off to Cleveland State and never came home. We were as close as a zebra and a lion. She became a dental hygienist, married a dentist, and had two houses, two cars, two kids, and two dogs, neither of which were trained. The kids, I mean.

"Cleveland, right?" Shavelson said.

"Yes," my sister said.

"You talk again, I'll disconnect you and give your share to the Salvation Army. Understand?"

There was silence for a moment, and then Marilyn said, "Yes."

"That goes for everyone. You're Jimmy's family, not mine, and I don't give a rat's ass about any of you. I got two more wills to do today, plus a shit-storm divorce mediation, so we're going make this short and sweet. Any objections? Don't answer. It's rhetorical. I don't care."

He took a pack of Pall Malls from his pocket and lit one—he now had three different packs of cigarettes on his desk, one from each of them burning in the ashtrays—sucked half of it down, chased it with Johnnie Black, blew hot smoke into the air, and said, "I James Patrick McCall, being of sound mind and sound body, hereby, upon my death, disperse and dispose of my earthly possessions as follows: To my cousin John in San Diego, I leave my blue suit in the hope that he'll wear it and get a job for a change. To my Uncle Mike in Tampa, I leave my Volvo, though I'm leaving the keys to his wife, Bonnie. Sober up, Uncle Mike. To my brother, Kevin, I leave my house in the Poconos. It needs a new roof, but the fishing's good, and all my gear's inside. Catch one for me, Kev."

He paused, sucked down the rest of the Lucky Strike, rubbed it out while finishing the coffee, lit another one, filled his glass with Johnnie, and continued.

"To Marilyn, I leave the only thing she cares about: money. I hereby direct my attorney to sell what's left of my earthly possessions, except for the box, deposit the money in my savings account, and transfer the balance to Marilyn. I hope she buys something that reminds her of me, but I doubt she will."

He took a final drag of the Winston and, with that smoke still in his mouth, immediately hit the Pall Mall. Then he lit another Lucky.

"It is my further wish that my remains be cremated as soon as possible and put in a suitable urn. I'd like there to be a little ceremony, but I'm not too particular about what kind. My final words are just this: Whatever you think you know, you don't. That's the only thing I know."

Shavelson picked up a loose piece of pastrami and dropped it in his mouth. "I took care of the cremation over the weekend, so that concludes my business with all of you. Stay on the line, and my secretary will handle the details. If you have any questions, ask anybody but me."

He clicked off the call, picked up the Pall Mall, and sat back in his chair.

"I get the box?" I said.

"You get the box."

"What's in it?"

"The business. He left you his business. The urn's in there, too. His gun. Some other shit I didn't look at. Don't grill me, all right? I'm not in the mood."

"Jimmy was murdered," I said. "Somebody shot him in the eyes."

"Talk about seeing it coming."

"Any idea who killed him?"

"I narrowed it down to seventy-three people. Ask Harriman; it's his case."

I knew that name. Detective Harriman. I was right. He was calling to tell me about Jimmy. "He's the homicide cop?"

"Thirteenth precinct. My secretary's got his number. She's got the box, too." He gestured at the door while lighting cigarette number six. Another Winston. "Pick it up on your way out."

"That's it?" I said.

"Unless we're on a date."

I stood up and moved to the door, but I turned back to him before I left. "It's your divorce, isn't it? The mediation today?"

"It's a shit storm," he said. "She wants everything, including the bear."

4

THE HOUSE OF EMOTIONAL TICS

THREE THINGS TROUBLED ME AS I TOOK THE M104 BUS DOWN Broadway and transferred at 86th Street to the connecting M86 crosstown through the park on my way home from Shavelson's office. The first thing was that even though the MTA New York City bus system operates the world's largest fleet of buses—close to 4,500 of the things run around the clock to all corners of the five boroughs—I can never get a seat. The second thing was that Jimmy's box wasn't big, and it wasn't heavy. Being a private investigator was Jimmy's whole life, and if that life could fit inside a cardboard box that I could easily hold while standing on two different buses, what did that say about Jimmy? What did it say about his PI business?

I got off the bus at 86th Street and Second Avenue, walked south to 83rd Street, turned left, and continued east to the five-story, walk-up brownstone where I was the resident manager. It was home to as quirky a collection of New Yorkers as was ever assembled. The House of Emotional Tics, I called it.

The building was owned by Dai Ying, a Chinese real estate company with offices in, well, China somewhere. My job was to keep the apartments occupied, collect the rent, deposit the money in a Chinatown bank, and oversee the maintenance and cleaning of the lobby, the laundry room in the basement, and the garden in the back. For these tasks, I received a break in rent. I paid four hundred sixty dollars a month for a two-bedroom railroad flat. For the island of Manhattan, that's the equivalent of free.

I climbed the steps, unlocked and opened the door, moved into the lobby, and let my eyes adjust to the light.

Like the rest of the building, the lobby had a beat-up, 1940s feel to it. The floor was tiled with tiny white, black, and aqua-blue hexagon, mosaic tiles that were faded and worn. Old-style lighting fixtures gave the long, narrow room an amber glow at all hours of the day and night. It was always three-fifteen on a dreary afternoon in that lobby.

The stairs were set along the right-hand wall. To the left was the door to my apartment, 1A. Also to the left, but further down the lobby, were the mailboxes for the building. At the end of the lobby and to the right were the stairs down to the base-ment, home of the laundry room, boiler room, incinerator, backdoor to the garden, and Fu's apartment.

As I stepped into the lobby with Jimmy's box, Fu was mopping the lobby floor, and Ray and Edie Mazzone were retrieving their mail.

"Hi, Fu," I said. "Did you fix Mr. Cutter's toilet?"

"Fu say no," Fu said.

To repaint vacant apartments, shampoo stained carpets, fix leaky faucets, rewire faulty outlets, prune the trees, vacuum the halls, take out the trash, mop the floors, and fix the toilets, Dai Ying sent me Fu Chen.

Fu was forty-two. He was five feet seven inches tall, my height exactly, and as wide as a double doorway. Though he probably weighed two hundred and fifty pounds, there wasn't an ounce of fat on Fu. He was clean-shaven with short, black, spiky hair. His back, chest, arms, legs, and hands were huge.

When I first met him, I imagined he could crush concrete with his fingers. I had since seen him do it.

He arrived at the brownstone two days after I did, speaking exactly six words of English: "Fu say yes," "Fu say no," and the words "you" and "too."

He was a moody man, a criminal back in China sent here on some kind of Asian witness protection program after testifying against the Chinese mafia, for which he was an assassin, or something like that. It was hard to get the facts straight because Fu could only respond with "Fu say yes," or "Fu say no." Conversations that would normally take two minutes took twenty until finally Fu was fed up, and then the conversation ended badly. Fu didn't like me very much, and I didn't like him either.

"Didn't I ask you to fix Mr. Cutter's toilet in 5A?"

"Fu say yes."

"So can you fix it today?"

"Fu say no."

"But it's broken today. What is Mr. Cutter supposed to do without a toilet?" It was a dumb question. Actually, it was a good question, just pointless, since Fu only answered yes or no questions.

"Can you tell me when you're going to fix it?" I said.

"Fu say no."

"Do you want me to call China and tell them you won't fix Mr. Cutter's toilet?"

"Fu say yes."

"Fu you, Fu."

"Fu you, too."

He lifted his mop and bucket and went downstairs, passing the mailboxes without even looking at Ray and Edie, trailing water across the lobby.

"You're dripping, Fu," Edie said as he went by.

"Fu you," Fu said.

"Fu you too, Fu," Edie said.

"It came," Ray said to me, showing off a small package he had taken from the mailbox.

"What's that?" I said, putting Jimmy's box on the ground and unlocking my door.

"The Viagra. I ordered it, and it came. My sexual youth is around the corner."

Ray and Edie Mazzone had owned a small dry cleaning and laundry business on First Avenue and 63rd Street for fifty years. They opened it with their honeymoon money, promising each other they would honeymoon later and then never got around to it. They had no children. Ray was seventy-seven. Edie was seventy-five. He was a disheveled man with a thin nose, thin mustache, thin everything. She was (still) a beauty parlor blonde, always well dressed. He had spent five decades in the back of the store, sucking in dry cleaning chemicals and pressing slacks in the steam. Her station had been the counter, where she was in charge of looking good, tailoring the clothes, and handling the customers. She did the books and the sewing. He did the detergent.

They moved into apartment 2A after their wedding and never left—except to go to their store six days a week, twelve hours a day, fifty-one weeks a year. For one week, Christmas to New Year's, they went to Pittsburgh to visit Edie's family. They sold the store at the same time that Fu and I arrived at the brownstone. Retirement had made Ray a little loopy, or possibly it was the chemicals.

"I can't hear you, Ray," I said. "When you talk about Viagra and sexual youth, my ears automatically disconnect from my brain. It's an animal instinct, like protecting your young."

"That's a good trick, Kate. Can you teach me how to do that one day?" Edie said.

She was wearing a red evening dress with matching shoes. Her hair was done and she had put on makeup. They weren't going anywhere but down one flight of stairs to get their mail, and she was dressed for the opera at Lincoln Center. Ray was wearing baggy slacks with suspenders and a white T-shirt. He had no shoes on. The big toe on his left foot was poking through a hole in his sock.

"If it's true what they say about it, you'll be hearing all kind of things," Ray said, showing me the plastic container of blue pills.

"With all my heart, Ray, I hope not," I said, opening my door and lifting the box.

"I'm going to try it now," he said.

"Don't bother," Edie said, starting for the stairs. "I just got a thirty-six-hour migraine."

"That's a good trick, Edie," I said. "Can you teach me how to do that one day?"

"What's in the box?" Ray said, following his wife up the stairs.

"My father," I said, stepping into my apartment.

"He's a lot smaller than he used to be," I heard Ray say as I shut my door.

5

RULE NUMBER ONE—DON'T DO MURDER

MY APARTMENT WAS A RAILROAD FLAT, LONG AND NARROW, WITH the rooms laid out in a straight line, like the cars of a train, which is where the name came from in the first place. From front to back there was the living room, which had a wide plate-glass window, covered with bars, that looked out on 83rd Street, then my bedroom, then my guest bedroom, which I used as a walk-in (or, actually, walk-through) closet and dressing room, then the dining room, and then the kitchen, which had the same huge plate-glass window as the living room, and the same bars, although it looked out over the garden. The bathroom was a separate room off the kitchen.

There were no windows besides those in the living room and kitchen. You might think it would have been creepy-claustrophobic to live with bars on your windows, and you would be right. But for four hundred and sixty dollars a month, I got used to it.

I had a fair amount of furniture that I'd acquired over the years at thrift stores and sidewalk sales, so my house was full and homey-looking. I have eclectic taste, but it all came together somehow in a French countryside kind of way that was bright and cheery but not overly girly. I'm a good cleaner, but a bit of a pack rat, so though you wouldn't catch any diseases in my house, it was always kind of messy or, in any case, cluttered.

Magazines, books, playbills, programs, posters, stills, scripts, and mementos of my long and unusual acting career were everywhere. Framed photographs of Matthew at momentous events—birthdays, graduations, first steps, first days of school, proms, Little League games—and a few family pictures of Marilyn and me and our parents, before our mother died, covered the walls.

I carried the box into the living room, put it on the coffee table, sat on the sofa, lifted the cordless phone, retrieved the piece of paper Shavelson's secretary had handed me on my way out, and dialed the number for the Thirteenth Precinct. While the phone rang on the other end, I opened the box.

Inside was a bottle of Wild Turkey, Jimmy's ashes in a ceramic urn that looked like a German beer stein with a lid, his .45 automatic Colt pistol (which he rarely carried and, as far as I know, only used once), two boxes of bullets, a sealed manila envelope with my name written on the front, a satellite cell phone, a digital camera that fit easily in the palm of my hand, a very small photo printer, a six-inch restorer's pry bar, two brown, legal-size, expanding envelopes (with an accordion bottom and a flap on top with a cord to keep it shut), one labeled *Closed Cases*, the other *Open Cases*, and an old-fashioned brass nameplate, the kind that's affixed to a door, that read: *McCall & Company, Private Investigations.*

"Thirteenth Precinct. Sergeant Mancuso."

"Detective Harriman, please."

"Hold on."

Years ago, when I was between jobs and short on cash,

Jimmy talked me into getting my New York State private investigator license and working for him part time. The money wasn't bad, so I kept my individual, proprietary license current, which meant I paid the fee every two years and did basic PI work on and off whenever Jimmy needed me—as long as I wasn't otherwise employed and it didn't interfere with my acting career.

And that was the third thing that had troubled me on the bus ride home from Shavelson's office. I was an actor, not a private investigator. I didn't want Jimmy's PI business. Not in a million years. I already had a day job—I was walking dogs through Central Park for Upper East Side investment bankers and advertising executives—and sometimes investigation work meant nights and weekends, and my nights and weekends were spoken for. That's when I rehearsed, took singing, dancing, and acting classes, and lived the life I was meant to live. There was no possibility that I was going to be a private investigator. None. I didn't want Jimmy's brass plate, his camera, his printer, his files, or his gun, especially not his gun. How could he not have known that? What in the world could he have been thinking?

"Mike Harriman."

"Detective Harriman?"

"That's right. Who's this?"

"Kate McCall. Jimmy McCall's daughter. He was murdered last Thursday night. You left me a message. I didn't realize what it was about until late Friday night, and you don't work weekends."

"Try not to. I'm sorry about your father, Miss? Mrs?"

"Kate."

"I'm sorry about your father, Kate."

"Thanks. Do you know who killed him?"

"Not yet. Do you?"

It doesn't take more than two episodes of *Law and Order* to know when you're being interrogated. "No."

"In my file, it says you're a private investigator."

"My father was a private investigator. I'm an actor."

"That's good. Been in anything I would know?"

Of all the questions in the world, that was my least favorite. "It's possible," I said.

I opened the manila envelope and removed the papers that were inside it. There were incorporation transfer documents, official-looking city and state papers, Jimmy's business and individual licenses, and a handwritten letter that started like this: *Jimmy's Rules of Private Investigation for Kate, Rule Number One—Don't do murder. It doesn't pay, and somebody's already dead. Murder leads to more murder. Maybe yours. Don't do it. It's bad for business.*

"I'd like you to come down to the precinct, Kate. We can talk about your father and anything else on your mind."

He had a nice voice, still somewhat smooth. Working for Jimmy, I had spoken with cops plenty of times before, and the older ones had an edge you could hear: disappointment mixed with frustration topped with years of witnessing human trauma and tragedy up close and in person.

"Are you going to question me, Detective?"

"Probably. Are you going to question me?"

"Probably."

"How about tomorrow at ten? My day is full, but I should be able to move some things around."

"My days are full too," I said, "Tuesdays are busy for me. I'm not sure I can make it." I had to adjust things on the fly all the time when I worked for Jimmy, the king of rescheduling, who drove me crazy with last-minute surveillance and other rush-rush private investigation business. I read: *Rule Number Two— Don't trust anybody who lives or works above the twenty-fifth floor.*

"Where's the Thirteenth?" I said.

"21st between Second and Third."

"What floor are you on?"

"Third floor. Homicide."

"See you tomorrow at ten."

He hung up, and I looked at the McCall & Company papers, the expanding envelopes, the Wild Turkey, the .45, the brass plate, and the beer mug urn that held Jimmy's ashes. I took in a deep breath, feeling uncertain and adrift. By the time I let it out, I knew just what I had to do.

6

JIMMY'S WAKE

THERE WAS AN INTERCOM SYSTEM AT THE FRONT DOOR, SO visitors (mainly delivery people) could announce their arrival and tenants could buzz them inside without having to come down to the lobby. There was another intercom by the mailboxes, so the mailman could call upstairs in case there was a package too big for the box or one that needed a signature. I used that intercom whenever I needed to talk to one of the tenants or pass a message along to everyone—if one of the dryers was on the fritz, for instance—or assemble a group for a burial ceremony in the garden, which was the first thing I did after I knew what I had to do.

Being the building manager, I was aware of everyone's schedule, so I knew who would be home at noon on a Monday in August. I stood at the mailbox intercom, Jimmy's box at my feet, the cases, the Colt, the company papers, the brass plate, the Wild Turkey, the Oktoberfest urn—and now my private investigator license—placed inside.

"So you'll come?" I said to Edie.

"Of course we will. We'll change our clothes and be right down."

"What you were wearing was fine," I said, but it was too late. She had already clicked off. She would no doubt be the most overdressed woman at a backyard burial in history. Ray's outfit would be anybody's guess. I took a breath and pushed the button for 5A: Al Cutter's apartment.

"This is Al," Al said.

"It's Kate, Al. My father died. I'm having a burial ceremony in the garden. You're home, so I'm inviting you."

"I'm not home right now, so leave a message, and I'll get back to you as soon as I can."

Al Cutter was a thirty-four-year-old insomniac who, rather than fight it, had decided instead that he would spend the entirety of his life awake. He drove a limo from eight o'clock in the evening until eight o'clock in the morning two nights a week, two more nights he deep-fried donuts at a shop around the corner, and the three remaining nights he hacked or watched TV or both. When the sun was up, he was a global eBay day-trader, trafficking in anything and everything on a massively powerful computer rig constructed with various and sundry eBay-purchased parts so seemingly disparate that only he could wire and work the Frankenstein-like contraption.

"I'm not sure I heard you, Al. Did you say you never wanted to see your newspaper again?"

"I have no toilet. Fu didn't fix it. I'm pissing in empty Gatorade bottles."

"I'm sure you see how that's a bad idea."

"I didn't know your father."

"His name was Jimmy. He was Irish. That's all you need to know."

"If he was Irish, it should be a wake."

"Okay, it's a wake. Be in the garden in five minutes."

"Will there be beer? I went to a wake once, and they had beer."

I looked down at the box. "I have Wild Turkey."

"What about pretzels? They had pretzels at the wake."

"How about Triscuits?"

"Cheez Whiz?"

"Fine. Five minutes, Al."

I clicked off the intercom and hit the button for 4B, the home of Warren White, a sixty-three-year-old, African-American night-shift doorman in an upscale, Third Avenue apartment building. He was a lifelong coin, currency, and stamp collector, which, as he told me on a regular basis, made him one of the very few men on the East Coast who was simultaneously a numismatist, a notaphile, *and* a philatelist. "Watch your mouth, Warren," was my normal response.

"Hello," Warren said.

"Warren, it's Kate. I'm having a wake in the garden."

"Are you dead?"

"No, I'm not dead."

"Then you're not having a wake."

"My father's dead."

"Then he's having a wake."

"Be down here in five minutes, Warren, or you'll be having a wake."

"I'm very busy, Kate. I know you know that I'm one of the very few men on the East Coast who's simultaneously a numismatist, a notaphile, *and* a philatelist."

"Watch your mouth, Warren. I have Wild Turkey, Triscuits, and Cheez Whiz. See you outside in five."

I clicked off the intercom, left the box on the floor, went back inside my apartment, grabbed a stack of Dixie cups, a box of Triscuits, and a can of Cheez Whiz, thought of Jimmy tied to a chair getting shot in the eyes, cried my guts out for fifteen minutes at the kitchen sink, composed myself, rinsed my face, returned to the lobby, put the wake supplies inside the box, carried the thing across the lobby to the stairs that led to the basement, went down the steps, crossed to the door that led to the garden, and walked outside.

Fu was already digging the hole by the elm tree in the far corner of the yard. Al and Warren were watching him. I crossed the brick patio, stepping around the wrought-iron furniture and the rusted Weber grill that Fu had turned into a birdbath, and met them by the tree.

"Thanks for coming," I said, putting the box on the grass.

"I'm bidding on five bins of oversized blue jeans, so let's get this over with," Al said, dropping Visine into his perpetually red eyes. "You're the one who said five minutes."

Al's eye sockets were set deep in his face, which made his nose look long and his ears look large. He was tall, but stoop-shouldered, with dirty-blonde hair that fell scraggily down to his shoulders. You could slide him in an envelope, that's how skinny he was. He never slept, he never ate; he was a mess.

"Is there a market for that?" Warren said.

Warren was short and bald, and a lifetime of sitting in a chair looking at coins, bills, and stamps had left him over-weight as well. I handed him a Dixie cup.

"You're my first customer," Al said.

Al was not a nice man. Or maybe he was, but that part of him was lost long ago in the absolute exhaustion of a life lived without rest. I gave him a Dixie cup too.

"Testy today, Al," Warren said. "Didn't you sleep well? You don't look rested. Long night?"

Warren wasn't a particularly nice man either. Forty-five years of opening doors for people who wouldn't give him the time of day if they were wearing two watches had worn his patience and self-esteem thin. Add to that the fact that he and Al, poster boys for the love-hate best-friends club, bickered and squabbled like emotionally co-dependent spinster aunts, and I knew Jimmy's wake would be more unpleasant than it had to be.

"Cheez Whiz for Al," I said, handing the can to Al, "and Triscuits for Warren. You're going to have to work together if you're going to eat." I gave Warren the box of Triscuits, poured Wild Turkey into their Dixie cups, and turned to Fu.

The full-sized shovel looked like a toy in his massive hands. With ease, he had dug a perfectly square hole for Jimmy's box. The thing that I knew I had to do first was say goodbye to Jimmy and his PI business for good. I put my private investigator license in the box, too, as a metaphor for burying the past and also so that something of mine, something Jimmy and I did together, would be with him forever.

I didn't offer Fu a Dixie cup of Wild Turkey because I knew he didn't drink, an incongruous characteristic for a Chinese mob assassin. Another odd thing was Fu's affection for birds. He loved birds. He had taken the rusted Weber grill, unused for a decade, turned it into a serene little birdbath, and spent hours in the yard watching the robins, orioles, blue jays, sparrows, and even hummingbirds play in the water. Like most New Yorkers, he had come to hate pigeons, so they weren't welcome in our brownstone garden. Remarkably, Fu had found a way to keep the rats-with-wings off the premises: an ancient, mystical Chinese trifecta that involved smashing them with a shovel, shooting them with a pellet gun, and poisoning them with tainted birdseed.

"Ray and Edie are coming," I said. "But why don't we start with a toast?" I poured myself a shot of Wild Turkey. Warren and Al had worked out a truce so they could eat Triscuits and Cheez Whiz.

"Go for it," Warren said.

"To Jimmy," I said, glancing down at Fu's hole. "He taught me how to box and throw a baseball like a boy. He came to every show he could and never gave me a bad review."

"To Jimmy," Al said.

"The best of the best," I said. And we all drank.

"How'd he die?" Warren said.

"He was murdered. Somebody shot him up close in the eyeballs," I said.

"What kind of crazy asshole would do that?" Al said.

"I don't know," I said.

"You going to find out?" Warren said.

"Yeah," Al said. "You're a private investigator. You should find the dude who whacked your father and string him up by the short hairs."

"I'm not a private investigator. I'm an actor," I said. "I'm burying my license with Jimmy. That's part of the wake."

"I saw you last night on that muffler commercial at four in the morning. No offense, but don't quit your day job," Al said.

"My day job is dog walking," I said.

"That's the one you should quit," Warren said. "Scooping up all that crap... being a PI's got to be better than that."

"Here we come, Kate, and we're bringing this nice man with us," Edie called, as she stepped outside.

She had put on a black evening gown that was covered with sequins and sparkled in the sunlight. To match the dress, she had covered herself from head to toe in jewelry, including a tiara. Ray was right behind her. He had not changed his clothes, but he had slid into his slippers, tied a tie over his T-shirt, and put a Panama hat on his head. Behind Ray was a man I had never seen before. He carried a large envelope that, in a manner of speaking, had my name on it.

7

——————

TO JIMMY

T HEY CROSSED THE PATIO AND THE GRASS AND ARRIVED AT THE elm tree. Ray glanced down at Fu's hole and Jimmy's box. "Hell of thing to bury your old man in a cardboard coffin. You're not worried about worms?" he said.

"They cremated him, Raymond," Edie said. "Ashes to ashes, dust to dust."

I handed Ray and Edie Dixie cups. And then I gave one to the man I'd never seen. "I'm Kate McCall," I said. "This is my father's wake."

"I'm Teddy Barkowski," the man said, holding up the envelope. "This is the workman's comp case that's going to put me in the poorhouse."

"I'm sorry?" I said, pouring everyone a Dixie cup of Jimmy's Wild Turkey.

"Me too," Barkowski said.

"I meant, 'What are you talking about?'" I said.

Barkowski was shorter than me by an inch, so five-six, and about as wide as he was tall, though not nearly as wide as Fu, who was standing by the hole near the elm, relaxed but with a subtle muscular tension in his arms, holding the shovel as if he would whack the guy like a trespassing pigeon if things got out of hand.

"Workman's compensation," he said. "This guy's playing me for ten million bucks I don't have. Says he fell off the scaffolding of a job I'm doing on MacDougal. Says he hurt his back so bad, he can never work again."

"I thought the point of workman's comp was benefits but no lawsuits," Al said.

"You can't sue your employer. That's the workman's compensation part," Barkowski said. "This guy's employed by one of my subs. He's not my employee."

"That's the workman's complication part," I said.

"Bingo," Barkowski said. "New York labor law says he can sue third parties under certain conditions."

"Like falling off scaffolding?" Warren said.

Barkowski nodded sadly. "Just like it. He's suing the owner and the general contractor, which, you probably figured out, is me."

"What's his claim?" Ray said.

"Pain and suffering, negligence, some other bad-sounding legal lingo you never want to hear your whole life."

"Don't you have insurance for that, Mr. Barkowski?" Edie said.

"Liability, sure I do," Barkowski said. "But you got to be a rocket scientist to understand that stuff. My premiums are through the roof. To keep them on this planet, I got deductibles as big as Baltimore. There's no way I can pay them. Everybody's got a sad story. That's mine."

Then he turned to me.

"I got triplets. Four-and-a-half months old. Cost me a hundred grand. Plus I got two kids in college. You know what tuition is these days? I got employees, business loans, school loans, mortgages, second mortgages, wraparounds...it's a big freaking nut. His doctor will testify against my doctor, it'll all be a pile of crap, and in the end, he'll win. So I'll settle, and he'll still win. Either way, I'll lose my house, I'll live in the van with the babies, my premiums will go straight to Mars, I won't be able to afford insurance, I'll never work again as a contractor, and I'll end up a Walmart greeter eating dog food out of a dumpster like Nick Nolte."

"I just saw that movie on cable. Four in the morning," Al said. "I was up."

"It's not so much for me," Barkowski said, "it's for the babies. Jesus, they didn't do nothing. Eat, puke, and shit, that's pretty much where they are."

He was probably sixty years old. I had the feeling the triplets were part of his second family, the children of Barkowski and his trophy wife, who was no doubt considerably younger and who probably wanted kids before the builder got too old to help her change diapers. Whoever she was, she and Barkowski had found a way to have three at the same time, a little surprise that had likely set the builder's bank account back twenty years. Anyway, Barkowski wasn't kidding about this being for the babies. There was fear in his eyes. The fear of failing his children. I knew that look inside out.

"What are you doing here?" I said.

"He just told you, Kate," Edie said, gesturing at Barkowski's envelope. "That man fell off his scaffolding and is suing him for ten million dollars."

"*Says* he fell," Barkowski said. "No one was there. No witnesses."

"I mean why are you *here*?" I said. "At my father's wake?"

"Shavelson sent me. Said you were a PI. Said this was your kind of case. Said you could help me prove the guy's running a scam."

My jaw fell open, but nothing came out.

"Can we drink this yet?" Al said. "I got Triscuit mouth."

"Not without saying something about Jimmy. You have to have a toast at a wake if you want to drink," Warren said.

"He fits in that box now, that's one thing about him," Ray said. "When he was alive, he never would've fit."

"To Kate's father, a man who, all his life, never would have fit in a small cardboard box," Edie said.

"Good enough for me," Al said and downed his shot.

Warren, Edie, and Ray downed their shots, too. So did Barkowski. I drained my Dixie cup and poured everyone another round.

"My father was the private investigator. Not me," I said. I had only done it because Jimmy asked me to.

"That's not what Shavelson told me," Barkowski said. "Shavelson said you had your license and now you owned the company. He said you were the man, so to speak."

Fu opened Jimmy's box and removed the brass plate—*McCall & Company, Private Investigations*—and held it and my PI license up for everyone to see.

"I have to agree with Mr. Barkowski and this Shavelson person," Edie said. "You're the man."

"I'm not the man," I said.

"Fu's got the proof," Warren said.

"Fu you, Fu," I said.

"Fu you, too," Fu said.

"So you'll do it?" Barkowski said to me.

"Not so fast," Warren said.

"What's it pay, Teddy?" Al said. "Kate's not working this case for peanuts."

"Kate's not working this case at all," I said to them. "Kate's in rehearsals. Kate's burying her license in the ground with her father's ashes. What do you think you're doing?"

"We're negotiating. It's what your old man would've done," Ray said.

"He would've driven a hard bargain, Kate," Edie said.

"To Jimmy," Warren said. "He never settled."

"To Jimmy," everyone said and threw their shots down.

None of these people knew my father. They had no idea whatsoever whether or not he would have settled. But it was a toast. I drank too and refilled the Dixie cups.

"Do you have a price in mind, Mr. Barkowski?" Edie said.

"Everybody has a price, Edith," Ray said.

"I'll bet Jimmy had a price," Al said.

"You know he did," Warren said. "Jimmy's price was written in stone."

"Shavelson said I should offer two hundred bucks a day plus expenses. He said that was fair."

"Sorry, Teddy. We'd like to help you out here, get this con man off your back, but two bills won't cut it," Al said.

"It's what I can afford right now," Barkowski said.

"That's too bad. Plenty of PIs make more than that," Warren said.

"I'll bet Jimmy made more than that," Ray said.

"To Jimmy, who probably made three bills a day," Al said.

"To Jimmy," we all said and downed our shots.

Aside from the surreal conversation, it was almost an actual wake. I refilled the Dixie cups.

"Anyway, bad luck, Barkowski," Warren said.

"Thanks for coming, though," Al said.

"But Shavelson said she'd do it," Barkowski said.

"She won't do it," Warren said.

"There's no way she'll do it," Ray said

"She absolutely won't do it," Edie said.

"I'll do it," I said.

Like most actors I knew, money was an issue for me—the issue being I never had enough of it to catch my breath. Debt is as American as cheeseburgers, and I had accrued my share, thank you very much, Mr. Visa. I made much less than two hundred dollars a day walking dogs. Plus, Warren was right;

cleaning up multiple piles of crap for canines that don't belong to you is no walk in the park, even if you're walking in the park.

It came down to one question: Was I an actor who made two hundred dollars a day plus expenses, or was I an actor who picked up dog shit? I would take this one case, put some money in the bank, and then I would bury Jimmy under the elm tree and be done with private investigating for good.

"To Jimmy," Al said, "who would've held out for three bills."

"To Jimmy," we all said.

8

NEVER KISS A COP ON THE
FIRST DATE

It was late Tuesday morning. We were in a small interrogation office on the third floor, the homicide floor, of the Thirteenth Precinct, an eight-story building located on 21st Street between Second and Third Avenues. We had been here for more than an hour.

It would have made their lives much easier if I had turned out to be the psychopathic daughter who blamed her father for everything and killed him because mysterious voices had told me to. But I was at a *Blood Song and Dance* rehearsal on Thursday night until eleven, and then I went to an all-night Mexican place near the D-Cup with a group of the Schmidt and Parker Players. We drank Tecate in cans and ate huevos rancheros until three in the morning on Friday, exactly the time the security guard at the Monument Life Insurance office building on 23rd and Broadway discovered Jimmy's seated and eyeless dead body in the elevator. My alibi checked out.

I didn't kill Jimmy, and my son was an up-and-coming assistant district attorney in the borough of Manhattan. Detective Mike Harriman and his partner, Lewis Logan, accepted these facts with varying degrees of displeasure.

Harriman was the handsome one. He was forty years old, about six feet tall, and built like a triathlete, muscular but thin and wiry, as if he could run and swim and bike all day with ease. He had cobalt-blue eyes that could melt glass and brown hair just long enough to make him look a little like a rebel. He wore a nicely tailored suit and a tie that was loose around his neck. He had a killer smile that never betrayed the seriousness with which he took his job. It was like being interrogated by Steve McQueen.

Lewis Logan, on the other hand, was a crusty, longtime homicide cop who, with every ounce and fiber of his being, put out the following vibration: I don't believe a goddamn thing anybody ever says, and that includes you and the fucking horse you rode in on. He was fifty-eight, about five foot ten, and in good shape for his age. Jimmy once told me homicide cops were rarely the fat guys on the squad. He said it had to do with their awareness that life was shorter than most people realized.

"So if it wasn't me, who was it?" I said, taking a drink of the worst cup of coffee I had ever tasted in my life. "Didn't you canvas the building?"

"Still canvassing," Harriman said. "Uniforms and crime scene guys are in there as we speak."

"You ever been in the Monument Life building?" Logan said.

"No," I said.

"Monument takes twelve floors, block to block. Eighteen hundred people work there, every one of them either selling policies or processing claims. Counting money is what the life insurance business comes down to," Logan said.

"Counting it and keeping it," Harriman said.

"The other twenty floors are lawyers and accountants, financial advisors, real estate investors, bond brokers, commodity traders, architects, importers, exporters, middle-men, managers, and marketers," Logan said. "In other words, another three thousand or so of the white collar crowd. That's at least forty-eight hundred people going in and out of that building on a daily basis, not including the messengers, mailmen, and delivery boys buzzing back and forth like flies on feces all day long."

"Plus building maintenance and management," Harriman said. "And security."

"The one thing they all got in common, except security, is that they're out of the building by seven, eight, nine o'clock latest. Most of them call it a day by five or six. You got a feel for where I'm going with this, Miss McCall?" Logan said.

"Jimmy was killed around midnight," I said.

"You see that, Mike? She really is a private eye," Logan said.

"I'm an actor," I said. "Not a private eye."

"She did tell me she was an actor, Lew," Harriman said.

"Who isn't?" Logan said. "Either way, I got one question for you: In what universe do you suppose NYPD Homicide has the money, manpower, or motivation to ad infinitum interrogate all forty-eight hundred Monument Life Insurance building occupants, none of who were there to witness the murder for which we have exactly no leads or evidence, physical or otherwise, with which to begin a homicide investigation?"

"It could have been any one of them for any reason," I said.

"Or none of them for no reason," Logan said. "The point is, you need to tell us what your father was doing in that building that encouraged someone to tie him to a chair, blow his eyes—not to mention his brains—out the back of his head, and then send him down to the lobby for no apparent explanation other than to mess with our minds."

"I wish I could help you," I said. Barnes had it right in the D-Cup bathroom—sticking his nose someplace it had no business being, that's what Jimmy was doing in the Monument Life Insurance building on a Thursday at midnight.

"Go ahead, Miss McCall," Logan said, leaning over the table

so his face was even with mine. "Play it that way if you want to. But keep this in mind: You may have an alibi, but you are now on my shit list. I'll be watching you."

"That's over the line, Lew. She's his daughter," Harriman said. "Her kid's a DA."

"You know what's over the line, Mike? She's his daughter, her kid's a DA, and she won't play ball."

And then he left the room, shutting the door hard behind him.

"He doesn't care much for private investigators," Harriman said.

"No kidding?" I said.

"He's frustrated because we've got nowhere solid to start. We spoke to Shavelson. We know you inherited the business and have your license. Lew was thinking, since it was your father, since your son was on our side, that you would tell us what cases Jimmy was working, give us a reason for him to be in that building. I guess he left it to me to say, 'Please.'"

"This is good cop-bad cop, isn't it?"

He smiled, and I thought, *this man has broken a million hearts.*

"Only if it's working," he said.

I smiled, too. "How could there be nowhere to start? What about the guards?"

"Eight during the day, four at night. We showed them all a photograph of your father. None of them had ever seen him in the building. Aside from finding him in the elevator at three in the morning, they didn't hear or see anything."

"Cameras?"

"Off line. Under repair."

"What about the cleaning crew?"

"Less than nothing."

"What about the elevator itself? There had to be something there."

"You'd think so. But there were no prints, no fibers, no foreign substances, and no bullets, just a guy with his eyes blown out. And blood. There was blood all over him, all of it his, but no splatter on the elevator walls or floor. Crime scene's going through the hallways and elevator lobbies on every floor. They're not going to find anything."

"Because Jimmy wasn't killed there," I said. "That's why there was no blood in the elevator. That's why there were no bullets."

"That's why there were no bullets," Harriman said.

"So you really don't know anything."

"I know one thing," he said. "It was a professional job. Somebody connected with that building wanted to send a message to anybody even thinking about looking around in there."

"And that message is?"

"This will be the last place you ever look."

His eyes are so damn blue, I thought. But was I thinking that to distract myself from picturing Jimmy in the elevator, or because his eyes were so damn blue?

"You think it was the mob?" I said.

"No. The mob is loud and messy. All kinds of evidence screaming, 'Look at me...me first,' soon as you walk in. This was clean and quiet, professional all the way. Somebody was paid a hell of a lot of money to make no mistakes. And guess what? They didn't."

"Do you know who?"

"I have ideas."

"Would you like to share them with the rest of the class?"

"Would you like to tell me what your father was doing in the building?"

Jimmy's Rules of Private Investigation for Kate, Rule Number Three popped into my head: *never kiss a cop on the first date.*

"Can I see the crime scene first?" I said.

He sat back and smiled again. I noticed he wasn't wearing a wedding ring. I'm sure he noticed that I wasn't either because he looked directly at my left hand and then into my eyes.

"A question like that makes me think you're going to investigate the murder all by yourself. That kind of uncooperative behavior will piss off most of the detectives I know. It'll send Lew through the roof."

"Call it closure," I said.

"Call it anything you want. You still didn't answer the question."

"Neither did you."

"No," he said. "You can't see the crime scene until we get a sense that you're going to cooperate. It's general NYPD policy not to help an inexperienced private investigator run around the city looking to avenge her father's murder and then kill the wrong guy, or get herself killed, in the process. Especially when she's the mother of an assistant DA. You can see how that head-line could come back to haunt us."

The fact that Matthew was a city prosecutor didn't change things for me or, more importantly, for Jimmy. "I'm not planning to avenge my father's death," I said, looking into Harriman's eyes while Logan, no doubt, watched me from behind the one-way glass. First things first, I wanted to see where Jimmy was killed. After that, I would reassess.

"I want to believe you..." Harriman said.

"But."

He smiled an effortless, stop-traffic smile. "But you're an actor."

I stood up and grabbed my purse; it was time to go. I had business that afternoon on the Upper West Side and needed to get back to the House of Emotional Tics to change. Not to mention Harriman said I had lied, or I would lie, or I was lying, or all of the above. Either way, he had called me a liar to my face and was trying to charm his way through it. It must have worked. Though I should have been pissed off, I returned his smile instead.

"Detective Harriman, that's the nicest thing you said to me all morning."

9

———————

QUITE THE WARDROBE WAREHOUSE

I COULDN'T HELP HARRIMAN AND LOGAN FOR TWO REASONS. First, I hadn't read Jimmy's case files yet and didn't know what was in them, and, second, Jimmy's cases were none of their business.

People hire a PI because they're looking to keep their affairs quiet. That's why it's called a *private* investigation—privacy being the key concept as far the investigation goes. Whatever their sordid reasons may be, clients count on the privacy part of the equation to keep those reasons secret. It's the confidential nature of the client-private investigator relationship that attracts them in the first place. That's why they're willing to pay two hundred dollars a day plus expenses. If, instead, they want to save their money, they can always contact a *public* investigator, also known as a cop.

On the 6 train home from the Thirteenth, I decided that despite my reservations about getting involved in Jimmy's business, I would have to read his cases carefully to find out what he was doing in the Monument Life building at midnight. As I walked from the 86th-and-Lexington subway station to the House of Emotional Tics on 83rd, I concluded that no matter what those cases revealed, I wasn't telling the detectives anything until I saw the murder scene. And, as I went into my apartment and headed straight for my closet, I promised myself (and, really, Jimmy) that even after I read the files and saw the murder scene, I wouldn't willingly compromise his clients. Harriman's eyes weren't that blue.

Between my bedroom and the dining room was the second bedroom, which I had turned entirely into a closet. Every inch of wall space was covered with shelves interspersed with dressers, a large armoire, and, to the left, a low-sitting vanity table with drawers on both sides of the makeup workspace, a huge mirror, and plenty of lighting.

I wasn't particularly a clothes hound. I was a comfortable-blue-jeans and soft-sweater girl at heart, maybe with black ankle boots, or slip-on leather Keds, with Ray-bans on a sunny summer day. But, like most women everywhere, I enjoyed dressing up sometimes too. I owned a fair amount of fashion-able designer apparel, most of it purchased over the years for one employment situation or another, not that I minded wearing any of it whenever I was the mood. I was living in Manhattan, after all.

My real-life clothes, however, only occupied about one third of the room. The rest was filled with the jackets, dresses, slacks, skirts, scarves, blouses, shoes, wigs, hats, gloves and accouterments, including the faux jewelry, purses, and bags, of the characters I had played for the last twenty-seven years on way-off-Broadway stages, in late-night ambulance-chaser commercials, and in no-budget independent films. One advan-tage of the less-than-legitimate world of stage and screen is that very often, to cover budgetary shortfalls, the costumes are avail-able for purchase at rock-bottom prices. I had acquired quite the wardrobe warehouse along the way, and all of it still fit me like a tailored suit.

I took off my interrogation clothes—a dressy black T-shirt, a red and gray summer-weight sweater, black pants, black flats—looked at myself in the vanity's nearly full-length mirror, thought about Harriman and Logan at the Thirteenth, and concluded, not for the first time, that in the city of New York, everyone you meet comes right out of central casting. What I mean is that everyone looks like someone famous, a fact not necessarily true in cities like Detroit or Denver. Only in Manhattan and Los Angeles—where I flew, every few years, to participate in TV pilot season—is your bus driver a dead ringer for Danny Glover, your pharmacist the spitting image of Patti LuPone, and your waiter the honest-to-God clone of Tobey Maguire. Only on the coast is your homicide detective Steve McQueen's long lost twin brother. As for me, most people said Sandra Bullock would play me in the movie of my life.

It was true, to an extent.

Though we were about the same size and general body type, Ms. Bullock was prettier than me (arguable), more talented than me (let's not get crazy), and seven or eight zeros richer than me, but I was probably a little curvier than she was and could definitely beat her up. Not that I would ever try. She's a terrific and funny actor, and I was a fan. Though I wouldn't have asked her for an autograph; I was an actor too, after all.

I could beat up Sandra Bullock and most women (and some men) because Jimmy and Raul had taught me how to box. Which is also why my wardrobe still fit me. I was in very good shape.

When my sister Marilyn left for Cleveland State and it was just Jimmy and me, my father decided it was time for his little aspiring actor to learn how to defend herself. He knew the trainers at Raul's Boxing in Hell's Kitchen, near the Port Authority—a small, second-floor space with a ring, two heavy bags, two speed bags, two spit pails, and not much more—took me down there, and set me up with Raul himself. I resisted at first, but Jimmy made me go, and Raul made me train, and one day, when high school first baseman Tom Warner wouldn't stop at first base after I said, "No," I used a devastating body shot to the solar plexus and a right cross to the jaw to make my point. Warner was my first TKO, and I felt so good and so strong that I fell in love with the Sweet Science and had been a boxer ever since. I drew the line at sparring, however, because I didn't like to get hit. I was an actor, and my face was my calling card, so all I did was train, and I had been doing that religiously, four sessions a week, for more years than I'd like to admit. I could handle myself in a dark alley, and I looked great for forty-five; let's leave it at that.

I flexed my muscles and shot off a few quick jabs at the mirror. As I ducked an imaginary left hook, my phone rang. I had an extension on my vanity, and I hit the speakerphone button.

"Hello," I said.

"Mom."

"Hi, Matthew."

"When you're summoned to an interrogation by homicide detectives, you have to call me."

"I'm fine. How are you?"

"When I have to find out from them, and I'm clueless on my end as to the particulars, that's not good."

"They called you?"

"You think?"

"Which one?"

"Harriman."

"He's the good cop. Logan's the bad cop. What did he say?"

"You know what he said."

"I haven't even read Jimmy's files. I'm not sharing them with the police yet."

"Define yet. And your definition better include the words 'exceedingly soon.'"

"Jimmy's files are confidential."

"They're your files now, not Jimmy's. And they're not confidential. There's no client-private eye privilege in the state of
New York. It's not like doctors and lawyers. Harriman can get a
judge to order you to turn them over."

"He won't do that."

"Why not?"

"Because you're going to explain that my definition of 'yet'
includes the words 'pretty soon.'"

"Exceedingly soon."

"Soon enough."

He groaned with frustration on the other end of the phone
while I put together an outfit for my meeting on the Upper
West Side. I would be a banker, I decided, and so I grabbed the
gray pinstripe pants suit with the white blouse, the black
pumps, and the short blonde wig I wore in *Catch of the Day*, a
three-thousand-dollar slasher film about a New York City fisherman who lived a second life as a serial killer. I played victim
number two, the banker who loaned the fisherman money for
his boat, called in the loan, and met a grizzly end. I considered
tortoiseshell glasses and green contact lenses.

"Are you still rehearsing the show?" Matthew said.

"Yes. Are you coming?"

"When is it?"

"Four weeks. We open Labor Day weekend."

"Do you think that's a good time to open a vampire
musical?"

"Do you think there is a good time to open a vampire
musical?"

I regretted the question as soon as I asked it.

"You have to stop, Mom. This is the last one. You're forty-five
years old. You can't be an aspiring actor forever. You can't be an
aspiring anything forever. At some point you have to stop
aspiring to be something and actually be something."

I was enormously proud of my son, and I loved him the way

all mothers love their boys: with every beat of my heart. With a little help from me and Jimmy, Matthew had put himself through NYU law school, clerked for a superior court judge, and become an assistant district attorney by the age of twenty-seven. He was smart, logical, practical, and reasoned, traits he got from I have no idea where. Not me, that's for sure. Though we were as close as we could be, we were not on the same wavelength, and we hadn't been since he was, oh, about three years old.

"I don't agree with your premise, Matthew. I don't think there is such a point. Aspiration is a quality we should never let go of. We should be aspiring from the cradle to the grave. The day I stop aspiring to be an actor is the end of the world."

How could I explain what being an actor, aspiring or otherwise, meant to me? It wasn't something I felt, not a profound conviction of some kind, not even a passionate promise to myself but much more than that. It was a feeling of oneness with the universe, the sense that as long as I was an actor, all was right, not necessarily good or easy, but right. I put in the green contacts, adjusted the wig, applied my makeup, slipped on the tortoiseshell glasses, and felt like a banker in my bones.

"Mom, a friend of mine's a mid-town broker. He just went out on his own. He does commercial real estate. He's looking for someone to manage his office. I told him about you. He'll pay for you to get your license. I want you to call him."

On the one hand, it was very sweet to have my adult son parent me as if I were an irresponsible teenager. On the other hand, it really wasn't all that sweet. It was a little insulting, to tell you the truth. I could have taken it that way if I wanted to, but I chose to believe he was worried about me as opposed to embarrassed by me.

"How's Nina?" I said, changing the subject.

"Good."

I couldn't bear Pompous Nina. She was a pretentious NYU

film studies associate professor. Her specialty was film appreciation, and she considered herself an expert, no, *the* expert, on what films (and pretty much every other damn thing) should be considered great and why the audience should or shouldn't like them. What crap. She couldn't tolerate me either, but Matthew loved her, and I was his mother, so we never let our relationship escalate to all-out war. She was a person who deserved an adjective at all times, at least in the privacy of my own mind.

"I'm glad to hear that. You should bring her to my show. I think she'd like it."

"Or I could stick hot needles in her eyes."

"Okay, that's mean, so this is where I hang up. I'm late, anyway."

"I'm sorry. I didn't mean it to be mean. Harriman said he didn't want you anywhere near the Monument Life building. That's not where you're going, is it?"

"Probably not."

"Definitely not."

"That's where they found Jimmy."

"You cannot, under any circumstances, investigate Jimmy's murder. Tell me right now you're not going to the Monument Life building."

"I'm going to the West Side. I have to see a man with a bad back."

"I don't want to know what that means."

"Will you talk to Harriman?"

"Exceedingly soon. Yes, I'll talk to him."

"Soon enough. I love you, Matthew."

"Love you, Mom. Wait, I want to give you my friend's number..."

I hung up before he could do it.

10

———

DON'T MAKE CONTACT WITH THE TARGET

THE NAME OF THE MAN WHO ALLEGEDLY FELL FROM TEDDY Barkowski's scaffolding and hurt his back to the tune of ten million dollars was Ken Curry. He was wearing an ostentatious lower back brace and grocery shopping at a speed so slow as to be incalculable. His cane was in his shopping cart, so he leaned on the cart for support, pushing it down the aisles in a pain-filled gear that was nearly reverse. If something on the far side of the store had a two-week expiration window, it would spoil before Curry could get to it.

I wondered why in the world he was grocery shopping if his back hurt this badly? Didn't he have even one friend in the world that would grab him some bacon and eggs and spare him this kind of stop-motion agony?

Surveillance at any pace can be mind-numbingly boring, hours and hours for days on end in a car, or on a park bench, or in the corner booth of a side-street diner, but at this kind of crawl it was especially hard to stay focused.

We were in the Gristedes on Columbus and 84th Street. I was shopping too, crisscrossing the aisles in such a way that I could keep a constant if not continuous eye on him. I couldn't simply follow him down a single aisle; it took him ten minutes to get a jar of applesauce off the shelf and into his cart. If I shopped at his speed in the same aisle, trailing behind him like a shadow, either my cover would be blown or someone from Gristedes security would pull me aside to ask me what the problem was.

So I passed him at the English muffins, watched him from one end of the bread aisle, and then did a loop and watched him from the other end. I varied my directions, my speeds, the foods I put in the cart. I never traversed the same aisle twice in a row. To the afternoon Gristedes crowd, I was just another sharp-looking blonde banker filling my fridge between high-powered money meetings.

Curry was at least six feet two inches tall, broad-shouldered and barrel-chested. He had to weigh in the neighborhood of two hundred and sixty pounds, a solid mass of working man. His chest and stomach were one and the same, both huge and wide and imposing. He wasn't muscular, but he wasn't fat either, just large and powerful-looking. The kind of guy you've seen on a construction site a thousand times—lugging four by fours, hauling bags of concrete, pushing huge wheelbarrows of debris, eating meatball subs out of a suitcase-sized lunchbox, shouting obscenely at pretty girls as they pass by.

He was maybe forty-three years old and good-looking: brown hair, brown eyes, and surprisingly nice teeth. He was wearing blue jeans, New Balance running shoes, a Bruce Springsteen T-shirt with the sleeves cut off and the Boss's tour dates on the back, and a Life is Good baseball cap. He had a colorful and aggressive tattoo of a rugby-playing rhinoceros on his left arm and another of a sweet, elderly woman holding up an apple pie—the woman and the pie underscored with the word "Grandma"—on his right arm. He was a tough guy cut to the quick by a brutally bad back. Or so he said. Barkowski, of course, said otherwise—and he was the one paying my way.

I had been following Curry since he left his apartment building around the corner from the Gristedes. It took him twenty minutes, instead of two, to arrive at the store, and I had been circling the aisles around him for another twenty minutes. In all that time, he never made a move contrary to a man with an excruciatingly bad back. Given that I was spending a fair percentage of the time mindlessly shopping in other aisles, when Curry was out of sight, my thoughts drifted back to Detective Harriman.

Specifically, they drifted to that instant we both realized neither of us was married and acknowledged that realization with a locked-eye look. That didn't mean we weren't otherwise occupied in a relationship, or even a serious relationship, it meant we could ask about it if we chose to. It meant the whole range of "I noticed you're not wearing a wedding ring" conversations, if we wanted them to, if it worked out that way, could commence.

I wasn't seeing anyone at the time. Since Tom Mullin, Matthew's biological father, now a hair stylist in the Castro, went West Coast twenty-eight years ago, I had dated often, sometimes seriously, had my heart broken in jagged pieces a dozen times, broken some hearts myself, and was now, at forty-five years old, as happy to be alone as with a man who never heard a word I said. That being the case, I was wide open for a steady, honest, positive, caring, and monogamous romantic relationship.

As I rolled past the pasta, I pictured myself with the Thirteenth Precinct homicide detective who was handsome enough to play one on TV. It was a blurry vision of some kind of first date. We were having pizza, maybe at John's, possibly Nick's, drinking wine, laughing at nothing. Then we were back at my place with low lights and soft music. Three things killed this daydream five seconds after it started.

First: Why was a guy that gorgeous not married? It could be

an innocent answer, but then again it could be a nuclear response. Was infidelity an issue? Was intimacy a problem? What about commitment-phobia? I'd only seen that trio a thousand times before. Maybe when the lights went down he was kinky in an off-putting way. It wouldn't have been the first time I'd seen that either.

Second: he was younger than me. Some men have an allergic reaction to envisioning themselves with older women, even only five years older, but I didn't think that was the case with Harriman. There was definitely some kind of spark between us. And, really, there was no reason for him not to be attracted to me. It was true I had been told more than once I was in possession of a first-class rear end. It was also true that one sad Sunday morning, when I mentioned that men had told me they admired my ass, the divorced, world-famous magazine editor I had just slept with said to me, "That's what all women with small tits say."

"Like you would know," I said to him. "Your tits are bigger than mine."

How I ended up sleeping with a bald, big-breasted, world-famous magazine editor was a long, regretful story I wasn't planning on reliving while pretending to shop for groceries on the Upper West Side, so I stopped myself and accepted the fact that I was a grown woman and that grown women make bad dating decisions every day of the week.

That's one example of how your mind can wander while on surveillance.

Third: Harriman was investigating my father's murder and had only just this morning forbidden me from surveying the crime scene. Beneath his Steve McQueen exterior, he was Logan's partner, and Logan was right about one thing: with no motive, no witnesses, no murder weapon, no ballistics, no forensics, and no suspects, the NYPD would soon move

Jimmy's death to the back burner and then off the stove completely.

From Jimmy, I had inherited some distinctly Irish DNA that had compelled me since childhood to do precisely whatever I was forbidden to do. If Harriman and Logan didn't want me anywhere near the Monument Life building, then that was where I was going next. I had to see it for myself. I had to do it for Jimmy.

Matthew wouldn't be happy about that either, but if after reading Jimmy's files and seeing the Monument Life building with my own eyes I couldn't add anything to the equation, then I would call Matthew's real estate broker friend, get my license, and lease office space for the rest of my days, though I would keep acting as well, no matter what my son said.

I turned into the snack food aisle and found myself face to face with Curry. I had made too sharp a turn into the aisle and couldn't avoid him. I had to stop directly in front of his cart or crash into it. I did a little of each.

"That was a close one," Curry said.

"Sorry." If Jimmy were here, he would have chewed me out like there was no tomorrow. I had been on the job for less than an hour and had already violated *Rule Number four* of *Jimmy's Rules of Private Investigation for Kate*, which was: *don't make contact with the target.* Jimmy had told me a hundred times that a PI's judgment was compromised if they had to be conscious of their own behavior. *They're worried about themselves instead of the target*, he would say to me. *You have to be a first-class screw-up to make that mistake.* He was right. I immediately and simultaneously felt idiotic and worried to the point of nausea, and I had only been standing here for eight seconds.

I also felt trapped. I had somehow wedged my cart against the snack shelves and Curry's cart in such a way that I couldn't make a graceful escape.

"Would you mind helping me for a minute? I can't reach up," he said.

"Sure. What do you need?"

Jesus Christ. I was having a conversation with him. I was helping him shop.

"Cheez Whiz," he said.

I could use some myself, I thought. Al and Warren had devoured mine at Jimmy's wake.

"No problem," I said, reaching up and grabbing a can.

"Would you mind putting it in the cart?" he said. "I can't bend down either."

"Glad to," I said and put the can in his cart, beside the applesauce.

"Guy who invented Cheez Whiz had to be stoned," Curry said. "Couldn't wait one minute to cut a real piece of cheese. Had to shoot it out of a can that second."

"There's no cheese in it," I said. "Nobody knows what it is."

"Nobody cares. Kind of tastes like cheese. It's orange."

"Food coloring," I said, backing my cart away from his in order to swing around him. But before I did I said, "How did you hurt your back?"

"Construction," he said. "I fell off the scaffolding. It wasn't rigged right."

"I'm sorry."

"Shit happens."

I was around his cart and almost past him when I had an idea that translated into action before I could judge the rationality of it, the consequences and the risks. As I passed Curry, I accidentally on purpose spilled the contents of my purse all over the snack aisle floor at his feet.

Would he go for it? Would he instinctively bend over to help me gather my things? Would he, in a weak moment, betray himself to me without knowing that I was the private investigator hired to expose his lies and deceit?

No. He just stood there helplessly.

I acknowledged his immobility with a nod and commenced to crawl around the floor and collect my things. *He's got a bad back,* I thought. Barkowski was negligent. Curry fell off the scaffolding, and now he's got a bad back. I hoped Mrs. Barkowski the younger had some kind of marketable skills because she was going back to work when Curry cleaned out her hubby's bank accounts.

I had surrendered the case by the time I stood up, but what I saw when I looked into Curry's eyes turned me one hundred eighty degrees around.

He was standing where I'd left him, and though he hadn't moved a muscle, his hands were all over my body. When his eyes found mine, he gave me a macho glance that said: Blondie, I may look disabled, but give me half a sign, and I will take off this brace and screw you to the bedpost for the next three hours. If you don't believe me, unbutton that top blouse button and see what happens.

He gave me no physical indication that he was anything but badly injured, but that look in his eyes was as true as it was unmistakable. I smiled, flirting like an embarrassed banker, and pushed my cart down the aisle. I could still feel his eyes on my ass as I turned the corner. I left the cart by the dairy case and headed for the exit.

I had wanted to get a glimpse of Ken Curry before I started digging. Instead, I had gotten a really good look, although not as good as the one he got of me. Though he hadn't moved one incriminating muscle, he had flinched big time where it really counted: on the inside. I was going to need a bigger shovel.

11

WHAT DID YOU SAY YOUR NAME
WAS, MISS?

OVER THE COURSE OF MY UNUSUALLY VARIED, TWENTY-SEVEN-years-and-counting career, I had been in many dozens of large-scale office buildings, but never before in one where my father had been murdered.

It was four fifteen when I arrived at Monument Life's thirty-five floors of stone, steel, and glass near the Flatiron Building. I was still dressed as a blonde banker and had been internally processing my Ken Curry surveillance results since leaving the Upper West Side Gristedes and taking mass transit to 23rd and Broadway. But the grocery cart crash, the ensuing conversation with the target, the accidentally-on-purpose spilling of my purse, and Curry's lecherous look all went out the window as soon as I stepped into Monument's marbled lobby.

The building was in the middle of the block. There were three entrances, all from Broadway: two sets of double doors closer to 23rd Street, two sets of double doors closer to 24th Street, and a large revolving door, flanked by double doors on each side, in the center of the building, which was close to half a football field wide, so that there was a good deal of yardage between the three entrances.

I entered through the revolving door. To my left and right were identical lobby seating areas made up of modern, black-leather furniture. There were plenty of large, potted plants all around, giving the lobby an upscale, indoor-park kind of feeling.

To my left, beyond the seating area, one building security guard kept watch near the 23rd Street entrance door, and to my right, another guard did the same near the 24th Street door.

Straight ahead, in the middle of the lobby, was a huge, oval, reception-security desk. The building's directory was constructed into the desk so that the two guards inside the oval could check out the people locating tenants, answer questions, and issue visitor passes after confirming appointments on a computer screen.

Still straight ahead, past the reception desk, at the back of the building, were two elevator banks. There were six cars in each bank, three cars on either side. The cars faced each other and opened into an elevator entry area where visitors and tenants waited to be fetched and lifted up to meetings, conferences, spreadsheets, reports, and policies. In other words, the elevator doors did not open facing Broadway, which was the front of the building, but instead they opened facing each other.

Each elevator entry area was cordoned off by fancy ropes in such a way that visitors and tenants alike were funneled through a security checkpoint where two more guards examined opened purses, briefcases, and just-issued passes. Unless you had approved business in this building, you weren't taking an elevator anywhere.

I counted eight guards: one by the 23rd Street doors, one by the 24th Street doors, two in the oval security desk, and two more at each bank of elevators.

People were all over the lobby: tenants, clients, messengers, deliverymen, salesmen, mailmen, executives, managers, marketers, and more, including, to my right, three uniformed police officers positioned at the entrance to the 24th Street elevator bank.

That's where they found Jimmy, I thought. I walked straight toward the policemen to see what I could see, but that turned out to be not much because I couldn't access the elevator entry area. I could, however, see that the middle car on the north side was sectioned off with yellow crime scene tape.

The car had been taken out of service. The door was locked in the open position and the police had set up hyper-bright spotlights in the entry area, shining them into the elevator in the hope of illuminating even one shred of evidence.

Three or four crime scene investigators—I couldn't see into the car, so it was hard to know for sure how many—were still going through their paces and procedures, though Logan and Harriman had made it clear earlier that morning that nothing substantive had been learned and was likely not to be no matter how many men put in no matter how many hours in the glare of no matter how bright a light.

While pass-holders rubbernecked their way past the murder car into the five remaining and still operational elevators in the 24th Street bank, I thought, *I have to see it for myself. I have to know what happened. I have to figure it out.* As I was finishing that thought, a woman exited the elevator area right in front of me.

"Hi," I said, politely blocking her way. "I'm sorry to bother you. Do you work for Monument?" Logan had said there were eighteen hundred Monument employees out of forty-eight hundred total in the building. Pretty good odds.

"Yes," she said.

"I'm Brandy Bay," I said. "I'm with Citigroup. I have a last-minute meeting with someone in human resources, but my assistant lost the name. I feel like an idiot. Can you help me? All I know is he's the class clown of company communications.

Very loud. Practical joker. Endless emails. Social butterfly. Kind of a flirt. Been here a while. Any chance you know him?" Every office I'd ever worked in had a human resources guy like that, and everybody knew him.

"Rick Steinberg," she said. "Twenty-first floor. Life of the party."

"That's it. Thanks. Are you in human resources too?"

I figured there was at least half a chance she sold insurance, and I had never once met an insurance agent who, given half a chance, wouldn't try to make a sale.

"Whole life. I'm an agent. Carole Forrester."

"Nice to meet you, Carole. Brandy."

"Nice to meet you too."

"Listen, do you have a card? I'm in the market. You almost never meet an agent you like." I said that in such a way as to imply that Carole and I could be best buddies long before the ink dried on my new Monument policy.

"Sure," she said, and she handed me her Monument Life business card.

"I'm getting new cards next week," I said. "But I'll call you after Rick tries to ask me out."

We both laughed.

"Good luck," she said. "Call me. I can help you."

"Talk to you soon," I said, holding up her card, and off she went.

I looked into the elevator entry area again and then at Carole's card. I took a breath and walked to the oval desk. One of the guards was crusty and the other was young. I chose the young one.

"Hi," I said. "Jeannine Watkins. I have an appointment with Carole Forrester. Whole life. Twenty-second floor. I'm dropping off a policy."

I studied the directory while the young one typed Forrester's name on the keyboard and checked the computer screen. We shared a fake smile while we waited for Forrester's visitor list to appear.

"What's going on?" I said, gesturing at the police by the elevator.

"Murder investigation. Some guy got killed in the elevator."

"That's terrible."

"Tell me about it. We're one car down and all hell's breaking loose."

It wasn't terrible that Jimmy was murdered, mind you. It was terrible how that tragedy had impacted the young one's life.

I had an I-hate-this-city moment and said, "It's never easy, is it?"

He rolled his eyes in agreement, looked at the computer screen, and said, "You're not on Ms. Forrester's schedule. You don't have an appointment."

"That's ridiculous. Of course I have an appointment. Can you call her?"

He sighed, lifted the receiver, dialed a number, and said into the phone, "Yeah, this is the lobby. Jeannine Watkins is here for Ms. Forrester. Dropping off a policy. She's not on the computer."

I waited. He covered the phone and addressed me. "Ms. Forrester's not in."

"That's fine. I just need to drop off the paperwork."

"Says she just wants to drop off the paperwork."

He waited. I could tell by the look on his face that I was fast becoming part and parcel of the one-elevator-car-short debacle that had ruined his week.

"Says she doesn't have you down in Ms. Forrester's book, which is why you're not in the computer."

"No kidding? Tell her that I am very busy, I'm between meetings, I have two minutes to finalize this contract, and if she can't see me, her boss can't have my business."

My voice was louder than I wanted it to be, and it caught the attention of the crusty guard, who put his business on hold and turned to me.

"What's the problem?" he said.

"The problem is," I said, gesturing at my purse, "that if Ms. Forrester's secretary can't figure out a way to let me deliver these papers, she can tell her boss to cancel my policy. Would you explain that to her, please? I'm running late. Did I mention that?"

I enjoyed playing the first-class bitch and always fell right into character.

The guards looked at each other as if to say: *Is this not the worst freaking job in the universe?*

"Whether you're running late or not, no one goes upstairs without a pass, and no one gets a pass without an appointment or a voice confirmation. Those are the rules," said the crusty one. The young one looked at the screen as if trying to will the name Jeannine Watkins onto it so this episode could instantly end.

"Tell Ms. Forrester's secretary that if she doesn't voice confirm me in the next thirty seconds, she will, by the end of the day, become Ms. Forrester's soon-to-be-replaced secretary."

Bluffing is a funny business. The bluffer never knows if he or she has crossed the line until the line is crossed and it's too late to call back the bet.

The crusty one put his hand in the air and gestured toward the 23rd Street elevator bank like he was calling for a waiter across a busy dining room. A tall, skinny security guard saw the signal, locked his jaw as if he'd been itching for a fight all day and was glad he'd finally found one, and started toward the oval desk. He had bars on his shoulders. He was the captain of the team.

When the guard floating near the 23rd Street entrance saw the captain on the move, he started toward the oval, as well. He was a black man the size and weight of a grizzly bear.

Behind me, a line of unhappy New Yorkers—who really were between meetings, or were late for meetings, or somehow had meetings hanging in the balance—were making impatient noises as only unhappy New Yorkers can make them.

"What did you say your name was, Miss?" the crusty one said as the captain and the grizzly arrived.

"Jeannine Watkins. Vice President of Community Affairs for Citigroup. Would you like me to call the Citigroup attorney? Maybe I should get all of your names."

"The first thing you got to understand, Ms. Watkins," the captain said, "is that you're not getting a pass without a scheduled appointment or..."

"Or a voice confirmation, yes, so I've heard. The first thing you need to understand is..."

My voice stopped on a dime because the uniformed policemen by the 24th Street elevator were also watching us with concern. Standing among them was Detective Mike Harriman.

"What we need to understand is what?" the grizzly said.

Harriman and one of the uniforms started across the lobby. The crowd behind me was riled up. *When did I cross the line?* I wondered. It had snuck up on me and suddenly I was on the other side. I didn't think Harriman could pick me out from twenty-five yards away—I was a blonde in a business suit with tortoiseshell glasses and green eyes—but up close and personal? I had done nothing with my voice. No accent, no pitch fluctuation, no speech impediment—it was me talking. I knew I couldn't just suddenly affect a change when Harriman arrived because the other guards would mention it and there would be trouble. It was possible, I thought, that Harriman would see right through my act even if I had become a British banker, say, or a banker from the deep South. But with my true voice? After meeting with him half the morning? Big risk.

I could have done it. If Harriman hadn't been there, I could have talked my way past the young one, the crusty one, the grizzly, and the captain. I was a much better actor than any of them and more committed to the moment than they were. It was another crappy day on the job to them and it was Jimmy's murder to me. It would only have been a matter of time until they decided to give me the damn pass. But with Harriman only ten yards away, time was something I didn't have.

"What you need to understand is…I have wasted more than enough time on a life insurance policy I can get anywhere in the city. Thank you very much for nothing. Tell Ms. Forrester to cancel my plan."

Harriman and the uniformed cop arrived at the far end of the oval. Any unusual behavior in this building was now his concern. The handsome detective looked across the big desk and our eyes met. He had a moment of confusion, like he knew me from somewhere but couldn't place me, like my eyes were familiar somehow but different at the same time, which, of course, they were—they had been brown this morning at the Thirteenth. He even half-heartedly pointed at me as if wondering: *Hey, have we met?*

I took a last look at the directory, turned, walked with great purpose toward the 23rd Street door, and was on Broadway headed south before anyone could stop me. I didn't look back until I was at the corner of 21st Street and Sixth Avenue, where I paused and took a moment to feel bad for Carole Forrester, who had lost a client she never knew she had.

12

PROBLEM: POWELL WAS NEVER MARRIED

There was no one in the lobby when I got back to the House of Emotional Tics. The day crowd usually returned to 83rd Street after work at about the same time and pecked around the mailboxes like squawking chickens, complaining about their chaotic jobs, their hard-ass bosses, their ungrateful customers, and their pitiful paychecks.

I wondered if Fu had fixed Al Cutter's toilet. I considered knocking on Fu's door in the basement before going into my apartment, but if Fu hadn't been to 5A yet, I would have to escort him up the stairs and personally watch him unplug the problem. I squashed the idea when I remembered Al was pissing in Gatorade bottles that had to be somewhere in his apartment: on the kitchen counter, on the dining room table, on various window sills, lined up on top of the TV, all of the above. In any of those locations, it was a vision I could live without. Plus, I had an appointment in the West Village in an hour, and then I had rehearsal and didn't want to get stuck up there for half the night.

I went into my apartment, walked straight to my closet,

changed out of my blonde banker ensemble, and thought about Ken Curry.

What was he doing shopping for groceries if he was in so much pain? Gristedes will deliver for an extra fee and back pain like the kind Curry was claiming would be worth that fee for sure. But there he was for the world to see, creepy-crawling up and down the aisles like a disabled old man.

And then I realized that was it right there: he was putting on a show. The name of the show was *Ken Curry Hurt His Back And Can Never Work Again*. He knew Barkowski would have someone watching him. He knew hiding wouldn't help his case. He was intentionally playing the game in public, where he could create witnesses—"I saw that poor man shopping; what a bad back he had"—and discourage skeptics—"Sorry Barkowski, he had to have that blonde lady help him put the Cheez Whiz in the cart. If you can't lift a can of Cheez Whiz...I mean, come on." Maybe he even knew I was the one Barkowski had hired. I didn't think so, but I wouldn't be a blonde banker next time, that was for sure.

I put on jeans and a nice, button-down, blue-and-white, pin-striped blouse, slipped on comfortable flats, walked through the dining room into the kitchen, poured a glass of white wine, made an omelet with feta cheese and sautéed mushrooms, fixed a small salad, toasted a bagel, and read Jimmy's case files while I ate dinner.

Shavelson had called all of Jimmy's clients and told them Jimmy was dead. He also told them that I had inherited the business. It was up in the air whether or not the clients would want to continue with the PI's daughter in lieu of the PI. I would have to make contact with all of them, explain that I was an actor, and bow out gracefully. I would have to do that soon, but not now. Now I had to read.

There were the two expanding envelopes: one labeled *Closed Cases* and the other labeled *Open Cases*. Inside each envelope were a dozen or so individual file folders. Each file folder contained a single case.

Jimmy kept a top-sheet for every case that listed all the pertinent details: the issue at hand, the name, address, and contact information for the client, the client's employer, the client's bank (including account numbers and balances), the target (or targets), witnesses, relatives, business associates, friends, enemies, and anything else that could sum up the case on the front and back of one page.

Clipped to the top-sheet were Jimmy's notes in chronological order. Some of the entries were one-liners: *Wednesday, March 12—Surveillance—6 a.m. to 6 p.m.—target never leaves the house*. Other entries were considerably longer. Case notes could be three pages or thirty pages or more, depending upon Jimmy's level of success and the patience and pocketbook of the client.

Photographs Jimmy had secretly snapped while on surveillance followed the case notes. There were some crazy angles and compromising positions that both the clients and targets were always unhappy to see when Jimmy presented them as evidence—clients because the pictures were proof-positive that whatever it was was true, targets because they were caught in the act.

It wasn't a fancy filing system, but it was clear, quick, and effective. Jimmy had neither a computer nor an office. He worked at his dining room table (or the dining room table of the woman he was sleeping with) and wrote with the cheapest Bic pen he could buy. His four big expenses were his Colt .45, his cell phone—a satellite model that could catch a signal more or less anywhere on Earth, and so anywhere in the New York metropolitan area, his camera, which was digital, miniature, and state-of-the-art, and a small, high-quality digital photo printer. They were all in the box I got from Shavelson, so they belonged to me now.

I opened the envelope marked *Closed Cases* and read quickly through the file folders, which covered only this past year—Shavelson said he had years and years of Jimmy's case files in deep storage somewhere. Many of the closed cases I knew about from conversations with Jimmy or because I had helped him with either surveillance or research. There was nothing in any of the closed cases that tweaked my radar.

Though I hadn't memorized the Monument Life building's directory, I had gotten a good look at the tenant roster while trying to bluff my way into seeing the crime scene. There were no names in Jimmy's closed case files that matched the list of people that worked in the building where Jimmy was murdered. There was no mention of the building itself. No surveillance had been done there at any time. There was nothing on the surface connecting Jimmy to that address. No reason for him to be dead in that elevator.

A few of the open cases were also familiar. They covered the range of PI puzzles: infidelity, embezzlement, missing persons, estate theft, robbery, alimony, identity theft, child custody, and conspiracy to commit...something, usually robbery or murder. If the conspiracy to commit murder became an actual murder, Jimmy's own rules would probably have compelled him to drop the case. Probably. Jimmy was notorious for breaking his own —or anybody else's—rules if he thought breaking the rules was called for. None of the open cases pointed me back to that building either.

Buried at the bottom of the *Open Cases* envelope, not in a folder, was a scrap of paper, a cocktail napkin from a place called Cutter's Tavern. On the front of the napkin Jimmy had written: *Terry Kramer—Smithtown—Half sister—Same father— Half brother is Ron Powell—Powell dead—Massive heart attack— Terry and Powell had recently spoken—Powell in perfect health—10 million life insurance policy—Policy written by Monument Life— Every penny left to ex-wife—Problem: Powell was never married.*

13

———

MISSION IMPOSSIBLE

IF IT WAS ONE OF JIMMY'S CURRENT CASES, WHY DIDN'T IT HAVE A folder or a top-sheet? If it wasn't, why was he poking around Monument? And what had he found?

One thing was certain, Jimmy had hit a raw enough nerve that someone had hired a professional killer to send a message to anyone else thinking about snooping around the marble Monument halls. But who? These were the questions that Harriman and Logan would soon enough stop asking when more murders arose, which they would as sure as the sun. Where would Jimmy be then?

And then I thought, *Whoa.*

Wasn't this just the kind of hand-written-cocktail-napkin thing I should turn over to homicide? Shouldn't Logan and Harriman take it from here? Hadn't I told Matthew I would cooperate with the police? But even as I answered yes, yes, and yes, I knew I wasn't going to do it.

Terry Kramer had gone to Jimmy, not the police, so it wouldn't be right for me to send the police to her. Not yet. Not until I had talked to her and filled in some blanks about Monument. I had every intention of eventually helping Harriman, just not now.

I carried my dishes to the sink, rinsed them quickly, finished the last of my wine, brushed my teeth, made myself presentable, walked back through my dining room, closet, and bedroom, and stopped in the living room to find my script before heading downtown.

I hadn't thought much about Farina LeBleu since last Friday night's rehearsal, when Paul Barnes had showed up to tell me Jimmy was dead. I knew I needed to get myself into a singing-vampire frame of mind, but I couldn't stop thinking the following thought: *How could I take on a monster like Monument Life when Jimmy had tried and ended up with bullet holes in his eyes?*

Jimmy called his business McCall & Company because he had me to pitch in and play the role of "company" when he needed an extra pair of eyes. Who did I have?

I thought of Peter Graves in *Mission Impossible*, opening his file, choosing from a menu of special agents: Martin Landeau, Peter Lupus, Leonard Nimoy, Leslie Ann Warren, Greg Morris, Barbara Bain, Sam Elliot, Lynda Day George. Graves would never have cracked those cases without them.

I grabbed my purse, put on a lightweight blue blazer, lifted my *Blood Song and Dance* script, opened my door, and stepped into the lobby.

Charlie and LaTanya were home from work, collecting their mail. LaTanya Bellamy from 3B saw me first. Roughly my age, she was a cab driver who shared ownership of a medallion with her twin brother. She drove the cab, a yellow Volvo station wagon, from six in the morning to six at night; he drove the night shift. All day long, she listened to the radio and was convinced she should have her own show. She could talk a blue streak on anything and was as outspoken and opinionated as she was black and a woman, which is to say completely.

"Where you at, McCall?" LaTanya called across the lobby. "LaTanya's in the house, let's get this party started."

"I have a meeting in the West Village, and then I have to be a singing vampire," I said. "You'll have to start without me."

"This town don't need no more vampires," LaTanya said. "We got vampires coming out our ass."

"Blood suckers on every corner," Charlie Nye said.

Charlie lived in 2B. He was fifty, a tow truck driver for the city, jacking naughty cars to the pound all day, every day. He had been jacked to the pound himself three times in his life, in three separate states, for breaking and entering—cars, houses, stores, offices, whatever. Working for the city was part of his early release. He wanted to be a professional poker player and entered local tournaments most weekends. I'm sure he hid aces up his sleeve.

Charlie shut his mailbox and shook his head. "Just today, some midtown vampire gave me a bag of shit for towing his Escalade. He's in a no-parking-under-any-circumstances-at-any-time-of-the-day-or-night-no-matter-what-your-bullshit-emergency-is zone. Never offered me a dime to look the other way. I can still feel his fangs in my neck."

I thought about them and the other tenants while I walked to 86th and Lexington to catch the 6 train downtown: their quirky contributions to humanity, their special talents, their concurrently functional and dysfunctional lives. Those thoughts led to other thoughts, which led to more thoughts, which led to the realization that like Peter Graves on *Mission Impossible*, I did have a file of associates to help me with Ken Curry and Monument Life. In fact, I had two files to choose from. The first file was labeled *House of Emotional Tics*. The second was called *Schmidt and Parker Players*. They weren't Nimoy, Landeau, and Lupus by a long shot, but they would do.

14

BARKOWSKI'S TRIPLETS

ONCE UPON A BEAUTIFUL TIME, GREENWICH VILLAGE REALLY WAS a village. But as the years pressed on, it became much more than that. Hip cafes and upscale retail stores had moved in and become cozy with the coffeehouses, headshops, clubs, bars, galleries, and ethnic eateries that had long defined the neighborhood. Upwardly mobile attorneys, marketers, promoters, and financiers now shared the narrow, twisty roads, the townhouses, brownstones, and sun-filled lofts with ancient hippies, wanderers, dealers, dopers, and a never-ending infusion of students. It was true that NYU had left its modern fingerprints on everything old, but somehow Greenwich Village had held onto its charm. At the right time of day, it was still quaint.

On MacDougal Street, between Bleeker and Minetta Lane, in the heart of the West Village, Barkowski was constructing a six-story, thirty-unit apartment building, similar in size to the other residential buildings on the east and west sides of the street.

It was after hours for his crew, but Barkowski had asked three of his men to stay for our meeting. When I arrived, the four of them were hanging around the trailer that served as the construction office, smoking cigarettes and drinking cans of Miller Genuine Draft.

"Hello, Ted," I said as I walked up to them.

We shook hands. He looked tired. As a small, independent, New York general contractor, he was no doubt used to hauling heavy financial pressure. But on top of the normal load he had piled on his shoulders was now the additional weight of Ken Curry and his ten-million-dollar lawsuit. It couldn't have been easy lugging that around all day.

"This is Rodriguez, Talley, and Collins," Barkowski said, gesturing at each of them in turn. "They all worked with Curry. You can ask them anything you want. They got no special love for the guy. This is Kate McCall. She's the PI I told you about."

"Nice to meet you," I said. "Thanks for sticking around. Ted gave me a file with the basics: name, address, job description, emergency contact, those kinds of things. What I'm looking for is everything else. What do you know that's not in the file? Nothing's too small to mention."

"Dude can eat. Inhale like three lunches in twenty minutes, no shit. People be like, 'Fucking dude can eat,'" Rodriguez said. He was the youngest of them, maybe twenty-three. He wore a blue bandanna on his head like a pirate and was filthy, as they all were, from a day on the job.

I nodded, though the information was useless. One look at his size and weight and even a preschooler could figure out that Curry could eat.

"He's strong as shit," Talley said. He was a little older than Rodriguez, but not by much. He had a thick Boston accent and wore a Red Sox baseball cap. I imagined his life, probably somewhere out in Queens, to be one bar fight after another: Yankee fans, Mets fans, I'll take the whole fucking lot of you on.

I nodded and smiled gratefully, but this wasn't going anywhere fast.

"I've seen him," I said. "I know he's a big, strong man who

eats a lot of food. What wouldn't I know just by looking at him?"

"He's not just strong, he's really fucking strong," Collins said. He was the oldest, maybe thirty-three, and spoke with the confidence of a foreman. "Like he can carry four eighty-pound bags of pre-mix concrete on his shoulders, two on each on side, like they were feather pillows, like some kind of pack mule or something. Point is, Curry's got like the strongest back in the history of the world."

"So you don't think he hurt himself?" I said.

"I doubt it. Ted's real careful about rigging the scaffold," Collins said.

"No fucking way," Rodriguez said. "Dude's light on his feet."

"Nimble motherfucker," Talley said.

"Twinkletoes," Collins said. "He's not the type to fall. You got to be an idiot to fall off the scaffold, and Curry's no idiot. He's careful, and he's smart."

"How is he smart?" I said.

"He knows about a lot of different shit. Politics, history, science. He's smart, that's all I'm saying." Collins said. "And he's careful."

"Was he an asshole or one of the guys?" I said.

"Asshole, definitely," Rodriguez said.

"But he wasn't an asshole asshole," Talley said. "I hung with him one time after work. We ate dinner with his grandmother; he lives with her. She's like five hundred years old, not all there. Then we shot pool at this Second Avenue bar he hangs out at. Fast Eddie's. He goes every Thursday night. I had about ten beers, couldn't make shit, but he couldn't miss, so we made some money. He was kind of a prick, don't get me wrong, but I mean, he worked here, didn't get fired or nothing. I guess he was just one of those smart, careful assholes who could've been worse. Except now he is."

The other men agreed with Talley's assessment. Curry was

light on his feet, strong as an ox, could eat like a horse, and was a smart, careful, pool-shooting asshole, though not an asshole asshole until now.

"Want to see where he says he fell?" Barkowski said. "Where he didn't fall?"

"I'd like to recreate it," I said. "Can we do that?"

Barkowski turned to his men, gestured toward the back of the site, and said, "Set it up the way it was that day. Rodriguez, you be Curry."

"Why I got to be him?"

"Typecasting," Collins said, as they walked away.

"What do you think?" Barkowski said.

What I thought was that *smart* and *careful* were not the words I wanted to hear. What I thought was that stupid and careless would have been better. What I thought was that it wasn't going to be easy catching Curry in a lie. I might never catch him. I might try and try and never prove he was faking it, and maybe I couldn't make that kind of commitment after all; that's what I thought. I was on the fence, falling toward the sorry-to-say-this-but-I'm-out side. I opened my mouth to say those very words when a Honda minivan pulled onto the site and parked beside the trailer, the passenger side facing us.

A woman in her late fifties got out of the van. She had shoulder-length gray hair pulled back, soft facial features, wide hips, and thick legs. She was neatly dressed and carried herself like someone who had lived a lot of life but was ready to live a lot more. It was a hopeful quality that contrasted with the look in her eyes, which matched the look I had seen in Barkowski's eyes at Jimmy's wake: one part concern, one part fear.

She came around the front of the Honda and slid the passenger-side door open. There, sitting in three matching car seats, were Barkowski's triplets.

"This is my wife, Denise," Barkowski said, moving to the minivan. "Denise, this is Kate McCall."

"Nice to meet you, Kate," Denise said, taking a three-seat stroller from the Honda. "I'll shake your hand when I get the kids situated. They need a little fresh air, and they need it now."

I wanted to say something like, "Nice to meet you, too, Denise," but when I opened my mouth, nothing came out. Actually, the truth was that I had nothing to do with opening my mouth. It fell open on its own in direct response to the fact that Barkowski's triplets were as black as outer space and gorgeous.

"That's what most people say. Nothing," Barkowski said as he and Denise laughed, kissed, and got the triplets out of the car and into the stroller. "They're from Rwanda. Their parents got killed in a raid. Pretty much their whole village got wiped out. The entire family, right, Denise?"

She nodded. "We saw them online on CNN. They were two weeks old and all alone in the world in Africa. Our hearts broke, and we fell for them. We couldn't help it. Know what I mean?"

Jesus Christ, yes. I knew just what she meant. They were the most beautiful babies I had ever seen. I had fallen for them before she finished the question. I nodded, my mouth still hanging open.

"Two girls and a boy," Barkowski said. "It was a nice combination."

"We've been married twenty-eight years, our youngest two are in college. The older ones are on their own. We're empty-nesters," Denise said.

"We said, 'We got so much, and they got nothing. No hope, no future, no life. We could help them. Give them a home, give them a chance, give them a leg up,'" Barkowski said. "Everybody needs a leg up, right McCall?"

I nodded again.

"We cut through the red tape—a hundred grand can do that sometimes—and got them here in two months. It was a fight-

and-a-half from the word go. Everything's political. But Denise went to get them, and she got them. They're great babies. This is Laura, this is Emily, and this little pistol is Nicolas."

"Hi," I said, my voice finally returning. "I had no idea."

That was the understatement of the year. I had imagined that medical science had given the sixty-year-old builder three for the price of one with a young second wife, when, in fact, Ted and Denise Barkowski were candidates for the Greatest-People-in-the-World award.

"Not too many people do," Barkowski said.

"Well, I'm going to take them for a little walk," Denise said. "Again, it's nice to meet you, Kate. I hope you can help us."

We shook hands, and she pushed her babies down MacDougal toward Bleeker.

As I watched them go, *Jimmy's Rules of Private Investigation for Kate, Rule Number Five* hit me in the head like a brick: *Find a reason to care about the case. It's business, but it's personal too. That's the kick in the ass that keeps you going when everything else says, "Call it a damn day and go home."*

"You ready to see this now?" Barkowski said, gesturing at the back of the building where Rodriguez, Talley, and Collins were waiting.

"Ready," I said.

We walked through the first floor, which was still steel framing, rough plumbing, and loose wires everywhere, and arrived at the back side of the building.

Rodriguez was standing on scaffolding high enough off the ground for you not to want to fall from it, but not so high that it would instantly kill you. Talley and Collins were looking up at him.

"How high is that?" I said.

"Ten feet," Barkowski said. "Million dollars a foot is what he's suing me for."

"Jump on it," Collins said to Rodriguez.

Rodriguez jumped up and down, up and down, pounding his feet on the scaffold. It didn't budge.

"So if it didn't give, what happened?"

"The railing was unlatched, and he fell backwards through it," Barkowski said. "We heard him calling for help, ran back here, found him on the ground. Show her, Talley."

Talley sprawled out on his back in the dirt. I couldn't help thinking that in the dirt was where this Boston brawler belonged. I walked to the scaffold, checked the railing.

"Was it unlatched?" I said.

Barkowski sighed. "Yeah. When I got here, it was off. We all saw it. It was secure in the morning, that's all I know."

"Didn't unlatch itself," Collins said.

"You think Curry did it," I said.

"His word against mine," Barkowski said. "Cases like this go south all the time. Worker wins or you settle for millions before it gets to court. His doctor's an asshole and his lawyer's an animal. Just beating the shit out of Shavelson and the insurance company. I'm out of ideas. What about you?"

I thought about crawling around the Gristedes floor, gathering the contents of my purse while Curry looked at my ass. He was smart and careful. I thought about the Barkowski Rwandan triplets, Laura, Emily, and Nick, being pushed happily down Bleeker Street by Saint Denise. I thought about Jimmy with his eyes blown out, and I knew exactly what he would do.

"I've got one," I said.

15

IT'S COX AND KENNEDY

THERE WAS A DEADLY, LOVE TRIANGLE SUBPLOT IN *BLOOD SONG and Dance* that built throughout the play and climaxed with the main plotline—Farina LeBleu's cabaret aspirations. The triangle included Farina, Orlando Bilzi, and Mariah Muldoon. Roger Platt, the fifty-two-year-old, twice-divorced janitor, was playing Orlando. A young actor named Chloe Burns was playing Mariah. We were rehearsing on the D-Cup stage. Posey was at the piano. Dennis was on the apron. Thankfully, for all of us, it was a fang-free scene.

At the table read, Dennis had explained that Orlando was a genius cabaret pianist who, because of his paralyzing stage fright, had not played in front of a live audience for many years. The Bilzi backstory was that while performing to his accompaniment, Orlando's longtime lover and musical muse had died, her heart exploding like a hand grenade in her chest cavity, and he blamed himself for pushing her to hit a note beyond her range.

In the first act, after leaving a cabaret audition for which she does not get the part (she later kills the casting director and drinks his blood in a champagne flute), Farina hears Orlando playing in an empty, abandoned nightclub.

The music makes her cry—"Oh these tears, these cold, cruel vampire tears," she sings—and she enters the bar. She sings her blood-sucking soul out to his mournful melodies, a bond between them is forged, and a deal is struck: he will teach her to be the greatest cabaret singer of all time and, by becoming his new musical muse and true love, she will mend his broken heart forever.

She will do this—the forever part—by turning him into a vampire (when the time is right) to consummate their love and musical partnership for all eternity, though that part of the deal is the teeny little secret she keeps from him. It is for fear that her love will be unrequited that Farina hides the fact that she is a vampire. That was the only part of the show that seemed real to me.

Throughout the play, as Farina and Orlando's relationship progresses, Mariah Muldoon watches from the shadows. She is from faraway Philadelphia and works in the ticket booth beside Farina. Over time, she becomes Farina's confidante and best friend. For Mariah, however, it is much more than the sisterly sharing of secrets: it is true love. Mariah is a closet lesbian lover of vampire women. *Her* back-story, as explained by Dennis and Posey at the table read, was indecipherable.

Late in the second act, before the vampire and her musical mentor are poised to make their cabaret debut—and cement their love for all eternity—Mariah, her affection for Farina unrequited, meets Orlando beneath a street light and betrays the first of Farina's two dark secrets: that she is a vampire. The second secret, that she sells train tickets at Grand Central, Mariah does not reveal. Instead, she convinces the pianist to buy a late-night, one-way ticket out of New York, knowing full well—when Farina learns Orlando is leaving her—what the tragic and deadly result will be. For reasons no amount of back-story could explain, Orlando agrees.

"I want a one-way ticket to the end of the world," Roger said, without recognizing that the ticket vendor was his singer and vampire lover.

"Why would a man like you want to travel to the end of the world?" I said, pretending to take Roger's money and hand him a ticket in return.

"Because the woman I love is not a woman at all. She is a monster," Roger said. "She is the Vampire of Grand Central Station. The truth has been told. The song has been written. She will never have my love, and she will never have me. I will not teach her to be the greatest cabaret singer of all time, and she will live forever in loneliness and obscurity."

"If you go, you will inflame her anger," I said to Roger, "and break her heart."

"A vampire has no heart," he said. "And this one has no stage presence either."

At the piano, Posey played the opening chords of the next song. It was Chloe's big solo: "Her Love Will Come To Me Now" (during the finale, after Farina drinks Orlando's blood, she learns it was Mariah who betrayed her. She kills Mariah, too, singing, "Philadelphia, Philadelphia, How Bittersweet is Your Blood," and when everyone is dead, there is a reprise of "Railroad Street," in which all of Farina's victims return to the stage to sing and dance).

Dennis had been silently mouthing all our lines, expressing every emotion in the scene—Orlando's bitterness, Farina's rage, Mariah's joy—but now he said, "Let's stop right there, please. Chloe, we want you to try something different with this song tonight. Posey had an excellent idea we think you're going to like. Kate and Roger, give us ten, if you don't mind. We'll take it again from the top in just a bit. All right, then, off you go."

Roger and I left the stage, walked to the back of the loft, and sat in the last row. The D-Cup was otherwise empty. Roger, Chloe, and I shared several scenes together and tonight's rehearsal was just the three of us. It was Tuesday night. Jimmy had been murdered last Friday at three in the morning. It was just yesterday, at Jimmy's wake, that Barkowski had come to me with Ken Curry's case of workman's complication.

"I know what they want her to try," Roger said.

"Singing it in key?"

"You read my mind."

We both wanted to laugh, but didn't.

"I'm sorry about your father. You doing okay?"

"Surviving."

"That's how it was when my dad died. But he didn't get murdered, so I guess I don't really know what that's like."

"It's hard either way."

"Right. Look, if there's anything I can do..."

"Actually, Roger, there is something you can do."

"Name it, Kate."

"I want you to bring back Carl Kennedy."

"Bring him back where?"

In *Mississippi Boppin'*, a rollicking D-Cup Ku Klux Klan musical comedy in which I played a widowed Mississippi gas station owner who marries her African American mechanic and then sings and dances the local Klansmen into harmony (literally) with bebop rhythms, catchy melodies, and lively two-step numbers, Roger played the role of Detective Carl Kennedy, a New York fish-out-of-water cop investigating the murder of my husband (his brother, the New York fish-out-of-water gas station owner), who dies a mysterious Mississippi death. Kennedy never solves the crime, but he goes on to support the romance of his widowed sister-in-law and her mechanic. His performance was convincing. He was a cop down to the donuts.

"I inherited my father's private investigation business. My

first case is a workman's comp gone bad. I want us to interrogate someone."

"Us?"

"I'll be your partner. Detective MacKensie Cox."

"Kennedy and Cox. I like it."

Just like an actor, I thought.

"Sorry, Roger. It's Cox and Kennedy. I have to take the lead on this one."

"No, of course, I understand. It's your case."

On stage, Dennis and Posey had lowered the key in Chloe's solo, but it hadn't helped, so now they had raised it.

"Who are we interrogating?" Roger said.

"The weak link," I said. *Jimmy's Rules of Private Investigation for Kate, Rule Number Six—Every case has a weak link in its chain. Break that link, you bust the chain.*

"What?" Roger said.

"The guy's grandmother," I said.

"What guy?"

"The guy who says he fell off the scaffolding and can never work again. His grandmother is old and losing it. They live together. We'll pay her a visit and see if we can get her to tell us the truth."

"That the guy's not really hurt?"

"Exactly. You still have your badge from *Boppin'*?"

"Of course."

"I played a New York cop once in a low-budget indie. I've got that badge."

"When's the performance?"

"The guy always goes to the same bar on Thursday night. Grandma should be home alone. We'll wait until he's gone, then we'll knock on her door."

Dennis and Posey, having found no success by lowering or raising the key, changed the song from an Ethel Merman

Broadway belter to a twangy, Country Western number. It suited Chloe, so they set about adjusting the lyrics.

"One question," Roger said. "Isn't impersonating a police officer a crime?"

"Yes," I said.

"You're not worried about breaking the law?"

"I don't like it. But my client's got adopted, Rwandan baby triplets, and if I can't prove the scaffolding guy's a con man, they're going to be living in their Honda."

"What about getting caught, you're not worried about that either?"

"We're not in anybody's law enforcement file, so even if they figure out it wasn't really the NYPD that questioned grandma, how are they going to come looking for us? And on the plus side—"

"There's a plus side?"

"—what actor anywhere wouldn't take a role with real risk?"

Dennis and Posey had settled on a Texas two-step for Chloe's solo, and they were talking about rewriting her lines and lyrics to show she was from Dallas and not Philly.

"Count me in," Roger said.

I nodded. "I'll call you with the details."

Dennis signaled for us to return to the stage. As we stood up and walked back across the D-Cup, I said, "It's a real gig, Roger. I'm going to pay you."

"I'm a professional, Kate," Roger said. "Of course you are."

I smiled and said, "They'll have to change my song, too. 'Dallas, Dallas, How Bittersweet is Your Blood.'"

"Six of one, half dozen of the other," Roger said. "Like an order of donuts."

Spoken like a New York cop, I thought.

16

AN APPOINTMENT AND A REFERRAL

I CALLED TERRY KRAMER AT NINE THIRTY ON WEDNESDAY morning, introduced myself, told her I had found the "Problem: Powell was never married" Cutter's Tavern cocktail napkin at the bottom of an expanding envelope labeled *Open Cases*, and informed her that Jimmy had been murdered one week ago. There was a long, silent pause when she heard about Jimmy, and then she said, "I knew it."

Terry's half-brother, the late Ron Powell, was fifty-three when—according to the medical examiner's report—he died of a massive heart attack and left the full ten-million-dollar payout to his supposed ex-wife. Terry said otherwise on both accounts. She also said whoever at Monument was responsible for Ron's death might have killed Jimmy too. Jimmy was murdered one month after Powell was found dead in his bed.

Terry and Ron had connected for the first time four months ago, after they happened to meet at a party—their father had left one life for another many years earlier and had never conjoined the two. Terry's husband was an accountant at the same firm that handled Powell's business account, Gottlieb and Gorman. When they discovered their blood connection, they tried to catch up quickly as brother and sister, speaking almost daily and meeting for dinner numerous times on Long Island or in the city, often at La Luna, Ron's favorite place in Little Italy.

The reason Terry thought someone at Monument Life Insurance was "responsible" for Ron's death was that Ron had been in perfect health. Not good health, Terry told me, *perfect* health. He had low blood pressure, low body fat, high muscle mass, an ideal blood panel, clean lungs, and a strong heart. He had never smoked, drank two glasses of red wine per week (and no other alcohol), ate an optimal balanced diet, cross-trained for two hours every day, was an early-to-bed-early-to-riser, and was also, according to his half-sister, a confirmed bachelor who dated fitness instructors half his age—which, Terry said, wasn't surprising since Powell's life revolved around fitness.

He owned three popular fitness centers—one in Fresh Meadows, one in Tribeca, and one in Paramus, New Jersey. They all went by the name "Powell's Power Plant." He was successful, he was happy, and he'd had a physical three months before his death, at the time he'd finalized his Monument ten-million-dollar policy, which was just three days before he connected with Terry at the Gottlieb and Gorman party. There was no indication from the insurance physical that Powell was a coronary risk.

"Monument lied," Terry said. "Why would they do that unless they were hiding something? And if they lied about that, what else are they lying about?"

Terry had paused when Ron first told her he had just bought a ten-million-dollar life insurance policy. He had no children, no cousins, no uncles or aunts, no grandparents, no relatives of any kind—except her, though he didn't know she existed until after he'd bought the policy. "I asked him who he was leaving these millions to," Terry said.

Powell told her his Gottlieb and Gorman accountant had

mentioned that he could leave a large insurance payment to his favorite charity upon his death and could introduce him to an agent who would write that kind of policy. Ron liked the idea of helping people even after he was gone. He had charities he supported, he could afford a policy that size, and so he bought one...three months before his death. It was the physical examination he'd passed with flying colors that had sealed the deal.

The reason Terry thought whoever at Monument was responsible for Ron's death was also responsible for Jimmy's death was her encounter with Olivia Russell, the Monument agent who sold Powell the ten-million-dollar policy.

"I was in shock, of course," Terry said. "But I was confused, too. How could a man like Ronnie die of a massive heart attack in his sleep? I couldn't believe it. So I tried to get some answers. I started with his insurance agent, Olivia Russell. She's a Monument bigwig: high-value policies, exclusive clientele, Snob of the Year.

"I wanted to know who Ronnie's ex-wife was," Terry said. "He told me he'd never been married, but maybe he didn't want me to know for some reason. I doubted it, but maybe. Anyway, if he had an ex-wife, whoever she was, maybe she would know about some secret heart thing Ronnie had that caused his coronary. But Russell wouldn't tell me anything. She was rude beyond belief and cold as Canada. She threatened me several times. That's why I think Monument's involved somehow, the *way* she threatened me. She never came right out and said, 'I will kill you too,' but she definitely let me know bad things happen to people who don't mind their own business. But I kept trying. For Ronny. After about two weeks, I got a letter from the Monument legal eagles saying that I was harassing one of their agents. They were going to bring a huge suit if I didn't stop. My husband said, 'Cut it out,' and I called Jimmy."

Jimmy had told Terry that Monument was a tall order, so he wouldn't officially take the case unless, after looking around a little, he felt he could break it himself (that's why it was on a cocktail napkin and not a top sheet). If it turned out to be too big for him, he would recommend one of the larger PI outfits. He had poked around for a week, gotten his eyes blown out, and Terry was hearing about it one week after that.

I thanked Terry for talking to me, told her I would pick up where Jimmy left off, and call her when and if I found anything. Then I called Monument Life.

"Olivia Russell, please," I said to the Monument operator.

"Ms. Russell's office. This is Bradley. May I help you?"

His voice was dripping with condescension.

"Olivia Russell, please."

"Who's calling?"

"Dana Hawley," I said.

I heard him clack-clack-clacking on his keyboard, checking Russell's computerized Day Planner. "I don't see that you're scheduled for a phone appointment, Ms. Hawley," Bradley said as if I was a world-class moron for cold calling the great Olivia Russell in the first place.

"I need an appointment to talk to her on the phone?"

"An appointment *and* a referral," Bradley said. "Ms. Russell is exceptionally busy and does not accept unsolicited, unreferred requests for her time. I can recommend another Monument agent, if you like."

"But I want to make an appointment to see *her*. I'd like to buy a very large policy and leave the payment to charity. I know she writes that kind of policy."

"Yes, but she does not take calls or meetings without a referral from one of her existing clients or close associates. Is there anything else I can help you with?"

"Listen, Bradley. I am the president of a Wall Street hedge fund with assets in the billions of dollars. That's billion, with a B. If you'd like me to have my attorney contact Ms. Russell, that can be arranged."

"I'll pass on your legal threat, Ms. Hawley. I'm sure that will entice Ms. Russell into meeting with you as soon as possible. Are we done?"

"Oh yes, Bradley, I think we are."

I hung up the phone with Bradley at five past ten. By five past ten and thirty seconds, I was on my way up the four flights of stairs to 5A, Al Cutter's apartment. As I climbed, I wondered what kind of businessperson required an appointment *and* a referral for a freaking phone call. The kind who wouldn't tell a dead client's grieving sister who the ex-wife was, the kind who, instead of offering professional condolences, offered threats, the kind who had a snot-faced Bradley answering her phones, that's what kind.

I knocked on Al's door. He opened it and stared at me. It had been two seconds and he already looked impatient. He also looked like shit. He hadn't slept in sixteen years, since an unexpected hostage encounter with his roommate when Al was eighteen and a freshman at Fordham had left him forever traumatized.

"I have a hypothetical question," I said.

"Make it fast. I'm the middleman in an international eBay blockbuster. I got twenty-five thousand silk ties from China at a buck apiece going to Holland, where they turn into two thousand bags of Darwin Hybrid Tulip Bulbs at fifteen per bag."

"Where do they go?"

"Tulsa."

"Oklahoma?"

"No. Tulsa, Argentina. Yes, Oklahoma, McCall. I trade them there for seventeen hundred pairs of custom cowboy boots at twenty bucks each, and they go to the Panhandle, where I make some serious green. What's the question?"

Behind him, through the half-open door, I could see his computer rig glowing like the bridge of an alien spaceship. He had three huge monitors and three smaller ones, each with its own tower, as well as speakers, keyboards, printers, scanners, and two six-foot-tall mainframes, like he was the CIA or the FBI or Homeland Security.

Because sleep wasn't one of the requirements in his life, Al had plenty of extra time on his hands. What he did with that time, beyond the occasional limo driving, donut making, and international eBay blockbuster trading, was hack. He would one day be curious, say, about Stanford University's endowment fund, or the mayor of Minnesota's family photographs, or the government of Thailand's top-secret documents and see if he couldn't find his way in and have a look around.

"If you wanted to hack into the Monument Life Insurance Company computer system appointment database, could you do it, hypothetically?

"It might take all day and night to override and circumvent their security codes and passwords, hypothetically."

"Will you be up all day and night, hypothetically?"

"I might be, hypothetically."

Near the computer were dozens of Gatorade bottles lined up like little yellow soldiers. I put them out of my mind.

"Well then, hypothetically, I would like Ms. Gillian Breiner to have an appointment with Ms. Olivia Russell of Monument Life at eleven o'clock Friday morning. She should be referred by one of Ms. Russell's clients."

"Do you know which one, hypothetically?"

"Ron Powell, hypothetically."

Al nodded. "Hypothetically, I'll see what I can do."

I gestured at the platoon of yellow bottles. "Has Fu been up here, yet?"

"Not that I can tell."

"Sorry about that."

"Yeah. Hey, you want something to drink? I got Gatorade."

I shook my head. Gatorade might be the last thing I would

ever drink for the rest of my life. "You won't get caught, will you? Hypothetically, I mean."

"No," he said. "Hypothetically, every time I hack, I program it so all my threads lead to Elliot Morgan."

"Good," I said and started down the stairs.

Pre-med Elliot Morgan was Al's freshman roommate at Fordham. One night, when Al was sound asleep, Elliot woke him up holding a loaded Smith & Wesson .357 Magnum in one hand and his cell phone in the other. He was talking to his biology professor, who was failing him. Elliot threatened to blow Al's head off if the professor didn't change Elliot's F to an A. The police arrived, and the standoff lasted a tense ten hours, nine of which featured Al sitting on his bed with the barrel of the gun in his mouth.

Eventually, Elliot surrendered and his wealthy Park Avenue parents had the charges reduced so that with a smidgen of counseling and a dab of community service Elliot's debt to society was paid. He graduated NYU without fanfare and was now a Wall Street commodities trader living somewhere in the East Village.

Thursday morning, my phone rang at eight twenty. I was on my way out the door to Raul's Boxing in Hell's Kitchen for a few hours of smacking the heavy bag while imagining it was Bradley.

"Ms. Olivia Russell is meeting Ms. Gillian Breiner at eleven fifteen tomorrow morning," Al said. "It's confirmed on her schedule, written in non-delete code."

"I specifically said eleven, Al. Eleven fifteen is the best you could do?" I said, busting his balls.

"Hypothetically," he said.

17

IT'S LIKE FIVE THOUSAND LITTLE ICE CUBES IN THERE

NEW YORKERS SPEND SO MUCH TIME SWEPT UP IN THE ENERGY OF eight million people living on a tiny island, so completely focused on themselves in the hot flow of the city, so intent on controlling the moments as they race by, that they often miss the obvious while searching for the subtext. Case in point: though I had followed Curry from his house to the Gristedes around the corner (only two days ago), it didn't occur to me how nice a building he lived in until I met Roger across the street from it, the two of us dressed like NYPD detectives, sitting on a bench on the east side of Central Park West, watching the front door, waiting for Curry to catch a cab to Fast Eddie's.

I was wearing gray slacks with a matching jacket, a blue blouse, and comfortable, but not unfashionable black shoes. I had chosen a shoulder-length red wig and blue contact lenses. My NYPD badge from the low-budget independent film *Cannibal Cop*, in which I played a detective who gets eaten by her partner, was clipped to my belt. Also clipped to my belt was a middle-of-the-back holster with the realistic but not real *Cannibal Cop* revolver I never got the chance to pretend to use because my partner blindsided me before eating me for brunch. I never even considered carrying Jimmy's Colt. I don't like real guns in my real life.

Roger wore a blue suit with a blue-and-red striped tie, his *Mississippi Boppin'* NYPD badge on a lanyard, which hung around his neck, and a shoulder holster with a plastic police pistol. We really did look like New York detectives.

"I'm in the wrong business," Roger said when he first arrived. "Last time I checked, construction workers didn't make this kind of dough."

"He's a pack mule for the concrete crew. There's no way he can afford this place," I said. It was called The Fairview, and it was high swank.

"Grandma Curry must be loaded," he said.

I told him what I had learned about Curry's grandmother—that her name was Dolores, that she was eighty-six years old and not all there, that her son was Curry's father, that she played cards, went to the movies, and still occasionally went ballroom dancing—and reiterated that we were trying to get her to say Curry's back was fine, that it was all an act, that he never really fell off Barkowski's scaffolding.

"Piece of cake," Roger said. "Then what?"

"Then this," I said, showing him the small piece of jewelry pinned to my lapel. "It's really a tiny wireless microphone tuned to a miniature digital recorder in my pocket."

Jimmy had bought it for me to catch a PTA president who had embezzled eleven grand from her daughter's elementary school and bought a super surround-sound home theater from Best Buy.

Roger leaned toward me and said directly into my lapel, "Detective Carl Kennedy always gets his grandma."

Just then, Curry came through the doors of his upscale CPW apartment building. The night-shift doorman, a five-foot-tall Mexican gentleman named Miguel Ortiz—who I had earlier asked about Dolores Curry while posing as a southern consensus taker with black hair and black eyes—held the door open as Curry limped into the night.

Curry was wearing his back brace and leaning heavily on his cane. He could barely move one foot in front of the other, but he somehow managed, in what seemed like a lifetime, to get to the curb, where Miguel hailed him a cab. Watching Curry contort himself inch by painful inch into the back seat, with Miguel helping him, was a sight to see.

"Jesus," Roger said. "Poor guy."

"Roger."

"I meant poor guy, what a terrible actor."

The cab pulled away, and Roger and I crossed Central Park West.

"Miguel Ortiz," I said in a tough New York City accent, "I'm Detective Cox, and this is Detective Kennedy."

Roger and I flashed our fake badges. Miguel froze, eyes wide. He might have had a green card, but then again he might have had a baseball card.

"Relax. We don't want to talk to you. Not yet, anyway," Roger said.

"We're looking for Dolores Curry," I said. "I'm betting you know who she is."

Miguel nodded.

"Call her, Ortiz. Tell her she has visitors," Roger said.

Miguel lifted the building phone, punched Dolores' apartment number: 1204.

"Mrs. Curry. It's Miguel the doorman."

He waited as she said something.

"I know your shows are on. But two detectives down here want to talk to you."

He smiled nervously at us, listening to Dolores, and then he said, "She want to know if she in trouble. She pretty sure she pay her bus fare." Then he covered the phone and whispered, "*Loquita*. Little crazy."

"Tell her she's not in any trouble," I said. "We just want to talk to her."

"No trouble, Mrs. Curry. They just want to talk to you."

He nodded, hung up the phone, pointed at the elevator, and said, "1204."

Roger and I stepped off the elevator on the twelfth floor and walked down the hall to 1204.

"I don't want to be here all night, Roger. Let's just get her to say it and get out."

"Is your mic on?"

"Good to go."

"We'll be a memory in three minutes."

I knocked. An eye filled the peephole. A voice came from the other side.

"Who is it?"

"Detective MacKensie Cox and Detective Carl Kennedy," I said.

"Put your guns away."

Roger rolled his eyes. "Maybe ten minutes."

"You're looking at us through the peephole, Mrs. Curry. You can see we don't have our guns out. We just want to talk," I said.

"Not until you put away those pistols."

"Maybe twenty minutes," Roger said.

"Okay, Mrs. Curry. We put our guns away," I said.

The door opened, and Dolores Curry narrowed her eyes and smiled a thin smile. "Call me Dolores. Mrs. Curry makes me feel like an old broad."

She moved aside, and Roger and I went into the apartment.

"The place is a mess, and I don't care. I'm eighty-six, I got better things to do than wash windows."

The place was hardly a mess. In fact, it was hardly a place. It was a huge and beautiful home in the sky. We were in a foyer the size of a studio apartment—with high ceilings, crown moldings, a chandelier, and antique furniture—whose only function was to provide an elegant place to wait while you took off your coat and decided where in the house you wanted to go. I could have lived in just this room.

Straight ahead was a wide living room with a thirty-foot wall of windows overlooking Central Park. From the foyer, I could see a fireplace, multiple sofas, chairs, and tables covered with framed family photographs, and a grand piano. To the right was a long hallway that led to the bedrooms. I counted eight doors down that hall. I figured four of them had to be bedrooms. To the left was another hall that led to the eat-in kitchen, butler's pantry and dining room, which also had a fireplace.

Jesus, I thought, *Concrete Curry lives like a king.*

"Nice place," Roger said.

"Kenny calls it the Taj Mahal. How the hell would he know? He's never even been to Burbank. Maybe he saw it in a movie once, but I doubt it. Nobody's made a decent movie since *Anchors Aweigh*."

"Frank Sinatra and Gene Kelly," Roger said with a smile.

"1945," Dolores said.

"I love that movie," Roger said.

"Sure you do, Detective, because you got class. I could see that as soon as I opened the door."

"See that, Cox?" Roger said to me, "I got class."

"Who would have guessed?" I said.

Going with the premise that everyone in Manhattan (and Los Angeles) looks like somebody famous—and speaking of movies—Dolores Curry was a dead ringer for Ruth Gordon. Specifically, the Ruth Gordon in *Harold and Maude*. Any minute, I expected Bud Cort, with a noose around his neck or a Samurai sword sticking out of his stomach, to come traipsing down the hall from the bedrooms, dripping buckets of fake blood.

"Why don't we sit down, Dolores?" I said, starting for the

living room. I wanted to get a look at Curry's family photos. "We'll ask you a couple questions and let you get back to your shows."

Before I took two steps, she cut me off, took me by the arm, and redirected me down the hall to the kitchen. "Why don't I make us a pot of tea instead? I got Fig Newtons. Kenny bought them for me at Gristedes."

I know, I thought. With her other hand, she had Roger by the arm, too, and was dragging him along with us. She was surprisingly quick and unbelievably strong. There was no possibility I could shake her off and get to the living room. We would have to do this over tea and Fig Newtons.

It was a large kitchen, nicely done in a modern country style, with a round, mahogany, pedestal table that could easily seat six in the middle of the room. She sat us at the table, moved to the stove, lifted a cast iron teapot, crossed to the sink, and began to fill it with water.

"So what do you want to ask me about?"

"Your grandson," I said.

"Such a shame. Strong as an ox one day, can't lift a kitten the next. Did he break the law? I'll tan his hide but good if he did."

"No, but there might be criminal charges pending against the contractor," I said. "If he really fell."

"If he really fell?" Dolores said.

"They're serious charges, Dolores. That contractor could be in deep trouble. Before we go down that road and press charges, we have to be sure that your grandson really fell off the scaffolding."

"You can tell us, Dolores," Roger said. "Maybe he's not hurt as bad as all that. Maybe that's not the real truth."

"It always comes out in the end, doesn't it?" Dolores said.

"Always," I said. "Better now than later for everyone involved. The contractor, Ken, you."

"Me?" She was at the sink, her back turned to us.

"You're a part of this now, Dolores," I said.

"A big part," Roger said. "Being that you live with him, you would have to know the real truth. And because you would know the real truth, you would tell us because you wouldn't lie to the police. You know why?"

"Why?"

"Because you got class, Dolores," Roger said.

"If I were thirty years younger, Detective, I'd show you some class."

"I know you would, Dolores," Roger said. He winked at me to let me know he had her just where he wanted her.

"This teapot weighs a ton. Could you give me a hand?" Dolores said, smiling at Roger over her shoulder.

Roger got off his kitchen chair and moved to the sink. At the same second he arrived to help lift the teapot, Dolores half spun around to him and accidentally stepped square on his foot.

"Ow, shit...Jesus Christ," Roger said, instinctively bending over to grab his foot. "You broke my foot."

"I'm so sorry," Dolores said, spinning around the rest of the way, absent-mindedly swinging the cast iron teapot out of the sink, and—wham—whacking Roger a hundred miles an hour in the side of the head.

Roger staggered backwards like a punch-drunk prizefighter, slammed into the kitchen counter, and fell to the floor, not unconscious, but seeing stars and hearing birds, ready to be counted out.

"Oh my, now I've done it. Assaulting an officer," Dolores said, dropping the teapot like a discharged firearm. "Take me to jail, Detective. I confess. Slap on the handcuffs. I'm ready to face the music." She put her hands out in front of her like a crook caught red-handed.

I didn't have handcuffs. Even if I did, I was already on my

way to help Roger, whose eyes were rolling around in his head like loose marbles.

"Jesus, Roger. Are you okay?" I said, kneeling beside him. The entire left side of his face was already swelling up and turning purple. His eye would be shut tight for a few days for sure.

"My head," Roger said. "My foot... my head..."

"I thought you said his name was Carl," Dolores said, her arms still stretched out, her wrists still cuffless.

"Roger's his middle name," I said. "All his friends call him Roger."

"He don't look too good," Dolores said. "You want some ice?"

"Yes, ice would be great," I said.

She opened the freezer, grabbed a bag of frozen peas, and handed them to me.

"It's like five thousand little ice cubes in there, except they're green and round," she said.

I put the bag on Roger's eye and helped him to his feet. He was weak in the knees.

"You better get him to a doctor," Dolores said. "He's going to have a hell of headache and a shiner to match."

"I think you're right," I said. "Can you walk, Carl?"

"I can try," Roger said. "I think she broke my foot."

"I thought all his friends called him Roger," Dolores said.

"It's interchangeable, Dolores," I said, turning to her. "Carl and Roger." She was leaning against the counter, relaxed, arms folded in front of her.

"That's good," she said. "I like that. I wish I had two names. I'd have been Dolores and Vivian." She led us down the hall to the foyer, opened the door, and smiled.

"I've been thinking about the real truth," she said, leaning into my lapel and speaking directly into the jewelry pin microphone. "The real truth is that contractor owes my grandson ten million dollars, and that sounds like a lot of Fig Newtons to me. So you go ahead and press charges against him. Don't you worry about it for one minute; we got you covered. I'll tell Kenny to be on the lookout for anybody trying to step on your case. I'm sure he'll be extra careful. Take care of Carl and Roger. Bye now."

She shut the door and I helped Roger to the elevator. I'd had a fleeting moment in the Curry kitchen, while applying the peas to the left side of Roger's head, where I thought, *That was not an accident. Not the foot or the teapot. That eighty-six-year-old broad did it on purpose to get us out of the house in a hurry.* But in the next moment, the thought seemed unlikely, if not impossible, so it vanished as if it had never been thought at all.

It wasn't until she leaned into my lapel that I'd realized the whole time we were playing her, the real truth was that she was playing us. Her grandson would be on red alert from this point on.

"Well," I said, as we stepped into the elevator. "At least we learned something."

"What's that?" Roger said, holding the peas in place.

"There's nothing *loquita* about Dolores Curry."

18

THE MOST BEAUTIFUL EXECUTIVE
ON THE BLOCK

"WHAT MAGAZINE DID YOU SAY YOU WERE FROM, MS. BREINER?"

"*Club Solutions*," I said. "As I'm sure you know, Ms. Russell, Ron Powell was a very successful fitness club owner, and covering the operation of first-class fitness clubs and their owners is our bread and butter business. Ron's sudden and unexpected death is a sad sidebar to our story."

The great Olivia Russell sat behind her modern, glass and steel desk, typing something into her computer. Her office was expansive and included her aircraft carrier-sized desk with four black leather chairs in a semi-circle facing her, two wildly-expensive black leather sofas anchoring a seating area, a glass-and-steel conference table that matched her desk (encircled by eight more black leather chairs), a wall of video equipment displayed in custom-made glass and steel shelving, and pricey-looking modern paintings and sculptures scattered around the room to demonstrate her exquisite taste and bulging bank account. The floors were blonde oak covered with imported Asian rugs. As enormous as her office was, it was hardly large enough to hold both Ms. Russell and her ego. I barely slid into the room between them.

I stood by the wall of windows that looked out over the city. Russell's office was on the twenty-seventh floor. As *Jimmy's Rules of Private Investigation for Kate, Rule Number Two* advised, I didn't trust her for that reason alone.

"As a matter of fact, I wasn't aware of your magazine until you stepped into my office," Russell said. "I wouldn't recognize your bread and butter business if it were served to me on a silver platter."

She was thirty-three years old. Dark hair, shoulder length and stylishly cut, dark eyes, perfect skin. She was the kind of dazzling that pops out of a fashion magazine in a feature called *The Most Beautiful Executive on the Block*—carefully constructed nose and cheekbones, casually gorgeous makeup, strikingly feminine business attire that cost more than a car, shoes so exclusive no one has ever heard of them.

"Served on a silver platter. I like that," I said. "Can I use it somewhere in the story?"

"Take a seat, Ms. Breiner. We'll discuss it while we wait."

"While we wait for what?"

"The reply."

What reply? I thought as I sat across the desk from her. To become Ms. Breiner, ace reporter from *Club Solutions*, I had chosen a brunette wig of wavy hair, hazel contact lenses and a simple suit. I was all business, but not overly dressed. I looked like I could write one heck of a fitness story if I could only get some quotes. Served on a silver platter would be a good one.

Bradley had placed a bottle of designer water on the matching steel-and-glass end table that accompanied each leather chair. I opened the bottle and took a sip of the water, which was, not surprisingly, chilled to perfection.

Ms. Russell's obnoxious little pit bull was the personification of my image of him: bone-thin body, narrow eyes, long nose, and prematurely receding hairline. Entering his outer office with an undeletable appointment to see his unseeable boss had been one of the highlights of my week.

"I didn't schedule this appointment for you, Ms. Breiner," he said as I came in.

"Of course you did, Bradley. We had a nice chat. I'm surprised you don't remember."

"I remember everything, I don't make mistakes, and I don't write in non-delete code. We have never spoken, and you don't have an appointment with Ms. Russell."

He didn't remember speaking to me because I was using a mildly Midwestern accent and had lowered the pitch of my voice. He glared at me through narrowed eyes the entire time I waited for Ms. Russell to make herself available. I smiled and told him that squinting causes crow's feet, which he'd have the rest of his life. I said I'd learned that from years of covering health and fitness.

"I'm not sure what I can add to your story," Russell said. "I didn't write a business policy for Mr. Powell. I have no special insight as to what does or doesn't define the professional administration of a chain of health clubs."

"But you knew Ron on a personal basis. I want to humanize him for our readers, present the man behind the health clubs, the Powell behind the Power Plants."

"I'm sure I didn't know him as well as you think I did."

"But you knew him in a way my readers didn't, and even if you didn't know him all that well, you know people who did."

"People?"

"Relatives, wives, ex-wives. Don't you speak with close family members when writing a large policy for a new client?"

"Not very often, no."

"You didn't speak with his ex-wife? He left her the full ten million, didn't he?"

She smiled a thin, unpleasant smile, one eye on her computer screen.

"I write so many high-value policies, Ms. Breiner, I'd have to pull up Mr. Powell's file to check the exact terms of his payout."

"Do you mind?"

"Would you like to know who she is, as well?"

"That would be great, thanks. So far, she's the mystery ex-wife. I can't find her anywhere, and I'm a pretty good reporter. I'm sure she'll know the real Ron Powell. I mean, they were married, right? In order for her to be the ex-wife, she would have to be the wife first. Mrs. Ron Powell. You must have their marriage license on file. And the divorce documents. Probably scanned them into Powell's digital file. That's the way we do it at the magazine."

"I'm sure you understand that Monument Life considers Mr. Powell's personal information to be confidential."

"Just the ex-wife's name would be great. I could take it from there."

"And you wouldn't tell anyone where you got it?"

"Reporters don't divulge their sources if they want to stay reporters."

"Even health club reporters like you?"

"The health club circuit's a small world, Ms. Russell. I'd have to say especially health club reporters like me."

"That's interesting because while we've been chatting, I emailed the editor of *Club Solutions* and asked him to confirm that a reporter named Gillian Breiner was on his staff since there was one in my office at this moment asking me for confidential information regarding a deceased client and his grieving ex-wife. Apparently, you're not listed as a staff writer."

She was even sharper than she looked. "I'm a freelance reporter. I'm not actually on the *Club Solutions* staff. I'm sorry, I should have made that clear when I booked the appointment with Bradley."

"Don't be sorry. I asked the editor to confirm his staff *and* freelance reporters. There's no Gillian Breiner anywhere in his files." With her eyes still drilling me, she called out to Bradley in his outer office. He appeared in the doorway.

"Bradley, call the woman who claims to be Mr. Powell's half-sister and ask her if she's recently hired a private investigator. If so, tell her we're suing her for harassment. Then call IT and have all my access codes changed and re-secured."

Bradley narrowed his eyes and glared at me again.

"I don't make mistakes," he said.

"Crow's feet forever," I said to him. He sneered at me and vanished.

"I don't authorize non-delete code on my schedule for this very reason," Russell said. "One of the annoyances of the high-payout insurance business is the steady stream of inexperienced private investigators falling all over themselves to undo the facts of a paid policy. I knew you were an investigator by the smell of your low-cost perfume. What is it? Ballantine Ale? If you want access to Mr. Powell's file, you'll have to download it from my office computer. Would you like a disc?"

"Please," I said. "But I'm not a private investigator. I'm a reporter. And I didn't know Powell had a half-sister. Can you tell me *her* name?"

"Bradley, escort whoever this is out of the building," she said.

Perfect. If nothing else I could punch Bradley in the nose before making my unescorted exit. Jimmy used to say, *Some people go begging for a good punch in the nose, and it's your job to give them what they want.* I decided on a right cross and stood up.

But filling Russell's doorway wasn't her skinny, asshole aide. Instead, it was an ex-Marine in a gray Armani suit. He was forty years old, built like a marble statue, with a huge jaw and buzz-cut blonde hair. He was probably six feet four inches tall, two hundred and thirty pounds. I would have trouble even reaching his chin with a right cross. He wore a Monument Life Insurance

Company identification badge on his chest. Under the Monument Life logo it read: *Bradley Olsen, Director of Security.*

"What are the chances?" Russell said to me. "Two Bradleys in one office. This Bradley was a Green Beret for fifteen years. Now he's in charge of security on my floor. Isn't that right?"

"Yes, ma'am," Green Beret Bradley said. He was Southern. His eyes were ice blue and cold as Christmas. Why he wasn't playing professional football was a mystery.

"I imagine I can't prove that you hacked into my scheduling software," Russell said. "I'm certain your digital trail leads someplace obscure."

"You could try," I said, thinking of Elliot Morgan: cell phone in one hand, .357 in the other, the barrel in Al Cutter's mouth for nine hours.

"And since the appointment was, in fact, on my schedule, I don't suppose there are grounds for criminal charges in your physically being here, even if you are impersonating a non-existent fitness club reporter."

"I want to be a real fitness club reporter, and I thought if I could write a personal piece about Ron Powell, *Club Solutions* would have to hire me."

"That's your story?"

"That's the truth."

Snot-faced Bradley appeared in the doorway beside Green Beret Bradley. The big one could have eaten the little one as a snack. Green Beret Bradley took two giant steps toward me, ready to guide me out of the office, into the elevator, down to the lobby, and out of the building. Before he could put his massive hand on my elbow, Russell came around her desk and stood before me, face-to-face.

"Please understand, today Bradley is gently escorting you off the premises. I promise you the next time will be demonstrably less pleasant."

She was my height, thinner than me, and hyper, Type A fit.

She had to work out two hours a day, seven days a week. Still, I wanted to punch her perfect little nose.

"Are you threatening me, Ms. Russell?"

"I'm offering you cost-free professional advice. It's never too late to reexamine your disability insurance."

Green Beret Bradley deposited me outside and watched as I walked away. Like Ken Curry and his grandmother, Olivia Russell now had her radar turned way up. I hadn't fooled her one bit. She'd given me nothing about Powell, his ex-wife, his policy, or his improbable coronary. But I hadn't come away empty-handed either. I could see why Terry Kramer thought Olivia Russell knew something about Powell's death. And if she knew something about that, it was likely she knew something about Jimmy's murder as well. I was still at square one on both cases, but at least I could see square two.

19

THINK OF THE SYMMETRY

I HAD BECOME ONE WITH THE VAMPIRE TEETH. SINCE LAST Friday's rehearsal—one week ago, when Barnes told me Jimmy had been murdered—I had spent an excessive amount of time molding and shaping the teeth to conform more naturally to my mouth. Still, no matter what contortions I wrought upon the plastic fangs, some kind of oral distortion remained, resulting in hysterics for the Schmidt and Parker Players when I spoke my lines and sang my songs.

The breakthrough occurred earlier that afternoon, after my meeting with Olivia Russell. As I was changing out of my Gillian Breiner outfit, I unknowingly knocked the teeth off my makeup table onto the floor and stepped on them on my way to the kitchen. I cursed the fangs, carried them to the sink, rinsed them off, and noticed that the force of my foot had caused a shift in the overall dimensions, a sea-change in the very posture of the fangs that I would never have considered or been able to accomplish by hand even if I had.

I slipped them into my mouth and knew instantly they were no longer just any vampire fangs...they were *my* vampire fangs.

I could speak, I could sing, I could laugh and cry and

threaten to suck neck without initiating waves of laughter from the cast. I could act effortlessly and with uncluttered concentration on Farina LeBleu, her eternal thirst for human blood, her insatiable hunger for entertaining nightclub crowds.

It had been an energetic rehearsal. Freed from the fear of fang failure, I hunted my prey with a gusto I had not until now discovered. Startled cast members, taken aback by Farina's unabashed lust and newfound enunciation, cringed with fear as I swooped in for the kill.

Roger, whose foot was not broken, whose eye did not close, and who was diagnosed as non-concussive by the emergency room doctor who examined him after we left Dolores Curry, performed admirably, despite a shiner the size and shape of Rhode Island and a still-stellar headache.

Of course, everyone wanted to know who was driving the truck that slammed into the side of Roger's face. I told them the abbreviated version of how I inherited Jimmy's PI business on account of his being found dead in the Monument elevator and how my first case was Teddy Barkowski's workman's complication lawsuit. I painted a picture of the Barkowski triplets and Saint Denise, so they would know what was at stake, then I replayed my shopping cart collision with Ken Curry at the Upper West Side Gristedes, and Roger and I reenacted our tea party with Grandma Curry. Chloe Burns won rave reviews for her performance as Dolores, although she got a carried away when pretending to swing the teapot and actually smacked Roger in the face with the back of her hand.

Rehearsal ended, and Dennis and Posey sent everyone home except me. I was scheduled for extra time at the piano. But before I sang a note, Posey wanted to know what my next move would be.

"I was thinking I would put the fangs in and we could work on my solo in the second act," I said.

"Your fangs *are* in, sweetheart," Dennis said.

"I mean your next move with Ken Curry," Posey said. "You can't let him get away with it. Think of the triplets. And poor Denise."

"Maybe the doctor," I said. "Curry's orthopedist, Dr. Martin Miller on East 63rd. He's the one swearing up and down that Curry's back is beyond treatment. Even if Barkowski's insurance company doctors say otherwise, Miller's still claiming Curry's disabled."

"So there's doubt," Dennis said.

"Yes, and doubt means settle out of court for everything Barkowski's got," I said.

"Can't he go to court?" Posey said.

"Sure, but to a jury of his peers, all of them thinking, *One slip in the office lunchroom and that's me*, doubt means asking is there any limit to the amount of money we can award the poor guy, or do we have to stop at ten mil?"

"Barkowski's the big loser either way," Posey said.

"So you're going to try to crack the doctor?" Dennis said.

"I'm not having any luck with Curry and his grandma."

"What's your plan?" Posey said.

"I need someone to act like they're pretending they got hurt on the job. I'll suck Miller in on a scam like Curry and his grandmother did. If I can get him to diagnosis a fairy tale, then Barkowski's case looks good."

Dennis and Posey's eyes went wide at the same moment.

"That year," Posey said.

"In the Berkshires," Dennis said.

"Summer stock," Posey said.

"I played the plumber," Dennis said.

"With the bad back," Posey said.

"Sharp pain shooting up and down my legs," Dennis said.

"You could hardly walk," Posey said.

"I was in agony," Dennis said.

"I was worried about you, and I knew you were acting," Posey said.

"We can do it," Dennis said to me.

"Do what?" I said.

"I'll be your father," Dennis said. "A commercial plumber looking to retire in high style after a life of laying pipe. You'll be my daughter."

"And I'll be your mother," Posey said. "A family of grifters. Like Dolores and Ken Curry."

"Jesus, my back," Dennis said, going into character.

He moved away from the piano and stagger-stepped his way to a chair that he could barely sit down on.

"Oh Angela," Posey said to me, while moving to Dennis. "Look at your father. He's in terrible pain. I don't think he'll ever be able to work again."

"Never again," Dennis moaned.

And then they looked at me like young actors at an audition, hoping that this time they really-truly got the part.

"Angela?" I said.

"If I'd had a daughter, that's what I would have named her," Posey said.

"Say yes, Kate," Dennis said.

"Think of the symmetry," Posey said.

"Symmetry?" I said.

"The three of us on one side, the Rwandan triplets on the other," Posey said.

"Kismet," Dennis said.

"I don't know," I said, certain it was a bad idea. "I have to think about it."

And then the bell rang, signaling visitors on the way up, and I was saved, until the elevator door opened, and everything changed again.

20

HOW DO YOU KNOW I'M A VAMPIRE?

Detective Mike Harriman stepped off the elevator, spotted us by the stage, and walked toward us, across the loft.

Dennis and Posey had a steady stream of actors visiting their theater at all hours, including during rehearsals. When one would arrive, Dennis or Posey, sometimes both, would call out for them to leave their head shot in the box by the elevator door. The actors would do as they were directed and take the elevator back down to the street.

But Dennis and Posey didn't call out to Harriman. I imagine they knew he was no actor. I imagine they knew he was a cop. Their silence, I'm sure, was due to the fact that he was such a damn good-looking cop.

He was wearing a beautiful gray suit with a blue shirt and a blue silk tie that was loose around his neck. He needed a shave the way all movie stars need a shave.

"Dennis Parker, Posey Schmidt," I said, as Harriman arrived at the piano, "meet Homicide Detective Mike Harriman. He's investigating Jimmy's murder. Detective, this is Dennis and Posey, co-founders and co-creative directors of the D-Cup Musical Theater."

"Nice to meet you, Detective," Posey said with a voice that implied "Jesus Christ, are you handsome."

"Nice to meet you, too," Harriman said, nodding at Dennis and Posey. "What show are you doing?"

"*Blood Song and Dance*," Dennis said. "It's a vampire musical."

"Can never have too many of those," Harriman said with a smile.

"Exactly," Posey said.

"Do you have a minute, Kate?"

"We're sort of rehearsing," I said.

"We were just taking a break," Dennis said.

"The man is investigating your father's murder," Posey said. "Take five."

Harriman and I walked away from the stage into the shadows of the theater toward the bathroom, where I'd first learned of Jimmy's death.

"How did you find me?" I said.

"I'm a cop. I find people for a living."

"So did you find the guy who killed Jimmy?"

"Not yet."

I was disappointed, though I knew before I asked that his answer would be no. You can see good news in a person's eyes. Harriman's eyes had only questions.

"Then what are you doing here?"

"I got a phone call today from a guy named Bradley Olsen. You know him?"

Green Beret Bradley. Olivia Russell's muscle. "No," I said. "Who is he?"

We reached the far side of the loft and sat in the same two chairs that Roger and I had sat in only three nights ago, on Tuesday, when I'd asked him to reprise his role as Detective Carl Kennedy, a decision, I'm sure, in retrospect, he regretted.

"He's the director of security for Olivia Russell. Do you know her?"

"Everybody knows her. *Robin Hood. Gone With The Wind.* She must be in her nineties by now. Why does she need security? Oh, wait. I'm thinking of Olivia de Havilland. What did you say her name was again?"

"Russell. Olivia Russell. She's a VP at Monument Life Insurance. Writes complicated policies for high-net-worth clients. Very exclusive."

"Are we getting to the point why you're telling me this?"

"Just about there."

On the D-Cup stage, Dennis was practicing his bad-back routine. Posey was offering him her professional critique: less stagger-step, more agony.

"That's where your father was found, the Monument Life building on 23rd. You might remember I told you that," Harriman said.

I might never forget, I thought. "Yes," I said.

"So anything unusual that happens in that building now, questionable behavior, for instance, is my concern. I made sure all the tenants knew that."

"Has there been questionable behavior, I mean besides Jimmy sitting on a chair in the elevator with his brains blown out?"

"Just this morning, in fact. That's why Bradley Olsen called me. A woman pretending to be a health club magazine reporter hacked into Ms. Russell's computer system and got herself an appointment. And this is the part why I'm telling you, they think she might have been a private investigator."

"You think it was me?"

"Was it?"

"It depends. What was the woman investigating?"

He pulled a small note pad from his pocket, flipped a few pages.

"A health club owner named Ron Powell. Died of a heart attack. Left ten million to his ex-wife. His half-sister's disputing the payout. Says he left it to charity."

"Meaning her, probably."

"I don't know what she means. Was it you?"

"Did Powell kill my father?"

"No."

"Then it wasn't me."

Harriman nodded. "I had to ask. Private investigator, a woman, poking around the Monument Building..."

"I'm not a private investigator."

He smiled. "You're an actor."

I smiled too.

We both looked at the stage, where Posey was helping Dennis from the chair to the piano and back again.

"Is he okay?" Harriman said. "Looks like he's in a lot of pain."

"It does look that way," I said. "But he's fine."

We both sat there for a moment longer and then, in the very next moment, a kind of awkwardness settled on us. I didn't know where it came from; it wasn't there when we were talking about Bradley Olsen and Olivia Russell and questionable behavior at Monument Life.

"Can I ask you a question?" Harriman said. He was trying to get the detective out of his voice. I could hear him pushing it aside.

"Sure," I said. Jesus, I was pushing the actor out of my voice.

"It's probably inappropriate, or a conflict of interest, or something like that, but you want to go out for dinner, see a movie, maybe get a drink, catch a ball game?"

"All in the same night?"

He laughed. "Doesn't have to be. We could spread it out."

Our eyes met. I'm sure he knew my answer, but I said it anyway.

"I'd like that."

"Me too. I have a busy week; how about next Friday?"

Cops. Like they're the only ones who have a life. "I'm busy too. Next Friday sounds good."

We both smiled. No matter how old you are, that first date proposal makes you feel fifteen. We stood up and walked to the elevator.

"You like Chinese?" Harriman said.

"I do," I said, and I thought of Fu, which made me think of Al and his piss-filled bottles of Gatorade, probably the exact opposite of a romantic thought.

"I know a great place," he said. "A hole in the wall."

"I'm in."

We reached the elevator. He leaned close, as if he was going to kiss me. I actually got ready for a kiss, but instead he said, "I can't wait to see you play a singing vampire."

"How do you know I'm a vampire?" I said. "Maybe I'm one of the victims."

"I don't think so," he said. "You still have your fangs in."

I put my hand up to my mouth. It was true. The whole time I was talking to him I'd been wearing Farina's fangs.

"I'll call you," he said, and then he stepped into the elevator and pulled the gate closed.

I'm dating a cop, I thought as I walked to the stage. Jimmy would kill me, if somebody hadn't already killed him.

21

───────

PRETTY LATE TO BE FARMING, CHARLIE

DENIS AND POSEY KEPT ME LATE AT THE D-CUP, TRYING TO convince me that the idea of conning Curry's doctor—with them playing the role of my parents—was not only a brilliant bit of PI strategy, but could be expanded and adapted into a musical if I would only option the rights to the story to them. I told them I'd have to think about it. Not the musical, I was down for that as soon as they offered me the lead, but for taking them to see Curry's doctor as part of the con. That piece was harder to get a handle on.

I got back to the House of Emotional Tics at one thirty in the morning. The humidity had evaporated, the temperature had dropped, and a gentle wind had kicked up, cooling the city in such a pleasant way that I opened the window in the front room, despite the sound of sirens, garbage trucks, and barking dogs that I knew would come in with the breeze. I walked through my living room, bedroom, and closet into the kitchen to open the back window too, but froze when I saw a flashlight beam flickering around in the far corner of the backyard.

I debated waking Fu as I crossed the lobby and walked down the stairs to the basement but decided against it and went past his door. It was two in the morning, and who knew what Fu would be like at this hour. Instead, I grabbed his pigeon-killing shovel, in case I had to whack somebody, went through the door, and crossed toward the light, which was moving in a herky-jerky pattern behind a row of shrubs.

What I found was Charlie Nye making a marijuana garden. He was on his knees, planting twenty baby pot plants, holding the flashlight in one hand and digging with a small spade with the other.

"Pretty late to be farming, Charlie," I said.

"Trying to make an honest living," he said, tamping the dirt down around one little reefer baby.

Charlie Nye making an honest living, forgetting for the moment that his business of choice was an illegal pot plantation, was a funny thought. He had been in prison for stealing cars, a skill he had so thoroughly developed that the City of New York had recruited him right out of his jail cell to collect delinquent autos for them.

He had also done time for breaking and entering in Ohio. And had once been a guest of the Pennsylvania Department of Corrections as well.

I thought to remind him about this, and to tell him the Chinese investment group that owned the building would no doubt take a disapproving point of view as to his growing weed in their yard, but some other thought must have been unconsciously at work because instead I said, "I need after-hours access into an office building for a case I'm investigating, and I'll pay you fifty bucks if you help me."

He was smoking a joint while he dug little holes in the ground for his cannabis. At the mention of fifty bucks, he stood up, or maybe it was the after-hours access that got his attention.

"I heard you were a PI now," he said.

"I'm not a PI. I'm an actor," I said.

"You're investigating a case."

"Trying to make an honest living."

He was five feet eleven and thin, I'm sure, because of his diet, meaning he drank his dinner as often as he ate it. He'd grown up in hardscrabble Scranton, Pennsylvania, left to do a stint in the army, and never went home. The army made him a mechanic, and he learned all about starting vehicles under less-than-ideal conditions and doing it in a hurry, lest the enemy blow your ass up while you were fumbling to turn the engine. It had been the ideal apprenticeship for a car thief.

He had gray hair and gray eyes and some scars and tattoos from his army and prison days that made it clear he wasn't afraid of a fight. He liked hookers and poker and now, apparently, pot.

"What's in it for me," he said, "besides the fifty?"

"The Chinese never find out about your garden. And neither do the police."

He offered me his joint.

"It's Kush," he said. "That's what I'm growing. Kush, a little G-13, and some BC Bud guaranteed to light up your life."

"No thanks," I said.

He took another hit, held the smoke, blew it into the night, and gestured at his plants.

"What about Fu?" he said.

"He was a hit man. I don't think a little pot's going to bother him."

"He hates pigeons."

"Talk about your stoned non-sequitur."

"I'm just saying."

"Charlie. Focus."

"I get to keep the plants?"

"Yes."

"What are we fishing for?"

"Information."

He thought about that for a second and said, "Deal me in. I'll take the fifty in advance."

"Fine. Thanks, Charlie. I'll let you know the details," I said, turning and walking back to the building.

"When?" he said, hitting the joint again.

"As soon as I know them," I said.

22

———

IS THAT GATORADE OR PISS?

Al Cutter woke me up at five thirty with a phone call.

"McCall?"

"What?" I'd been up until two with Charlie Nye. Like most people, I don't function very well on three and a half hours of sleep. Al, however, hadn't slept three and a half consecutive hours in decades.

"I've composed my suicide note in the form of an email. Would you like to hear it?"

"Can you send it to me?"

"No."

"Okay. Go ahead."

"'Dear Dai Ying, My name is Al Cutter. I am a tenant in your building located on East 83rd Street in Manhattan, New York. For weeks and weeks, I have asked your building manager, Kate McCall, to repair the toilet in my apartment. Either out of incompetence or spite, she has ignored my requests. As a result, I have now filled countless cases of empty Gatorade bottles with my own urine. I drink the Gatorade so I can have the empty bottles and then fill them with that same Gatorade. This mindless cycle has driven me into a deep depression, and I can no longer live under these piss-poor conditions. Therefore, I have decided to end my life by drinking my own pee out of the Gatorade bottles until I die. Kate McCall is responsible for my death. It is McCall alone who needs to answer for this avoidable tragedy. Sadly and sincerely, Al Cutter, 5A.' It's five thirty in the afternoon in Beijing. All I have to do is hit send."

"I never liked you, Al. I want that to be your last thought."

Two hours later, Fu and I were in apartment 5A with Fu on his hands and knees in the bathroom, doing something with the pipes. Al stood in the doorway, holding a disturbing bottle of yellow Gatorade. I was leaning against the sink, watching Fu.

"Is that Gatorade or piss?" I said.

"I'm not sure," Al said, taking a sip. "Why? Thirsty?"

"No. I have a job for you, and if you're dead from urine poisoning, you won't be able to help me."

"What job?"

"I have to sneak into an office building for a case I'm working, and I need to know the building's service vendors and schedules and things like that."

"Monument?"

"Yes."

"Ms. Olivia Russell didn't cooperate?"

"Not particularly."

"Nobody likes non-delete code."

"Especially her."

I noticed Fu was listening. He didn't want me to know he was listening, but his banging around got a lot quieter when I brought up sneaking into an office building.

"After you get the vendors and schedules, I need you to come with me, access her PC, and download what I need onto one of those cigarette lighter memory things."

"Zip drive."

"I'll pay you fifty bucks. Will you do it?"

"Fu say yes."

"Fu you, Fu. That's my fifty," Al said. "She didn't ask you. She asked me."

"Fu you too," Fu said.

"Be quiet, Al," I said. "Fu, are you saying you want to help with the case?"

"Fu say yes."

It was pointless to ask him why. With Fu, it had to be a yes-or-no question. In order to begin a sentence with "Do you want to come because..." I had to have at least some idea of *why* just to finish the question. Maybe it was because he was bored fixing pipes and mopping floors and wanted to be a part of something that reminded him of the old days, when he was a hit man for the Chinese mob. Or maybe it was because he wanted out of his witness relocation purgatory as a handyman in New York and getting arrested for breaking and entering would reshuffle the deck and land him in some other identity that couldn't be worse than poisoning pigeons at the House of Emotional Tics.

Probably it was both. And looking at him now, this massive block of hit man up to his elbows in Al Cutter's sewage, I had a moment, a tinge, of empathy. Nobody likes to feel washed up. What actor doesn't know that kind of emptiness?

"Okay, Fu. You're in. I'll pay you fifty. You can be the lookout."

"Fu say yes."

"Same deal for you, Al."

"I should get more."

"Fu, let's come back some other time and finish these pipes..."

"Okay, okay. Fifty. Jesus, life never stops kicking you in the nuts. I'm doing all the important work, and I'm making the same as the look-out man."

"There's no "I" in team, Al."

"Yeah, but there's an 'M' and an 'E' and that spells me. People forget that."

"You really need to get some sleep."

"Tell me about it. So it's me, you, and Fu..."

"And Charlie," I said.

"Charlie does the break in, I do the download, Fu does the look-out, and you run the job?"

"Something like that."

"Who drives?"

"I'm working on it."

Al finished the rest of the yellow Gatorade, looked at his toilet in pieces on the bathroom floor, sighed, held up the empty bottle, and said, "Time to drain the snake."

Peter Graves never had to deal with anything like this, I thought.

23

SOMEBODY HAS TO DRIVE

"Jimmy didn't just roll over in his grave," LaTanya said. "He stood straight up and said, 'Have you lost your mother-fucking mind?'"

She had driven the yellow Volvo cab for twelve hours, criss-crossing Manhattan a thousand times, and now was barbe-cuing chicken on the communal gas grill Dai Ying had bought for the building. She was drinking a cold bottle of Michelob with one hand and smoothing a thick, dark sauce on her chicken with a long barbecue brush that she held in her other hand. She used the brush as a pointer, like an elementary school teacher emphasizing the important parts of the lesson. I was the only student in the class.

"It's just one date," I said. I left out the part about Jimmy's ashes being buried in a beer stein by the elm tree just thirty feet away.

"With a cop," LaTanya said.

She had given me one of her Michelobs. It was six thirty, still brutally hot and humid as hell, one of those summer Saturdays where an idiot somewhere in the city actually tries to fry an egg on the sidewalk. After Fu and I finished with Al, I went back to bed, then to rehearsal, then to the gym, where Raul worked me to the bone for two solid hours. I came home, showered, saw LaTanya firing up the grill and drinking a six-pack of Michelob and joined her in the early evening heat. The cold beer was heaven.

"What's he look like?" LaTanya said.

"Like Steve McQueen in *Bullitt.*"

"He got them eyes?"

"Big time."

"He may be pretty, McCall," she said, pointing the brush at me. "But at the end of the day, he's pure po-lice."

"If I get to the end of the day, I'll let you know," I said.

"And don't leave nothing out."

We clinked beer bottles and laughed.

Two and a half years ago, we'd moved into The House of Emotional Tics on the same day. Jimmy, who was helping me move in, and LaTanya, both big fans of ZZ Top, had a time and a half talking tunes while lugging boxes into the building. They had the same musical taste, the same filthy mouth, and the same loud laugh. Jimmy liked working class people. He was one. He and LaTanya and her brother (and partner), Anthony, who was helping her move in, were all fast friends.

Anthony was six feet eight inches tall and weighed three hundred fifty pounds at least. No one called him Anthony. He was known as Mountain.

While LaTanya and Mountain were on the third floor delivering another load of LaTanya's stuff, someone stole their yellow Volvo taxi. They had just purchased their medallion. The Volvo represented all the money they had in the world, and now it was gone, lost forever somewhere in Manhattan. LaTanya sat down on the curb and cried. Mountain sat beside her, looking, for the first time in his life, small and helpless and lost.

Jimmy told them not to worry. He was a private investigator, and he would find their cab *and* the guy who stole it. Then he looked at me and said I would help him.

We found the cab—and the prick that took it—one week later. I actually broke the case with the help of a chop-shop snitch I knew. Jimmy roughed the guy up (*some people go begging for a good punch in the nose, and it's your job to give them what they want*), put him in the back seat, and I drove the Volvo to The House of Emotional Tics, where LaTanya and Mountain were waiting for us. The look on the guy's face when Mountain stood up to introduce himself was worth the week it took to find him. LaTanya and I had been close ever since.

The gas-fired flames licked at the chicken, turning the sugary barbecue sauce into a sweet-and-sticky blackened crust. With no breeze to blow it away, the smell of the burning charcoal and the carmelizing chicken hung in the air, blanketing the yard with a mouth-watering aroma that smelled good, though not good enough to make me forget about Jimmy, dead as dirt in the Monument elevator.

"I need a driver," I said.

"Where you going?" LaTanya said, looking over the top of her sunglasses. She was forty-nine years old, heavy set, with big boobs, a wide waist, thick thighs, strong arms, beautiful brown eyes that could see bullshit coming five miles down the road, a head full of dreads, and the whitest smile on the island of Manhattan. In all ways, she was an exaggerated woman.

Except for her patience, which was the size of a tiny bug—a mosquito or a gnat or maybe a flea. LaTanya Bellamy did not suffer fools gladly, as the saying goes. Just ask her ex-husbands —all three of them. Her first marriage lasted three days. Her second marriage lasted three weeks. Her third marriage lasted three hours (although, to hear Mountain tell it, three hours is a generous assessment). Her marriages, if you could call them that, were forbidden topics of conversation. Although romance, meaning mine, not hers, was always a safe bet.

"Monument Life."

She pointed the brush at me and said, "Only about a thousand cabs, buses, and subways running here to there. You got thirty seconds to tell me what you're really asking. Twenty-nine. Twenty-eight. Twenty-seven..."

"Jimmy was found dead in a Monument elevator. Olivia Russell, first-class bitch and world-class Monument life insurance agent, has information in her computer system I need to see. Information about a dead guy whose long-lost half-sister hired Jimmy to investigate the ten mil Monument payout to the dead guy's ex-wife, even though the dead guy was never married."

"There's no ex-wife?"

"I can't find her."

"Insurance bitch won't play nice?"

"Not so far. I went to see her pretending to be a health club magazine reporter—the dead guy owned fitness clubs—and she threw me out, or her Green Beret bodyguard did, before I could get what I wanted. So I'm going to access her office after hours with Charlie and Al and Fu, and somebody has to drive."

"Access after hours sounds a whole lot like breaking and entering, which sounds a whole lot like against the law."

She was right. It *was* breaking and entering. But *Jimmy's Rules of Private Investigation for Kate, Rule Number Seven* was: *don't break the law for just anyone*, and Jimmy wasn't just anyone. If I had to sneak into Monument Life to get the information about Powell to find out who killed my father, then it was Olivia Russell's fault.

"Depends how you say it."

"What if we get caught?"

"We won't, if the plan works."

"You going to tell me the plan?"

"As soon as there is one."

She flipped the chicken with metal tongs. I drank my beer.

"You doing it for Jimmy? To find the cocksucker who killed him?" LaTanya said.

"Yes. I'll pay you fifty bucks."

She took a sip of Michelob and looked at me out of the sides of her eyes, tilting her head like a dog that thinks you've lost your mind.

"Shit," she said. "I'll pay *you* fifty bucks."

24

———

FORTY YEARS OF LAYING PIPE AND NOW LOOK

Dr. Martin Miller's nurse, a bone-thin hawk named Harriet, came out from behind the reception area divider and asked if there was anything she could do for my father.

Too late, I thought, *my father was murdered nine days ago*. But what I said was, "Cross your fingers and hope that Dr. Miller can pull a miracle out of his hat."

It was Wednesday afternoon. I had met Dennis and Posey on the corner of East 63rd and Third at two thirty. If Roger had happened by at that moment, he wouldn't have known us. We were unrecognizable.

Dennis had dyed his hair black as night and slicked it down and back for his role as Gus Marinaro, a commercial plumber from Jersey City. He was dressed like a low-level member of the mob: two-toned button shirt, gray slacks, black loafers, and pinky ring. Posey was Gus's wife, Marie. She had poofed her hair up high and big and frozen it in place with glossy spray. She wore heavy makeup and red lipstick to match her red fingernail polish, her red pants, shirt, and jacket, and her red shoes. Even her perfume, which preceded her arrival by half a block, smelled red.

I wore a short black wig, black contact lenses, big round glasses, black jeans, black flats, and a light blue sweater. It was my outfit (plus a neck brace) for an injury lawyer commercial I had shot in Brooklyn several years ago. "DeAngelo and Freidman got me more money than I ever thought possible. If I can't have my health, at least I've got cash," was my line. It ran on a local cable channel at three a.m. on Thursdays for twelve weeks. I made thirty-five whole dollars. That was then. Today, I was Angela Marinaro, the only child of Gus and Marie. We all spoke with Jersey accents.

I called Dennis and Posey on Monday morning to tell them I had decided to let them help me catch Curry's doctor in a lie. My reasoning, I told them, was simple: Curry and Grandma Dolores currently had the upper hand. To turn that around, I would have to think outside the box, and I didn't know how I could get any further outside the box than by enlisting the help of Dennis Parker and Posey Schmidt. They were thrilled and in agreement: if outside the box was what was called for, they were perfect for the parts.

They went right to work, creating character sketches with intricate histories for Gus, Marie, and Angela. We met at the D-Cup on Tuesday and rehearsed for an hour. Posey, in particular, was especially in the moment as Marie. Dennis said he was holding back, saving his best performance for the doctor.

Miller's office was on East 63rd between Third and Second. It was in a brick apartment building, on the first floor, with an entrance right off the street. A small brass sign affixed to the building read: *Dr. Martin Miller, Orthopedics.*

The waiting room was small but nice, especially if you liked to fly fish. If you liked to fly fish, even if you had a bad back, like Gus Marinaro supposedly did, your pain would fade into the woodwork upon entering Miller's orthopedic, fly-fishing paradise. There were four upholstered chairs and a sofa arranged like a living room, with an oak coffee table and matching side tables, all of them covered with magazines, including dozens of back issues of *Field & Stream*, *American Angler*, *Fly Fisherman*, *Fly Rod & Reel*, *Fly Fishing in Saltwater*, *Northwest Fly Fishing*, *Southwest Fly Fishing*, *Fly Tyer*, and a hardcover book called *Fifty Places to Fly Fish Before You Die*.

The walls were covered with photographs of what had to be Miller himself, fly fishing in nearly all of the fifty places. Between the pictures were mounted fish, all manner of trout pulled from a variety of streams, rivers, and lakes. Between the photographs and the mounted fish were antique rods and reels, carefully hung and displayed with pride. Between the photographs, the mounted fish, and the rods and reels were box-framed, colorful, hand-tied flies. Miller was serious about fly fishing, and he wanted you to know it.

After our Marinaro rehearsal on Tuesday, I called Miller's office and pleaded for an appointment for my father, Gus, who that very afternoon had fallen from the scaffolding on a construction job in Weehawken. Gus was in tremendous pain, and another construction worker, a guy Gus met in the city, a guy who also fell off some scaffolding, a guy whose name, I said, I couldn't remember now but would remember later, recommended Dr. Miller to us. Miller's receptionist, Harriet the hawk, checked the schedule, found an opening at two forty-five, and fit us in.

Dennis wasn't kidding about saving his best stuff for the doctor. He was on the sofa, demonstrating excruciating discomfort, grimacing, moaning, swearing, and blaming his boss for screwing up the scaffolding.

"McGuire, that son of a bitch. He did this to me. Forty years of laying pipe and now look. What am I going to do, Marie? How am I going to put food on the fucking table? Oh Jesus it hurts. Jesus H. Christ, I'll never work again..."

"What can I do, Gus?" Posey said. She was sitting beside him, furious and worried to death at the same time. "You tell me what to do, and I'll do it. You want me to go to McGuire's house and bash his head with an eighteen-inch Stillson wrench? I can do that. I swear to God, Gus, it's just tearing me up seeing you in so much pain. Angela, look at your father. He's dying here."

"That's why we're at the doctor," I said. "After this, we're going to the lawyer."

The thought of perfectly round Posey banging on the fictional McGuire's fictional door somewhere in New Jersey and then banging on his fictional head with a Stillson wrench nearly pulled me out of character. Who were we kidding? There was no way this was going to work. I was crazy to let Dennis and Posey talk me into this. Out of the box is one thing, out of your mind is another. But just as I was about to call it off, Harriet the hawk was saying something to us through the window.

"Dr. Miller will see you now."

25

ALL WE NEED IS A DIAGNOSIS THAT WILL STAND UP IN COURT

"Where, exactly, does it hurt?" Dr. Martin Miller said.

He looked just like his fly-fishing photographs, except better. He was forty-eight years old and male-model gorgeous. Sandy hair, hazel eyes, square jaw, dimpled chin. He was an outdoorsman, even in his white doctor's coat. If there were an office pool for such a thing as the Ruggedly Beautiful, Fly-Fisherman, Orthopedist-of-the-Year Award, I'd put my money on Miller.

He was about six feet tall and weighed one hundred seventy or so pounds, solid and trim at the same time. He had white teeth and smooth skin. He was self-confident and straightforward. He was successful. For the first thirty seconds after he walked through the door into the exam room, I couldn't see a single weakness. He appeared to be a perfect specimen, an unblemished orthopedic naturalist. But in the next thirty seconds, as he smiled at himself in the mirror while he washed his hands in the exam room sink, and, for every second after that, his fatal flaw was clear.

Dr. Martin Miller was the movie-star version of himself—and also his biggest fan. He was a first-class narcissist. There was nothing too good in the world that he didn't deserve. He wore eighteen hundred dollar, custom-made Berluti shoes. A thirty-five hundred dollar Armani suit. Even his white doctor's coat was custom tailored, with his name hand-stitched in gold-plated thread. When he washed his hands, his sleeve pulled up. On his wrist was an eighty-one thousand dollar Rolex Masterpiece watch, with dozens of diamonds and a glacier-blue dial.

"In my wallet," Dennis said.

"Excuse me," Miller said, drying his hands with a laundered cloth towel embossed with his name. The fly-fishing theme had been carried into his exam rooms, but here the flies and rods and reels and fish and photos were intermixed with his many and sundry diplomas. He had gone to Columbia for both undergrad and med school.

Dennis, who had been lying on the exam table, groaning, Posey holding his hand and wiping his forehead with a handkerchief, sat up without pain. "I'm not sure I'm ever going to be able to work again. Know what I mean?" he said.

Miller leaned against the counter and crossed his legs. "Not so far. You don't seem to be in any distress. Although, you were when I first walked in."

"It comes and goes," Posey said. "Don't it, Gus?" She was wearing Jimmy's miniature microphone. It went with her red ensemble.

Dennis seized up and fell back onto the table, unable to bear the pains shooting from his back down through his legs and up through his neck. "McGuire, that stupid son of a bitch. I can't feel my feet. What's that mean, Doc, when you can't feel your feet? How am I going to walk? How am supposed to live when I can't even stand up? It's McGuire's fault. He did this to me. Tell him, Marie..."

"Please, Dr. Miller. Do something. Gus is a good man. A good husband. He don't deserve this kind of pain."

Dennis sat up, pleased with his performance.

Miller stood there for a moment and then narrowed his eyes ever so slightly. "Are you hurt or not, Mr. Marinaro? And who is McGuire?"

"I'm as hurt as you need me to be. McGuire's the general contractor on the office building we're putting up in Jersey. I work for a sub. I'm a plumber."

"Yes, I read that on your chart," Miller said. Then he looked at me. "And who are you?"

"Angela Marinaro. I'm the daughter."

"Are you hurt?" he said to me.

"Only in my heart," I said.

Miller nodded, then turned to Dennis and Posey. "If you're not really hurt, I can't imagine why you're here."

"I could paint a picture," Posey said.

"Please," Miller said.

"My husband was on the job site, on scaffolding about eight feet off the ground. Is that right, Gus?"

Pain began to overwhelm him. "Eight, nine feet. Something like that," Gus said.

"McGuire didn't do the guardrails on the scaffolding. Forgot to screw them down tight, didn't he, Gus?"

Dennis fell back down on the exam table. "He's going to pay for this," Dennis moaned. "He's going to pay big."

"Gus fell though the rail and landed on his back. Nobody was there. Nobody saw him. They found him on the ground. Just like he is now."

Dennis groaned, immobilized on the table.

"We got a good case of workman's compensation," Posey said. "We can sue the contractor..."

"McGuire," Miller said.

"Third party," Gus said.

"All we need is a diagnosis that will stand up in court," Posey said.

Miller considered that for a half a second and then said, "But you're not hurt."

"Do I *look* hurt?" Dennis said, nearly blacking out with agony.

"Yes," Miller said.

"Then he *is* hurt," Posey said.

Miller nodded, smiled a paper-thin smile. "Why me?" he said. "There are thousands of orthopedists in Manhattan. Probably thousands more in New Jersey. It can't be because of my good looks. Well, it could be, but I doubt it is."

"Guy I know has the same kind of case," Dennis said, sitting up again, his pain magically dissipating. "You're his doctor. He's suing for millions. McGuire's got insurance up the yin yang. I got a right to cash in. You got a right to a piece of the pie. That's what my guy said."

"Are you going to tell me your guy's name?" Miller said.

"He said you'd know," Posey said.

"He said no names," I said. "He said that's the way you work."

"You want me to issue a medical statement that says your workplace injury, though difficult to precisely diagnose, has incapacitated you to the point where your ability to earn a living wage in the future has been terminated. Something along those lines?"

"We're thinking ten mil," Dennis said. "You get twenty-five percent of whatever we win."

"We're thinking your piece is two point five mil," Posey said.

"We're thinking you could catch a lot of trout with that money," I said.

"I'm thinking you have three minutes to leave my office, or I'll call the police and turn you in for fraud and extortion. You're a crook, Mr. Marinaro. I don't deal with crooks."

"But we got a guy," Posey said. "You got a guy."

"You're a liar, Mrs. Marinaro. A very bad liar."

"Nobody talks to my wife that way," Dennis growled. Then he leaped off the table and grabbed Dr. Miller by the front of his tailored white jacket, scrunching up the gold-plated, hand-sewn letters spelling out Miller's name.

Posey and I were too stunned to stop him or even make a sound. We just stood there.

Miller, a drop-me-in-the-wilderness-with-a-match-and-a-pocket knife-and-a-spool-of thread-and-I-will-kill-a-bear-catch-a-trout-and-live-for-weeks kind of guy, instinctively lifted the Joel Gray-sized Dennis Parker off the ground and tossed him across the room.

Dennis hit the side of the exam table and smashed hard to the ground.

"Ooooh," he screamed. "*Ooooooh.*"

It didn't sound anything at all like his preplanned moaning and groaning. He couldn't make words. His eyes were closed tight. He was hurt. It was not an act.

Posey knew it right away. She ran to him, kneeled beside him, speechless for a second, and then turned to Miller, who was in a state of shock at the course of these unpredictable events. Creating his own patients, apparently, was not part of his usual orthopedic routine.

"What have you done?" Posey screamed at him, panic in her voice.

"Can't breathe..." Dennis gasped, turning blue on the floor.

Miller threw open the door and called down the hall. "Diane, Harriet. I need help. Hurry."

Within two seconds, Miller's nurse, Diane, and Harriet the Hawk were in the exam room helping Miller deal with Dennis, who was suffering in a way you can't fake. He was simultaneously gasping for breath and in excruciating pain. With Diane's help, Miller gently rolled Dennis onto his back, which elicited a terrible, gasping shriek from Dennis that sounded like paralyzing pain.

"You hurt him." Posey said to Miller, tears flowing, fear in her voice. "You really hurt him."

"He attacked me," Miller said, though not with any degree of confidence. "He attacked me and I...I..."

He was flustered enough that he couldn't finish the thought. As he tried to locate the broken ribs and punctured lung we all knew he would find, I realized that I was the reason for Dennis' suffering, and I couldn't watch one more minute of it. With everyone's full focus on Dennis, I left the room unnoticed.

26

WHEN THAT DIDN'T WORK, WE WENT TO PLAN C

What I meant to say was: Dennis was suffering in a way you can't fake...unless you're an accomplished actor with a special talent for depicting near-death pain.

Jimmy's Rules of Private Investigation for Kate, Rule Number Eight was clear as a Colorado day: *make sure your backup plan has a backup plan for its backup plan.*

Our first objective was to get Miller to climb on board and agree to make an extra two point five million with the Marinaros somewhere down the road in Scam City. When he didn't bite, Dennis and Posey went to the backup plan: try to get him to name Curry as "the guy" he was helping with the con job we outlined. When that didn't work, we went to plan C.

When we first discussed the idea of Dennis challenging Miller physically, forcing the doctor to push back and then turning that reaction into a serious distraction so that I could leave the room and not be missed, I said, "Are you people insane?"

But the more we spoke about it, the more I came to think it would be our best chance and most likely outcome. I'd been right about that.

With Miller, Nurse Diane, and Harriet the Hawk preoccupied with Dennis and Posey, who, as I slipped out of the room and hurried down the hall, was shrieking, "You killed him, you killed my Gus," I knew I had two minutes at most to find Curry's file.

I had worked as a medical receptionist for half a dozen different doctors, so the wall of color-coded file folders was familiar to me. I searched the alphabetically arranged shelves, arrived at "Calhoun," scanned quickly down the row until I reached "Culver," then slowed down and went file by file—Cummings, Cuppler, Curdman, Curibe, Curonna, Curran, Curreck...Curstan. No Curry. I read them again, checking to make sure I didn't skip it, that the Curry file didn't mistakenly stick to the Curreck file or the Curstan file. Or somehow slip inside them. No luck. I went back to the beginning. Nothing. I searched the Ks. Not there. No Ken Curry. I had confirmed that Miller was Curry's physician through the legal documents that Barkowski had given me. He had testified on Curry's behalf. The file had to be here somewhere.

Down the hall, Posey was raising her voice, threatening lawsuits and physical damage: "I got a Stillson wrench in my purse, you asshole. You don't fix my Gus, I'm going to beat your brains all over the floor."

Dennis was gasping for breath so loudly that he nearly drowned out Posey, who was screaming and crying and no doubt rending her garments. It was the climax of their performance. They couldn't maintain that intensity without Dennis either dying or Posey joining him on the floor with a coronary. I had sixty seconds.

If I were Miller, I asked myself, *where would I keep a file that I didn't want anyone to see?* The answer was easy: in my office.

Directly off the general office-administration area, where Harriet sat, was a half-open door. Like all the doors in Miller's office, this one had a shiny, brass, identifying nameplate. The engraved letters spelled out *Dr. Martin Miller*.

I went through the door and into Miller's office, which featured more expensive furniture, more fly-fishing paraphernalia, and more accolades, diplomas, and photographs. I moved behind the desk. If I were hiding a patient's file that implicated me in a ten-million-dollar insurance fraud and possibly tied me to a murder or two, I would lock that puppy in my desk and hide the key.

Miller's desk was covered with patient files and letters, a multi-line phone, a computer, a laser printer, some half-tied flies, a mug of cold coffee, framed photographs of a wife and children, and various newspapers, newsletters, and magazines. I was able to open every drawer except the file cabinet drawer on the lower right hand side. That one was locked.

There was no time to search for the key. I had thirty, maybe forty seconds. I reached into my purse and grabbed the six-inch restorer's pry bar that Jimmy had left me in the box I got from Shavelson at the reading of the will. It came in its own little carrying case that read: *For precision prying without damaging delicate surfaces*. I debated bringing it to Miller's office, decided not to, and then put it my purse on my way out the door. *Oh hell*, I thought as I was leaving, *what if I need it and don't have it? How stupid will I feel then?* Now, I needed it, and here it was. I smiled at how smart I felt and set to work prying open Miller's private file drawer. It took five seconds.

Down the hall, Posey was screaming: "If Gus dies, you all die." She had been part of an improvisation group in Buffalo and, in our Marinaro rehearsal, was confident that she would know what to say when the time came to say it. "I've got friends who've got friends. I'll track you down and make you pay, you sons of a bitches..."

I opened the drawer. Inside, there was one hanging file

folder with five manila folders resting inside it. Ladd, Murphy, Williamson, Downing...and Curry, Ken.

I opened Curry's file on the desk, took the small digital camera (more or less the size of a credit card) from my purse, and photographed the pages inside Curry's file. I didn't have time to get them all, though, because from down the hall I heard Dennis yell out: "It's all right, Marie. Nothing to worry about. The only thing bruised is my pride."

I took one last shot, closed the manila folder, put it back, shut the drawer, threw the pry bar and camera in my purse, sat in Miller's leather chair, and waited. Five, four, three, two...the door flew open and Miller, nostrils flaring, steam shooting out of his ears, stood in the doorway.

"What are you doing in my office?" he said.

"I couldn't take it," I said, laying Angela's Jersey accent on as thick as I could. "To see him in pain like that. Dying on the floor. He was such a strong man when I was a little girl in Weehawken. I couldn't watch him go like a baby."

"Harriet, call the police," he said.

Somewhere behind him, I heard Harriet lift the phone.

"Time to go, Angela," Posey said, also somewhere behind Miller.

"Come on, sweetheart," Dennis said. I want to miss traffic."

"Lock the door, Diane," Miller said, moving out of his private office and into the general office. "And arm yourself. The Marinaros aren't going anywhere."

I stood, came around the desk, and went through the door. Harriet the Hawk was on the phone with the police, explaining, and these were her words: "...it's a home invasion. They're from New Jersey, so there's no telling what they'll do." I pulled the phone from the wall as I walked around her and went into the reception room.

Miller had positioned himself in front of the door, jaw set like he meant business, and Diane had taken her loyal place beside him, holding one of those little physician's hammers used to test knee reflexes. Maybe she was going to get me to kick myself.

Dennis and Posey were cracking under the pressure. I could see it in their eyes. A police lineup was not what they had in mind when they signed on. Posey, in particular, was wide-eyed. Miller had called her bluff. There was no Stillson wrench in her purse after all. Dennis looked at me and said, "Do something."

He didn't have to say it. I was already on my way to Miller, who took a forceful step toward me as I strode to the door, as if we were going to get in each other's faces and argue about it. Instead, I hit him as hard as I could, square in the nose, with a brutal right cross that sent him to the floor like a bag of rocks.

"Oh Christ," Miller said. "Oh, Jesus. You broke my nose. I'm bleeding..."

He *was* bleeding, out of both nostrils, a thick, steady, stream that stained his fancy white doctor's jacket. I had definitely broken his nose, possibly in two or three places. It was one of the best punches of my life, and he walked right into it.

I held my fist up to Diane, who dropped the tiny hammer and moved out of the way. I unlocked the door, opened it, and turned to Dennis and Posey.

"Mom, Dad, we're done with Dr. Miller."

Posey and Dennis exited the office in a hurry. I smiled at Diane and Harriet and followed the Marinaros out, stepping over Miller as I left the office, leaving him in a heap, holding his nose, trying to stem the red tide.

27

SUBTEXTUAL SIGNIFICIANCE

On Friday, at seven fifteen, I still wasn't dressed, though Harriman would be here for our Chinatown date in fifteen minutes. I couldn't decide what to wear. It was very unlike me to be indecisive about what to wear on a date. I blamed my hesitancy on the heat, which arrived with a bang on Wednesday afternoon, just two days ago, as I was busting Martin Miller's nose.

It was a ridiculous amount of oppressive air accompanied by an absurd amount of humidity. The forecaster on the Weather Channel, the macho one who sticks his jaw out in defiance at hurricanes, warned New Yorkers to stay indoors, drink lots of liquids, and keep an eye on pets, grandparents, and infants, in case they spontaneously combusted in the one-hundred degree inferno that New York would become for the next five days.

Outside Miller's office, after telling Dennis and Posey that I had taken pictures of the hidden file (and assuring them that not only were they were convincing as Joe and Marie, but that I would insist they play the parts in the musical), I came home to the House of Emotional Tics and printed the pages of Curry's orthopedic medical records.

I didn't know what, exactly, I was expecting, but as the pages came through the printer I inherited from Jimmy, nothing incriminating appeared. Miller's comments all pertained to his examination of Curry's condition after the accident at Barkowski's West Village construction site and lined up nice and neat with the story Curry was telling his lawyer and his lawyer was telling the court.

"Hard to pinpoint, vis-à-vis exam and X-ray, the precise location of injury, but nerve inflammation, and probably damage, due to realignment, shifting, and jarring of vertebrae due to fall from scaffolding is likely, if not certainly, the cause of patient's pain and suffering," said Miller, in one way or another, in notation after notation. "Prognosis is difficult to predict. No surgical solution is evident. Physical therapy and pain medication are likely prescription. Successful, pain-free outcome is not guaranteed. Patient in need of relief."

It was clear why Barkowski was worried. With notes like that from a reputable fly-fishing orthopedist and Curry's lawyer spitting nails in every direction, a settlement before the case ever got to court was a foregone conclusion. If the lawsuit was for ten million, Curry might settle for four or five. Peel off a few bills for the lawyer and the doctor and there would still be three or four million left for Ken and Grandma Dolores.

I reached for the phone. It was the end of the line for me. I didn't know where to go next because there *was* nowhere to go next. All roads ended with bad news for Barkowski, Saint Denise, and their Rwandan triplets. My heart was heavy with disappointment. But as I dialed Barkowski's number to tell him I was done, I saw a note in the margin on the last page: *Munson Construction...2001...ask Bajaria for deposition transcripts.* I hung up the phone.

From the file folder Barkowski had given me, I knew Bajaria was Boris Bajaria, Curry's lawyer. I called Matthew at the office and asked if he knew anything about Bajaria. He called me back within ten minutes. Bajaria, he told me, was a vicious beast for whom total destruction was the only measure of victory. There was a rumor in the New York State court system that he had once taken a bloody bite out of the opposing attorney's arm during the trial. No one disputed it, including Bajaria. "Don't go anywhere near this guy, Mom," Matthew said. "He's a sadist."

He may be a sadist, I thought, *but he was Curry's attorney, and Curry's orthopedist had asked him for deposition transcripts from a 2001 case involving a construction company called Munson.* It was a lifeline, a place to dig deeper.

It was seven twenty. Harriman would be here in ten minutes. If it was one hundred degrees in New York, it was one hundred fifteen degrees in Chinatown, where the laws of nature did not apply. Meanwhile, I still wasn't dressed.

When I called Matthew on Wednesday about Bajaria, he also told me that his girlfriend, Know-It-All Nina, would be on the Upper East Side for dinner and invited me to join them at Nick's. Dinner with Nina was low on my list of favorite things, but I love Matthew, and I love Nick's, so I said I would meet them there.

Nick's Pizza on Second Avenue is a restaurant I highly recommend. Matthew, Ghastly Nina, and I shared chicken parm with spaghetti and an order of sautéed spinach. It was heaven. Nick's red sauce is served family-style to the Gods on Mount Olympus. It doesn't say that on the menu, but all of Nick's regulars know it to be true.

Infuriating Nina went on and on about a new, off-Broadway production of *Little Shop of Horrors* she had just seen, outlining in holier-than-thou, professorial, art-appreciation language how "the organic quality of the outer-space plant, its innate, Afro-centric, masculine humanity, is what grounds the play and makes it accessible to audiences, particularly women of child-bearing age. This is precisely the type of subtextual significance that your vampire musical should be striving for. Is there anything at all in your play, Kate, that connects the audience to the universe at large while resonating a deeper, more personal, more vibrant voyage? Is there any intrinsic emotional value whatsoever? Or is it simply an exercise in shock-value theatrics?"

While I think Vile Nina is entirely full of crap, she did give me an idea for getting into Olivia Russell's office after hours, so I smiled, drank my Chianti, and decided to be nice. "In the second act alone, I drink the blood of twenty-two New Yorkers, Nina, including a gas-bag, NYU, art appreciation professor, while singing and dancing like Ginger Rogers. I think the subtextual significance of that speaks for itself, don't you?"

Contemptible Nina smiled while murdering me with her eyes.

On Thursday, I worked out at Raul's, searched the Internet for Munson Construction, told Charlie Nye my plan for accessing Monument Life, and had a run-through rehearsal for the second act of *Blood Song and Dance*, which included, for the first time, buckets of fake blood spurting everywhere. The special effects weren't in sync, so blood gushed without warning or reason not only from actors who weren't being bitten on stage, but also from actors who were off stage, standing in the wings, waiting for their entrance. When Roger strode into Grand Central Station to buy his one-way ticket out of New York already shooting red spouts in the air, like a whale crossing the Atlantic, even Dennis and Posey had to laugh.

The clock read seven twenty-five. I had five minutes until Harriman arrived, and I still had no idea what I was wearing. *Maybe I'm coming at it the wrong way,* I thought. Maybe I should start by figuring out what *he* would be wearing. Maybe imagining his clothes first would help me decide.

I had only seen him three times, once when he interrogated me at the Thirteenth with his partner, Logan, the bad cop, once at the Monument Life building, when I created a scene at the main reception desk, and once when he came to the D-Cup to ask me out on the date we were going on in, shit, four minutes, and each time he'd worn a tailored suit and tie. Would he change after work? Would he be dressed more casually? More formally? I didn't know, and so I stood there in my underwear thinking about what? About Charlie Nye.

This morning, Friday morning, Charlie told me he had everything taken care of for "the Monument job."

"I just told you the plan yesterday," I said. "How did you manage that?"

"Don't ask, don't tell," he said. "We go tomorrow night."

"Tomorrow night?"

"Carpe diem."

"Excuse me."

"Seize the day. Or night, as the case may be. Carpe nightem."

His eyes were red. He'd been smoking his own crops.

"Okay, Charlie. Tomorrow night it is."

I spent the rest of the day doing my laundry, cleaning my house, paying my bills, running my lines, and figuring out what I was going to wear on my date with Harriman, which was scheduled for seven thirty, which it became while I stared at my clothes. *Maybe he'll be late*, I thought. Even ten more minutes would help me. If I had ten more minutes, then I could...my door buzzer went off. He was here.

And then it dawned on me, the source of my indecision: It wasn't the heat. It was Harriman.

28

A WORLD-FAMOUS CHINESE JOINT
BELOW MOTT STREET

DETECTIVE MIKE HARRIMAN CAME STRAIGHT FROM THE JOB wearing a charcoal-gray suit, a blue silk tie that was loose around his neck, and a shoulder holster, complete with NYPD revolver, as an accessory. He was unshaven (in a really good way), and he must have put on cologne in the Thirteenth Precinct bathroom before he picked me up because he smelled great: a bit of musk, a hint of sex, a touch of mystery.

He drove a vintage, 1968, fully restored, jet-black Camaro with black leather seats, that was rough and rugged yet sleek and beautiful, like him. Sitting in it, heading downtown via Second Avenue, I was glad I had chosen a silk, black-and-white, sleeveless blouse, with a black sweater, a black skirt, and white wedge sandals. We matched. On the most superficial of levels, we were off to a good start.

We listened to music on the way to Chinatown, a compilation CD Harriman had burned that included The Killers, The Ramones, Nine Inch Nails, Guns N Roses, Blue Oyster Cult, and Cream. Harriman liked to rock to but only on the inside because he didn't sing or move his head in rhythm (not even to "Human," by The Killers), though I did a little of both.

We chatted about the heat wave and what effect it either did or didn't have on crime in the city—I said: crime goes up because people get crazy; he said: crime goes down because people get lazy—and about the best place to be in the middle of a heat wave—I said: with friends, drinking cold beer while floating down a river in big inner tubes; he said: with friends, drinking cold beer while working under the hood of a muscle car in a greasy, sweaty garage with a ball game on the radio. I asked him what restaurant in Chinatown we were going to, and he said, "The one and only," and I knew what he meant: Wo Hop.

At 17 Mott Street, down a flight of stairs, so, basically, in the basement of another street-level restaurant (with, inexplicably, the same name), waits Wo Hop, an iconic Chinese restaurant that has been cultivating a legion of devoted fans for five decades (or more). While standing in line for a table, you will, in all probability, strike up a conversation with a couple from Dallas, back for their third time this trip, an old hippie from the West Village, students from Columbia University, well-to-do philanthropists in tuxedos and gowns (straight from a charitable gala), firefighters from Staten Island with their wives and girlfriends who are celebrating someone's birthday, totally gothic teenagers (who have been here ten straight nights), soap opera stars, Brooklyn garage bands that can't rub two nickels together, Jewish families from Fort Lee, New Jersey, operating room nurses from Beth Israel, and an actor, currently in rehearsal for a vampire musical, on a date with a homicide detective investigating the murder of her father.

The restaurant itself is something of a dump. Open around the clock (I've been here, after a rehearsal or with Jimmy, after surveillance, at four in the morning), the service is brisk and usually brusque; the tables are small and packed tightly together so that even if you're not seated with people you've never met (and, at any time of day or night, there's a good chance that will happen), you might as well be; the checks are written in Chinese, so you have no idea what you ordered or how much you're paying for it; the smell of cigarette smoke drifts down from the street and mixes with the smell of hot oil, garlic and ginger, and the food is anywhere from good to very good to bland to too greasy. But the beer is cold, the portions, like the menu itself, are huge, and you have the sense that you're eating in a true-blue, New York institution. It's not a dining experience, per se, but a loud, funky, fabulous time in a world-famous Chinese joint below Mott Street, a one-of-a-kind New York event that you repeat over and over for most of your life.

We were seated at our own table, meaning the next table with a young Nashville couple on their honeymoon was two inches away. Harriman ordered the beef chow fon (a sign that he'd been here before), I ordered the honey crispy chicken (a sign that I had too); we both started with hot and sour soup and ordered cold Chinese beer.

The food comes fast, as if they're cooking your dinner before you order it, so Harriman and I talked while we ate, sharing each other's dishes, drinking beer, and letting the Wo Hop vibe erase the rest of the week. And then I said, "This was one of Jimmy's favorite places," and we both remembered that we were investigating my father's murder.

"What was he like?" Harriman said. "I mean I know he was a PI and a good one, I've heard stories about him, you know, as part of my investigation, but as a dad, what was he like?"

"He was tough, but he was fair, always fair. If you were right, and he was wrong, he'd say so and apologize or let you have your way or whatever. He had a bad temper, but a very long fuse. I mean really long. I would torture him for hours, and he'd just take it, and then finally he'd blow his top, and that was never fun."

"How did you torture him?"

"Name it. School, boys, money, back talk, fighting with my sister, missing my curfew, getting pregnant at sixteen, wanting to be an actor. Pretty much everything across the board a teenage girl could do to drive her father crazy, I did. It went on from there. My twenties and thirties weren't much better. When I messed up, he let me know. But he never let me down. And he always told me he was proud of me. And that he loved me..."

And then right there, in Wo Hop, on a date with a homicide detective (something that would have made Jimmy nuts), I started to cry. I'd been crying at some point during the day every day since Jimmy was shot in the eyes, but I sure as hell wasn't planning to cry in my food on my date with Harriman.

Harriman reached across the table and took my hand. "I'm sorry," he said. "I didn't mean to upset you."

"It's all right," I said. "I just miss him." And then I cried all over again.

He let me cry, and when I finally stopped, he smiled and said, "Your honey crispy chicken is wet now. Would you like me to order you another one? It will be here before you blow your nose. You won't even know they replaced it."

I laughed, and still he held my hand. I looked down at his hand on my mine, and then I held *his* hand. We looked into each other's eyes, then Harriman ordered us two more beers, and all I could think about was the two of us holding hands.

29

SO WHAT DO YOU DO FOR FUN, HARRIMAN?

Maybe it was the six-pack of cold Chinese beer we shared or my weeping-willow interlude during dinner, but whatever it was, the ride from Wo Hop to the House of Emotional Tics was night and day when compared to the ride from the House of Emotional Tics to Wo Hop.

Some guys loosen up by cracking jokes they normally wouldn't tell a woman. Others let you know that they're comfortable being with you by confiding the truth of the end of their last relationship. Still others, after they've gotten you pregnant at the age of sixteen, tell you it was a mistake. Not that you're pregnant at sixteen, mind you, but that *they* got you pregnant. The reason that's the mistake is because they've realized they're gay, and they're moving to San Francisco to take classes at the Institute of Esthetics and Cosmetology, never to return again, so you'll have to raise the baby by yourself, so long, sister, good luck with the rest of your heterosexual life. Or maybe that's just me.

Harriman, though, loosened up in a way I had rarely seen and hadn't expected: he softened. He was still Steve McQueen-handsome and Steven McQueen-tough, but his perfect blue eyes, always on alert for killers and clues, let their guard down in a gentle way. His mouth relaxed. He smiled easily. He moved his head in rhythm to "Don't Fear the Reaper." He talked about himself.

"Where are you from, Harriman?" I said. "There's a lot of New York in you, but you don't seem like a New Yorker."

"Army brat," he said. "My dad was a Marine Corps colonel, a weapons specialist. We moved a lot. I wasn't from anywhere until I got here twelve years ago."

"Weapons specialist?"

"That's what he said. Wherever we were, he'd fly to the Pentagon four, five times a year and advise them about weapons. That's all I knew. His job was 'Top Secret.' When I was ten, he said he could tell me about it, but then he'd have to kill me."

I laughed, but Harriman looked at me with those eyes, and I stopped laughing.

"I don't think he was kidding," he said.

And then, taking in the suddenly serious look on my face, he laughed too, which made me laugh again.

"Is he still alive?" I said.

"In Tampa. He retired from the military. Fishes all day, every day."

"Your mom?"

"She died. Pneumonia, of all things. I was fifteen."

"I'm sorry."

"Long time ago. I'm an only child, and my dad was gone a lot of the time, so for most of my life it's just been me."

He smiled in a way that said his mother's death still made him sad, and I thought, *Oh Christ, here I go...I like Harriman.*

We flowed with the traffic up First Avenue, and I remembered when my mother died. It was a cold, all-encompassing sadness, like a blanket of snow I thought would never melt, except it did melt, leaving an empty feeling, though not a cold one because the memories of her were so warm. Jimmy's death was nothing like that. Jimmy's death was a brick to the head. I felt like I was walking around with a concussion, the entire world off-kilter. I had the sense that I could live in this new world but might never be part of it. Looking at pictures of my mom, which I did from time to time, made me both sad and happy. I didn't know if I would ever be able to look at Jimmy's face again. It was hard to believe, given the amount of grief we gave each other, that I could miss him that much. But I did.

I told Harriman about my mom, Christine, and my sister, Marilyn, and our family, and he listened and laughed at the funny parts, especially the stories of me harassing Marilyn. (If there had been a league for annoying older sisters, I would have been an All Star.) He got quiet when I told him about my mother dying of cancer when I was ten, and we held hands again, sharing the loss of our mothers. The city blurred into one long block, and Harriman took surface roads, weaving his way uptown to avoid traffic.

I'm all for contemplative introspection but not when I'm on a date with Steve McQueen, so to break the mood, I said, "So what do you do for fun, Harriman?" I didn't realize that he had turned onto East 83rd Street and was parking in front of the House of Emotional Tics.

"Invite me in for a drink and let's find out," he said.

30

AMERICA THE BEAUTIFUL MEETS I'M A YANKEE DOODLE DANDY

IT HAD BEEN A LONG TIME SINCE I KISSED A MAN THE WAY I KISSED Harriman. I hadn't consented to sex with anyone in eight months, so I was ready, maybe a tad too ready. His lips on my neck were burning hot. I had forgotten how sex, when you really want it, makes your skin feel like it's on fire. We were on the couch in the living room, making out heavy, and my hands went exploring new territory. Harriman said something like, "Slow down, Kate," to which I said something like, "No way." Then I stood up, out of breath, my hair wild, my body one big flaming mess of horny, and said, "You. Bedroom. Now." To Harriman's credit, I didn't have to tell him twice.

Some guys get so lost in their own pleasure that they forget they're with someone else. But Harriman was always looking for me, always connecting, finding my mouth with his mouth, my eyes with his eyes. We were in each other's arms the entire time, except when I went to the bathroom. Even then, he came with me to the kitchen to drink a glass of water and keep me company.

We made love two times, and they were both like the Fourth of July. Sex with Harriman was "America The Beautiful" meets

"I'm A Yankee Doodle Dandy"—red lights flashing, sirens screaming, bombs bursting in air. We had great sex our first time together, and that is not a bad indicator of where a relationship can sometimes go. It's not the be-all-end-all by a long shot, but it can point to potential.

He left at four fifteen in the morning to drive four hours to Syracuse for a vintage car show he was committed to. We kissed at my door, and he said, "Good date."

"Not bad," I said.

"Want to do it again?" he said.

"Let me think about it," I said. "Yes."

He laughed and said, "Me too."

We kissed again, and he left.

After he was gone, I stayed in bed, all warm and glowy, wondering if Harriman was soon to be my boyfriend, thinking about how ironic that would be but also about how nice it would be, how much I really did like him, how gentle he was, how funny and sensitive and smart and handsome and strong. Guys like Harriman don't fall off the truck every day, so when one does, you have to be open-minded, even if they're a cop. I was ready, I decided, for whatever romantic possibilities awaited Harriman and me. I also realized that I had never once asked him what he was doing about Jimmy's case and that he had never asked me what I was doing about it either. Which was just as well because if he had, I would have lied to his face.

31

ALL PLANT PEOPLE ARE PERVERTS

IT WAS SATURDAY, SIX THIRTY P.M., TWO WEEKS AND (MORE OR less) one day since Jimmy was murdered, one week since I had hired, for fifty bucks each, Charlie Nye, Al Cutter, LaTanya Bellamy, and Fu to help me "access" Olivia Russell's twenty-seventh floor Monument Life Insurance office after hours, three days since Dennis and Posey watched as I busted Dr. Martin Miller's nose with a haymaker, and fourteen hours since Harriman and I made love for the second time that night.

Charlie, Al, and LaTanya were in my apartment trying on their jade-green, Manhattan Plantscape jumpsuits, which featured a large logo across the back and a name stitched on the front pocket. LaTanya was in my walk-through closet; Charlie and Al were in my kitchen.

I was in my living room, wearing my Manhattan Plantscape jumpsuit, looking at the Manhattan Plantscape van that was doubled parked on 83rd Street in front of the House of Emotional Tics. Fu was standing guard by the van, already in his jumpsuit. Charlie had gotten Fu an XXL. The body fit Fu fine, but the sleeves and legs were too long, and so they were rolled and cuffed. Fu didn't particularly look like an interior plant maintenance person, but who did?

I watched Fu throw an empty beer bottle at a pigeon and reviewed the plan, which was inspired by Odious Nina's snarky lecture about the "depth of intellectualized emotionality relating to the sexual subtext" of *Little Shop of Horrors*, a musical that features a talking plant from outer space. Thinking of that exotic plant reminded me that Olivia Russell had extensive, expensive, and extraordinary trees, shrubs, flowers, and plants placed all over her twenty-seventh-floor fortress. Some company, I reasoned, was being paid a princely sum to care for those plants after insurance-company hours. My plan was for Al to hack into Monument's contractor database and find out who those plant people were, for Charlie to secure one of their vans and some of their uniforms, for my House-of-Emotional-Tics team to impersonate the plant people, drive to Monument in the plant-people van, waltz past security, take the elevator to twenty-seven, keep a careful eye out while Al downloaded Russell's file on the late Ron Powell, gather up our borrowed plant-people gear, take the elevator to the basement, and drive back to 83rd Street without incident. I would then find out what really happened to Powell, and that would lead me to whoever killed my father.

"I look like shit in green. You couldn't get no blue plant people?" LaTanya said, entering the living room. *Monique* was the name stitched on the front pocket of her jade-green jumpsuit.

"Sorry, Monique," I said.

"Look at this. Can you fucking believe this?" Al said, coming into the living room, Charlie right behind him. "Of all the fucking plant people in the world, I get this one?" He pointed at the name on his Manhattan Plantscape jumpsuit. It was *Elliot*, the name of the roommate who pushed Al into insomnia. "And Charlie won't switch with me."

"I like being Walter," Charlie said, showing me the name on his jumpsuit. "He's probably from Wilkes-Barre or someplace in Pennsylvania. Probably was a cop who retired, ran out of money, and got into the plant business. Fucking Walter. Didn't plan for the future, but he's got a hell of a green thumb."

"Are you stoned, Charlie?" I said, rhetorically.

"Walter's a pervert," Al said. "All plant people are perverts."

"I knew a plant person one time," LaTanya said. "Name was Buddy. He wasn't no pervert. His right leg was two inches shorter than his left leg, and he grew rhubarb in the alley, but that don't make him no pervert."

"Would anyone mind if we talked about plant people perverts later?" I said, handing each of them a pair of latex gloves.

Charlie, LaTanya, and Al moved across the living room to the door.

"Walter's not a pervert," Charlie said over his shoulder, putting on the gloves. "He's just fiscally irresponsible."

"Can't be no plant person if you look like shit in green," LaTanya said, following him out, pulling her gloves on too.

Al stopped in front of me and shook his head in disgust. "Elliot," he said.

The Manhattan Plantscape van was jade green with red and yellow graphics that made it seem like the city was an over-grown tropical rainforest and help was on the way. LaTanya was behind the wheel, I was in the front passenger seat, and Fu, Al, and Charlie were seated uncomfortably on large plastic buckets in the back, surrounded by Manhattan Plantscape gear. LaTanya drove the van with ease. She had been a big-rig driver for five years before settling down and buying the medallion with Mountain. She moved through traffic in one fluid motion, like the van was ice-skating in Central Park. She never missed a light, never jammed the breaks, and never blew the horn. She timed her turns down surface roads so the van would never have to stop. She drove with her right hand. Her left hand tapped a soft rhythm on the van door.

It was a hot night, but we had the windows open because the van smelled like chemicals and peat moss. Charlie and Al couldn't let the Walter-Elliot-jumpsuit-name thing go. They bitched back and forth, asking Fu, with yes or no questions, who was right and who was wrong and betting twenty dollars on the outcome. Fu said they were both wrong and told them each "Fu you" for good measure. This lead to further arguing, and everyone participated.

But the further south and east we went, the quieter we got. By the time LaTanya made a right onto 23rd Street from Lexington, drove past the south end of Madison Square Park, went across Broadway and Fifth Avenue, and pulled into the garage beneath the Monument Life Insurance Building, we were silent as sand.

32

EVERYBODY'S AT THE BEACH
BUT ME

LaTanya parked the van near the entrance to the Level One elevator lobby, killed the engine, and turned to me. "Get what you need and get the hell out," she said.

"We won't be long," I said.

"You best not be."

I nodded and climbed out of the van. Charlie, Al, and Fu got the gear out of the back and moved it toward the double elevator lobby doors. There were buckets of pruning and digging tools, spray canisters of chemicals, and a watering rig—a rolling platform with a twenty-gallon tank, an electric pump, and a coiled hose with a long, skinny, spray-gun attachment at the end.

"We're plant people," I said. "We take care of plants. We don't talk. Except me. I supervise and do all the talking. You got your zip drive?"

Al pulled it out of his pocket. It was smooth and silver. Soon it would hold all of Ron Powell's information. "I can't believe I'm doing this for fifty bucks," he said. His eyes were bloodshot. His hair was stringy and greasy. I wouldn't let him near my plants.

"Jesus Christ, Elliot. Keep your shit together," Charlie said. "Last thing I need is this gets fucked up. Taking a plant van's one thing. Corporate espionage is some real different shit."

"You call me Elliot one more time, I'll make you eat this," Al said, showing Charlie the zip drive.

They were nervous. So was I. Fu was tense, too, but not nervous. He was focused. We all wore gardening gloves to cover the latex gloves.

"Let's go," I said.

I opened the elevator lobby door. We moved our gear into the lobby and were confronted by the young one, the first guard I spoke to when I was pretending to be Citigroup Vice President of Community Affairs Jeannine Watkins, dropping off a policy —without an appointment—for Carole Forrester less than two weeks ago. The crusty one, the grizzly, and the captain had intervened when it became clear that Watkins was more than the young one could handle.

He was seated behind an old, battered desk that didn't look right in the room, which was marble, mahogany, and modern. I glanced up and saw the security camera was disabled. Harriman had said it was out when they found Jimmy. It was still offline.

"Manhattan Plantscapes," I said, laying on a heavy New York accent. "Twenty-seventh floor."

The young one looked at his log. He had no computer at his desk. "You're early."

He had either been demoted from his shift at the command center during the day to the sad, lonely, night shift in the garage elevator lobby or had drawn the short straw when someone called in sick. Either way, I'm sure he was hoping nobody dropped off a dead body with the eyes blown out. That would just ruin *his* night.

"City's empty. We got here in like two minutes."

He looked us over. When I was here eleven days ago, I was a

blonde banker in a business suit with tortoiseshell glasses and green eyes. To become *Donna*, the name on my Manhattan Plantscapes jumpsuit, I had put my hair up under my hat and worn blue contacts and no makeup.

"Everybody's at the beach but me," the young one said, as if we weren't standing in the elevator lobby waiting to pretend to go to work.

"It's like almost seven," I said. "Probably nobody's at the beach."

"Yeah," the young one said. "You're an hour early."

"Are we going to have this conversation again, or are you going to let us take care of Ms. Russell's plants, which cost more than either one of us makes in a year?"

He shook his head: Why was every minute of his life so complicated? Why wasn't he at the beach, or at least back in the main lobby working the command center?

"Sign the sheet," he said.

He spun a clipboard around, I wrote "Manhattan Plantscapes/Donna" on the line, we moved our tools and supplies into the service elevator, which was around the corner, and rode it up to the twenty-seventh floor.

It was Saturday, seven p.m. No one was here. The lights were on in every room. The white-noise hum from the overheads and the steady whoosh of air from the central air conditioning system made the whole floor cold and numbing. It reminded me of someplace, but I couldn't put my finger on it. During the planning stages of the break-in, I had to decide whether to take the service elevator off line and keep it on the twenty-seventh floor or let it go and call it back when we were ready. Keeping it would attract attention after a few minutes but not having it here if we needed it seemed like a bigger risk. I opted for "hold and hurry." We took it out of service and left the plant gear inside.

I had taken the main elevator for my meeting as wannabe-fitness reporter Gillian Breiner, so it took me a moment to find my way from the service elevator to the long hallway that led to the huge corner office of Olivia Russell. Her suite door was shut. I knew it was locked before I tried it, but I tried it anyway and then turned to Charlie.

"Quickly, Walter," I said.

Charlie moved to the door, took a handful of personal, professionally engineered tools from a felt sack he'd had in his jumpsuit pocket, and worked the lock. The tools were oiled and polished, in mint condition. Charlie tried one and then another and then another. No luck.

"Is there an alarm on the door," Charlie said.

"I don't know," I said.

"You don't know?" Al said. "Shit, McCall. How can you not know?"

"Donna," I said. We had agreed to call each other by our Manhattan Plantscapes names on the contentious ride down from East 83rd Street. "What was I supposed to do, ask her? If there's an alarm, we have to hurry."

"If there's an alarm, we screwed the pooch," Al said.

"The real plant people have a key," Charlie said.

"The real plant people have the alarm code," Al said.

"The real plant people don't come until eight."

I recognized the voice as I was turning to face it. It was the strong, deep, Southern sound of Olivia Russell's director of security: Green Beret Bradley Olsen.

Click. Charlie flipped the lock, and I remembered the cold and numbing place that reminded me of the twenty-seventh floor of the Monument Life Insurance building: the city morgue.

33

FU TAKE BIG ONE

"Go, Elliot," I said. "Ron Powell. Everything she's got. Stay with him, Walter, in case he needs help. Me and Robert will talk to security." Robert was the name on Fu's XXL jumpsuit.

"Don't call me Elliot," Al said.

"Now," I said, pushing them into Russell's office and shutting the door.

Green Beret Bradley had two Monument security guards with him, a pit bull about five feet five inches square, and a wire brush about six feet tall. They all wore gray suits with Monument security nametags on their lapels. Bradley wore a blue tie. The pit bull and the wire brush wore red ties.

"I want the door to Ms. Russell's office opened, and I want everyone in the hall and against the wall in the next ten seconds," Bradley said. He was talking to me but also to the pit bull and the wire brush, because those two started toward us with serious intent, the pit bull in a hurry. Bradley followed them very slowly, his eyes on Fu.

I was sure the young one had called Green Beret Bradley and told him the plant crew was here an hour earlier than they were supposed to be. He did this not because he cared but because he thought it might score him some points from the parking garage and land him back in the command center. I made a mental note to introduce my fist to the young one's nose at a later date.

I can usually find a way out of a sticky situation, but I was frozen. Charlie and Al were in Russell's office, breaking about a dozen laws, and Fu and I were about to be thrown against a wall by Bradley's attack dogs. A call to the cops would be next, illegal activity in the building would trigger an automatic response from Harriman, my team would be arrested, Fu would be deported, and I would have, as Al said, screwed the pooch. I had almost packed Jimmy's Colt .45, but decided not to at the last minute because I don't like guns, though I could have learned to like them at that moment. Now it was too late. I was out of ideas at the precise moment that I was also out of time.

The pit bull arrived first, eager to earn his stripes in front of his Green Beret boss. He reached out to physically spin Fu around and shove him face first to the wall. Instead, Fu grabbed the pit bull's arm with his right hand and, in one blinding, brutal motion, snapped it back with such speed and force and at such a terrible angle that it broke on the spot. The pit bull screamed in agony but only for a moment, because Fu grabbed him by the head with his left hand and thrust his face down while lifting his knee with incredible power. The collision was epic. The pit bull's nose was smashed to a pulp and his cheekbones were crushed to bits. Blood was all over the pit bull's face, his arm was broken, and his gray suit was ruined. He gurgled his own blood and then slipped into unconsciousness.

Fu let the pit bull fall to the floor and looked at me. Bradley and the wire brush were running at us. "Fu take big one," Fu said.

Fu take big one? Son of a bitch, Fu could talk. All this time, Fu could talk. I had less than a second to process this mindblower because *Fu take big one* meant *You take wire brush*, and the wire brush was here.

I don't think the wire brush was expecting much of a fight from a forty-five-year-old woman, so his hands were down. If I learned one thing from Raul it was this: when the hands are down, pound the face. I hit the wire brush flush on the eye with a wicked left jab that staggered him. I followed that with a strong right cross to the jaw that dropped him to one knee. *Son of a bitch*, he was probably thinking, *what the fuck?* I answered that question for him by landing a hellacious hook to the side of his head. The wire brush collapsed, and I glanced down the hall at Fu and Green Beret Bradley. I will never forget this vision for the rest of my life.

They were kicking and punching and bashing each other in an awesome display of mixed martial arts, both of them third degree black belts, trading blows that would incapacitate pretty much anyone else on the planet. The six-foot-four-inch Bradley towered over the five-foot-seven-inch Fu, but the bigger man was frustrated: How could this block of Chinese granite be that fast, that strong, and that completely unafraid of an American military killing machine? Bradley rushed forward, throwing punch after punch, deciding to overwhelm Fu with a tidal wave of size, speed, and strength. He cracked Fu in the head with a forearm, Fu moved back with the force of the blow, a reed in the wind, and Bradley stepped in for the kill.

But at the same moment the Green Beret lunged forward, Fu shot out a sidekick that caught Bradley's kneecap straight on. The knee buckled backwards with a terrible sound, everything broken and ripped to shit, bone exposed, blood pouring through his torn suit, and Bradley went down hard.

Fu was on him in an instant, grabbing the Green Beret by the front of his suit and jerking him forward a hundred miles an hour, cracking him head to head, knocking him stone-cold unconscious. It was the most devastating headbutt I had ever seen...or heard. (It sound like a car crash.) Fu let Bradley fall to the ground and then stood up. He was bleeding from the nose and ear, and he was out of breath.

"Jesus, Robert," I said.

"We go now, Donna," Fu said.

I opened the door to Olivia Russell's suite and yelled across snot-nosed Bradley's outer office into Russell's inner sanctum. Her door was open, and I could see Al and Charlie at Russell's computer. "Elliot. Walter."

"We're not done," Charlie said.

"Yes we are," I said.

"I need three minutes," Al said.

"We don't have three seconds," I said.

"Three minutes," Al said.

"Goodbye, Elliot," I said.

"Shit," Al said, pulling his zip drive from whatever the hell port it was in. He and Charlie hurried out of the office, and we all took off down the hall, past the incapacitated pit bull and Green Beret, toward the service elevator.

As we turned the corner, the wire brush, on his knees, pulled his walkie-talkie and said loud enough for us to hear, "Code red on twenty-seven. Code red on twenty-seven."

34

YOU CALL THIS A PLAN?

"Hold and hurry" turned out to be a good choice. The service elevator was waiting for us like a well-trained dog. We piled in, hit the release, and the door closed as the wire brush, wobbly as a bowling pin, turned the corner at the far end of the hall.

No one spoke for the first twenty-one floors down to the Level One garage. The sight of Green Beret Bradley unconscious, knee bones exploded through his pants, blood everywhere, *and* the unconscious pit bull, face bashed in, arm twisted at a hideous angle, *and* the wire brush seeing stars, face down on the floor, was enough to shut even Al's big mouth. Al and Charlie were both a bit freaked out. They looked at me for some kind of explanation. I looked at Fu.

Why in the world had he chosen to say only six words since moving to the House of Emotional Tics when he could, apparently, speak quite a few more? I asked him in a way that he couldn't answer yes or no.

"What else do you have to say, Fu?" I said.

Charlie and Al looked at Fu, who wiped blood from his

nose with the folded-up sleeve of his jade-green jumpsuit and said, "What mean code twenty-seven?"

"Code twenty-seven means fifty bucks is a fucking joke," Al said.

"It means we're all going to jail," Charlie said.

"No one's going to jail," I said, thinking that we were all going to jail.

The elevator doors opened, and LaTanya was standing in the elevator lobby, one arm's length from the young one, who she had backed up against a marble wall by holding the blade end of huge pruning shears to his throat.

"What the hell did you do, Donna?" LaTanya said, never taking her eyes off the young one. "This moron was waiting to take you down when those doors opened."

"You're all going to jail," the young one said.

"Will everyone please stop saying that?" I said.

A police siren, somewhere a few blocks away, was getting louder by the second.

"Here they come," the young one said.

I turned to Fu, Al, and Charlie. "Get the stuff in the van. Hurry."

They double-timed it to the back of the Manhattan Plantscapes van and loaded the gear into the back. I took two steps toward LaTanya.

"Put that thing down, please, Monique." I said.

Still glaring at the young one, she lowered the shears. In that same instant, I stepped in and punched him as hard I could, square in the nose. He went down on his knees like a grade-school cry baby, wailing that it hurt, that it might be broken, that he had a deviated septum so now what had I done to him, and on and on. It was all about *him*.

"Want me to cut off his head," LaTanya said, snapping the shears, half kidding.

"Yes," I said, the siren getting closer. "But we have to go."

We left the young one on the floor in the elevator lobby, ran to the van, and jumped in. LaTanya turned the engine, put it in gear, and rolled away just as the stairwell door to the elevator lobby opened and two more security guards arrived.

LaTanya pulled away from the elevator lobby, made a left turn, went to the end of the garage, made another left and hit the gas down the long straightaway toward the 23rd Street exit.

"Go east on 23rd," I said.

"Oh, now you the driver?" LaTanya said.

"Trust me," I said.

"Trust you?" Al said from the back of the van. "Aren't you the one who said, 'Piece of cake. In and out. Walk in the park. Easy as...'"

He stopped mid-sentence because as we approached the exit, which was also the entrance, a cop car blasted into the garage, lights flashing, sirens blaring. Seeing us coming at him, the car skidded to a stop in such a way as to try and block our escape, but it didn't have a great angle, so there was room behind it.

There were two officers in the car, and they got out to wave us down.

"Go, go, go," I said.

"Hold on," LaTanya said. She ran the van to the right and smashed through the opening on the back side, destroying the squad car's trunk and rear quarter panel, making the cops jump away for their lives, and flew out of the garage onto 23rd Street.

"Left, left," I said.

LaTanya turned the wheel sharply, the van went up on two wheels, grabbed the road, righted itself with a jolt, and took off down 23rd toward the East Side of Manhattan, our front left headlight bashed in.

"Start talking, McCall," LaTanya said.

"We had a little run-in with security," I said.

"A little run-in?" Al said.

"World War III," Charlie said. "Dead bodies everywhere."

"Nobody died," I said. "It just looked like it."

As we crossed Fifth Avenue and came to Broadway, picking up speed, the lights turned red, and another cop car came screaming down 23rd from Avenue of the Americas, behind us. We would be stuck between Fifth and Broadway if we stopped. I heard other sirens in the distance.

"Go through it," I said.

"You crazy?" LaTanya said.

"You worried about a ticket?" I said. "Really?"

LaTanya floored it across Broadway through the red lights, weaving like a stock car racer, horns honking all around us, cars skidding, tires screeching. Fu, Charlie, Al, and the plant gear got tossed around in the back of the van like pants in the dryer.

"Left on Madison. Now, turn now," I said.

LaTanya made another very sharp left, and we shot up Madison Avenue, Madison Square Park on our left, banks and office buildings on our right.

"Faster, LaTanya," I said. "They're all coming now."

"I hear them," LaTanya said. "You got any more bright ideas?"

"Just one," I said. "Everybody take your jumpsuit off."

"That's not a bright idea," Al said. "You think getting rid of the jumpsuits is going to make us go faster. What do they weight, nine, ten pounds all together in a pile?"

I turned in my seat, already slipping out of my jade-green coveralls. "Do it, Al. It's part of the plan. You too, Fu. Charlie."

Charlie and Fu took off their jumpsuits, no easy task as the van hurtled past 26th and 27th streets, LaTanya pushing the speedometer to eighty while changing lanes without warning.

"Plan?" Al said. "You call this a plan? Killing two security guards with your bare hands is your idea of a plan?"

"Not dead," Fu said. "Hurt bad."

"Fu you, Fu," Al said.

"Fu you, too," Fu said.

As we crossed 28th and Madison, two more cop cars joined the chase. They were a full block behind us. We were flying. They were flying faster.

"LaTanya," I said.

"It's a plant van," LaTanya said. "Horsepower isn't exactly a priority."

The light at 29th and Madison turned red. LaTanya and I saw it at the same second.

"Don't say it," LaTanya said, and we shot through the red light, just missing a Pottery Barn delivery truck.

"Right on 30th. Right, right, right…" I said.

LaTanya turned right, and we fishtailed through the turn and exploded forward. The light was red at the corner of 30th and Park, and traffic was badly backed up.

"Sidewalk," I said.

"Way ahead of you," LaTanya said.

"There," I said, pointing to a Toyota parking on the north side of the street.

LaTanya hit the gas, and we went into the opening and up over the curb onto the sidewalk, the Toyota clipping us on the rear end as it backed into the space.

Behind us, the three police cars made the turn from Madison onto 30th. If they wanted to catch us, they would have to drive on the sidewalk too.

New Yorkers of all shapes, sizes, and colors dove out of the way in surprise and panic as the plant van barreled down the sidewalk toward Park Avenue—even in New York, a plant van doing eighty-five on the sidewalk doesn't happen every day.

The light turned green just as we reached the corner. We sailed off the curb and crashed down in the intersection, ahead of the cars that were in line, and picked up speed heading east on 30th toward Lexington.

"We lost them," I said, checking my side mirror. But then I

saw two more cop cars turn onto Thirtieth from Park, one from the north and one from the south. They were three quarters of a block behind us.

We caught the light at Lexington at nearly ninety miles per hour, the van shaking and groaning and ready to come apart at the seams. Charlie, Al, and Fu bounced around the back like beach balls, cursing each other, the police, the plant van, and me.

The cops missed the light at Lexington and had to slow down to go through the red so they wouldn't crash into the crossing traffic.

"Left on Third," I said.

"First is faster," LaTanya said.

"Left on Third," I said.

"I'm a cab driver," LaTanya said. "You're an actor."

"Thank you," I said. "Now left, LaTanya, left on Third."

We almost missed it, but LaTanya cut the wheel and just caught the corner. The cop cars were still on 30th. Their sirens were screaming at us.

At the corner of 31st and Third, I pointed to a gap between a light pole and a mailbox and said, "Through there."

LaTanya drove the van up on the sidewalk between the light pole and the mailbox, past the Super Cuts and into the long, narrow, tree-lined, park-like courtyard entrance of an apartment building.

"By the trees, park by the trees, stop the van," I said. I think I was shouting, maybe the entire time, but this was when I realized it.

The van came to a shrieking, rubber-burning stop by the courtyard's very own gazebo.

We sat there for a moment, stunned, then LaTanya, already taking her jumpsuit off, said, "Now what?"

"Everybody out," I said.

We fell out of the van, and I could see that Al, Fu, and

LaTanya were confused and, for the first time, afraid. Where the hell were we? Why did we stop? Why did we get out of the van? Why did they ever listen to me? Al was so blown away that he couldn't even complain about the money. No one knew what to say except me.

"Charlie," I said, and he pointed through the trees to a 1975 Lincoln Continental Town Car parked in the street beyond the brick and wrought iron fence. It had a powder blue body and a white vinyl roof with porthole windows behind the rear doors. There was a huge chrome grill and a carpeted trunk bigger than a studio apartment. Charlie had presented it for my approval when I was making sure my backup plan had a backup plan for its backup plan, which was *Jimmy's Rules of Private Investigation for Kate, Rule Number Eight.*

The sirens were getting louder. The cops would turn onto 31st Street in less than a minute.

"Over the fence," I said. "Hurry."

We ran past the gazebo and through the trees to the wrought iron fence. The iron fence posts were spears, more or less, but if you put your foot between the "blades," you could make it up and over without impaling yourself.

When we were all on the sidewalk, we ran to the Town Car and climbed in, Charlie behind the wheel, me riding shotgun, Fu, LaTanya, and Al in the big back seat.

Charlie started the car and pulled into traffic, heading west on 31st Street. Behind us, two police cars turned the corner and then two more after them. They spotted the van in the trees, stopped their cars, and jumped the fence with their guns drawn.

We made a left on Lexington, a right on 30th, and a left on Third. By the time we passed 31st, there were three more police cars on the scene and more than a dozen cops with no one to arrest.

35

NO RADIO, OR CD, OR CASSETTE, OR EVEN AN EIGHT-TRACK

On Tuesday, I drove to Westwood, New Jersey, to meet with Gilbert Munson, owner of Munson Construction, the company referenced in Dr. Martin Miller's Ken Curry file. Miller had made a note in the margin of Curry's orthopedic records asking Boris Bajaria, Curry's cannibalistic lawyer, Boris of Borneo, for the Munson Construction deposition transcripts of 2001. It had been three days since we inconvenienced Green Beret Bradley and his attack dogs.

The car had no sound system. It was a Toyota Corolla that I sometimes rented from Warren White, the numismatist, notaphile, *and* philatelist doorman, who purchased it stripped down to its bare bones to keep his cost lower than low. I like to listen to music or news or talk when I'm driving because it distracts me from the fact that I don't like to drive. I'm not good at driving, so I don't like it, so I don't drive much. Or I don't drive much because I don't like it because I'm not good at it. Either way, it sucked eggs that there was no radio, or DVD, or cassette, or even an eight-track for me to listen to. But Warren only charged me twenty-five bucks a day, so I couldn't complain. It was the quietest car on East River Drive, the quietest car crossing the George Washington Bridge, the quietest car on Route 4 west, and the quietest car on Route 17 north. There was nothing to do but think about the last three days.

After we'd abandoned the Manhattan Plantscapes van, we drove the Town Car to Fiftieth Street, parked it, left it for the authorities to find, and went our separate ways. Fu walked back to the House of Emotional Tics, Charlie went to a bar on 51st Street, and Al grabbed a cab that he made me pay for. "No way cab fare was part of the deal, McCall," he said, holding up the zip drive as a bargaining chip. I was too drained to fight about it, so I gave him a twenty, and he handed me the drive. LaTanya called her brother, and he picked us up in the yellow Volvo. We went out for pizza and drank too many beers. By the time I got back to East 83rd Street, I was drunk, and it was late, but I went down to the basement anyway and knocked on Fu's door. I had questions, and now I knew he had answers. He wasn't giving them to me tonight, however. "I know you're in there, Fu. You can run, but you can't hide," I said to the peephole, proving again that when I drink too many beers, I say ridiculous things to peepholes.

Olivia Russell, not surprisingly, had all kinds of encoded protection surrounding her hard drive. When Al finally did break through, he discovered that her *real* hard drive wasn't integrated into the Monument main frame. It was offline, which is why we had to visit her office after hours in the first place. On her *real* hard drive, there were codenames and number sequences that, even if you knew them, would be hard to navigate, and it took Al longer than expected to get over, under, and around her digital gates. Once he was in, it took him a few minutes more to find Powell's file, and just when he did, Fu head butted Green Beret Bradley into the twilight zone, and I declared it Time to Go. It turned out that Al really did need three more minutes.

Even inside Powell's personal file there was serious security in place. The documents were named by number and were broken into pieces, with each piece having its own password as well. The correct combination of words and numbers, initiated in the right order, was required to bring all the right pieces together at the same time. Despite all that, Al found a path almost all the way in and downloaded whatever he could without knowing precisely what pieces of what documents he was grabbing.

On Sunday morning, nursing a hangover, I looked at what we got. It turned out to be a hodgepodge of Powell papers that were frustratingly incomplete: pages eight through eleven, sixteen, and nineteen through twenty-two of the policy, several pages of Powell's Monument physical examination results, a few pages of the medical examiner's report and other random, internal, Monument procedural documents. There were no surprises.

According to Russell's records, Powell left ten million dollars to his ex-wife (whose name, address, and phone number weren't part of the Powell pages) and not to his favorite charity, as Terry Kramer said Powell himself had told her over clams and Chianti at La Luna; Powell was in perfect health just three months before his massive heart attack; Powell owned three fitness centers; Powell was of sound mind; Powell was this; Powell was that; Powell was perfectly positioned to be the ten-mil centerpiece of whatever the hell had happened to him. I did, however, learn something that sparked a bit of a plan. The signature page of Powell's medical examiner's report was among the disparate pieces of the puzzle downloaded onto Al's zip drive. The M.E.'s name was Dr. Arnold Stone. I penciled him in for a visit.

Sunday afternoon I had a *Blood Song and Dance* rehearsal at the D-Cup. It was the understudy run-through. Dennis and Posey, understudies themselves for most of their careers, insisted that everyone in the show (in every one of their shows) understudy someone else in the show, learning all the lines, all the songs, and all the dances for that role in addition to their own role. I understudied Chloe Burns, who played Mariah Muldoon, closet lesbian lover of vampire women, originally from Philadelphia but now from Dallas, because Chloe couldn't hit her off-off-off-off Broadway notes and so all her songs were rewritten as twangy Texas tunes.

I liked the understudy run-through. As rehearsals progress, everyone becomes accustomed to everyone else's performances. The characters of the play, as depicted by each cast member, become familiar. It's easy to become complacent with your own performance because you become complacent with the performances around you. The understudy run-through either confirms the cast's best hopes or heightens their worst fears—but usually does some of both. For me, it was as eye opening to see Chloe, who was my understudy, tackle the role of Farina LeBleu as a country-western cowgirl as it was for me (I was Chloe's understudy) to play the role of Mariah Muldoon from Dallas. What fun to go from a centuries-old, New York-nightclub-singing vampire to a two-stepping, backstabbing, Texas lesbian.

Harriman called me Monday morning at ten.

"Hi," he said.

"Hi." I said. "Was it vintage?"

"Four hundred twenty-six cars worth."

"Sounds like fun."

"It was. What did you do?"

"Rehearsal, laundry, cleaned my house, drank beers, paid bills, went to the gym."

"The drinking beers part sounds like fun."

"It was."

"Want to drink beers with me? We could catch a movie, go to a ballgame, have dinner, walk in the park..."

He was setting me up. I could hear him smiling, and so I could see him smiling. What a nice, warm vision for a Monday morning. I smiled too.

"All in the same night?"

"Doesn't have to be. We could spread it out."

"I'd like that."

"How's Friday?"

"Too long. How's Tuesday at seven?"

"Tomorrow night?

"You really are a detective."

He laughed. "I've got softball. Sorry. How about Wednesday?"

"Rehearsal. Thursday?"

"Card night."

"Friday it is."

Later that day, I met Matthew for lunch at a midtown Japanese restaurant. We ate sushi and talked about Nauseating Nina and *Blood Song and Dance* and how we both missed Jimmy, and then Matthew said, "Did you do something at Monument Life Insurance I should know about?"

"Like what?" I said.

"Like pretend to be a plant crew, break into Monument on Saturday night, beat two security guards close to death, steal information from a very successful, very powerful, very pissed off insurance agent, then participate in a car chase that ended on 31st and Third?"

"What an imagination, Matthew? You should be in theater."

"Was it you, Mom? You better tell me the truth, because this is a big deal now. The people at Monument are seriously bent out of shape, and Detective Harriman, the one who questioned you about pretending to be a magazine reporter in the same Monument office that was just broken into, the one who wants you to hand over Jimmy's files, he left me two messages this morning."

"What did he want?"

"He just said to call him. Are you investigating Jimmy's murder? Is that what this is? Was it you or not?"

"I'm terrible with plants."

"Mom."

"I'm not answering that question. It's insulting and disrespectful. So there."

I kissed him good-bye, told him he was a terrific prosecutor, went back to the House of Emotional Tics, and set up a meeting with Gilbert Munson at The Iron Horse in Westwood. The rest of Monday I spent wondering why Harriman was calling my son. And why he didn't say anything about it to me. And then it was Tuesday, and I drove to New Jersey in Warren's Toyota with no sound system and plenty of time to think.

36

GUILTY AND NEGLIGENT

WESTWOOD IS A CUTE, CONSCIOUSLY COSMOPOLITAN TOWN OF almost eleven thousand that sits in the center of the Pascack Valley in the northeast corner of New Jersey. It was incorporated as a borough in 1894, but its history trails back to the Lenni-Lenapi Indians, who had already been hunting here for many moons when the settlers arrived in the 1700s. There's a real American Main Street with a big, four-story bank on the corner and a soda fountain luncheonette—regionally famous for tuna sandwiches and chocolate Easter bunnies—that is so incredibly old, the story is it was opened by the Lenni-Lenapi Indians in the 1700s when the settlers arrived. There's a wine shop, a bagel shop, a pizza place, a music store, fashionable jewelry and clothing boutiques, and dozens of other mom-and-pop places that fight for their lives against the national chains that arrived like locusts. It's a prosperous town, but there are still pockets of struggling, working-class families that live here in smaller, older homes that are around the corner but worlds away from the McMansions of their suburban-professional neighbors. Not everyone in Westwood can keep up with the

Joneses. It's a town with shadows and cracks that people can hide in and slip through.

I parked Walter's Toyota on a street around the corner from The Iron Horse, went inside, sat at the bar, and ordered a glass of white wine. The bartender, a pretty, twenty-two-year-old redhead named Patty, told me the place had been here for forty years and that her father, a Pascack Valley firefighter, had been an Iron Horse bartender for a few decades to make extra money. She said that kind of family connection was what The Iron Horse was all about. She also said it was all about their stuffed cheeseburgers.

I opened the menu to find out what the cheeseburgers were stuffed with, and a man sat in the stool beside me. "You can buy me lunch and play twenty questions if you want to," he said, "but if Ken Curry's saying he busted his back on your job and can't work for the rest of time, I got two words and only two words to say: 'You're fucked.'"

He was wiry, maybe sixty-eight years old, with a bushy, wild-west mustache and droopy blue eyes that were still sharp. He wore jeans, work boots, and a zip-up New York Giants hoodie. His hair was thick and full and gray-going-white. His mustache was already white. He wore a watch but no wedding ring. The vibe coming off of him in waves was bitterness, the acceptance that life had royally screwed him for no good reason, and there wasn't a damn thing he could do about it.

I put my hand out and said, "Kate McCall."

He looked at my hand as if not trusting it, as if he didn't trust anything ever.

"Girl at the front said you were at the bar wearing a blue jacket."

He didn't take my hand, didn't say, "Gil Munson, nice to meet you." He had no use for social niceties whatsoever. They were irrelevant to him. He smelled like cigarette smoke. Three packs a day was my guess. His voice was pure gravel. His skin was deeply wrinkled and weathered like rawhide. He had been outdoors all his life, no doubt breaking balls on construction sites, barking orders, taking shit from no one, getting the job done and done right.

"Would you like to sit at a table," I said, gesturing through the railroad-themed bar to the large, railroad-themed dining room.

"Club soda," he said to Patty the bartender. Then he turned to me, still without introducing himself, and said, "I started in construction when I was seventeen. I was a contractor at twenty-seven. I built offices in Paramus, Patterson, Fort Lee, Fair Lawn, Montvale, Hackensack, every fucking place. Thirty years. I was married. Kids. House in Hillsdale. You understand? That was my life."

Patty arrived with the club soda. She put it in front of him on a coaster. He didn't acknowledge her or the drink.

"Twelve years ago, I'm fifty-five, I hire Curry to work a job in Ramapo. Three-story medical building. Fifteen thousand square feet. I did plenty of them. You understand? People working for me."

I said nothing. He wasn't looking for an answer.

"One day, he's in the dirt, fell off the scaffold. No one saw him fall. They just saw him in the dirt. You understand? Nobody saw him fucking fall. He's screaming, crying, can't fucking move. His back, his back, he's saying it's his back. We call an ambulance, take him to the hospital, the whole thing. He gets a lawyer and a doctor and sues me for seven mil. Curry's his grandmother's name. That's the one he uses. But he sues me with his father's name, Buchanan. Don't matter, either way I'm fucked."

He drank half his club soda and reached inside his hoodie pocket for a pack of Marlboro, then remembered he couldn't smoke inside and left them on the bar.

"I'm just a small-time Bergen County contractor. I got a

good life but no savings. I got big deductibles, fucking huge, just so I could work. If I sell everything, every fucking thing, I still can't pay them. We go to court, and his lawyer, some fucking animal named Boris, beats the shit out of everybody. His doctor, Miller, an arrogant prick, talks in circles and doesn't say a damn thing. And Curry never gives it away. Not for one second. He's got the worst back injury anybody ever saw, except nobody saw it because he didn't fall. Scaffold was checked twice a day, before each shift. There was nothing wrong with it. But there's no way to convince anybody he's lying. No way. I hired a PI, a good one, but Curry never slips up. Never. And you know what, I lose. I lose every fucking thing."

"I'm sorry," I said.

"I lose my contractor's license and can't get work on account of I'm guilty of negligence in a seven-million-dollar workman's compensation case. Everywhere I go, that's what they say: I'm guilty and negligent and nobody can hire me because of *their* insurance. 'Tough tits, Gil. Wish I could help, but my hands are tied.' I can't make my house payments. Can't make my car payments. My wife leaves me and takes the kids to Connecticut. I go through a bad spell with booze and end up selling tools at Home Depot. I'm on my lunch. Got the vest in the truck. I live in a trailer. Costs me five-fifty a month. I got a mutt from the pound. A trailer and a mutt. You understand?"

"I think so," I said. "Like I told you on the phone, I'm investigating Curry for a similar kind of case."

"Yeah," he said, "that's why you're fucked. And your contractor's fucked worse than you. When Curry beats your ass, you'll go back to investigating other shit like nothing happened, and your contractor's life will be over. Between Curry, his lawyer, and his doctor, you got no chance. The only way you get him is if you're a fly on the wall in his house, stuck to him like glue every minute of the day. Maybe then he slips. You understand? I got to smoke."

He got up off the stool, walked across the bar, and went outside. I finished my white wine, discovered that The Iron Horse Original Stuffed Cheeseburgers are stuffed with your choice of American, Swiss, cheddar, mozzarella, or bleu cheese and are served with railroad tie fries. After twenty minutes, I realized he wasn't coming back.

I can't say I was surprised or even disappointed. Munson had said what he came to say, and every bitter word was stuffed with a different kind of pain, like the cheeseburgers on The Iron Horse menu. Also, every word was true.

There was no way to make Curry slip, no way to catch him in the lie that would bankrupt Barkowski and send him, Saint Denise, and the Rwandan triplets—Laura, Emily, and Nick—spiraling down to the gutter like Gil, who said, as if to put the final nail in the coffin: "Curry never gives it up. Not for one second."

Munson was right. I was fucked, and my contractor was fucked even worse. I thought about letting Patty the bartender get me drunk enough to call Barkowski and tell him the bad news, and then *Jimmy's Rules of Private Investigation for Kate, Rule Number Nine* went off in my head like an explosion: *the last thing in the world you'd ever do is the next thing in the world you have to do.* The brain blast must have jarred something loose because at the same time as it went off I saw the next step I had to take.

"The only way you get him is if you're a fly on the wall in his house, stuck to him like glue every minute of the day," Munson said. It was the last thing in the world I would ever do, so it was the next thing in the world I had to do: starting Thursday, I would date Ken Curry.

37

ARE YOU HERE TO BUY TICKETS?

I DROVE BACK TO THE CITY, FILLED THE TOYOTA AT A GAS STATION on Route 4 near the bridge—I had to return the car with a full tank, like Warren was Hertz or something—changed my clothes, and took a bus to the D-Cup. We were two weeks and two days from opening night, and Chloe Burns couldn't remember her lines, her lyrics, her blocking, or her dances.

She was from Akron, Ohio. Her entire family, literally every single member of the clan on both sides, worked for Goodyear Tire and Rubber Company dating back to the very beginning—it was Burns' family lore that someone on her father's side, a distant uncle or cousin, was one of the first thirteen workers in 1898, when the factory was founded. If you wanted to have a conversation about vulcanized rubber, a Burns' family barbecue was the place to be.

She came to New York to be an actor less than six months ago, a career path encouraged by her family, who believed a Burns could make it big on Broadway. She landed in Queens, found work as a waitress, and set out to audition for her first play. *Ever*. That was the crazy thing about Chloe: Acting wasn't her life's work. It was a whim, an idle idea that drifted into her brain on a breeze. She had never been in a play before driving her sister's Chevy Malibu to New York. She just one day decided that she could be a star and the next day packed her things.

After she was settled and serving Irish soda bread for Sunday brunch at an Irish Pub in Queens, she took the elevator to the D-Cup Theater to audition for the role of Mariah Muldoon in the original vampire musical *Blood Song and Dance*.

She had very little talent in any regard. She couldn't really sing, dance, or act. But what she could do was make any play *look* better. She was fashion-magazine beautiful: blonde Ohio hair, sky-blue eyes, flawless skin, big boobs, curvy hips, flat stomach, shapely legs, perfect lips, cheek bones for days, a nose to die for. In an off-off-off-off Broadway situation, Dennis and Posey decided, she could be an asset on the D-Cup stage, if they could keep a lid on her shortcomings. They had mostly succeeded, including rewriting her character's back-story, dialogue, dances, and lyrics, until this particular Tuesday night, when the wheels on the Chloe express came off.

No matter the scene or song, she stopped and said, "Line," literally every other minute. Finally, she broke down, crying and confessing not that she was overwhelmed with stage fright but that she was actually becoming Mariah Muldoon, closet lesbian lover of vampire women, that the line between Chloe and Mariah was now so blurred she could no longer tell the difference between them. Real-world dialogue and D-Cup dialogue had meshed in her mind to the point where she couldn't discern which was which or what was what.

Dennis and Posey stopped the rehearsal and commenced the psychotherapy that actors—including me—often require. The cast left the stage. As I headed for the seats with the rest of the Schmidt and Parker Players, the elevator opened, and my son stepped into the theater.

I could tell by the look in his eye and the line of his jaw that he wasn't here to buy tickets.

"What a nice surprise, Matthew," I said. "Are you here to buy tickets?"

"No, Mom. Is there somewhere private we can go to talk?"

I took him to the bathroom and locked the door behind us. He leaned against the sink, just like Paul Barnes had done when he told me Jimmy had been murdered.

"What's with the drama?" I said.

"I spoke to Harriman."

"When?"

"An hour ago. Just as I was leaving the office. I hung up and came here."

"What did he say?"

"We'll get to what he said in a minute. First we'll talk about what the Monument Insurance Company security guard in the basement elevator lobby said about the people who imperson- ated the Manhattan Plantscapes crew during the break-in on Saturday night."

He was so handsome in his Brooks Brothers' suit and tie, so focused and sure of himself. I was so proud of him that I almost forgot I was on the witness stand.

"Basement elevator lobby security guard?" I said. "Sounds like the low man on the totem pole. What did he say that we have to be locked in the bathroom to talk about it?"

"He said that the leader of the crew, the woman who said she was, pretended to be, *acted like*, a plant maintenance person, was a woman in her late forties, about five-seven," Matthew said. "That's the same physical description as the woman who said she was, pretended to be, *acted like*, a health club magazine reporter in the same office."

"That is a coincidence," I said, thinking I'd like to punch the young one again for saying I looked like I was in my late forties.

"But there must be a million women in the city who are five-seven and in their early-to-mid forties."

"Not who are professionally trained boxers."

It took every ounce of self-control to keep my emotions out of my face.

"I don't know what that means," I said.

"I think you do. The guard said the woman broke his nose with a Golden Gloves punch. She set her feet and hands like she was in the ring, he said. Like she'd been professionally trained."

"If you think it was me, then I don't even know what to say. I'm your mother, Matthew. What do you think you're doing?"

"I'm trying to help you. This isn't some off-off-off-off Broadway play where you dress up as a fake health club magazine reporter and no one gets hurt. This is breaking and entering. This is assault and battery. There's a Green Beret in the hospital with a busted knee and a bad concussion, for Christ sake. This is a felony conviction waiting to happen. This is a powerful victim with plenty of money to press charges and a vindictive streak from here to Hartford."

"Is that it?"

"The guard said one of the plant people was an Asian man the size of a Volkswagen bus. Know anyone like that who lives in your basement?"

It was circumstantial at best. He knew that. He also knew I wasn't telling him the truth. And he knew I knew that he knew.

"Is it time to talk about what Harriman said?"

"Yes. Harriman said he still wants Jimmy's files. I told him I would ask you again, and he said if I could do that before Friday that would be good because he was seeing you Friday night, and you could have them ready. He said you were dating."

"One date."

"Are you crazy? He's probably investigating you."

He shook his head in a way that I had never seen before, and I had a sinking feeling that I had lost him somehow, that he had decided he wouldn't—or couldn't—save me from my own questionable behavior anymore, that I was finally, irretrievably, in too deep. If he had told Harriman about Fu, then that would be my answer.

"Harriman thinks I broke into Monument Life on Saturday night with Fu?"

He crossed to the door, unlocked it, then stopped and turned to me. "Harriman doesn't know about Fu yet," he said.

"I love you, Matthew," I said.

"I love you, Mom. But Harriman gets Jimmy's files on Friday or Fu becomes part of his investigation."

"Matthew..."

"Friday."

Then he opened the door and walked out.

I had three days before my second date with Harriman, two days before I started to date Ken Curry, and one day before my unannounced date with medical examiner Arnold Stone.

The bathroom door opened, and Chloe Burns walked in. She had stopped crying, but was still something of a mess. She walked to the sink, splashed water on her face, and looked at me in the mirror.

"Did you ever lose track of who you were or what you were doing?" she said.

"Only every day," I said.

38

NAOMI POWELL

AND THEN THERE WAS THE TIME I DROVE WITH MY FATHER TO THE hinterlands of Pennsylvania so he could interview the coroner in a case that revolved around a disputed death. On the never-ending ride from the streets of Manhattan to the farms of western PA, Jimmy made sure I understood the difference between a coroner and a medical examiner. Here it is: A medical examiner is always a real doctor, a forensic pathologist. After four years of undergraduate pre-med mania, then four years of medical school, then several years of specializing in pathology, then a few more years of focusing on forensics, he or she is appointed to his or her position in a medical examiner's office.

A coroner is not necessarily a forensic pathologist. Depending upon the county in question, a coroner is not even necessarily a doctor. He could be a grocery store clerk, or a farmer, or, like the guy Jimmy drove us to see at the far end of Pennsylvania, the owner of the local U-haul. The more rural the county, the more likely there isn't a trained forensic pathologist in the area to appoint—or a lab to examine dead bodies in even if there were one. In faraway farm country, there just aren't that many unexplainable deaths. There's hardly any violent crime. That's why forensic pathologists don't usually stay on the farm. They go to the city, where there's plenty of violence and boat loads of unexplainable death—and labs on every corner in which to autopsy it. With no appointees in town, rural counties usually elect a coroner. Somebody runs for and wins a political office in which the official function is to pronounce dead people dead.

Jimmy's client was an investor who had given fifty thousand dollars to an old army buddy to start a local feed store. The guy went out of business before he ever opened the store, and the investor wanted his money back on account of: "Are you fucking kidding me? He never opened the store, never bought any inventory, never paid a bill, never spent a dime, never did anything." When word got back to the investor that his army buddy had died, he hired Jimmy because he didn't believe it. He thought the army buddy had faked his own death to keep the fifty grand.

The U-haul coroner took us to the funeral home and showed us the body.

"See this man?" the U-haul coroner said.

"Yes," Jimmy said.

"This man's dead," the U-haul coroner said. "Choked on a chicken bone."

And that was that. (You could still see the chicken bone making the army buddy's neck stick out like Frankenstein.)

"That's why I like coroners," Jimmy said. "It's yes or no, dead or alive, black or white. With medical examiners, everything is doubletalk. You never know what the hell the guy died of."

Dr. Arnold Stone was a medical examiner, not a coroner. He had pronounced Ron Powell dead of a massive heart attack for reasons that were so opaque, convoluted, and mysterious that no one could decipher them. For all anyone knew, it could have been Stone's secret code for "choked on a chicken bone."

Nowhere in the report pages I had did it mention that Powell was in picture perfect health three months before he died.

I arrived at the Office of the Medical Examiner, a six-story building on the southeast corner of First Avenue and 30th Street, at nine thirty on Wednesday morning. I wore black leather pants, black ankle boots, a sheer, black top with a lacy, black, push-up bra, a platinum blonde, shoulder-length wig with serious bangs, and jade green contact lenses. It was my costume from a micro-budget Indy film called *Attack of the Killer Blondes*. I played a woman named Glorious Sexpot, and I morphed into a zombie who wandered Wall Street looking for investment bankers to hack with a cleaver for reasons I never understood. I wasn't alone. The movie never went anywhere because no one, including the writer, director, producers, and actors, had any idea what it was about. Still, I looked hot in the film, and I looked hot now. That was the point.

I entered the building, walked to the receptionist, whose nameplate read "Minerva," and said with a Southern accent, "Dr. Arnold Stone, please."

"Is he expecting you" Minerva said. She was black and maybe sixty-five years old. She was overweight by seventy or eighty pounds and stuffed into a purple jumpsuit that was unbuttoned halfway down her chest, which was huge by any measure. Her fingernails were two inches long and painted like flags, four of which I recognized: the Stars and Stripes, the Union Jack, Don't Tread On Me, and the Jolly Roger.

"Does he have to be?" I said.

She peered at me over her glasses and said, "Where you from, honey?"

"Charleston, South Carolina," I said.

"Don't people need an appointment to see a medical examiner in Charleston, South Carolina?"

"Since I have never been to see a medical examiner in Charleston, I don't know whether people need one or not," I said. "All I know is that I traveled far and wide to see Dr. Arnold Stone, and I will be devastated if you turn me away without even trying to find me a few minutes of his morning. Please is what I'm saying, Minerva. And nice nails. I'm saying that, too."

She sighed and said, "Who should I say you are?"

"Naomi Powell," I said. "Ron Powell's ex-wife."

That's why I had to look hot. Powell had to have been physically attracted to Naomi to the point where he married her, even though he normally dated women half his age. It was a character detail on my part that was wasted on Minerva, who didn't know anything about Powell, but could possibly mean something to Stone, who might have known about Powell's love life. Naomi could easily have been the exception is what I wanted Stone to think.

Minerva picked up her phone, punched a few buttons, and told Dr. Stone that I was here, or that Namoi was—I knew it was Stone she was talking to because she said, "Naomi Powell, Ron Powell's ex-wife, is here to see you."

I imagined that this message was a big surprise for Stone. I pictured him opening the chest cavity of an obese Brooklyn bus driver who had died running to catch a bus. I envisioned him reviewing the Naomi Powell possibilities in his head. Either he knew Powell never had a wife and so couldn't have had an ex-wife and so whoever was here saying she was his ex-wife was really someone else poking around, or he took a bribe after the fact to falsify Powell's autopsy report without knowing about the bogus ten-mil insurance payout. Either way, Naomi's arrival was bad news for Stone.

Minerva pointed the Jolly Roger at the elevators and said, "Third floor. 318."

I got off the elevator and followed the arrows down the hall to 318. With every step I took toward Stone's office, I thought of the same word: *death*. Powell was dead of a heart attack he never had. Jimmy was dead from someone shooting him in the eyes. Stone, it dawned on me, probably killed them both. Who knows more about death than a medical examiner? Who could get away with murder and call it a coronary better than a forensic pathologist? *Death.* Of course it was Stone. How could I not have figured it out until I was ten feet from his office door? The pathologist was the psychopath. He would kill me the minute I walked into his office because I was nosing around like Jimmy. He would kill me because he was the kind of handsome and debonair doctor who played Rugby in Central Park during the week, played first violin with the New York Symphony on the weekend, and murdered people for money between shifts in the lab. *Death.* He killed Powell in some arcane, untraceable way, and then he killed Jimmy by blowing his eyeballs out to send Logan and Harriman running in the opposite direction. He would kill me in a whole new way, with more pain and more brutality, just to make a point. I would be dead on his office floor, he would rig my autopsy report, and no one would ever know I had been murdered by a medical examiner. *Death. Death. Death.*

The door to room 318 was closed. I knocked on it, and a voice said, "Come in." I opened the door, entered the office, saw Dr. Arnold Stone seated behind his desk, and thought of a new word: jackpot.

39

STONY

Jimmy's Rules of Private Investigation for Kate, Rule Number Six—Every case has a weak link in its chain. Break that link, you bust the chain.

This rule should be easy because the thing about the weak link is that it's *weak*. You should be able to wake up and say, "Today I find the weak link," go out looking for a little while, discover it napping on a park bench, bash it up a bit, and solve the case. The problem is that the weak link *knows* it's weak and compensates for its weakness. It stays in the shadows, keeps a low profile, never even hints that it's a part of the chain in the first place. Finding the weak link may be the hardest part of being a PI. Most of the time, you break the case another way. You almost never find the weak link. That's how good it is at hiding its weakness.

And then sometimes you walk into a room and there it is.

Dr. Arnold Stone was a ghost of a man, forty-eight years old, soapy white and clammy as a cadaver. He was about my height, stoop-shouldered, and slight, though with a potbelly. He was mostly bald, used several strands of hair in a pointless comb-over, and wore wire-frame glasses with little round lenses. Medical school had done little if anything for his confidence. His suit was wrinkled, off the rack, and emblematic—he was the opposite of tailored in every way.

In and of itself, his appearance did not give him away as the weak link, though it didn't help. What gave him away was the expression on his face. One part anguish, one part relief, one part bemusement, one part abject terror. It was all of that plus the sign that was flashing on his forehead: you got me...you got me...you got me...

His office was modest and filled with medical books, diplomas, and hundreds of file folders stacked in skyscrapers on his desk and on the floor surrounding his desk that represented his overwhelming workload. Stone, seated behind his desk, obscured by these tall towers of the dead, was the poster boy for the catchphrase "People die every minute of the day." Seemingly, every one of them was here.

I walked to the window and looked out onto 30th Street. The glass was grimy. An old, window air-conditioning unit blew cool but not cold air into the room. I had been here sixty seconds, and I was already depressed.

"Nice view. I'll bet you never get tired of it," I said.

"I'm surprised to see you, Mrs. Powell," he said. His voice was mousy and thin, with a frenetic nervous quality, like the whole world was cheese in a trap.

"It was spur-of-the-moment," I said. "Last night, I was minding my own business in Charleston, and this idea came into my head with the wind. The idea said, 'Naomi, you have just got to go to New York for a few days and ask Dr. Stone for the truth.' The next thing I know, Stony, I'm sitting in your office. Can I call you Stony? I feel like we're going to be friends. You can call me Naomi. Mrs. Powell seems so formal now that we're getting personally acquainted."

"The truth about what?" he said.

"Bless your heart, Stony. The truth about my ex-husband."

"I don't know what you mean."

He was a rodent of a man, scanning his office for a gap in the wall to slip through. I moved from the window to the edge of his desk so he could see my breasts, which were impossibly pushed up and out into the room by my wonder bra.

"Do you know why he divorced me?"

"I can't imagine why."

"Because I couldn't satisfy his sexual appetite. Lord knows I tried, Stony. I tried and tried and tried and tried. But that man was a stallion. He was in the best shape of any man I ever met. It was his job, you know, staying in top physical condition. He was a professional fitness expert. You did know that about him, didn't you? You must have read his insurance medical report when you were doing his autopsy. A massive fatal coronary for a man in perfect health surely sent up a red flag."

"I don't remember. Look, Mrs. Powell…"

"Naomi."

"I can't talk to you about this. The two of you were divorced."

I came around the desk and sat on the edge right beside him. I could feel his pulse rate rise.

"Are you saying that Ronnie didn't love me?"

"No, I, uh, I, no, that's not what I meant. I meant only family members are allowed to—"

"Ronnie divorced me to have sex with twenty-five-year-old fitness trainers. But he left *me* ten million dollars. Not them. That says more than something about how much he loved me. It says exactly how much."

"I think you should leave now," he said and hit a button on his phone. "Security, this is Dr. Stone. Please send someone to my office right away."

I leaned down to him in such a way that my chest rubbed against his face as I whispered in his ear.

"Your know what I think, Stony? I think Ronnie didn't really have a coronary. I think he died of something else, and it's breaking my heart that I don't know what. You can tell me. His secret's safe. Was it syphilis? Gonorrhea? I'm a big girl. I can take it."

My arms were draped around him. I was breathing in his ear and on his neck. He smelled like formaldehyde and something else. Root beer.

"Please, I can't tell you," he said. "Leave me alone. Stop breathing on me."

I let him go and walked back around the desk toward the door.

"That's fine. If you can't tell me what really happened to Ronnie, then I'll ask one of your New York newspaper reporters to help me find out. They'll put your picture on the front page. You ready for your fifteen minutes, Stony, cause here they come."

"Wait. No. Don't do that," he said.

I stopped in the doorway. The weak link was about to break. In the next sentence, I would have the truth about who killed Ron Powell, which would lead me to the truth about who killed my father.

"It wasn't my idea. It was...

A security guard appeared in the doorway, a large Hispanic woman wearing a gun, a uniform, and a badge that read "Rosy." She put her eyes on me and said, "Everything all right, Dr. Stone?" She looked eager to physically escort me out.

Stone looked at her and, in that moment, like a rat, found a gap in the wall to wiggle through. He wrote his cell phone number on the back of his business card and held it out to me. "Call me right after work, and I'll meet you somewhere," he said.

I walked to his desk and took the card. "If you don't answer, Stony, my next call is to the *New York Times*."

"If I don't answer," he said, upper lip beaded with sweat, voice disappearing down the wormhole of despair, "it won't matter."

40

WE'RE THE ONES IN THE WATER

I GOT BACK TO THE HOUSE OF EMOTIONAL TICS FROM THE medical examiner's office at ten thirty-five. Stony wrote his cell phone number on the back of his business card and told me (Naomi) to call him right after work. I had a *Blood Song and Dance* rehearsal at seven thirty that night, so I decided to call him at six sharp. That meant I had seven hours and twenty-five minutes to kill.

I changed out of my Glorious Sexpot outfit, put on a comfortable pair of faded blue jeans and a vintage Meat Loaf *Bat Out of Hell* T-shirt, sat at my kitchen table, paid my bills, and balanced my checkbook. Then I made myself a grilled cheese sandwich and studied my lines while I ate lunch. I did some shadow boxing, some sit-ups, some push-ups, and a little yoga. I chatted with Ray in the lobby (he gave rave reviews to Viagra, which ended our chat in a hurry). I checked my emails, my voicemails, and my text messages. I wrote a get-well card to a friend who was sick, a thank-you card to a friend who had taken me to dinner, and a miss-you card to an actor friend who had moved to Los Angeles to try her luck in TV.

All of that took me to two forty-five. I still had three hours and fifteen minutes before I could call Stony. I grabbed my cleaning bucket from the broom closet in the kitchen, a roll of paper towels from under the sink, and the vacuum from my walk-through closet, where it was currently being used as a hat rack, and commenced to clean the living room, which was a cyclonic mess. Jimmy had been murdered nineteen days ago and, in the rush of Ken Curry and Monument Life and *Blood Song and Dance* and Mike Harriman, the maid (me) had not lifted a finger since.

I started with the sofa, but after thirty seconds of primping and prettying the cushions, I found a photograph hiding between them that buckled my knees.

It was a shot of Jimmy and Matthew on Long Beach Island at the New Jersey shore in the early spring when Matthew was maybe five years old. It was a crisp, clear day, and the ocean was freezing. Jimmy had taken us for a picnic and decided that the men were going for a swim. I told them the water was way too cold, but Jimmy wouldn't hear it, and so Matthew wouldn't hear it.

"We're a couple of polar bears, right Matt?" Jimmy said, lifting his grandson and carrying him to the Atlantic. "We can take a little cold water."

"We can take it, Pop," Matthew said, smiling back at me like the world could not be any more perfect than it was right then.

I took my camera to the water's edge and caught them as they exploded out of the surf. My father was holding my son above his head, their eyes were locked, and they were both laughing and screaming in pain. Their joy for one another was so pure at that moment, their bond so impossibly all-encompassing and infinite, their love so deep and true, that tears came to my eyes.

"What are you crying for?" Jimmy said to me. "We're the ones in the water."

"I'm a polar bear, Mom," Matthew said, lips bluer than blue, teeth chattering.

Grief has no time limit to respect, no schedule to keep. I know this because nineteen days after Jimmy was murdered, at two fifty-two on a random Wednesday afternoon in August, I sat on the couch and cried as long and as hard as I had ever cried in my life. My head hurt, my heart hurt, and my muscles ached from the loss of Jimmy's love. No one would ever love me like my father did. That kind of unconditional connection is reserved for fathers and daughters, for grandfathers and grandsons. And now it was gone. Many things about the loss of my father made me sad, but today it was the brutal realization that his love for Matthew and me was murdered along with him. It was a memory now, a feeling to recall. I was never, for the rest of my life, going to see him again.

I sobbed myself to sleep on the couch and dreamed about Jimmy building a tree house for my sister and me when we lived in Brooklyn in a small home with a small yard that had a small tree. Jimmy was hammering nails, but turned his head to me and said, "Get up, Kate. It's time to get going."

I opened my eyes and looked at my watch: five after six. It was just like Jimmy to keep me on the case, even in my dreams, even after he was dead. I looked at the ceiling and said, "Thanks, Daddy." Then I walked to the kitchen, lifted Stony's card off the table, and dialed his cell phone.

41

FU SAY TRAP

Stony answered on the first ring.

"Arnold Stone."

"It's Naomi."

He tried to cover the phone with his hand, but he did a poor job because I heard him say to someone else, "It's her."

His voice was weak and filled with worry.

"You there, Stony?"

"Yes, I'm here."

"You going to tell me where to meet you, or are you going to make me guess?"

"My house. Saturday night at eleven."

"I can't make it Saturday. It has to be tonight."

"Hold on."

He covered the phone again and said something to the other person. They argued for a minute, but it was muffled. There was no way I could place the other voice, but it sounded like a woman more than it sounded like a man. Whoever she was, she was damned angry. When Stony got back on the line, he was shaking. Literally. I could hear the phone rattling in his little rodent hand.

"Saturday or nothing," he said.

"I'll call the *Times*, Stony. You know I will."

He covered the phone completely this time, so I heard silence until he came back.

"Go ahead," he said. "Show them your marriage license while you're at it."

He had called my bluff and raised me a Saturday night.

"Where do you live?" I said.

"Queens. 150-01 87th Avenue. Off Parsons. You know where that is?"

"I'll find it."

"Eleven o'clock."

"You going to be okay, Stony? You don't sound so good."

There was a little cry in his throat. It was pathetic and terrified. "I have to go now," he said and clicked off the phone.

I hung up and replayed the call in my mind, pacing across my kitchen. Stony had spoken to somebody after I left his office, and that person had thought it important enough to be in the room when I called him after work. Whoever that person was, they weren't afraid of me contacting the *Times* because they knew I wouldn't, which meant they also knew I wasn't Naomi Powell, because they knew there was no Naomi Powell in the first place.

The person who killed my father was in the room with Stony, I thought, and a chill went through me and raised the hairs on my neck.

But why wait until Saturday for the meeting? Now that they knew someone was onto them or, if not onto them, onto something that would lead to them, now that they knew that, why wait? While I worked the angles for answers, I looked up and out the kitchen window and saw Fu in the backyard communing with the neighborhood birds.

He was wearing red sweatpants, sandals, and a silver and black Oakland Raiders sweatshirt. He was sitting cross-legged, still as stone, arms outstretched, hands open and cupped, palms up. A pile of birdseed filled each hand. He was the largest and most deadly birdfeeder in the city of New York. A sparrow sat on his right thumb, picking at the seeds. Another sparrow was perched on his left forearm. A third sparrow was on his right knee. A fourth sparrow was on his head.

I opened my kitchen window and called down to him through the bars.

"Now that I know you can talk, you have to talk," I said.

The spell was broken, and the birds flew away. Fu glared up at me and then dropped the birdseed in his special bucket, a bright-yellow, plastic beach pail.

"What Fu say?"

I had no idea what I wanted him to say, so I said the first thing that came to my mind. "Why didn't you kill the Green Beret at Monument?"

"No more kill. Kill too many. Kill enough."

There was regret in his voice and on his face. He took a handful of birdseed and let it run through his fingers into the yellow pail.

"I got the name of the coroner from the files Al down-loaded. I went to see him at his office. I know he knows who killed my father. He knows I know he knows. He wants me to meet him at his house in Queens on Saturday night at eleven," I said.

"Fu say trap."

"I know it's a trap. You think I don't know it's a trap? Of course it's a trap."

"Fu go too."

"Oh really? Just like that? Fu go too?"

"Take car, not train."

"You're not the boss of me, Fu. We take the car if I say we take the car."

"What you say?"

"I say we take the car."

"Fu say good idea."

"Fine."

"Fine."

"Good."

"Good."

I shut the window. He took two fistfuls of birdseed, opened his hands, stretched out his arms, and waited for the sparrows to return.

42

THAT SMILE IS STINKY HOT SEX

As I was leaving the House of Emotional Tics to head downtown to Barkowski's MacDougal Street construction site to pick up a check for PI services rendered, I saw LaTanya's yellow Volvo double parked outside. It was Thursday afternoon, twenty past twelve. I went back into the lobby, to the intercom by the mailboxes, and punched the button for 3B.

"Whoever you are, you best not be selling me nothing, or I will come down to the lobby and kick your ass from here to Harlem," LaTanya said.

"What are you doing home?" I said.

"I made chicken pot pie for dinner, and it was damn good. I came back to eat some for lunch. Where you at?"

"Going to the West Village to pick up a check. Want to give me a ride?"

"Last time I gave you a ride, I had to drive a hundred miles an hour on the sidewalk."

"No idea what you're talking about."

"Had to run red lights, crash into cop cars, drive on the sidewalk, and fuck up traffic for five hours while the po-lice tried to figure out what the hell happened and who the hell did it."

"Matthew thinks it was me."

"It was you."

"What was me?"

"You're funny, McCall. *Last Comic Standing* and shit."

"Thank you."

"And after all that, you didn't get nothing, did you?"

"I got the coroner who knows who killed Jimmy. I'm going to see him Saturday night at his house in Queens."

"It's a trap."

"Would people stop telling me that? I know it's a trap. Are you going to drive me or not?"

She took Park Avenue. She was wearing a beautiful, sleeveless sundress, aqua blue-green with a starfish pattern that looked gorgeous against her skin. We listened to the radio until 63rd Street, when she turned it off and said, "You still dating the cop or what?"

"Homicide Detective. Yes, we're going on a second date tomorrow night."

She turned the radio back on and then turned it off again at 62nd Street.

"You like him or what?" she said.

"I think so. I think I like him, he likes me, and we like each other. I think that's why we're going on a second date, because the first one was good. Very good, actually."

We stopped at the light at 61st Street. She peered at me over the rim of her sunglasses, reading me like a romance novel.

"You tell me right now you didn't sleep with him on your first date. You say, 'LaTanya, I did not sleep with the policeman on my first date.' You got ten seconds. Nine. Eight. Seven..."

"I did not..."

"You did. I know you did. You know how I know?"

"How?"

"You smiled at me when you told me your first date was

good. But you smiled at yourself when you remembered why. I know that smile. That smile is stinky hot sex. Don't deny it."

Talking about the sex made me think of Harriman in my bed, and I smiled again.

"There it is," LaTanya said. "Sure as shit. You slept with the po-liceman on your first date." She looked up and through the roof of the Volvo to heaven, where my father was now presumably residing. "I'm sorry, Jimmy. I'm doing the best I can, but your daughter's a horny slut."

The light changed, and we moved with the traffic. LaTanya turned on the radio and then turned it off again at 60th Street.

"He's probably investigating you," she said.

"That's what Matthew said."

"That boy has some sense."

"Why can't he just like me? Why can't he just find me attractive, want to take me out to Wo Hop, and then have stinky hot sex with me? Why does he have to be investigating me? Why can't we be two consenting adults who like each other's company and want to drink Chinese beer and have stinky hot sex?"

"Ask him," she said.

"I will," I said, and my cell phone rang. I answered it. "Kate McCall."

"Hi." It was Harriman.

I immediately turned ten shades of crimson.

LaTanya saw me go red. "It's him, right? Thank you, Jesus, for minor miracles."

"Be quiet," I said to LaTanya.

"What?" Harriman said.

"Not you," I said into the phone. "I'm in a cab, and I told the cab driver to be quiet so I could talk to you. She's a very noisy and nosy cab driver, and now she has to shut up, so I can have a conversation that isn't any of her business."

"I'm going to let that one go," he said.

"I don't blame you," I said.

"Ask him," LaTanya said.

"How are you?" Harriman said. "I haven't spoken to you all week."

"I'm crazy but good. How are you? Are your ears burning? Because we were talking about you."

"Who's we?"

"Me and the cab driver."

"Ask him if he's investigating you," LaTanya said.

"Were you saying something nice?" Harriman said.

"*I* was," I said.

"The cab driver wasn't?" Harriman said.

"She thinks you're investigating me," I said.

"Not just me," LaTanya said.

"She does?" Harriman said.

"Yes. So does my son. Are you investigating me, Harriman?" I said.

LaTanya and I made eyes at each other. My eyes said: *I asked him*. Her eyes said: *Because I made you*.

"I don't think you killed your father, Kate," Harriman said. "But I do think you have information that would help me find out who did. So I'm definitely trying to pull you back from the dark side so the force can be with you. But no, I'm not investigating you as a suspect in that sense."

"I like *Star Wars* a lot," I said.

"Me, too," he said. "But in another sense, I would very much like to continue my physical investigation of you. And I would like you to continue your physical investigation of me too. So tell the noisy and nosy cab driver yes, we're still investigating each other after dinners and movies and drinks and ballgames and everything else we're going to do."

"All in the same night," I said.

"We could spread it out," he said.

His voice was calm and confident and understanding and

something else: warm. I smiled and turned red again. If I had been on the fence as to whether or not I liked Harriman, I was now off the fence. I liked him.

LaTanya saw me smile and said, "Stinky hot sex."

"Maybe we can continue our investigation tomorrow night," I said, feeling like a fifteen-year-old high school sophomore on the phone with her brand-new boyfriend.

LaTanya rolled her eyes as if that's how I sounded too.

"About that," Harriman said. "Any chance we can change Friday to Saturday? Sorry to ask. If we can't, okay. But if we can, that would help me."

"I can't," I said. I have an early rehearsal, and then I have something else I can't change." *Walking into a trap*, I thought. "Are you sure tomorrow's okay?"

"Yes," he said. "I'll work it out. See you Friday. I'll pick you up at seven thirty."

"I'll be waiting," I said and clicked off the line.

"So is he investigating you or not?" LaTanya said.

"I think he is," I said. "But he's being really nice about it."

She looked once more to heaven and said, "Ain't nothing I can do." Then she turned on the radio and left it loud until we reached MacDougal.

43

—————

SWEETEST GIRL IN THE WORLD

BARKOWSKI'S CONSTRUCTION TRAILER WAS FILTHY FROM TOP TO bottom. Mud was caked on the floor and walls and mismatched metal chairs, where workers walked and leaned and sat, and a coat of dirt covered everything from the beat-to-hell file cabinets, to the army-issue desk, to the sad and sagging couch, to the make-shift drafting table, to the disparate tools and gear in the corner, to the visitor hard hats hanging on a rack, to the microwave, sink, and small fridge, to the cases of bottled water stacked nearly to the ceiling, to the conference table buried beneath books and forms and files never filed. I couldn't imagine how the computer and printer were computing and printing through the dust, soot, grime, and muck. Barkowski himself, seated behind his desk in an old, worn, leather office chair, was covered in the stuff.

The only clean thing in the office was a framed photograph of Saint Denise and the Rwandan triplets on the otherwise grubby credenza behind Barkowski. He must wipe that picture a hundred times a day, I thought, as he signed his name on my check while barking into his walkie-talkie, "Get Talley in here."

A static-filled voice that sounded like Collins, Barkowski's foreman, came back from the other side: "He's on the way."

Barkowski handed me the check across the desk and said, "Are we getting anywhere?"

His eyes were heavier and sadder. The weight of Curry's ten-million-dollar lawsuit was breaking him, bone by bone, heart by soul.

"Yes and no," I said.

"Just tell me the part that's yes."

"I know all the roads we can't go down.

"Process of elimination?"

"Exactly."

"Are there any roads left?"

"Just one that I can see."

It wasn't the answer he was hoping to hear. But he was a pragmatic man and, really, one road was better than no roads at all.

"You want to tell me what that is?" he said, letting the slightest bit of hope slip into his voice even though it was against his better judgment.

"I can't. In case anybody ever asks you," I said.

"I can say no and not be lying."

I nodded. He sat back in his chair, reached behind him with his right hand, and lifted the photograph of his wife and triplets. He looked at them for a long moment and then put the picture on his desk in such a way that we could both see it.

"His lawyer called me. Bajaria. Looking for the names of my children, not the older ones, he had them, the triplets, in case I hid any money in their names, separate accounts, out of state, overseas. I know I'm supposed to behave. Shavelson told me the guy would call and harass me, but I couldn't help myself."

"What did you say?"

"I told him he was a sick motherfucker and that if he came

after my babies, I'd spend every minute of the rest of my life tracking him down like the fucking scumbag animal he is."

He meant every word, and I thought that being on Barkowski's bad side was a rotten idea. Then again, being on Bajaria's bad side was probably worse.

"What did Bajaria say?"

"He said he notated my threat and would use it to have them taken away and split up in different government-run foster care systems across the country. He said he would bury them so deep that no one would ever find them, that they would be forgotten and neglected and end up on the street as whores and drug addicts. I'm telling you, he's not human."

"No," I said.

He took a cloth from his desk drawer and wiped the dust off the photograph, smiled sadly, and put the picture back on the credenza.

Just then Talley knocked on the door.

"It's open," Barkowski said.

The door opened and the Boston brawler climbed the steps and stopped in the doorway. He looked at me and nodded, remembering me, then looked at his boss. "What's up?" he said.

"McCall has more questions about Curry," Barkowski said. You're going to sit here and answer them until she gets what she came for."

Talley moved into the trailer. Barkowski stood, came around his desk, walked to the doorway, then stopped and turned to me. "One last road," he said and disappeared, pulling the trailer door shut behind him.

"Did you miss me?" Talley said, smiling at me like we were in a bar, and he was hitting on me. His voice was filled with a kind of false macho bravado. He was nervous.

"Sit down, Talley," I said. "I'm not going to hurt you."

He made a sneering, snorting, you-couldn't-hurt-me-if-you-tried face, but I could tell he was relieved. There were two

Army-green, metal-framed chairs facing Barkowski's Army-green desk that, like the desk itself, came from the Korean War, or World War II, or the Civil War. I was sitting in the chair furthest from the door. Talley sat in the other one. A poof of dust came off his entire body when his butt hit the seat.

He was wearing blue jeans and a Death Valley T-shirt and was covered head to toe with a base of brown dirt and a white construction topcoat of drywall dust, cement dust, sawdust, and sugar dust from a half dozen doughnuts. Not surprisingly, he wore his ancient, soiled, sweat-stained Boston Red Sox hat. His hair, brown, though with the same white construction topcoat, stuck out under his hat like a tangle of wire. He had freckles and blue, wide-set eyes. His ears were small. He might have been a cute kid on the streets of Bean Town for fifteen minutes before his first nursery school fistfight. It had been all rolling around in the mud since then.

"After you shot pool with Curry and won a pile of money, it's hard for me to believe you only went out with him one time, a cash-poor slacker like you," I said. "What did he give you, twenty percent?"

He didn't know whether to be offended or caught red-handed. He chose a combination of the two: admitting it but pissed off to be called out. And he was indignant, proud of himself in the way that pride cometh or goeth or wenteth before a fall.

"More like thirty," he said. "So what? We drank beers a few times. You think I'm in on it?"

"No. I don't think you're smart enough to run a ten-million dollar scam."

He was confused. Was I ridiculing him for being an idiot, or was I saying he was honest? His eyes went narrow and then wide and then narrow again.

"Okay, then," he said. "Wait, what?"

"What kind of women does he go for?" I said.

He looked at me like he didn't speak English. I could practically hear the gears grinding and shifting in his head.

"I'm guessing he likes blondes, big boobs, tight jeans, low-cut shirts. Am I ringing any bells, Talley?" I said. "Single women, married women, who does he hit on when he's out drinking?"

"He don't like married women. I know that because he told me one time that married women are in it for them, you know, the sex. He likes women who are in it for him."

"Like who?"

"Hard to say. I seen him go for big tits, no tits, blonde, redhead, tall, short, every kind. Except no Asians. He told me one time Asian chicks freaked him out like Siamese cats. Everything else was in play. That's what he'd say after a few beers, 'See that one, she's in play.' The thing they all had in common was they acted like he was King Kong, laughed at his jokes, rubbed up against him, bought him drinks. It was all about him, not them."

This was bad news for me. Not because I couldn't act like a moon in his orbit, but because that kind of woman couldn't get close to him emotionally, and that's where I needed to be. Curry had no desire for a relationship. He couldn't care less what the woman felt or thought or wanted. She was useful to him only as long as she worshipped him, and the minute she stopped, probably after the first or second time she slept with him, he would drop her like a hot rock. If I was going to be a fly on his wall, I had to get closer than that. Now that didn't seem possible.

I stood up to end the interview, not knowing what else to do. "Thanks, Talley. That's all I wanted to know. He goes for women who've lost all self-esteem and never gets serious with any of them."

"Yeah, except one time, when we were loaded at Fast Eddie's," Talley said, "he told me he had been engaged."

I sat down. "Engaged?"

"He met her in Jersey. Down by Newark. She was a teacher, originally from Ohio. She taught the retards in special ed in a bad-ass school. Sang in the church choir. 'Sweetest girl in the world,' he said. The only girl he ever took home to meet his grandmother. Her name's Dolores. The grandmother. They didn't get married. Not Curry and Dolores; that would be sick. Curry and the Ohio girl. She died in a car crash after they got engaged. Her name was Veronica. They were kids, like twenty-two or something. He called it the saddest story he knew."

"Curry told you this?" I said.

"At Fast Eddie's, yeah. Like three in the morning."

I said nothing. I'm sure Talley could hear *my* gears grinding and shifting. I stood and slid past him to the trailer door.

"Where you going?" he said.

I opened the door and said to myself, "Down the last road."

44

HERCULES AND BREANNE

I STOOD IN THE MIDDLE OF MY WALK-THROUGH CLOSET, LOOKING at a wall of wigs and wardrobe from twenty years of plays, movies, and commercials, wondering what I was going to wear to Fast Eddie's, and all I could think of was the Hercules Diner and Breanne Murphy.

There is nothing in the world like a New York City Greek diner, and the Hercules, on Third Avenue and 54th Street, where I worked when I was twenty-three, was one of the best. Twenty-four hours a day, seven days a week, every single day of the year, every year for forty-seven years, customers had ordered almost any kind of food on the planet from a fantastical menu that was eighteen pages long, each page gigantically oversized, laminated, and as blue as the Aegean Sea.

There were thirty-five different sandwiches, two dozen different omelets, fifteen kinds of pancakes, seventeen varieties of muffins, twenty-one different soups, a full menu of Italian specialties, another full menu of Greek specialties, a third full menu of American specialties, two columns of soda fountain drinks, half a page of puddings, a page of salads, two pages of homemade cakes and pies, an improbable abundance of seafood, an astounding variety of vegetarian delights, daily specials from around the world, and gyros. And all of it, every item, was available any time of the day or night.

There's a place just like this on practically every block in the city of Manhattan. New Jersey has plenty of diners too, but in the Big Apple, diners are part of the cultural architecture, no different than the Empire State Building or the Statue of Liberty, just greasier.

Georgie Papamichael owned the Hercules. He was called Papa by everyone, including his father, August Papamichael, who was called Gus. Gus's father, Apollo, had originally opened the Hercules and still worked in the kitchen. In fact, all the Papamichael brothers and sisters and uncles and aunts and sons and daughters and grandchildren and cousins worked there. They all spoke Greek to each other and English to the three non-Greeks on the staff: me, a Lebanese busboy, and Breanne Murphy.

Breanne was my best friend at the Hercules. She was a small-town Indiana girl who came to New York to be a writer of children's stories but ended up being a girl-next-door model for store-bought picture frames—it's Bre's beautiful smile, already in the frame, that convinces you to buy that frame over another frame in drug stores and card stores and department stores across the country. She was my age, impossibly pretty, with soft hair and bright eyes and smooth skin, but her Midwestern glow came from the inside even more than it came from the outside. She was, I still think, the very nicest person in the city of New York, not naïve, though naiveté can often be associated with Midwesterners when they're transplanted to the City, but earnest, sincere, and well-meaning from her heart. In a word: honest.

I was something less than honest, even back then, so Bre's Indiana honesty warmed me like a campfire flame. For the seven months we worked together at the Hercules (before she was discovered by the picture frame advertising manager), we were inseparable. I was the single mother of a seven-year-old son at the time, and Bre took both Matthew and me into her generous heart without judgment. She had an easy laugh, a grateful-for-every-day attitude, and an uncanny ability to find the best in every person she met and focus on that.

We were opposites, but opposites attract and so we were fast friends. She taught me about Midwestern values like faith and loyalty and trust, and I introduced her to the Lower East Side. She shared her dry Indiana wit and sense of humor at Central Park picnics she planned for Matthew and me, and I got her loaded at Kenny's Castaways on Bleeker Street.

Just when her picture-frame-modeling career was taking off, her high school sweetheart, a car salesman in their hometown, chased her down at the Hercules, kneeled in the middle of the diner during dinner, and proposed marriage. Everyone applauded. Bre cried and cried and said, "Yes, yes, yes."

She moved back to Indiana, got married, found a job as a kindergarten teacher, bought a split-level house with her husband (now the sales manager) that had an above-ground pool and a picket fence, had three kids in three years, and continued to sell picture frames from coast to coast with the sparkle in her eye and the smile on her face. We've traded Christmas cards with pictures of our children and birthday phone calls ever since. She's too busy to take a New York vacation, and I'm an actor.

Talley said Curry had fallen hard for an Ohio girl named Veronica who was pure in heart and soul. Could I glow from the inside out? Dubious. Could I project faith, loyalty, and trust as my true nature? Debatable. Could I be a Midwestern woman in the marrow of my bones, earnest, sincere, and well-meaning from my heart? I was about to find out.

As I looked at my wall of wigs and wardrobe, thinking of the Hercules and Breanne, I knew it was honesty more than anything that would determine my success or failure. If I was going to get up close and personal with con man Ken Curry, there could be no wig, no colored contacts, no physical phony baloney. Honesty, I realized, was my best shot. I would have to find something truly honest in every moment I was with him, even though I would be lying through my teeth.

45

IT WAS THAT KIND OF JOINT

FAST EDDIE GLEASON WAS A CRANKY, CRUSTY, SEVENTY-FOUR-year-old pool shark from the South Side of Chicago. He was as tall and thin as a pool cue and had (dyed) jet-black hair slicked back, wore black denim jeans, black shit kickers, and a black T-shirt with the sleeves rolled up. Tucked into the T-shirt pocket was a pack of Marlboro. He was, he told me, a teenager from the 1950s who never grew up.

The thing about Fast Eddie is that he wasn't fast. It was an ironic nickname, like calling the neighborhood six-foot-ten kid Little John. He played pool at a snail's pace, marathon matches that took days and days: chalk the stick, line up the shot, chalk the stick, take a drink, line up the shot, light a cigarette, chalk the stick, check the time, flick the ashes, take a drink, chalk the stick, smoke the cig, line up the shot, take a drink, chalk the stick. Fast Eddie was the slowest pool player in the Windy City or any city. He had won and lost millions over a fifty-year hustling career, took this six-story brownstone on Third Avenue in an epic game of nine ball when he was sixty-eight years old, and opened Fast Eddie's as a place to hold court at his own pace.

The building was long and narrow. The mahogany bar was on the left and ran half the length of the room. A smoky mirror was behind the bar, broken only by shelves of booze. Directly across from the bar, tall, black, leather booths also ran half the length of the room. They were deep, dark, private, and candlelit, perfect for disappearing into your drink with someone who wasn't your husband or wife. It was that kind of joint.

The back half of the room was devoted to pool. There were four championship tables, two side by side and then two behind them. Tall cocktail tables with stools to match—to wait your turn, watch the action, scope the crowd, and down shots of bourbon—ringed the pool tables. Racks of pool cues and framed black-and-white posters of pool halls and gin joints across the country were mounted on the walls. Wooden scoring beads and Tiffany-style lights hung over the tables.

There was a good crowd, pockets of people in their twenties and thirties planning the future in the booths, old timers reliving the past at the bar, and a robust gathering of men and women in their forties, fifties, and sixties shooting stick in the back. All four tables had games going. A jukebox played hits from the '50s and B-sides free of charge.

It was the back room that got my attention. Though the whole bar was dated and dusty, the men and women looking to hook up over a game of eight ball were anything but. The women were made up, dressed up, teased, squeezed, primped, primed, and looking for action. They were mid-level bankers and retails sales managers and residential real estate agents who got stuck in careers and suddenly discovered they were forty-eight and alone. They were divorcees looking for good times before the clock ran out. They had money for clothes and salons, facelifts and personal trainers. They were loud laughers, sexually confident, and hard drinkers. They looked good in the dim light of Fast Eddie's.

The men were much the same, though maybe a touch younger and rougher around the edges. They were advertising executives, commercial airline pilots, firefighters, and diesel mechanics. They were single, or acting that way, and looking to escape their endless days. They were macho to a man, shooting pool like pros, though Fast Eddie could play lefty and take their last dimes. They were rugged and handsome and smelled like gallons of aftershave. Ken Curry was among them.

He wore a blue-and-white-striped Oxford button-up shirt, untucked over a pressed pair of dressy jeans. His sleeves were rolled up, and he had a gold watch on his right wrist and a manly gold bracelet on his left wrist. He wore coffee-colored Top-Siders with no socks. You could see the outline of his back brace beneath his shirt.

He was half-sitting/half-leaning on a tall bar stool at a cocktail table in the back right corner of the room. When he moved, he moved slowly, battling back pain, nerve pain, and whatever other kinds of pain came along with a fake-fall-from-the-scaffolding injury. He was drinking something on the rocks. It was ten thirty. I had been here an hour. He had already been here when I'd arrived. He'd had three drinks.

I was wearing a V-neck, sky-blue, cotton sweater that told everyone I had swell boobs but didn't show very much skin, a white skirt that stopped just above the knee line, and pretty white sandals. I had washed lighter brown highlights into my hair, pulled it back in a loose pony tail, and taken enough time putting on soft makeup so it looked like I wasn't wearing any. At the last minute, I put on a pair of glasses in case Dolores decided to go with her grandson. I wouldn't underestimate her again.

I had two white wines at the bar, started a conversation with three women, two of whom were named Lisa, co-workers at a business-to-business publishing company, who all admittedly came to Fast Eddie's on Thursdays to meet men, pointed at the pool tables, and said, "Well, they're back there, and we're up here."

We all laughed, lifted our drinks, and took our turn at the table right next to Curry's corner.

One Lisa could play pretty well; the other was inept. The third one, Debbie, couldn't concentrate on anything but Curry. She flirted with him before her shots, during her shots, and after her shots. She draped herself on his arm, brushed the hair from his forehead, whispered in his ear, casually rubbed her tits on his massive arms.

She was about my age, a salon blonde with big round boobs, nice legs, and a fake tan. I imagined it was her Thursday-night-at-Fast-Eddie's tan, sprayed on an hour before she left her apartment. She laughed too loud and too long at jokes and moments that weren't that funny. She drank too much. She was too loose in every way. It's not that she wasn't nice; she was nice enough. It was more like she had awakened that morning to discover everyone was happy but her. She was desperate to feel happy, to feel like she was a person who deserved to feel happy. And if she could only score Ken Curry, even with his bad back, well, that might fill her sails with wind. (Don't drink when you're down in the dumps is the moral of Debbie's story.)

Despite Debbie's desperate come-on, Curry kept looking at me. I was having fun—the Lisas were good company—and plenty of guys were gathered around our table providing pool pointers, drinks, jokes, and running commentary. I was demure in a way that separated me from most everyone else in the room. I was not from here. I was from somewhere else, somewhere softer, more forgiving, and more innocent. I was fully in the moment, one and the same with my character, comfortable in my Indiana skin.

At one point, Curry caught my eye and smiled. I smiled back, embarrassed (some serious truth in that moment) and saw him lean over and say something to a guy he was with. The look on that guy's face gave it away. It was the same look Talley had when he told me about Curry in Barkowski's construction trailer. *I'm in play*, I thought.

46

GOOD TO MEET YOU, STEPHANIE

I SHOT DOUBLES WITH THE GOOD LISA AND TWO GUYS FROM A marketing company. I shot with Debbie and two guys who laid cable. I shot with the bad Lisa and two guys who painted bridges. I had fun with all of them. Whenever I glanced over at Curry, gently exploring the possibility of flirting, he was watching me.

At half past eleven, I missed a shot right in front of him. I stood up, expressed a minor amount of disappointment, and said to him, "I'm not very good at this."

"Doesn't matter how good you are. Matters how much fun you have," he said.

"That's a good outlook," I said. "I'm going to remember that. Thanks."

"No problem."

He held out his fifth drink (I was counting), which looked like scotch neat, and we clinked glasses.

"Ken Curry," he said.

"Stephanie Garner," I said.

"Good to meet you, Stephanie."

"Good to meet you too, Ken."

Around midnight, the crowd thinned out. The Lisas left without male companionship, Debbie moved into a dark booth with a real estate manager, and I was left shooting with three guys who were slurring their words, having a ball, and being nice about it.

Curry waved me over after I missed a bank shot.

"You hit it too hard. You got to let the rail do some of the work," he said.

"How do I let it do all the work?" I said.

He laughed out loud, and I laughed too. We had a nice laugh together.

"Want to show me how?" I said.

"More than anything," he said. "But I can't. I hurt my back pretty bad."

"I'm sorry. It's no fun to be hurt."

He nodded and shifted his position, letting me know he was in pain but was fighting through it.

"Is it serious?" I said.

"Afraid so. I work in construction and fell off some scaffolding. I got nerve damage and other stuff. It's a mess."

"I'm really sorry."

"Thanks. I should be lying down, I feel better when I'm lying down, but I come here every Thursday. I like the crowd."

"Me too. I mean, I don't come every Thursday, this is my first time, but everyone does seem nice."

"First time?"

"I just moved here from Indiana three weeks ago, and a friend told me it was a good place to meet people." I smiled right at him and held his eyes. "She was right." Then I moved my eyes away, down into my drink, as if to say: *Oh no, what are you doing, Stephanie? That was a step too far.*

He smiled back. "So, Stephanie from Indiana, what are you doing in New York?"

"It's a little silly, but I'm taking a year to write a book," I said.

"I'm an elementary school teacher, and I want to write a book about what kids really mean when they say things they don't really mean. I woke up one day and said, 'If I don't do it now, I'll never do it.' I chose New York because, I don't know, it's where the publishing companies are, and I always wanted to live here. Know what I mean, Ken?"

"Exactly," he said.

At my table, my partner, a public school administrator named Roland, gestured that it was my turn again. As I stood up, Curry put his hand on my arm.

"Look, usually girls give me their number—I got two tonight—but yours is the one I want. Would it be all right, could I ask you for your phone number? Maybe we could have a cup of coffee. I know my way around the city pretty good. I could help you settle in. I'm a really nice guy. At least that's what my grandmother says. But she may be prejudiced, I don't know."

He smiled, and I looked at him and thought, *Damn, he's even more handsome than I imagined he was, his teeth are freaking perfect, his breath is minty fresh, despite the scotch, and he can flick on the charm like a Zippo lighter. He's smooth and confident and funny. No wonder girls give him their phone numbers.*

I looked away, suddenly shy.

"I don't bite," he said. "Just a nip here and there."

I made a face that said I got his double entendre, that it embarrassed me even more than I was already embarrassed, but that it didn't offend me either, that if I knew him better, I might even like a little nip here and there, that maybe, if I knew him better, I might even nip back.

"Do you have a pen?" I said, smiling into his eyes.

"It's in my shirt pocket. Can you get it for me? That position kind of hurts."

I put my wine glass on the cocktail table and reached into his shirt pocket, my eyes locked on his eyes, saying: *I'm really*

*nice too, Ken, and I'm from the Midwest where trust is everything.
Can I trust you?*

He smiled as I wrote my cell phone number on a Fast
Eddie's cocktail napkin.

"You're up, Indiana," Roland said to me.

I put the pen back in Curry's pocket and said, "You'll
call me?"

"I'll call you," he said.

I moved to the pool table, lined up a bank shot, made it, and
smiled at Curry.

He swirled the ice in his glass, tilted his head, and smiled as
if to say: *Trust me, Steph.*

47

SHE'LL FIND YOUR FAMILY AND CRUSH THEM TOO

IT WAS FRIDAY NIGHT, SEVEN THIRTY—THREE WEEKS SINCE JIMMY was murdered. Harriman's classic Camaro was double parked in front of the House of Emotional Tics. We were in my living room, sitting on the sofa. Copies of Jimmy's cases were on the coffee table. We were supposed to have a quick glass of wine at my place, during which I would turn over Jimmy's files, and then leave for our second date. Instead, Harriman opened the files—both the closed and open cases—sat on the sofa, and began to read through them, turning over the top-sheets, scanning the notes, taking in the photographs.

Matthew had said that if I didn't deliver Jimmy's cases—though he also said they were *my* cases now—to Harriman on Friday, he would tell the homicide detective about Fu living in the basement, the equivalent of pointing a huge Chinese arrow in my direction regarding the Monument break-in one week ago. Though I knew I had to do it in the end, I felt terrible handing them over, like I had failed Jimmy *and* his clients.

To keep my mind off of how upset I was, I thought about how much I was looking forward to our date.

We were going to an opening in a SoHo gallery for a thirteen-year-old artist and psychic named Gilda Gold, who painted visions of the future that were freaking people out. There was a buzz beginning to build that young Gilda was a prophet. One of her paintings, for instance, was a chaotic and colorful vision of a New York street scene so crowded with people and cars and cabs and dogs and trucks, so crammed and jammed with real-life dejection, unhappiness, rage, confusion, panic, violence, and hysteria, that viewers were bursting into tears just looking at it. Other paintings, like one of an enormously obese and bejeweled woman walking her ridiculously overweight Chihuahua in the park, both the woman and the dog on custom-fitted hover pads, elicited shrieks of horror from obese women with overweight dogs, of which the City had thousands.

"Is the teenage prophet really going to be there," I said, hoping to pull him out of detective mode and back into date mode.

"Everyone gets a bingo card when they enter," he said without looking up. "Gilda calls out the numbers during the opening. The winner gets a psychic reading. Yes, she's going to be there."

"Maybe she knows who killed Jimmy," I said.

Now he looked up.

He was wearing black casual slacks, black shoes, a dark gray silk shirt, and a gorgeous Tag Heuer sports watch. His hair was still wet from the shower and spilled over his collar in a damp, impossibly sexy way. I was wearing a navy blue skirt, a pretty, cotton, low-cut red sweater, and blue Charles David wedge sandals.

"There's nothing in here that connects your father to Monument," he said.

"I hate to say I told you so, but I really did."

"Is this all the cases?"

"Matthew told me to give you all the cases."

"Did you?"

I stood, crossed to the windows, looked through a gap in the curtains at the Camaro, and wished we were on our way to play bingo with Gilda Gold. "Yes."

But not all the scraps of paper, matchbook covers, and scribbles. And not the cocktail napkin from Cutter's Tavern that said *Problem: Powell was never married.*

He stood and paced to the other side of the living room, running his hands through his hair.

"If you're holding back information," he said, "you're making a mistake."

"Are you saying I'm holding back?"

He looked at me and said, "I'm saying it's all tied together. Your father's murder, the fake fitness-magazine reporter, the plant-crew break-in. Someone thinks the answer is in Olivia Russell's office, and I want to know why."

He took two steps toward me.

"Why the answer is in that office or why someone thinks it is?"

I took two steps toward him.

"Take your pick."

He took two more steps and stopped in front of the sofa.

"Why don't you ask this Olivia Russell woman, whoever she is? Maybe she knows who killed my father. It's her office someone keeps trying to get into."

I took two more steps and stopped in front of the sofa, facing him.

"Don't mess with her, Kate. She'll crush you without thinking twice. She'll find your family and crush them too. She has her own floor, for Pete's sake, with her own security team. She makes millions and millions for Monument and for herself. She reports to the Chairman of the Board directly. She makes her own rules. She takes no prisoners. Do you understand?"

"She's rich *and* powerful. Yes, I understand."

"It's not the money. It's the power. I tried to question her; she threatened to have me transferred to Oneonta. I got a call the next day from the assistant commissioner telling me to back off. She's connected, she's ruthless, and she shows no mercy. She is unlike anyone I have ever met."

"Why Detective, you either care a lot about her or a lot about me."

We both took a step toward each other. Maybe there was a foot between us. I could feel the heat from his body on my body. I could tell he was feeling what I was feeling.

"We have to work together, Kate."

"Cooperate?"

We leaned in to each other.

"Share information."

"That goes both ways, Harriman."

He kissed me hard. I kissed him harder.

"But it has to start with you," he said, pulling my sweater over my head, "because I'm the cop."

"I won't hold it against you," I said, unbuttoning his shirt.

We fell back on the couch and were hot and heavy in no time flat.

"Gilda is expecting us," he said in a low rush, our hearts pounding, his hands all over me, my hands all over him.

"She's a psychic," I said. "She already knew this would happen."

48

THIS WHY FU NOT TALK

Fu met me in the lobby at ten fifteen on Saturday night. He was wearing loose-fitting, black linen pants, the kind that you tied with a drawstring and maybe did jujitsu in, a black AC/DC *Highway to Hell* T-shirt, and black Toms with no socks. He looked like a huge, Asian, black bear. Except stronger.

I was dressed like Naomi Powell, if Naomi knew she was walking into a trap: lightweight, navy-blue sweater, comfortable blue jeans, and Nikes, in case she had to run for her life. Stony, and whoever was pulling Stony's strings, probably the guy who killed Ron Powell and my father, knew I wasn't Naomi; they knew there was no Naomi. I wasn't fooling anyone. Still, I wore the Gloria Sexpot platinum blonde, shoulder-length wig with the serious bangs and the jade green contact lenses. A disguise, I reasoned, was a good idea no matter how this shook out.

As we left the House of Emotional Tics and walked to Warren's Corolla, parked down the street, I told Fu we were going to take the Queensboro Bridge to Queens Boulevard to the Jackie Robinson Parkway to the Grand Central Parkway to Parsons Boulevard to 87th Avenue.

"How long take?" Fu said.

"Thirty, forty minutes," I said.

"Forty minute. No get ticket," Fu said.

"Don't tell me how to drive, Fu," I said as we climbed into the car. "I'm a very good driver."

"Fu better."

"How do you figure that? You don't have a license. You've never driven in New York one time. How can you possibly say you're a better driver than me?"

"Fu better."

"I'm not having this conversation," I said, settling in, checking the mirrors, and putting on my seat belt. "There's no way I'm having this conversation."

"Where radio?" Fu said. "Fu like music."

"There is no radio," I said. "No music for Fu."

"Fu have iPod," he said, holding a tiny little thing that looked like a postage stamp in his huge hands. He put the buds in his ears and leaned back in the seat.

I started the engine and put the car in gear. Distracted by the Italian opera blasting out of Fu's iPod, I glanced at him in disbelief for half a second and nearly hit a cab as I pulled into traffic on 83rd Street. The cabby honked his horn at me. I slammed on the breaks, jolting the car to a head-snapping stop, and sat there silently as the cabby gave me the finger, told me what a piss-poor driver I was, and explained exclusively in expletives how women shouldn't be allowed to drive in New York. He glared at me as I backed into my parking spot so he could get by, and then he burned rubber and blared his horn all the way down 83rd.

I looked over at Fu. His iPod volume was maxed. The very ends of his lips were ever so slightly turned up into a whiff of a hint of a wisp of a smile.

"Fu better," he said.

"Fu you, Fu," I said.

"Fu you, too," he said.

By the time we crossed the Queensboro Bridge, I'd had enough Italian opera.

"Fu. Fu. Fuuuuuuu..."

He turned down the aria, took the bud out of his left ear, and looked at me.

"How long have you been listening to opera?" I said. I hadn't prepared a question, and that was the first thing that came to my mind.

"All Fu life," he said. "Shifu listen opera when teach Fu fight."

"Shifu?"

"Shaolin Temple Master. Fu live in Temple."

"With your family?"

"Fu not have family. Father leave Fu at Temple. Fu seven. Never see one more."

"What about your mother?"

"Not have mother."

"Everybody has a mother."

"Not Fu."

I learned more in that conversation than I had in two years. And yet I had even more questions now than before. He moved to put the bud back in his ear. I put my hand on his arm and stopped him.

"Whoa," I said. "So you never knew your mother, and your father left you at a Shaolin Temple when you were seven, disappeared forever, and you were raised by a Shifu Master who listened to Italian opera when he was teaching you martial arts, so you could grow up to be a hit man in the Chinese mob? Is that what you're saying?"

Fu took a breath tinged with one part sadness, one part regret, and one part anger and said, "This why Fu not talk."

He put his ear bud in, cranked up the opera, and didn't say another word until I turned the Toyota onto 87th Avenue and pulled to the curb, half a block down and across the street from Stony's house.

"That's it," I said, pointing at a small, two-story, brick Tudor with a one-car driveway but no garage. "150-01 87th Avenue."

A brown, newer-model, Ford Explorer with the license plate "NYME" was in the driveway. The curtains were drawn. A single light was on in one of the downstairs rooms. The upstairs rooms were dark.

Fu opened the door and got out of the car before I could stop him.

"Fu go," he said, leaning back into the car.

"Fu go where?" I said.

"Into night," he said and shut the door. Then he ran to the shadows on Stony's side of the street, jumped a fence with ease, and was gone. *How could a man that size be so incredibly light on his feet, so agile and graceful?* I thought as he vanished into the darkness. And then I thought, *Shit, Fu. What the hell?*

49

HERE'S WHERE WE START THE TRAPPED PART OF THE TRAP

I PARKED THE TOYOTA ON THE NEXT BLOCK, 88TH AVENUE, AND walked to Stony's two-story Tudor. It was a few minutes before eleven o'clock, and no one was out. *After the news, I thought, at eleven-thirty, the dog walkers will meet on the street, talk about the weather, and clean up crap,* something I knew a good bit about.

I walked around the block and was standing in front of Stony's house at eleven o'clock. I took latex gloves from my purse and put them on. It was time to find out who killed my father.

There were two brick steps up to Stony's front door, which was red, and there was a cheap, red metal awning hanging above the entrance. To the left of the door was a curved bay window comprised of five long, narrow panes, each one wood-framed, with the frame painted white. There was a little square of lawn out front and some shrubs beneath the bay window.

It was a 1940s, working-class neighborhood, where New York cops and cooks and teachers and telephone operators raised their families. Their houses were tidy. Their grass was cut short and edged along their sidewalks and driveways. I could imagine kids in bathing suits running through sprinklers on summer Saturdays, dads taking pictures with Kodak cameras, moms emerging from their kitchens with pitchers of Kool-Aid. I was once one of those kids.

I walked up the driveway, climbed the two brick steps, and rang Stony's doorbell. As I waited, I reached into my purse and put my hand around Jimmy's gun. I don't like guns. I don't like how heavy they are or how they smell. I don't like accidents that can't be undone, and that's what a gun is. More than two hundred thousand people get killed in their houses by guns every year, Jimmy had told me once during a gun-safety lecture after Matthew was born, and a big percentage of those are accidents that can't be undone. I didn't need the lecture. If it were my child on the tragic end of a gun accident, I couldn't go on living. That's just me.

But sometimes, it turns out, when you're investigating your father's murder and walking into a trap at eleven o'clock in Queens, a gun, like Jimmy's Colt .45, is like a long-lost friend who has your back. *Starting tonight*, I thought, *that's just me too.*

No one answered the door. I rang the bell again and looked up and down the street. There was an elderly woman with her back to me walking her poodle. Maybe she caught the ten o'clock news, or was hurrying to catch the eleven o'clock news, or didn't watch any news at all. Maybe she just wanted to walk her dog. Maybe if *she* rang Stony's doorbell, someone would answer the damn door.

I rang the bell again. What the hell? "How can you trap me inside the house if you don't open the door and let me in?" I said softly to whoever wasn't answering.

I reached out to ring the bell one more time, put my hand on the doorknob instead, and turned the handle. It was open, as in not locked, as in, *Here's where we start the trapped part of the trap*, as in, *Whatever you do, don't go inside the house.*

I looked up and down the street. The elderly lady with the poodle was receding in the distance. There was no one else in view. I cracked the door open and slid inside, pulling it closed behind me.

I was in a small entry area on the far left side of the house. The stairs to the second floor were straight ahead of me. The living room was to my right. A lamp in the corner of the living room threw a low, amber glow across the first floor and halfway up the stairs. After that, it was pitch dark up there.

The furniture was from the 1940s and '50s. It looked like somebody's mother's furniture. It smelled like somebody's mother's furniture. I had the feeling that this was the house Stony grew up in, his mother's house. That feeling was confirmed by a photomontage on the wall to my left. There were half a dozen shots of Stony as a child, on ponies, in go-carts, on swing sets, and at the beach building sand castles. Apparently, he was as an only child. (He was the only child in the pictures.) There were a dozen more shots of his mother and father. Stony was a carbon copy of his dad, who looked like a milkman to me.

There was a can of root beer on the coffee table. Two blue Barcaloungers were positioned in front of a flat screen television that sat on a boxy TV cabinet that came from the 1950s. I imagined Stony and his mother watching The Discovery Channel, or The Food Network, or American Idol, eating cookies and drinking root beer, talking about days gone by and dead bodies in the lab, before turning in early. No one, however, was talking tonight. The house was silent.

I took Jimmy's .45 out of my purse.

"Stony. It's Naomi. You said eleven on Saturday, and it's eleven on Saturday. I let myself in because no one answered. Where are you? Come out, come out."

I took two steps into the living room, which had a wood floor covered with an oval hooked rug that was many shades of brown. I crossed the rug to the coffee table and touched the root beer can. It was more than half full, and it was warm. *That can't be good*, I thought.

"You're creeping me out, Stony. I came here hoping to find out what happened to Ronnie, and you're playing hide and seek, or Marco Polo, or Olly Olly oxen free, and I'm in the dark, and, like I said, you're creeping me out. Now come on, Stony. Tell me where you are, and let's talk about it." I tried to keep my Southern twang and tone of voice upbeat and unafraid, but that was getting harder by the minute.

I moved across the living room to the dining room doorway. From there, I could see through the dining room into the kitchen. A lace tablecloth, like the one my grandmother had, was on the dining room table. There was an old hutch with old china on the far wall. The table sat six, although nobody but Stony, and maybe his mother, had eaten here in decades. On the wall opposite the hutch was a framed swatch of knitting that read: *Bless this home and all who enter*. "Amen," I said softly.

Beyond the dining room, the kitchen was lit only by the moon, whose silver beams slipped in through the window above the sink and through the double sliding doors that led to the small brick patio in the backyard.

I told my legs to move me to the kitchen doorway, but my legs told me that they had gone far enough, thank you very much. Somehow I convinced them that standing still made me an easier target, and I walked through the dining room into the kitchen.

To my left were two closed closet doors on either side of the refrigerator. *Pantries*, I thought. Straight ahead was the sink, dishwasher to the left, gas stove to the right. A microwave and a toaster oven sat on the counter. At the end of the counter, next to the stove, were the sliding glass doors. Beyond them, at the end of the room, was a small kitchen table. Seated at the table, tied to a wooden chair, his eyes blown out the back of his head, was Dr. Arnold Stone.

50

GET HIM BEFORE HE'S GONE

MY FIRST THOUGHT WAS, *POOR STONY; HE NEVER HAD A CHANCE.* Whoever else was involved in the Ron Powell scam, and I felt sure Olivia Russell's name was on that list, realized, like I did, that they couldn't count on the medical examiner to keep his little rat-trap shut. The man who killed my father was reconfirming that whoever was still minding Monument's business instead of their own was going to wind up dead in a chair, without their eyes in their head, without any blood in the room, without any bullets in sight, and without any clues on the horizon.

After that, all I could think of was Jimmy.

This is what my father looked like when they found him alone in the Monument elevator three weeks and one day ago: head back and to the side, mouth hanging open, dried blood covering his clothes, everything limp and lifeless and too horrid to imagine.

What could he have been thinking, tied to a chair, gun pointed at his eye, knowing his life would be over in a flash-bang moment, that he would never see us again, that we would never see him? What were his last words, his last prayers? None of that had crossed my mind in the twenty-two days since he was murdered. I had kept myself busy since then, I realized now, just so those kinds of heartbreaking thoughts *wouldn't* cross my mind. But right here, in Stony's Tudor kitchen, looking at him dead in his own chair, horrific holes in his head, I couldn't think of anything else.

I told myself to focus, to do something smart, something investigative, search the house for a hidden note, for a secret phone number, but instead I took two steps toward him to get a closer look.

His skin had a bluish tint (backlit by the silvery moon, he almost looked like a special effect in a 3-D murder movie), meaning he'd been dead for a while. Like Jimmy, he'd been shot somewhere else and then brought back to the house in time for my visit. (Jimmy had been moved to the Monument Life elevator from wherever he was killed, possibly the same place as Stony.) This terrifying show on a quiet Queens street was for my benefit. Put another way, Stony was dead because of me.

No. Stony was dead because he rigged Ron Powell's autopsy report, or at least looked the other way, so Olivia Russell could collect ten million dollars, pay whoever she hired to kill Powell and Jimmy and now Stony, and keep the rest for herself. Stony was dead because he made a bad decision—and because he was the weak link.

He was wearing a Columbia University T-shirt and blue jeans. He was barefoot, and his feet, like his clothes, were splattered with his own blood. He had a watch on. A thick rope went around and round his chest, holding him up in the chair. His legs were tied together with another rope. Neither rope, I was certain, would have even a partial fingerprint on it. There would be no arrows pointing in the killer's direction anywhere in the house, anywhere on Stony, or anywhere else. Harriman was right; whoever was paid to do this was a professional.

I took another step. Stony's back was to the glass sliders. He was facing a wall (on the other side of that wall was the dining room) upon which were framed photographs of birds. One frame displayed a blue ribbon for bird watching. Stony, before someone shot his eyes out, was a competitive bird watcher. I was on his right side. He had a small tattoo on his right arm, just below the sleeve of the T-shirt, which was too tight and too small and was probably from his days as a young medical student, when he believed that the sky was the limit in his medical-examiner future. The tattoo, written in bold, black, capital letters, read: DAD.

I felt a lump in my throat that I couldn't control. And then there were tears in my eyes. "Oh shit," I said in a breathy whisper. "I'm crying."

What was I doing here in Stony's kitchen at seven minutes after eleven on a Saturday night in August? I wasn't a private investigator. I was an actor and a mother and the daughter of a man who had been recently murdered. I had no idea what I was doing here. The only thing I knew was that I missed my father and was still grieving my loss, fighting the feeling of helplessness that envelops those left behind. Stony's stupid little tattoo had taken me by surprise and now, goddamn it, I was crying.

The .45 was in my right hand. As I raised my left hand to wipe the tears from my eyes, a thin leather cord came over the top of my head and was pulled tight against the back of my hand, which was just then in front of my neck.

Someone was behind me, someone strong and quiet. I never heard them coming. They smacked the front of their right knee into the back of my right knee, trying to buckle me and get me to the ground. I staggered but didn't go down. They pulled tight on the cord. I was choking myself with my own hand.

Instinctively, my right hand came up to free my left hand

and to get the leather cord away from my neck. As my hand shot up, the gun went off beside my head, sending a slug into the wall. It was impossibly loud. Deafening. My ear exploded in pain. I saw stars. And still the leather cord kept digging down and in. I heard myself gagging and wheezing. It was hard and then harder to breathe. The killer smashed his knee into my leg. I still didn't go down.

The gun went off again and then again, both shots fired in Stony's direction. One hit his shoulder, the other landed with a thud in his chest.

I pushed back against the killer. We slammed into the wall with the framed birds. He pulled harder on the leather cord. My left hand was in blazing pain. My right ear was echoing and throbbing. I couldn't breathe. He hit my leg again, and I went down on my knees.

He was standing over me, pulling and pulling on the cord. I was looking straight at Stony, fighting with what I had left but losing power. I would blackout soon, and then I would die. I dropped Jimmy's gun and heard the killer kick it away, across the room into the shadows of a far corner. And then I was looking through the glass sliders, where a huge figure was flying through the backyard. It was Fu.

As he sprinted across the brick patio, he grabbed a wrought-iron chair, put it in front of him without stopping or even slowing down, and crashed like a heat-seeking missile through the double sliders into the kitchen.

Glass exploded everywhere. The doors were completely demolished. The frame holding them in place was ripped half out of the wall. The whole house shook. I felt the leather cord fall away from my hand and throat. I wanted to scream, but there was no way. I was gasping for breath and couldn't find my voice on a bet.

Fu tossed the wrought-iron chair to the side and hurried to me. He helped me up and sat me at the kitchen table. I looked at him and somehow said the following sentence, my voice a strained whisper, "He killed my father. Get him before he's gone."

Fu ran out of the kitchen, through the dining room, and into the living room. I concentrated on breathing. In, out. In, out. I looked at Stony, who was now covered with glass. *Jesus*, I thought, *another minute and there would have been two dead people at the table.*

Seconds later, Fu was back beside me. "Door open," he said. "Man gone. No find. You live?"

"Yes," I said. "I live."

Fu took in the awful vision that was Stony without his eyes and said, "This who you come see?"

I nodded. It hurt to talk, and my left hand was killing me.

"Trap. Like Fu say. Fu know whole time."

"What do you mean 'Like Fu say?' I knew it was a trap the whole time too. You're not the only one who knew the whole time."

The sound of police sirens filled the house. Some were in the distance, but two sounded like they were pulling up in front. Their shrill screaming felt like a dagger in my right ear, and I realized that I had a vicious headache.

"You walk?" Fu said.

"I think so," I said.

He helped me up, and we went through the atomic hole in the back wall of the kitchen that used to be the sliding glass doors. We hurried across the backyard, jumped a low fence, and made our way through the shrubs and shadows to Parsons Boulevard. As we crossed the turn-in to 87th Avenue, we saw three police cars parked in front of Stony's house. One of the cars had pulled up on the little square of lawn. Another was half in and half out of the driveway, angled as if it had jumped the curb in a great big goddamn hurry.

Up and down the street, Stony's neighbors were out in force, wondering if all of this hubbub would end up on the news that they were watching at that very moment before they hurried outside to see what was what.

Fu and I arrived at Walter's Toyota. There was no action at all on 86th Avenue, though people had heard there was something special happening on the next block and were on the sidewalks heading over there. All around us, police sirens were blaring. Soon, there would be uniformed officers knocking on every door in the neighborhood.

Fu walked me to the driver's side door. I opened it, and he put his huge arm out, blocking my way. Our faces were maybe two feet from each other.

"Fu drive," he said.

I wanted to protest, to tell him I was fine, that I was still a better driver than him, even after almost getting murdered, but instead I said, "Yes, Fu drive."

I handed him the keys. He walked me around the car, opened the door, and helped me in. Then he came around the front of the car and squeezed himself behind the wheel.

The ride back to the City was silent. For the first time ever, I was grateful that Walter had never put in a radio.

"Jimmy's gun," I said after a while.

"Too late," Fu said.

51

IMAGINE WHAT WILL HAPPEN WHEN
WE SEE EACH OTHER

Opening night for *Blood Song and Dance* was less than two weeks away, twelve days to be exact, including today, Sunday, the day after the man who murdered my father tried to murder me too.

It was Final Fitting at the D-Cup. The cast had been measured weeks ago, and now our costumes were in, and we were trying them on for Dennis and Posey and Posey's sister, Suzanne, the Schmidt and Parker Players seamstress.

It was an all-day affair. Two or three cast members at a time (I was here with Roger) would arrive at the theater according to an intricate schedule, try on a costume, and walk back and forth across the stage like Miss America in a spotlight, while Dennis, Posey, and Suzanne commented on the fit and look as if the actor weren't in the costume and on the stage walking back and forth like Miss America in a spotlight.

I had five costumes, including a black leather dominatrix get-up accessorized by black, ankle-high, lace-up leather boots with four-inch stiletto heels. (I wouldn't wear that one in the privacy of my own home.) Throw in my fangs, and I was somebody's worst nightmare—and somebody else's wettest dream.

"If only her boobies were bigger," Suzanne said.

She was older than Posey and even rounder. She had frizzed-out hair that was dyed fire-engine red, and she wore large sparkly glasses with extra-thick lenses.

"It's her tush," Posey said. "It's a bit out of proportion."

"I'm standing right here," I said, "with my small boobs and big butt. I can hear every word you say."

"Maybe if the heels were higher," Suzanne said.

"Or if the top was tighter," Posey said.

"Yes, a tighter top and higher heels," Suzanne said.

"Don't make me wear this, Dennis," I said.

"What are you worried about?" Dennis said. "You look gorgeous."

"She's worried about picking up clients," Roger said. "I'm thinking of signing on myself."

"I'm thinking of whacking you with a teapot," I said.

"Have you considered topless?" Roger said to the committee. "I think the play is screaming for a topless-dominatrix-vampire-nightclub-singer."

"Now that's an idea," Suzanne said.

Before I could say, "You will pay for this, Roger," my cell phone rang in my purse at the edge of the stage.

"May I get that, please," I said.

"Yes," Dennis said, "but keep walking. I'm letting the dark power of your boots wash over me."

"I don't want to know what that means," I said, as I walked to my purse and pulled out my phone. "Hello," I said, answering it.

"Stephanie. It's Ken Curry. From Fast Eddie's. Last Thursday. Remember me? I got your number and promised to call you. I'm the guy with the busted back."

I gave myself five seconds to focus, not enough time when you're dressed like a not-yet-topless-dominatrix-vampire-nightclub-singer and have to be an earnest, sincere, and well-meaning Indiana elementary school teacher.

I walked side to side and up and down the D-Cup stage, the four-inch stiletto heels killing my feet.

"Of course I remember. Hi. How are you? How's your back?" I said.

"Not good," he said. "I don't think I'll ever work again."

"I'm so sorry, Ken," I said.

"How's your back? I'm so sorry, *Ken*?" Dennis said, repeating my part of the conversation. "Do you hear this, Posey? She's talking to Curry."

I put my index finger in front of my lips and mouthed the words: *Shut up*.

"Thanks. Thinking about you almost makes the pain go away," Curry said. "I'm happy to hear your voice."

"I'm happy to hear your voice too," I said. "It's been kind of a rough few days." It was the truth and so it sounded true, even though it was true for me and not for Stephanie Garner, whose Indiana idea of a rough few days wouldn't include getting strangled half to death in Queens, which would be the worst few days *ever* for her.

Dennis and Posey came onto the stage and followed me like puppies, gesturing that I should let them listen to the conversation. I shooed them away and walked in the opposite direction. They ignored me, as puppies do, and kept signaling that they wanted in on the action.

"If we're happy to hear each other's voices, imagine what will happen when we see each other," Curry said.

"Are you asking me out on a date?" I said.

Posey's knees buckled. Dennis had to stop and support her. "The triplets, the triplets, the triplets..." she said. I kept walking.

"If I did, would you say yes?" he said.

"I would," I said.

"Then I'm asking you," he said.

Posey recovered, and she and Dennis were back in my face, insistent now that they be allowed to participate. It was against my better judgment, but I relented, figuring they had paid their dues as *The Grifters Marinaro* in Miller's office. I covered the phone with my hand and said to Dennis, Posey, Suzanne, and Roger (who had paid his dues with Dolores), "If one of you makes a sound, all of you suffer the consequences, which will not be pretty, I promise." Then I drilled them with my eyes so they knew not even to breathe and put my cell on speaker.

"Great," I said. "What should we do?"

"What do you want to do?"

"Something that won't hurt your back."

Dennis looked like he wanted to say something (or maybe vomit) like the words (or maybe the puke) were halfway out of his mouth. I warned him to zip it with a clenched fist, which, combined with my dominatrix outfit, silence him pretty quick.

"That's nice. Thanks. You like museums?" Curry said.

"I love museums," I said.

"Have you been to the Met?"

"Just once," I said. "I've been wanting to go again."

"Are you free on Wednesday at two o'clock? I don't want to interfere with your book."

Posey mouthed the words: *What book?* I rolled my eyes.

"I write early in the morning. Wednesday at two is good."

"You want to pick me up? I'll pay for the cab."

"Yes, sure, that's really kind of you, Ken. Where do you live?"

"Central Park West between 84th and 85th. The Fairview. 1204."

"Got it. I'm excited."

"Good. Me too, Stephanie."

"See you Wednesday."

"Bye," he said, and we hung up. Immediately, Posey, Dennis,

and Roger created a cacophonous sound that I more or less interpreted to be: What the hell was that? I held up my hands for silence. The four-inch stiletto heels gave me a stage presence that shut them all up. Maybe that's what Dennis meant by the dark power of the boots.

"I had no choice but to date him," I said. "Roger and I struck out with Grandma, and Posey and Dennis and I got nowhere with Miller, and Gil Munson told me I'd have to be a fly on the wall to break Curry's con, and the only way I could think of to get that close to him was to be just like the only girl he ever really loved, a teacher from Ohio, who taught special ed, sang church songs, and was the sweetest girl in the world, until she died in a car crash after they got engaged, so I'm a teacher from Indiana named Stephanie taking a year off in New York and writing a children's book. Any questions?"

"Clear as Clearasil," Roger said. "He's on to you."

"He's not on to me. He likes me. I mean Stephanie," I said.

"You can't be sure. We'll meet you at the museum," Dennis said. "Keep an eye on things. Watch your back."

"We'll have walkie-talkies, like secret agents," Posey said.

"I don't know what you're talking about," Suzanne said, "but you can never have too many secret agents. I'm in like Flint. We'll all go."

"Not this time," I said, putting my fangs in place. "This time I go alone."

52

THE COLT AND THE CHAIR

Dr. Arnold Stone was found murdered late Saturday night, so I understood why he didn't make the Sunday papers. But on Monday, after Raul put me through the ringer for a few hours as the sun was rising, I came home, poured myself a bowl of Cheerios, put a few fresh raspberries in there, and sat down at my kitchen table expecting to see a headline like "Manhattan M.E. Found Dead in Queens Without His Eyeballs" on the front page of my favorite New York daily. When it wasn't there, I went looking inside. Buried deep on the crime page was a small notice that Stony had been killed during a "home invasion." There was no mention of empty eye sockets or Monument Life.

I called Al and asked him to check all the other New York newspapers online to see if they had covered the medical examiner's murder in more detail. He said it would cost me ten bucks. I told him I was sending Fu up to his apartment to re-clog the toilet. He said he hoped I would burn in hell and hung up. Before I finished my Cheerios, he called me back to say Dr. Stone's death was reported in all the papers as a minor news item, but the especially violent nature of his demise was nowhere to be found.

I thought I knew why Jimmy's murder never made head-lines. Jimmy was one of hundreds of New York private investi-gators. His murder was barely news. Yes, having your eyes shot out of your head isn't your everyday cause of death, but it doesn't change the fact that the dead person is dead. At the time, three and a half weeks ago, I figured the papers didn't mention it because it was grim and why bother; the dead person was dead. If Jimmy had been killed by a vampire (like Farina LeBleu) and found on Madison Avenue with holes in his neck (instead of in the Monument elevator with holes in his eyes), then that would have been news. I remember being grateful that the graphic details of his murder were never published in black and white. I was glad no one else would know how he died.

But Stony was a New York City servant. His murder, in all its gruesome glory, should have been news. So why wasn't it? Jimmy had told me more than once that police and politicians tell the people only what they want them to know, withholding whatever they don't want them to know for whatever reasons they don't want them to know it. "Strategy," Jimmy said. "There's always an angle."

So what was the angle in holding back the truth about Stony?

Maybe I didn't know why Jimmy's murder never made headlines after all.

I spent the rest of Monday organizing my desk, doing my laundry, and fighting with Fu and Charlie about killing pigeons in the backyard—Fu had built himself a slingshot and was knocking them out of the sky like, well, clay pigeons. One fell on Charlie, who was tending his pot plantation, which is how the fight started in the first place. I rehearsed the first act of *Blood Song and Dance* from six to ten.

On Tuesday, I treated Harriman to lunch in the shadow of The Cathedral Church of Saint John the Divine, the largest cathedral in the world, where, on the corner of Amsterdam and Cathedral Parkway, an ancient Egyptian man, wearing a Joe Namath New York Jets jersey, served the best falafel outside Egypt from his funky, homemade cart, which he towed behind him while riding his bicycle (which still had training wheels!) from who knows where. There was always a line of fifty or more New Yorkers waiting for Joe's heavenly fried chickpeas and tahini—everyone called the Egyptian "Joe" because of the Namath jersey he wore every day of the year.

We waited on line for twenty minutes, we said hello to Joe, who spoke no English, had two teeth, and was in his mid-nineties, and then we found a bench by the Fountain of Peace, a fantastic and bizarre sculpture depicting sun worship, weird, mythical creatures in crazy, contorted positions, and the struggle between good and evil.

It was a gray August day. The sun seemed like it had tried to break through the clouds at first but then had lost heart. It was hot and humid and could even rain later if the breeze went one way instead of another. Still, there were trees in the park by the Fountain of Peace, and it was nice on the bench, eating lunch with Harriman, St. John the Gigantic dominating the skyline for blocks and blocks around us.

When we finished eating, we held hands, both of us looking at the fountain—the Archangel Michael vanquishing Satan, the nine giraffes cavorting like party animals, the lion and the lamb lying down together, Satan's decapitated head dangling beneath the crab's claw. Then Harriman said, "Last Saturday night, a medical examiner named Stone was murdered in Queens," and our lunch date went from sublime to surreal.

"A medical examiner?" I said.

"Yes. Arnold Stone was his name."

"Was he a friend of yours?"

"No. Never met him. Heard he was a wallflower kind of guy. Harmless. Non-descript."

I could describe him, I thought. *A rat in a trap.*

"It's out of my precinct," he said, "but the homicide detective who caught it, guy named Mark Morgan, called me to compare notes."

"Why did he do that?" I said, knowing the answer."

"Because they found Dr. Stone tied to a chair with his eyes shot out."

"Jesus," I said, letting go of Harriman's hand.

I thought I would have to act my way through that moment, feigning surprise, sadness, and grief at another murder like Jimmy's, so Harriman wouldn't suspect that I had been there, that, in fact, I had caught the case first. But those feelings and more washed over me for real as if for the first time. With my own eyes, I had seen Stony tied to a chair (without his eyes), so I knew in a palpable way what my father looked like in the Monument elevator. That terrible vision of Jimmy was fresh and raw and painful and shocking every time it came into my mind.

"Jesus," I said again, and then I said nothing for a long time.

Harriman let me work through it. The breeze died and the humidity came on with a vengeance. It was like someone hit the afternoon switch for unbearable heat.

"Is there a connection between Jimmy and Dr. Stone," I said, "besides how they were killed?" The connection, though I hadn't tied it together, was Olivia Russell, Ron Powell, and a bogus Monument Life policy worth ten million dollars. And there was also a connection between Jimmy, Stone, and me— Terry Kramer. But Terry was Jimmy's client, sort of his client, and Jimmy had been murdered for poking around Powell's questionable death on her behalf. I had inherited the case, and now Terry was my client, sort of my client, and I wasn't ready to turn her over to the police.

"I was hoping you could tell me," Harriman said. "Did your father know him?"

"He never said anything to me." That was true, just not the whole truth.

Harriman nodded. "First, your father was found in the Monument Life Insurance building," he said. "Then there was the fake magazine reporter, and then the Manhattan Plantscape break-in, and then Dr. Stone had his eyes shot to shit too. If we could tie Monument to your father and your father to Stone, that would be something to build on."

"What about tying Monument to Stone?"

"Over the last ten years, Stone was the M.E. on three dozen dead bodies that had Monument policies attached to them, twelve from Olivia Russell's floor. Car accidents, stabbings, strokes, heart attacks, drugs."

"That's got to be something."

"Feels like it, but Monument insures a hundred thousand people in New York. If you just play the percentages, every examiner in every borough will have a file of Monument bodies. Plus, your father's not connected to any of them. All by itself, Stone's Monument connection doesn't mean much."

"Except his eyes got shot out," I said softly

"Except his eyes got shot out," he said even softer than me.

We sat quietly. The sun, after a siesta, had regained its strength and was breaking through the cloud cover. There were little beads of sweat on Harriman's upper lip. He looked troubled, like something else was bothering him, something he didn't want to talk about but was going to anyway.

"Morgan said they found a gun," Harriman said.

I concentrated on keeping my composure. I knew they would find it. I was waiting for them to find it. How could they not find it? Still, hearing that the police had found my father's Colt at the scene of Stony's murder shook me up. "Morgan?" I said.

"The detective who caught Stone. He found a .45 caliber

Colt pistol in Stone's kitchen. Stone was tied to a chair at the kitchen table. You know the rest of that part."

"Yes," I said, seeing Jimmy in the Monument elevator all over again. "Is it the killer's gun?"

"They don't know whose gun it is yet. They're tracing it while they do ballistics. There was one slug in Stone's shoulder, one in his chest, and one in the wall behind him. Morgan thinks it's a match, but he won't know until the end of the week."

There were no prints on the gun or on the bullets or on anything in the house. They couldn't put me in Stony's kitchen no matter what. "Good," I said. "That's something."

"The back wall of the house was blown in from the outside, rocked off the foundation," Harriman said.

"Is that how the killer got in?"

"He doesn't leave a speck of dirt behind. It's not likely he's going to bust up the entire backside of a house."

"I guess not."

"There was a wrought-iron patio chair in the kitchen," Harriman said. "Morgan thinks someone picked up that chair and blasted through the sliding glass doors like a jet plane. It would have to be someone incredibly strong. Strong enough to snap a security guard's arm in half or beat the shit out of a six-foot four-inch Green Beret."

"What are you talking about?" I said, knowing exactly what he was talking about.

"Do you own a gun, Kate?"

"No. Why?"

"Is it your gun in Stone's kitchen?"

"What does that mean?"

"That means I think you're investigating your father's murder. I think you think the answer is in Olivia Russell's office, and you won't tell me why. I think you pretended to be that reporter, and I think you broke in with some other people, including the jet plane, dressed up as a Manhattan Plantscapes crew. I think you won't admit any of this, not because you don't like me, I think you do, but because I'm a cop, and you don't trust me. I think you're in way over your head, and, if you're not careful, you're going get too close for somebody's comfort without even knowing it, and whoever's running around shooting people's eyes out is going to shoot your eyes out next. I don't want that to happen, because I think I like you too."

"Are you done?" I said.

"Yes," he said.

"Can I kiss you now?"

"I wish you would."

We kissed in the heat, and the City disappeared around us, even the Fountain of Peace and St. John the Gigantic. After we kissed, we held hands again.

"The Colt and the chair, that's privileged information," he said. "Privileged and confidential. If you tell anyone, it'll be bad for me. Please don't say anything."

"I won't, Harriman," I said, resting my head on his shoulder.

53

───────

YOU A YANKEE FAN, SWEETHEART?

I LEFT THE HOUSE OF EMOTIONAL TICS AT TWENTY MINUTES until two on Wednesday afternoon. The heat and humidity were stupid, maybe the worst they had been all summer. The island of Manhattan was a steambath. I walked east on 83rd toward First Avenue to catch an uptown cab that would go two blocks north to 85th, then west through the park, then left to The Fairview, Curry's building between 84th and 85th on Central Park West.

I was wearing pretty khaki cotton shorts that stopped above the knee, a two-tone, brown canvas belt with a checkerboard pattern and a gold hoop buckle, a white sleeveless blouse, and white, comfortable, summer sandals with crisscross ankle straps and half-inch stacked-wood heels. I wore a simple watch on my right wrist and a little gold bracelet on my left wrist. I matched my makeup from the last time I saw Curry, staying soft and gentle but making subtle adjustments for daylight, and made sure the brown highlights in my hair weren't over-stated. At Fast Eddie's, I had pulled my hair back in a loose ponytail. I chose the same style for our museum date. Stephanie Garner was not a woman to fuss with her hair when the heat and humidity were stupid. I wore the same pair of glasses.

I arrived at the northwest corner of 83rd and First and waved for a cab. A checker pulled to the side, and I got in, got settled, and momentarily stopped blinking because covering every square inch of the top of the dashboard and every square inch of the ledge between the backseat and the back window were two hundred or more New York Yankee bobblehead dolls. Every generation of Yankee for a century was represented, as was every style of bobblehead from the beginning of bobblehead time. In addition to the bobbles, autographed pictures of Yankees and layers of Yankee headlines, articles and box scores were taped to the roof, the backs of the front seats, and the insides of the doors. It was like being inside a newspaper. A Yankee game was on the radio.

The driver was a sixty-five-year-old New Yorker named Ernie Shapiro—his name and date of birth were on his cabbie license, which was duct taped to the meter. When he saw that I was speechless, he turned to me and said, "You a Yankee fan, sweetheart?"

"From birth," I said with my Midwestern accent. "What about you?"

He laughed out loud, displaying a smile stained brown and yellow from decades of ingesting coffee and tobacco, most of it while sitting in this very cab.

"Where to?" he said. In his lap was a scorecard on a clipboard. Ernie scored the games while sitting at red lights and when stuck in traffic.

"85th and Central Park West. The Fairview," I said.

"Okay I cut through at 85th, then?" he said, turning around in his seat.

"Yes, okay," I said. Someone got a hit, I think for the Yankees, and Ernie wrote it on his scorecard before pulling into traffic.

"What about you?" he said, repeating my joke and laughing again. Then he caught my eye in the rear view mirror and said, "Where you from?"

"Indiana," I said. Then I thought, *I can't see the line.* Meaning: once you start lying, it's hard to stop. Meaning: Jesus, what a lying liar I had become.

It's the job of the playwright to lie to the reader while telling the most profound truth they can imagine, and it's the job of the actor to lie to the audience while projecting that truth with added truth of their own. It is, as Jimmy often told me, the job of the private investigator to lie to pretty much everyone without any regard for the truth whatsoever. He must have meant it, because *Jimmy's Rules of Private Investigation for Kate, Rule Number Ten* was: *Lying is a part of the job. You have to lie every day, sometimes all day. You have to be a champion liar to crack your case. You have to do it, but you never get used to it.*

I was never a lying liar until I accepted Barkowski's case and simultaneously started poking my nose around the Monument Life building. In that three-and-a-half-week window, I had lied to more people than I could remember, pretty much everyone, just as Jimmy had said. Truth be told, I didn't mind lying to Olivia Russell and her crew or to the Ken Curry crowd, but I had also lied, more than once, to Harriman and to my son. That bothered me a lot. I had lost sleep over lying to Matthew.

And yet I had to do it to crack my case. Jimmy was right: I would never get used to it.

Ernie pulled the checker in front of The Fairview just as someone hit a home run for the Yankees. He wrote it down on his scorecard while saying "That's what I'm talking about" and "Right back in it" and "Going, going, gone." Then he hit the meter and said, "They were stinking it up before you got in, sweetheart. What's your name?"

"Stephanie," I said. "Do you think you could wait for me,

Ernie? I'm going to buzz my date. He'll be right down, and you can take us back to the Met."

"You kidding me? I got to keep you in the cab so we can win this thing."

I smiled, climbed out of the cab, and walked to the front doors. Miguel Ortiz, Curry's diminutive Mexican doorman, was on duty. He looked at me as if he had never once seen me before and said, "Can I help you?"

"Ken Curry, please. 1204," I said. "Tell him Stephanie is here, and I have a cab, so he should come down."

Miguel nodded, lifted the intercom, and punched in 1204. He waited a moment and then said, "Señor Ken. It's Miguel in the lobby. Miss Stephanie is here for you. Says she has a cab, and you should come down."

Then he did something I didn't expect; he handed me the intercom.

"He want to talk to you, señora," he said.

I took the intercom and said, "Hi Ken. I have a cab."

"Hi Stephanie," Curry said. "Why don't you let the cab go and come up to the apartment?"

Oh crap, I thought, *he's onto me.*

"Are you sure, Ken? I mean, I don't want to be any trouble," I said.

"No trouble at all, Steph," he said. "I want you to meet my grandmother."

54

KENNY IS THE KING

I RANG THE BELL TO 1204 AND WAITED. IF IT WAS GOING TO BE over, I thought, it would be over in seconds: a knife in the gut, a bullet in the chest, a cast iron teapot to the side of the head.

The door opened and Dolores Curry—nicely dressed in dark brown slacks and a pretty, lightweight, mocha-colored sweater, her hair pulled back in a tight and tidy bun, her jewelry understated but expensive, looking like Ruth Gordon on her way to a charity brunch—put out her hand and smiled.

"Come in, Stephanie," she said. "I'm Kenny's grandmother, Dolores. It's nice to meet you."

I took her hand and returned her smile. "It's nice to meet you too, Dolores," I said, stepping through the doorway into the grand foyer.

She shut the door, turned to me, and said, "Kenny will be right out. Takes him twice as long to get ready now. Poor thing."

"I feel so bad for him," I said. "I know he's in a lot of pain."

She nodded and took me in, looking at me like I was familiar somehow, couldn't figure out why, but was damn sure going to in the next three minutes.

There was no reason she should recognize me. Detective MacKensie Cox was a no-nonsense, blue-eyed New Yorker with shoulder-length red hair, a hard look, a sharp voice, and an all-business attitude. Stephanie Garner was a soft, Midwestern, elementary school teacher with a gentle disposition and a trusting heart, the diametric opposite of Cox in every way. Still, I was nervous.

"Kenny says you're from Indiana. Where?" Dolores said.

"A little town outside Bloomington," I said. "Not even a dot on the map. You probably never heard of it."

"Try me," she said. "My sister lives in Bloomington. I've been all around there a hundred times."

Whether or not she had ever been all around Bloomington or even Indiana was irrelevant (and unlikely: she probably was an only child too.) She was testing me, giving me an opportunity to dig my own grave while making double sure the coast was clear.

"Ellettsville," I said.

"Small world," she said. "My sister's got a good friend in Ellettsville. I've been to your town before."

"You have not," I said, acting drop-dead surprised and thrilled, yet at the same time challenging her to prove it. *Two can play this game, Dolores*, I thought.

"There's a bike race every year," she said. "Big damn deal. Starts in Ellettsville. Can't remember the name of it."

Crap. She *had* been there. What had started as a quick pop quiz to see how I handled pressure had become a serious final exam in a matter of moments. She was looking at me for the answer. If I were really from Ellettsville, Indiana, I would know the name of the big bicycle race by heart. If not...I didn't even want to think about if not.

"The Hilly Hundred," I said. "Oh my gosh, I can't believe you know about that."

And then I thought, *Thank you Breanne Murphy of Ellettsville for telling me everything about your Indiana hometown from the very first day I met you at the Hercules Diner.*

Dolores smiled, and the muscles in her face, around her eyes, softened a bit. Her entire eighty-six-year-old body relaxed. She stepped toward me and took me by the elbow, precisely the same thing she had done when I was here as Detective Cox. That time, I'd tried to get into the living room to see the family photographs, and she had physically moved me down the hall, away from the living room, to the eat-in kitchen (where she'd brained Roger and given him a bag of frozen peas to tame the swelling). This time, I decided to let her lead the way without resistance or intention on my part. She guided me to the living room.

It was a huge, beautiful space. Maple floors, Asian rugs, handsome leather sofas and chairs, mahogany coffee and end tables, an antique card table with artfully mismatched antique chairs, and elegant lamps of all shapes and sizes were too much to take in at once, yet gave the overall impression of taste and money. A thirty-foot wall of windows straight ahead revealed a panoramic, north-south view of Central Park. A grand piano dominated the left side of the room. Behind it, floor-to-ceiling, built-in, maple bookcases were filled with hardcover novels. To the right, on the far wall, a fireplace with a massive mantel served as a counterweight to the piano.

It was a stunning living room, the kind of room you would never associate with a construction pack mule like Curry. No way he could ever afford the furniture, forget the grand piano, and, if he could, there's no way he'd lug bags of cement for Barkowski. Something was very wrong here.

Dolores walked me to a soft-leather sofa, and we sat together, the fireplace in front of us, the wall of windows to our left. We smiled at each other, and I thought, *What the hell is with these photographs?*

I had hoped that Curry's family photos, perhaps a recent shot of him lifting a car over his head, would reveal his scam. But the family photos weren't really family photos, not like any I had ever seen.

Picture after picture after picture after picture showed Ken Curry, in all his concrete-carrying, barrel-chested, thick-armed, broad-backed glory, from the age of eight until probably five or six weeks ago, winning medals, ribbons, and trophies (proudly displayed in box frames around the room) in spirited ballroom dancing competitions. The guy wasn't just good; he was, apparently, exceptional.

As many photographs as there were of Curry, there were half as many again of Dolores, stretching as far back as three quarters of a century. She was something in her youth. She had a dancer's body like nobody's business and ballroom style to spare.

There were many pictures of the two of them, with various and sundry partners, each holding up trophies for rumbas, sambas, mambos, and tangos, for fox-trots, cha-chas, lindys and merengues, for polkas, waltzes, jitterbugs, and jives.

"Wow," I said. "Did you and Ken win all of these?"

"I won plenty in my day," Dolores said, "but Kenny is the king. Before he hurt his back, he was one of the top competitive ballroom dancers in the Northeast, maybe the whole East Coast. I taught him everything he knows, but he's got the gift. Turn on the music and turn him loose."

"He didn't tell me."

"He's a humble man on the outside, soft as a field of feathers, but there's a ballroom fire burning in that boy that's never going out. He's like his grandma that way. Believe me, honey, if I could get out there and strut my stuff like Irene Castle, I'd still be at it like there was no tomorrow. And he's got the ballroom bug way worse than me. It's killing him that he can't put on his dancing shoes."

"That's so sad," I said.

Dolores nodded, wistful, looking at the photos and awards, letting them transport her back in time, before she and her grandson figured out how to con contractors out of millions in bogus workman's compensation claims.

"That's why I don't talk about it," Curry said, entering the room behind us, walking slow and slower to the fireplace, and gazing at himself in the photos on the mantel, where he was the ballroom king in sleek black ballroom pants and crisp white ballroom shirts. The poor guy was a shell of himself, unable to pull a pen from his own shirt pocket without pain shooting up and down his back. Or not.

"I'm really sorry," I said.

He nodded. "Thanks. You look nice."

I smiled, glanced at Dolores to let her know I was embarrassed to be complimented in front of her, and then looked back at Curry. "So do you," I said.

He wore pressed blue jeans, a blue-striped oxford shirt, a gold chain around his neck, a gold watch on his right wrist, and a gold pinky ring on his left hand. I was struck again by how handsome a man he was, how brushed and polished and manicured. And that smile. Those teeth. He was almost pretty, in a linebacker sort of way.

"I took ballroom lessons at the Arthur Murray in Bloomington," I said, meaning Breanne had taken them there. "I was pretty good, but nothing like this."

"Depends on your partner," Curry said, smiling at me. "Good partner makes all the difference."

If only I could blush on command, I thought.

"I'll tell you what's sad," Dolores said, ever so slightly narrowing her eyes at her grandson as if warning him to pull it back from the edge a bit, "that Stephanie might never find that out, that we might never see you dance that way again."

"That's what I meant," Curry said.

"I hope we do," I said.

"Yes, honey," Dolores said, patting my leg. "We can always hope."

I nodded and thought, *We can do more than that, Dolores.*

55

NO MATTER WHAT YOU THINK THIS IS, IT'S NOT WHAT YOU THINK

ON FRIDAY, FOUR WEEKS TO THE DAY SINCE JIMMY'S MURDER, I went to the gym and let Raul sweat me to death. I shadow-boxed, jumped rope, and hit the pads until my arms went numb. If only I could have hit the stupid things until my head went numb, or my heart. After an hour, I was soaked and ready to puke and Raul said, "Heavy bag. Fifteen rounds." Then he disappeared into his backroom office.

At three minutes a round with sixty seconds of rest between rounds, the heavy bag was a brutal way to spend an hour. I knew I would be drained in mind, body, and soul. Raul knew it too. That's why he made me do it. He knew I was thinking about Jimmy the whole time he was wearing the pads. I knew Jimmy was in his thoughts too. I could tell by the way he looked at me, like I reminded him of the years and years he had spent shooting the shit with my father. Somewhere in his office, Raul was going to hit his own metaphorical heavy bag.

As I started round six, my body screaming and burning and dripping rivers, Matthew walked through the gym door. He wore a Brooks Brothers navy blue suit, a crisp white shirt, and a blue and gold paisley tie. He carried his big black lawyer's briefcase, the one that looked like it could hold his paralegal in case he needed her in court, which is where he looked like he was heading before he decided to stop in at Raul's. *He's all business today*, I thought. *This can't be good news.*

He crossed the room to the heavy bag, nodded hello, and waited impatiently for me to stop. I wasn't stopping until the round was up, however, and, after about forty-five seconds, he said, "It's important, Mom. Take a break."

"Two more minutes," I said, gasping it out. "How are you? How's Nina?"

"I'm fine. Nina got an essay published in a big-deal psychology journal. That's not what I came to talk about. You need to—"

"About what?" Every time I hit the bag, pain shot up my arm and through my body to my brain, a terrible state in which to receive bad news.

"Mom."

"Essay about what?"

"How our cross-media obsession with vampires has led to the anesthetizing of American tweeners, particularly girls."

"At least she's not wasting anybody's time," I said as round six mercifully ended.

He made a sour face, maybe about Agitating Nina, maybe about something else.

"Kidding," I said, thinking that sixty seconds of rest seemed more like six seconds. "What do you want to talk about?"

"Detective Harriman called me again. Just now. I was in a cab on my way to court. I tried to call you, but you didn't answer. Then I remembered you were at Raul's, so I came here instead. It's Jimmy's gun."

"What's Jimmy's gun?"

"This is how you're going to act? Like you don't know anything?"

"I don't know anything."

"We do."

"We?"

"The police. The DA. We. As in not you."

My sixty seconds were up. I started round seven.

"What is it you think you know, Matthew?"

"It was Jimmy's gun at Dr. Stone's house."

I bobbed and weaved, pounding the bag with body blows.

"Makes sense. Whoever killed Jimmy took his gun, killed Stone, then left the gun to mess with the police."

"It wasn't the killer, Mom. It was you. That's what we know."

Jimmy had told me that guilty people freeze when finally confronted with their guilt. Some freeze for a second, he said, others for the rest of their lives, but all of them stop in their tracks when you reveal that you've got them dead to rights. It took every ounce of self-control I could muster to keep boxing without missing a punch.

"Really? How do you all know that? My prints are on the gun?"

"No prints."

"So what are we talking about? Why would I have Jimmy's gun to begin with? It was his gun, not mine."

"Harriman and Logan spoke to Shavelson about Jimmy's will. We know you inherited and took possession of the gun. You had it, you went to Stone's house, something happened, and the gun got left behind."

I was a lying liar caught in my lies. There was no point in finishing round seven, but I kept hitting the bag, sweating and breathing hard. "What Jimmy left me in his will is privileged information," I said.

"No it's not. Attorney-client privilege pertains to communication whose purpose was to obtain legal advice. All matters leading up to the execution of a will, including its contents, are discoverable. It's a murder investigation, not a statutory share dispute. No one's questioning Jimmy's intent. No one's questioning the validity of the will. The fact that you inherited and took possession of Jimmy's gun is admissible. None of that is the point, Mom. The point is the gun puts you at Dr. Stone's murder. The point is a bullet from the gun was removed from Dr. Stone's chest. The point is it looks very bad. The point is you're in trouble here. The point is it's finally time to tell the truth. Jesus Christ, Mom. What the hell are you doing?"

He looked at me with frustration, anger, disbelief, disappointment, and shame.

It was the shame part that killed me.

At that moment, I felt like the Worst Mother in America. That was a horrible feeling. I could see that he fully expected me to turn the corner right then and there, to stop hitting the bag and tell him what the hell I was doing. The round was almost over. I looked at him, still boxing.

"Well?" he said.

The round ended. I stopped hitting the bag.

"No matter what you think this is, it's not what you think," I said.

"Than what is it?" he said.

Jimmy told me he always knew when it was finally time to tell the truth. It was a gut feeling he got, he said, when the pressure was about to blow the lid off. With my assistant District Attorney son demanding an honest answer—not from some low-life, gang-banging, street punk but from his very own murder-suspect mother—I could feel the pressure shooting steam out every which way, so I checked my gut for a feeling. What I felt was that this wasn't the time, though the time was coming.

"It's something else," I said.

He was furious and disgusted, an ugly combination made way worse when it comes at you in waves from your child.

"All my life you told me how important it is to tell the truth, even when you don't want to, even when you think you can't, so you can look at yourself in the mirror and know you did the right thing, so you can be proud of yourself, so you can sleep at night, and now that it's your turn, the whole honesty thing, it doesn't apply to you," he said.

Of course it applied to me. Terry Kramer, Ron Powell, Olivia Russell, Arnold Stone, *Club Solutions*, Manhattan Plantscapes, Monument Life; it was all right there on the tip of my tongue. Except it wasn't the whole truth. Something was missing. A piece of the puzzle I still had to find that would make it the whole truth. I *couldn't* tell him.

"I don't know the truth yet," I said.

"Of all the things I thought you were," he said, "I never thought you were a hypocrite until right now."

"Innocent until proven guilty, Matthew," I said.

"Guilty sneaks up on you, Mom," he said. "You think you can outsmart it, but you never can. And then it's too late."

He turned and left the gym. My minute was over. Round eight started. I didn't know what else to do, so I hit the heavy bag with everything I had.

56

A GAME CHANGER TO FIT THE BILL

I WAS UNDER NO ILLUSION AS TO THE STATE OF THE OFF-OFF-OFF-off Broadway musical called *Blood Song and Dance*. With less than a week to go until opening night, the show was in deep doo-doo.

Chloe Burns, who played Mariah Muldoon, closet lesbian lover of vampire women, who had lost herself in her character and suffered an epic identity crisis just nine days ago, had now lost the show. While the rest of us were trying as hard as we could to present a musical drama along the lines of *Sweeney Todd*, dark in its humor, solemn and true to its emotionally intensified fictional world, Chloe was performing Catskills vaudeville, complete with tap dancing (there was no tapping in the show), funny faces and hand signals to the audience, an occasional Yiddish accent, and exaggerated laughter at moments meant to scare the crowd crazy.

It was Saturday (opening night was Friday), and we were doing an uninterrupted run-through of the second act. To Dennis and Posey, uninterrupted run-throughs meant no stopping for any reason. Whatever occurred on stage during the rehearsal—missed lines and entrances, wrong steps, forgotten lyrics, misplaced melodies—would be discussed immediately afterward at a cast meeting, where additional direction would be given. Today, there would be much to discuss and direct because, over the course of the second act, Chloe transported the D-Cup to the Borscht Belt.

Serious songs like "Her Love Will Come To Me Now" and "Railroad Street" became zany production numbers, with Chloe kicking like a Rockette and then shaking her ass like Charo. The moment when Farina LeBleu bites into Mariah's neck, a bittersweet and violent act laced with vengeance and agonizing heartbreak, was turned on its head when Chloe winked at the audience—*while I was biting her*—and ad-libbed the line, "Oy vay, does that tickle or what?"

It's not that she wasn't committed to her performance; she was all about it. In fact, the zeal with which she upended the show caused other actors, primarily in the chorus, to follow her lead. *Blood Song and Dance* was torn into two camps, neither of which was ready for opening night.

When it was over, Dennis and Posey took to the stage for the cast meeting and, for a moment, were struck dumb. Chloe's camp felt good about their performance and thought the show had at last found its footing. "Comedy is king," Chloe said, leading the rebellion. "*Blood* can't help itself from being a laugh riot. Once we started, we couldn't stop. It's not our fault. The play spoke for itself. We're actors. The material takes us where we must finally go. And this is where we went." On the one hand, it was hard to argue with that line of thought. On the other hand, Dennis and Posey were ready to kill someone.

Posey explained that they had not intended to write and, in fact, had not written a musical comedy and that they would be deeply offended, as the playwright and composer, if the cast interpreted it as such. As the producer, she said, she would hit them all in the head with an eighteen-inch Stillson wrench if they ever tried it that way again.

Dennis gave one of his melodramatic history-of-the-theater lectures, filled with metaphors and similes and anecdotes about plays gone by, and closed by threatening to strangle any actor who laughed while being bitten by a vampire, winked at the audience, tapped across the stage, or spoke one word of Yiddish.

Everyone got a chance to say something, and the consensus was that the show was adrift. The company concern was palpable. We opened in six days. It's not like we had weeks to work through this great divide. Between now and Thursday, we had a full-show run-through, a tech run-through, and two dress rehearsals; then the curtain came up, ready or not. There wasn't enough time to correct a schizophrenic fissure like this one with theater pep talks, death threats, or rehearsal time. Besides, figuratively killing Chloe (or literally killing her) wouldn't help; I was her understudy. And as capable an actor as I was, I couldn't bite myself in the neck.

What we needed was something that would unite the troupe under one banner, a game changer that no one was expecting, that everyone could rally around, that had nothing to do with *Blood Song and Dance* but would require talent, commitment, fortitude, savoir-faire, and guts. Fortunately, I had a game changer to fit the bill.

"I went on a date with Ken Curry," I said, while everyone was bickering.

The D-Cup went silent for two seconds as the cast and crew reconfigured their neural pathways.

"Oh my God, Kate. The Met," Posey said. "Last Wednesday…"

"We forgot," Dennis said.

"What happened?" Chloe said.

"We want the whole story," Roger said.

By "we" he meant the Schmidt and Parker Players, every one of who knew all about Barkowski and Curry and the lawsuit and the Rwandan triplets and Dolores and Martin Miller and Saint Denise and Fast Eddie and Gilbert Munson and Boris Bajaria and Stephanie Garner from Ellettsville, Indiana.

"It boils down to this," I said. "Before the date, I didn't have a plan. Now I do, and I need your help. I'm seeing him again for brunch tomorrow, and I need to know if you're in or out."

Dennis, Posey, and Roger were eager to get back in. Chloe, especially since she lost her mind nine days ago and was now leaning a little to the crazy side, was gung ho to get involved and to help nail Curry to the wall. Everyone else in the cast had approached me privately since they heard about Roger getting bonked in the bean by Dolores.

"Talk," Dennis said.

"Tell us everything," Posey said.

"We held hands," I said.

"Gross," Chloe said. "Where?"

"In front of Manet's *Boating*," I said.

"The Impressionists, of course," Roger said. "He's slick. I'll give him that."

"He's more than slick," I said. "I went back to his apartment to pick him up and go to the museum and in his living room, which is the size of Madison Square Garden, there are dozens of photographs of Curry winning ballroom dancing competitions. Trophies, medals, ribbons, there's tons of them. He's the workingman Fred Astaire. It's what he does. It's his life. When he's not ripping off contractors, I mean."

"What's your point?" Roger said.

"Ballroom is his Achilles heel," I said. "As long as he has a 'bad back,' he can't dance, and it's killing him. It's all he talked about on our date, how he couldn't face the rest of his life without ballroom, how he was praying every night for a miracle so he could dance in one more competition."

"Breaking Barkowski, that's the miracle he's talking about," Dennis said.

"Then his back will be good as new," Posey said.

"Dancing with the stars," Roger said.

"Ballroom here I come," Chloe said.

"That's the plan," I said.

"What's the plan?" Dennis said.

"That we either get on the same page, play our parts with conviction, pay attention to detail, follow the plan to the letter, and take Curry down, or we let the triplets live in the Honda. It's up to us," I said.

There was mumbling and grumbling as everyone shared, compared, and confirmed their feelings about Curry. I let it buzz around the room until it reached a crescendo, and then I said, "All those in favor of the plan say aye."

"Aye," everyone said.

"The ayes have it," I said.

The Schmidt and Parker Players cheered at the pronouncement, shaking hands and hugging and slapping each other on the back.

Then Roger realized something was missing, quieted the cast, and said to me, "Now that we're in, will you tell us the plan, please?"

I took out my fangs and said, "Yes, I will."

57

A CON-MAN SLUT AT HIS BEST

WE SAT IN SARABETH'S ON AMSTERDAM AND 80TH, ME AND KEN Curry, me as Stephanie Garner. Sarabeth's is another New York classic eatery—like Wo Hop, except quaint and fabulous and feminine and delicious to smell—specializing in about the best breakfasts anywhere in the Big Apple. Their popovers and omelets, in particular, are impossible to describe. You have to see them and then taste them to believe them. The popovers are heavenly miracles of milk, flour, eggs, and salt. The omelets are perfectly formed clouds of joy. That's the best I can do.

Curry wore a dressy, silk, Tommy Bahama Hawaiian shirt, deep blue with a palm-tree design, casual black slacks, and black, four-hundred-dollar, Bruno Magli loafers (with no socks). While his gold watch, bracelet, and pinky ring said, "I'm a macho, macho man," his shoes said, "I may pretend to be a concrete mule, but I took Munson for millions, and now I'm going to bust Barkowski." He had his medieval back brace on and indicated some level of pain and discomfort with every shift of position, sip of coffee, and bite of blueberry muffin. Hard sighs, soft grumbling groans, and contorted facial expressions were the tools he employed to let all the Sarabeth's brunchers know his back hurt bad.

I wore a sleeveless, soft-gray blouse with pretty ruffles down the front and cute, black capris, both of which came from Ann Taylor, a reserved yet not altogether unhip clothier that would have earned Stephanie Garner's Midwestern seal of approval. I wore black and white linen slip-on Keds. My hair was down and held back by a mother-of-pearl barrette. My jewelry was understated— mother-of-pearl earrings and a friendship bracelet from a late-night television commercial I was in about a bail bondsman whose signature line was "Makin' Friends Forever."

We were an attractive couple in an attractive restaurant eating an attractive basket of home-baked muffins, scones, and popovers. And almost every minute of it was bullshit. I wasn't Stephanie Garner, and Curry's back wasn't bad. What was real, I thought, was that Curry liked Stephanie.

On our first date, while we walked two steps a minute through the Met, he asked me about my Ellettsville life, about my parents and siblings, about my high school and neighborhood, about my kindergarten class and my first car and my favorite books, bands, teams, and cookies. Every answer was from *This is Your Life Breanne Murphy*, except for my favorite cookies, which I said were Fig Newtons. His eyes opened wide with the delight of coincidence—"Those are *my* favorite," he said—then quickly narrowed into a wincing moment of back pain.

He seemed so happy to hear about my teaching, the kids in my class, the sincerity of my desire to help them achieve a sense of confidence, to nurture and lead them on an exploration of their creative young minds. He delighted in my family stories, Christmas tales of my brothers (Bre's brothers) and me finding the presents in our parents' closet, vacation sagas of canoe trips and campgrounds, and, especially, anecdotes of learning to dance ballroom at Arthur Murray in Bloomington. Ken Curry, the scumbag conman, was falling for me, meaning Stephanie Garner, meaning Breanne Murphy. He had finally found his ballroom girl, earnest, sincere, and well-meaning from her heart.

I asked him about his life, too, pretending that I was falling for him in the same way he was falling for me, and he was cryptic at best. He was originally from Cleveland, he said. He had lived with his grandmother since he was nine because his mother had disappeared and his father had gone looking for her and never came back. That was the extent of the story of his childhood and family. Cryptic may be underselling it.

Dolores was born a ballroom beauty, he said, a professional dancer and dance instructor, and he was raised on the dance floor where she worked and competed in countless ballroom contests. She taught him everything she knew and then some. She entered him in every contest she could. He took to it like a cow to cud. At some nebulous point in his life, Dolores moved them to New Jersey, where she had either met a gentleman friend, or found work in another dance hall, or both. It was hard to remember, he said. Later, they moved to their home on the Upper West Side of New York. And then he met me, and his life, except for his back, felt like it was starting all over again.

As sketchy as his memory was about the rest of his life, he remembered with ease every ballroom dance contest he ever entered, every dance partner, seemingly every rumba, mambo, and merengue since Dolores had raised him in the dance hall.

"Ken," I said, after our omelets arrived, "Before I met you, a guy I know, his name's Norman, invited me to dance with him in a ballroom competition in a loft theater. He knew I took lessons back in Bloomington and thought it would be fun for me. He's gay, so it's just a friends thing. Anyway, the contest is called 'The Big Apple Ballroom Bash.' It's a new competition, my friend said, but it's going to be a big deal. All the best dancers in the City will be there, and it should be really fun. I know you can't dance, but will you go with me? You can give me pointers. If it's too hard for you to watch, because of your back, because you can't, you know, I'll understand. But I would really love for you to come with me."

"When is it?" he said.

"This Thursday night."

"Where?"

"It's called the D-Cup. It's some kind of off-off-off-off Broadway Theater. It's a big loft, my friend said. It's supposed to be nice."

"Are you asking me out on a date?" he said, smiling mischievously.

"Yes," I said, smiling back at him. "Will you go with me?"

We were sitting catty corner at a small table. His right elbow could tap my left elbow without much effort. I thought, *This is it. My last shot. If he doesn't say yes, it's goodbye Barkowski, thank you for playing, tell Saint Denise and the triplets I'm sorry about—*

And then he leaned over and kissed me on the mouth.

I was taken completely by surprise. Air-raid sirens started screaming in my head. My fight-or-flight instinct shouted, "Flight, flight, flight now, get flighting, flight away, be a flighter..."

While one part of my brain was screaming and flighting for its life, another part was exerting superhuman effort to not only remain calm but to make all the outward signs of enjoying it. Whoever invented the phrase "Baptism by fire" had this kind of moment in mind.

Yet another part of my brain was pleading, "No tongue, please, no tongue..."

And still another part of my brain was saying, "What a great kisser. He's got the softest lips in the business, and he knows what to do with them. Curry doesn't *need* his tongue."

The kiss ended, and I imagined everyone in Sarabeth's was

going to applaud, that's how good the kiss was. But brunching New Yorkers are more often than not wrapped up in their own eggs Florentine, so there were no ovations.

"That was nice, Ken," I said, thinking, *That is what's called acting, finding the one sliver of truth in a moment that is otherwise hideous, repulsive, and nightmarish and playing it as the whole truth.*

"There's more where that came from," he said.

He had leaned over to kiss me without a shred of back pain, and, as he leaned back, also without pain, he was inferring, as he had when he leered at (me) the blonde banker in Gristedes, who'd spilled her purse on the floor at his feet, that somehow his back would be fine if, after brunch, we went back to his palace on Central Park West and fucked for four hours. His smile was more genuine this time, but he was a con-man slut at his best, even when he had feelings for someone.

"One day, I'll find that out for myself," I said in a way meant to mean, *I like you, and I hope this goes someplace special, and it just might if we spend more time together.*

We ate our eggs and popovers, feeling really good about being together—he actually had a little glow going there for a minute—and then I said, "So will you come to the Ballroom Bash with me on Thursday?"

"That's my Fast Eddie's night," he said. "Thursdays are tough."

"I understand," I said, pouting enough for him to see my disappointment.

"But I'll see what I can do," he said.

I brightened, so he could feel the power of my Indiana hope, and thought, *In that case, asshole, I'll see what I can do.*

58

THE ONLY QUESTION LEFT IS: DID YOU KILL HIM?

Curry kissed me one more time, on the sidewalk outside Sarabeth's, after brunch, and I had an out-of-body experience, which, I imagined, was even more surreal than out-of-body experiences usually are because I was watching Stephanie Garner kiss Curry and not me, an out-of-someone-else's-body experience—except not really.

Then we said goodbye, and I grabbed a cab that took the park to First and dropped me at the northwest corner of 83rd. I missed the trip entirely because I couldn't stop thinking about the second kiss. I thought Curry might choose Fast Eddie's over the Ballroom Bash, so I did the last thing in the world I would ever do (*Jimmy's Rules of Private Investigation for Kate, Rule Number Nine*): I slipped him some tongue. Not too much, just a quick taste, but more than enough to make myself sick.

I had crossed an internal line, and there was no going back. Four weeks ago, I had promised myself that as a private investigator I would walk right up to the line, okay, but would never cross it. My line was *dignity*, and now it was gone. I was trucking along—a professional person, a working actor, a grown woman, a mother—and then Jimmy left me his business, and in the blink of an eye I was French kissing Ken Curry out of desperation. Jesus, what was next? Would I let him touch me? Would I fuck him for the case? Would I fuck anyone for a case? Where was the line now?

I was furious with my father. He had left me rules that were worthless in the end, especially *Rule Number Nine—The last thing in the world you'd ever do is the next thing in the world you have to do.* The problem was that "the last thing in the world you'd ever do" kept shifting shape, jumping time, changing its nature—and corrupting my soul. As a case progresses and new walls arise, the way around them, or over them, or under them, or freaking through them shift, jump, and change too. The pressure to crack the case for the client builds and builds. The last thing I would ever do was unknowable. I might do anything. The line keeps moving.

"Why did you leave me your business," I said to my father, inside my head. "You ruined my life. What were you thinking?"

"I was thinking you could do it," Jimmy said.

"I can't do it," I said.

"You are doing it," he said.

"It's too hard," I said. "It's too much to ask."

"Tell that to Barkowski."

"You tell him."

"I can't, Katie. I'm dead."

I burst into tears in the back seat of the cab. It was a total meltdown, with sobbing and gasping and nose blowing galore.

"What is wrong, madam?" the driver said with a thick Indian accent. He was a Sikh, with a royal-blue turban and a long, gray beard.

"I'm sad. My dad died, and I miss him so much," I said, my voice disappearing in another wave of weeping. "I loved him so much..."

"I am very sorry for you," he said. His first name was twenty letters long and impossible to pronounce. His last name was

Singh. He was eighty years old and looked like the ancient King of the Punjab—or at least the King's cabbie.

"Thank you, Mr. Singh," I said.

He let me cry it out for the rest of the ride, saying nothing until he pulled the cab to the curb at 83rd and First.

"We are here," he said.

"Thank you," I said, composing myself. "How much do I owe you?"

"There is no charge today, madam," he said. "To honor your father."

He smiled kindly. I nodded thank you and tried to tip him ten dollars. He politely refused, then pulled out into traffic. I watched him go and thought, *it's moments like that one that make New York the best city on earth.*

I walked west on 83rd to the House of Emotional Tics, blowing my nose one more time, wiping the last tears from my eyes. When I arrived at the building, Harriman was sitting on the front steps.

"You look like you've been crying?" he said as I sat beside him. He was wearing a black, V-neck T-shirt, worn, faded Lee jeans, and beat-up Nike cross trainers. He hadn't shaved, and his hands had a little engine grease on them, as if he had been working on the Camaro, doubled parked in front of the building, before deciding to drive to my place. I looked like Stephanie Garner from Ellettsville, eyes still a bit red and wet. We kissed, but he didn't mean it.

"I was. I had brunch at Sarabeth's and was thinking about my father on the way home and just lost it in the cab. I'm okay now."

He nodded. "What's it been?"

"Since he was murdered? Thirty days."

"Still pretty raw, I guess."

"It comes and goes, but yeah, still pretty raw."

There was an edge in his voice. It wasn't straight-up anger, or disappointment, or resignation, or impatience, or regret. It was a crazy cocktail of all of them that he had to swallow against his will and wishes.

"So what's going on?" I said. "Do we have a date that I forgot?"

"Why didn't you tell me the truth, Kate?"

"About what? The way I feel for you? Every word of that *is* true."

"About Monument and the fitness reporter and the Plantscape break-in and the busted-up Green Beret and your father's gun at Stone's house and the bullet from that gun in Stone's chest. Why didn't you tell me the truth about any of that?"

"You sound like you already have an answer."

"I do."

"And you came here to tell me."

"I did. You had the gun. Your father left it to you in his will. You took possession of it at Shavelson's office. You were at Stone's. I crosschecked the names on Stone's Monument policy-holder autopsy list with the names on Olivia Russell's deceased client list. There's only one name on both. Was your father investigating the death of Ron Powell?"

"I gave you his case files. You tell me."

He took a reluctant breath and nodded. "Okay," he said, "I'll tell you. I went back to Russell and told her that a medical examiner named Stone had been murdered in more or less the same way as your father and that the one name Stone had in common with her deceased clients was Ron Powell, the man you were asking about when you were the fake fitness reporter. You want to pick it up from here?"

"Not really."

"Russell told me that Powell's half-sister, a Long Island woman named Terry Kramer, was questioning whether or not Powell was ever married, questioning how he could have left his fortune to his ex-wife and not charity, which is what Kramer says Powell told her. Kramer says there is no ex-wife in Charleston. I know because I called her and she told me that she said the same thing to your father and then to you. Your father didn't have a case file, so Kramer never actually hired him. She never actually hired you either. But he was investigating Powell's policy on the side, and he got shot in the eyes for it, and you picked up the trail, which led to Stone. The only question left is: Did you kill him?"

"Did I?"

He leaned over and kissed me, and this time he meant it. "I hope not," he said.

I kissed him back. "Me too," I said.

We kept our foreheads together after the kiss.

"I'm worried about you," he said.

"Thank you," I said.

"It's going to be hard," he said.

"I know," I said.

"I'll be with you to the end," he said.

"I'm glad," I said.

He brushed my face with his hand. I kissed his fingers as they touched my lips.

"Is there anything I can do?" he said.

"You can tell me the truth."

"About what?"

"The way you feel for me."

He held my face and kissed me again. When the kiss was over, he looked me in the eyes and said, "And every word of that is true."

59

NOT SELLING SOMETHING

HARRIMAN SAID THE ONLY QUESTION LEFT WAS DID I KILL STONEY. By my math, however, there were three unanswered questions on the board (none involving me): Who killed Ron Powell, who killed Jimmy McCall, and who killed Arnold Stone? It would have been four questions (one involving me)—Who killed Kate?—but Fu smashed the back of Stoney's house to bits and saved my life. I hadn't formally thanked him for that yet, so I invited him for coffee and Danish in my apartment on Monday morning to show my appreciation at not being dead.

Early Sunday afternoon, after Harriman left, I went to the basement to do a few loads of laundry and found Fu sweeping the laundry room floor. He was wearing bamboo flips flops, navy-blue canvas yoga pants, and a vintage Mickey Mantle baseball jersey that had no buttons. A truly nasty knife-fight scar was carved across his chest, and four bullet-hole scars marked his abdomen.

"I want to thank you for saving my life last Saturday night," I said. "My father's favorite way to thank someone for a favor was to treat them to coffee and Danish, so can you come for coffee and Danish in my apartment tomorrow morning?"

"No coffee and Danish," he said, without looking up. "Tea and tea cakes."

"I just said it was coffee and Danish."

"Fu like tea and tea cakes."

"Well, this time, you're going to have coffee and Danish."

"Fu not want coffee and Danish. Fu want tea and tea cakes."

"Are you kidding me, Fu? You're the guest. You don't—"

"Chinese tea. Oolong. Wuyi Mountains."

"Are you listening? It's my house. I invited you."

"Oolong best tea."

"We're having coffee and Danish."

"Oolong. Wuyi Mountains."

"Would you please stop saying that?"

"Oolong. Wuyi."

"Fu—"

"Oolong."

"Fu—"

"Wuyi."

"Okay, okay, Oolong, Wuyi, whatever. But I choose the Danish."

"No Danish," he said, sweeping his way out of the room. "Fu bring tea cakes."

And so just like that my offer of coffee and Danish, Jimmy's gesture of choice, became a Chinese tea I wasn't familiar with and Chinese tea cakes, whatever they were.

I did two loads of laundry, put on a clean pair of jeans, red, low-cut Converse sneakers, and my favorite Lou Reed T-shirt and took the 6 train to Canal Street. From there, it was an easy walk to 75 Mott Street and TenRen's Tea and Ginseng Co.

There are plenty of good, authentic, Chinese tea shops in Chinatown, but TenRen's (TenRen means "heavenly love" in Chinese) was the favorite of Annoying Nina, connoisseur of all things cultured. But whereas Irritating Nina was full of shit when it came to theater, film, and television appreciation, she had her shit together when it came to Chinese tea. She was a practitioner of weekend Chinese tea ceremonies that she hosted for her university colleagues. At each ceremony, she taught them to lightly tap their fingers as a way to thank the "tea master," which is what she called herself, Matthew told me, while she poured the tea. My eyes glazed over—again—just thinking of Narcissistic Nina anointing herself a tea master, but, truth be told, she knew her Chinese tea and was a TenRen's regular.

Tea is not tea in TenRen's, I discovered. It is, instead, a miraculous way of life, thousands of years old, treated with reverence reserved for treasured gemstones, diamonds, and jewels. The loose tea is stored in a hundred huge metal urns that fill tall shelves that line the long shop from front to back. There are less expensive varieties to satisfy the tea-drinking masses, but there are teas that if you have to ask how much they cost, you shouldn't be buying them. Oolong, from the Wuyi Mountains in Fujian, where damp, cloudy weather and beautifully balanced soil produce outstanding teas of superior character, turned out to be such a tea.

I asked a Chinese woman behind the counter for two ounces of Wuyi Oolong, and she asked another woman, who asked another woman. There was much buzzing between them, and then a fourth Chinese woman disappeared into the back rooms. She returned with a small package, handed it to me as if it were the long lost map to the Fountain of Youth, and said with a thick Chinese accent, "Forty-eight dollar."

"For two ounces?" I said.

"You need lotus flower porcelain tea set," she said.

"Are you asking me or telling me?" I said.

"Fifty-five dollar," she said.

"How much?" I said.

"And clay panda," she said. "You need clay panda."

By the time I left TenRen's, I had spent two hundred fifteen dollars on Oolong from Wuyi, a lotus-flower teapot and matching cups, and various and sundry ceremonial-tea accoutrement, including several traditional clay animals for display while drinking to bring luck to my guests, in this case Fu, who arrived at my door early Monday morning, wearing a vintage, gray, pinstripe suit from the 1930s, including a bow tie and a gold pocket watch, carrying a plate of four delicately-decorated Chinese tea cakes.

Decorated is not a strong enough word to describe Fu's tea cakes. They were works of art, museum pieces, each one different than the others, yet all as intricate and elegant as a spider web. They were Chinese origami in icing on two-inch square pieces of delicate almond cake. There was a tiger, colored with bright orange, red, and black icing on the first cake, a green and yellow and blue dragon on the second, a flower done in multiple hues of violet on the third, and a perfect, white swan with cherry-blossom accents and chocolate eyes on the fourth.

"Where did you get these, Fu?" I said. "They're beautiful."

"Fu make," he said. "Taste good as look."

"Fu make? What do you mean, 'Fu make?' You made these? You didn't make these."

"Shaolin master teach Fu bake. Fu good baker."

"Fu good baker? Did you just say, 'Fu good baker?'"

"Fu decorate swan, dragon, flower, tiger. Shaolin master teach."

I tried to envision this massive Chinese assassin, with his knife-fight and bullet-hole scars, with his huge, concrete-crushing fingers and his penchant for poisoning pigeons, hidden away in the basement, listening to Italian opera while creating miniature miracles in brightly-colored icing, but my mind interrupted the vision with the memory of him headbutting Green Beret Bradley into oblivion.

All I could say was, "I don't know what to say."

We moved into the kitchen—Fu in his suit and me in an ocean-blue sundress with a seashell design, both of us barefoot —and he took control of the tea, presenting, brewing, and serving the Wuyi Oolong leaves with ceremonial precision passed down for centuries and centuries, rites he was taught as boy in the Shaolin temple, where his father had abandoned him and his master had turned him into a killing machine that could decorate cakes like Martha Stewart.

When Fu was finished, I put the lotus teapot with the matching cups and the tea cakes on a tray, and Fu carried them into the living room. It was a golden-amber tea with a wonderful, earthy aroma. We sat on the couch, lifted our cups, and my doorbell buzzed.

"Forget it," I said. "It's somebody selling something I don't need."

We sipped some Oolong—it was smooth and rounded with a long, lingering sweetness—and the doorbell buzzed again, more insistent this time.

"May I have the swan, Fu?" I said, pretending there was no one buzzing. He passed me the plate with the tea cakes, and I lifted the swan to my mouth. Before I could take a bite, the buzzer went off again: three angry bursts with one longer blast at the end.

"Not selling something," Fu said.

I put the tea cake back on the plate, placed my lotus cup on the tray, got up off the couch, crossed to the intercom on the wall beside my front door, and pushed the button.

"Building manager," I said. "Can I help you?"

"Miss McCall, it's Detectives Logan and Harriman. Open the door."

I turned to Fu. The porcelain lotus teacup looked like a dollhouse toy in his hand. His black bowtie leaned slightly to the left. He knew this wasn't good news. So did I.

"I'm having tea. Can you come back later?" I said, wincing at how stupid I sounded.

"Open the door now, Miss McCall," Logan said.

"Gun in Queens," Fu said.

"Yes," I said.

"Come to arrest," he said.

"Yes," I said.

He stood up like he was ready to rip someone's head off and said, "Fu stop."

"No. It's too late," I said to Fu, and then I hit the button and said to Logan and Harriman, "I'll be right out."

I walked from the living room to my walk-through closet, put on a pair of comfortable flats and grabbed my purse. Fu followed me.

"Charlie has an early harvest," I said. "Make sure he works way after midnight and keeps the lights low and the music down. Al's toilet is bad again. He bought three cases of Gatorade. Please fix his pipes before he drinks his own pee. Warren's Toyota is in the shop. He asked me to get it for him at two today. I think I'm going to be busy, so can you please do it? You're a better driver than me anyway."

"Fu say yes."

"Yes, you're a better driver or yes you'll do it?"

"Not funny now," he said.

"I know," I said. I stopped in the living room, picked up the swan, and crossed to the front door.

"You wait in my house until after the police leave; I don't want them to see you," I said. Harriman was convinced a human jet plane was helping me, and I felt no need to confirm that for him.

Fu nodded. I opened the door and took a bite of the tea cake.

"You're right," I said. "It tastes as good as it looks."

60

THAT'S WHAT I LIKE ABOUT MIRANDA

EDIE AND RAY WERE PASSING THROUGH THE LOBBY, CARRYING their laundry to the basement. Edie wore a ruby-red ball gown, high heels, full makeup, and an updo fit for a night at the opera. Ray wore a sleeveless T-shirt, black dress shoes with no socks and his boxers. Apparently, he had been unable to find clean pants and just said fuck it.

"Where are you off to, Kate?" Edie said as I locked my door.

"The police station," I said.

"Tell your detective boyfriend he can borrow my Viagra," Ray said. "I got a two-by-four down there now, I'm telling you what."

"Thank you for that vision, Ray," I said and walked outside, where Detective Lew Logan arrested me for the murder of Dr. Arnold Stone. Harriman stood on the steps below him. Two uniformed officers waited on the sidewalk. One squad car and an unmarked sedan were double parked in front of the building. Logan handcuffed me and, holding my arm, escorted me down the walk to the sedan. Harriman moved out of the way as we walked down the steps. Our eyes met. He was all business, but his mouth gave him away, the corners turned down in a small, sad frown. He said nothing to me, and I said nothing to him. I wondered if Logan knew we were dating.

One of the uniformed officers, a redheaded kid with an absurd amount of freckles, too young to be cop, opened the backseat door of the sedan, and Logan slid me into the car. There was a cage between the back seat and the front seat. Harriman took the wheel. Logan rode shotgun, turned halfway around, and read me my rights, while Harriman drove to the Thirteenth Precinct.

When I was fourteen, Jimmy told me that Miranda was his friend. "She's there when I need her," he said. "That's what I like about Miranda." Years later, I learned that Miranda wasn't a woman that Jimmy knew: it was his right to remain silent, his right to speak to an attorney even if he couldn't afford one. He had been arrested on several occasions, but the charges against him were dropped each time, when he'd pulled last-minute evidence out of his hat (or his ass, as he would say).

"I'm not talking," I said to Logan. "And I want to see my lawyer."

"Shavelson," Logan said to Harriman with disdain. "Asshole smokestack prick." Then he turned to the front and none of us said a word until we were at the Thirteenth.

61

BECAUSE YOU'RE IN A SHITSTORM OF TROUBLE

It took three hours to fingerprint, photograph, identify, and register me into the system. Logan was particularly unpleasant throughout the process. He didn't like me, and I didn't like him. We were even except that I was under arrest, and he wasn't.

After an hour and thirty minutes at the Thirteenth, for instance, while I was being fingerprinted by a woman who had to weigh four hundred pounds, I said to Logan, "Have you called Shavelson yet?"

"Yeah," he said. "I called him a dickweed."

Logan and Harriman sat at desks that abutted and faced each other, creating one, big, square desk that was positioned in the center of the third-floor homicide squad room. I sat on the side of their conjoined desks, still handcuffed. All around us, detectives went about their business, tracking down leads, following up phone calls, researching facts and figures on the internet, meeting by the assignment board, by the coffee counter, and in the glass-fronted offices that ringed the room.

Logan's desktop was chaotic, buried beneath waves of papers, files, photographs—of his family, of gruesome murders, of suspects—news clippings, and handwritten notes scribbled on candy bar wrappers, bar coasters, paper bags, pieces of cardboard, and hundreds of stickies in dozens of colors. Sitting in the center of this sea of paper was a vintage, antique Royal typewriter. I couldn't see the phone, but the handset cord was visible between the waves, snaking through like a water moccasin.

Harriman's desk was clean as a bean. His iPhone, his iPad, and one file, mine, were his only desktop items. He either didn't do paperwork or was highly efficient. I imagined it was a combination of the two: he did what he needed to do with forethought and efficacy, and he let Logan handle the bulk of their reports.

"You want to give us some phone numbers, McCall," Logan said, typing on the Royal, "next of kin, friends, colleagues, someone who can confirm you are who you say you are? Start with your sister and work your way down."

"We're finishing your file," Harriman said. "We send it to the DA, so he can draft a criminal complaint against you and assign your case a file docket number.

"The more you cooperate, the easier it is," Logan said.

One time, after he'd been released from custody—he'd been arrested for trespassing—Jimmy had told me it wasn't a good idea to tell the police anything about anything about your life, including any kind of contact information. I never fully understood why until I was handcuffed and questioned by an asshole homicide detective I detested.

I could imagine the phone call between Logan and my sister, Marilyn.

"Can you see a scenario where your sister would blow some guys eyes out of his head, maybe for revenge, maybe because she got nervous, maybe because she got careless?"

"How about all three? She was unstable when I left for Cleveland—you know she was pregnant at sixteen—and she got progressively more unstable the clearer it became that she was trapped in a downward spiral, wasting her life as a no-talent actor. Revenge? That sounds just like her. Nervous? Careless? Yes and yes again. Not only can I see a scenario like that, I would cast my vote "guilty as charged." Would I get paid to testify against her?"

"The easier it is for you," I said to Logan.

"I told Mike he was making a mistake going out with you, McCall. Thanks for making me look like a genius."

So he did know. "Looks aren't everything," I said, when I should have said nothing.

"Fuck you. You're going in the cage," Logan said.

A uniformed cop deposited me in the holding cell, and I waited three more hours before Shavelson showed up. He grabbed a chair, and we spoke through the bars.

"Sorry I'm late," he said. "My wife is squeezing my nuts. Twenty-five years of marriage, I have one stinking affair, and she's got my balls in a vice.

"That's interesting," I said, "but do you think we could talk about me, since I'm the one under arrest for murder."

He was unshaven, disheveled, and disorganized. He opened his briefcase in his lap and papers exploded out of it. He dove into them, looking for something with my name on it, I assumed.

"Your son's in court."

"You spoke to him?"

"Briefly."

"What did he say?"

"Not much. He doesn't like me. Calls me a fringe lawyer. Working on the fringe of the law, I guess he means. One time, your father and your son were..."

"Shavelson. Focus on me."

"Jesus, you and my wife. He said he'll see you in central booking."

"I'm not going to central booking."

"Why not?"

"Because they can keep me there two, three days until I'm arraigned, and I open on Friday."

He looked at me, cocking his head to the side like a dog that doesn't understand what the hell you're saying.

"Open what on Friday?"

"My show."

"It's Monday."

"That's my point. I have a dress rehearsal in two hours."

"That's not happening."

"Why not?"

"Because you're in a shitstorm of trouble."

He produced a piece of paper and handed it to me through the bars. I wasn't sure what amazed me more, that he had found what he was looking for or that someone had actually had an affair with him.

"What is this?" I said, scanning the document.

"Medical examiner's report. It says the gunshot to the chest, the one that came out of your gun, killed him. The other two, the DA is going to say, the ones in the eyes, were you trying to cover your tracks, send the cops on a goose chase, a copycat thing."

"That's not true."

"I know that, and you know that, but the medical examiner, guy named Gary Wong, he doesn't know that. And, right now, he's the one that matters."

"I mean it's not true, as in falsified, as in intentionally altered."

"How do you know that?"

"Because I was there."

"Oh good. The 'I-was-at-the-scene-of-the-crime-with-the-murder-weapon-defense.' Why didn't I think of that?"

He grabbed a pack of Lucky Strikes out of one pocket, a

pack of Marlboro out of another, considered both, put a Lucky in his mouth, and lit it.

"You're not listening. This report is bullshit," I said, handing it back to him.

"This report is the legal position of the City of New York. And due to the violent nature of the crime, the out-of-control revenge motive of the suspect, and the fact that the suspect slept with the homicide cop investigating her father's murder to stay close to the case, nobody's letting you go anywhere until you're arraigned. And then the judge is going to set your bail so high that Shaquille O'Neal won't be able to reach it."

A desk sergeant appeared in the doorway, barrel-chest, crew cut, Popeye forearms. "You can't smoke in here, asshole. Put it out, or I'll put it out for you."

Without even looking at the sergeant, Shavelson dropped the Lucky and killed it with his foot. The sergeant shook his head derisively and walked away. As soon as he was gone, Shavelson lit a Marlboro.

"It's time to take a plea. Temporary insanity, crime of passion, something like that. We'll get you a good defense lawyer. Dominick Tamburro. Defends mafia hitmen and serial killers. He's the guy you want at the table when their big guns are..."

I didn't hear the rest because I had a moment. It was an unmistakable sensation that started in the pit of my stomach, a gut feeling that the pressure was about to blow the lid off. Jimmy had told me I would know, and now I knew: it was finally time to tell the truth.

"Shavelson," I said, interrupting him midstream.

"What?" he said, gathering his papers while sucking half the cigarette into his lungs.

"Get me Detective Logan."

62

THAT'S WHAT THE DA IS GOING TO
SAY ABOUT YOU

AFTER SPENDING SEVEN HOURS AT THE THIRTEENTH, I WAS handcuffed and transferred by police van to 100 Centre Street, Central Booking, three blocks south of Canal Street. Along for the ride were three men and someone named Sylvia. The men were as different as ducks and Dobermans. One was sixty and dressed in a seersucker suit, one was thirty, covered with tattoos, and wearing a bloody, torn T-shirt, and one was an angry Asian gangbanger, barely twenty, with a dragon headband. The tattoos and the headband were tough guys, real criminals who, I imagined, had perpetrated some kind of violence, maybe as they were robbing someone, maybe as an initiation, maybe for the fun of it. The seersucker kept his eyes down the entire time and said over and over, "What have I done? What have I done? What have I done?"

Sylvia was an emaciated, fifty-year-old, black, transvestite hooker wearing a skin-tight, red-leather mini dress and ten pounds of mascara. I knew he was a hooker because he said to me, "The fuck you looking at, honey? Ain't you never seen no hooker before?" I knew his name was Sylvia because he said to the two cops in the van, "Sylvia don't like jail, Sylvia don't like cops, and Sylvia don't like you." I knew he was a transvestite because of the bulge in his mini dress.

The van delivered us to a rear entrance in front of a twenty-foot-tall, roll-up metal door. The cops jumped out, walked around the van, opened the back doors, and helped the men out first, because they were handcuffed and chained together and needed the help. One cop watched the men, and the other helped me out—I was handcuffed too, though not to Sylvia, who said, "The fuck I always go last?"

I had never been arrested and arraigned before, so the size and severity of the two monolithic buildings, connected by an umbilical walkway fifteen stories up, was enough to put the fear of God in me. *Son of a bitch*, I thought, *this is the last place anyone wants to be.* On the streets behind us, the neighborhood people went about their business—criminals were deposited in Central Booking every day of the year, and the sight of five handcuffed New Yorkers, three of them belly-chained together, was no different to them than five kids singing doo-wop on the sidewalk for small bills and loose change. But visitors stopped and stared. I would have stopped too, if I wasn't in handcuffs and standing next to Sylvia, who yelled out to one middle-aged gawker, "Wait for me, baby. I'll make you feel like a real man."

The policemen walked us to the metal door, looked up at the security cameras, and signaled that they were ready. A moment passed, and then the door opened like the jaws of death. When it was halfway up, the cops led us in. I heard the heavy motor reverse itself and sensed the door shutting behind us, but I didn't turn around.

We were led down a cinderblock hallway to a holding area that was gray and drab and depressing. We stood there in our handcuffs and bellychains while the escort officers checked their clipboard list of names with the clipboard list of names of the receiving officers. The officers signed and stamped each other's lists, and the receiving officers led us to a large, open, registration area where registration officers were waiting to question us about our names, ages, addresses, employment histories, relatives, arrest records, drug addictions, and, surprisingly, our health, especially our sexual health.

My registration officer was a woman named Helen. She was sixty years old and as gray and drab and depressing as the building she worked in. I had never met Helen before. I had never seen her or heard of her. We were total and complete strangers. And yet she asked me questions my gynecologist wouldn't ask me—How many men have you had sexual intercourse with in the last twenty-four hours, in the last forty-eight hours, in the last seven days, the last four weeks? What was the nature of those sexual experiences? Were they men or women or both? Were these relationships or singular affairs? Were you paid for the sex? What sex acts did you perform? What sex acts were performed on you? Was anal intercourse a part of the sex? Are you exhibiting any sexually transmitted disease symptoms now and/or have you ever exhibited any sexually transmitted disease symptoms and/or are you in treatment for any sexually transmitted disease? Do you perform or have you ever performed sexual acts in a public setting? And on and on and on...I didn't tell Helen about Harriman, but I did mention that she might want to question Sylvia along these lines.

What they were concerned about was that I might start an orgy in the Central Booking jail cells, or rape someone, or start taking tricks, and, if I did, they wanted to make sure I wouldn't infect any of the other criminals with the puss-infected sex sores I was no doubt concealing under my ocean-blue sundress with the seashell design.

Later, another registration officer, a latex-glove-wearing beast named Livonia, performed a full-cavity search and seizure—while Helen watched—to make sure I was as clean as I said I was. It was humiliating, dehumanizing, demeaning, and frightening. They had all the power, and I had none. When it was over, Livonia and Helen left the small, gray, drab, depressing exam room, and Matthew walked in. His skin was tight, as if he couldn't relax his cheeks or unclench his jaw. His mouth was a thin, tense line. His eyes were hopeless and help-less. We hugged each other. That was our small talk.

"I spoke to Shavelson again, after court, on my way here," he said.

"He wants me to hire a mafia attorney," I said.

"Shavelson's a slob, but he's right about Tamburro."

"He defends psychotic people."

"That's what the DA is going to say about you."

"Matthew, you're the DA."

He looked away, at the floor, to the side, anywhere but into my eyes. His voice was stuck deep down in his throat, strug-gling to get out. "We're charging you with first degree murder and about a dozen other felonies, breaking and entering, assault, eluding arrest, wreckless endangerment, impeding an investigation..."

The words became too soft for me to hear, and I was sitting right in front of him. He took a breath and started again.

"I can't help you," he said. "Every time I turn around it's a conflict of interest. They gave me five minutes off the record today. But that's it."

I touched his arm. "It's okay," I said.

"No, it's not," he said. "Life without parole. That's where this is going."

It was a sobering assessment for both of us: me realizing how much trouble I was in, him realizing there was nothing he could do to stop it from happening.

"I'm meeting with Logan at the Thirteenth right after this, then with Shavelson and Tamburro later tonight. They'll be here tomorrow at eleven. Harriman said he'd be here at nine. The Tombs are full, so you won't see the judge until sometime tomorrow."

"Who do I have?"

"Morrison."

"Is he good or bad?"

"She. Very bad. You won't make bail."

"Time to go." Another officer stood in the exam room doorway, a Volkswagen bus named Bernice.

"I told them you're my mother, and I asked them to watch you in there," he said, "but they can't be everywhere all the time, so be careful."

"Let's move, McCall," Bernice said, and she took my arm and led me away. I turned back and tried to smile at my son, but he looked so worried that I couldn't do it.

63

THERE'D BE ONE LESS
WITHOUT YOU

Nine women, including me, all of us under arrest and waiting to be arraigned, were gathered in a central area, accounted for in triplicate, and then escorted to double doors at the end of a hallway. The doors were unlocked by an officer with a pass card and opened for us by two additional officers, both women. Behind the doors were metal steps that led only down, so down we went, single file, two officers at the front of the line, two more securing the rear.

We descended three or four flights below the city of New York. I lost count because I couldn't stop thinking that these were the stairs to hell and that we would walk them forever. We didn't. We went through another set of double doors, traveled a long hallway—via the underground umbilical walkway, we were moving from the registration building to The Tombs next door—arrived at yet another set of double doors, were buzzed through, accounted for in triplicate, and then led to a large jail cell, a holding cell, as in iron bars that clanked shut when all nine women were inside, me included.

There were seventeen women in our cell. Juveniles, men, and women, I learned firsthand, are held overnight in separate cells. Sylvia, I assumed, was either with the men or the other transvestite hookers.

Maybe I slept twenty minutes, two minutes at a time. The lights were on all night and officers watched the cell around the clock. The toilet was out in the open. You can only hold it for so long, I learned, even in jail.

Harriman was coming to see me first thing in the morning. That's what got me through the night.

At eight o'clock, the officers brought us single serving boxes of corn flakes and little cartons of milk. I was still in my sundress. We were all wearing the clothes we were arrested in. We ate breakfast like a silent class of disobedient school children. There was very little eye contact. Maybe none. There was no place to brush our teeth.

When our corn flakes were gone, the officers opened the cell door, and we traced our path back to the registration building, except that this time we were led upstairs to a holding area behind the criminal courts. Another cell of women was added to our holding area. *Jesus Christ*, I thought, *could we all be criminals? How is that possible? How could there be thirty-six women waiting to be arraigned on the last Tuesday in August. Was this just another summer Tuesday? Or was it a full moon or something?*

"There's too many people in this city," I said unintentionally out loud.

"There'd be one less without you," a woman with black teeth and track marks on her arms said to me.

"McCall," an officer called out.

"Here," I said.

"Interview eight," he said.

I walked across the holding area, and two officers led me down a corridor, past half a dozen doors labeled "Interview 1," "Interview 2," and so on until we reached "Interview 8." They got me settled inside and left the room. It was painted a boring beige and had brown baseboards, a brown and beige linoleum tile floor in an uninspired diamond pattern, and fluorescent lights in the ceiling. There was a plain, wooden conference table in the middle of the room with four straight-back wooden chairs around it. It was a room to meet your attorney in and nothing else. Sixty seconds after the officers exited, the door opened and Harriman walked in. I wanted to cry, but I didn't. I wanted to kiss him, but I didn't. I wanted to hold him and never let go, but I didn't. Instead, I tried to focus on the moment. It wasn't easy.

64

I'M SORRY THAT ONE OF US IS

Harriman did his best to buck up, but he was shaken. The status of the murder of Dr. Arnold Stone was case-closed. There was nothing to investigate, no clues to uncover. The killer was in custody, waiting for arraignment, and he was holding her hands across the conference table in Interview 8.

His blue-blue eyes were filled with sadness. His voice was soft with concern. He was terribly sorry about what happened to me, about his part in it, about what was yet to come. "I'm so sorry, Kate," he said ten times in a row. "I'm so sorry. What can I do? Tell me what to do. I'm so sorry." He was turned upside down and inside out. He was wearing his heart on his sleeve.

He hadn't slept, he said, and he hadn't eaten. He'd been up all night trying to figure something out, trying to reason it some other way, but he couldn't do it. There was no other way. He looked beat up. He hadn't shaved, his hair was a mess, and he hadn't changed out of the slate-gray suit he'd worn yesterday.

He'd never looked more handsome.

We had been seeing each other for four weeks, sleeping together, whispering in the dark, sharing thoughts and dreams and secrets. We had talked about traveling, driving to Chicago and meeting my sister and her family, then heading south to Louisiana and New Orleans, Harriman's favorite city.

As troubled as he was, as worried and emotionally raw, I was worse. I wasn't falling for Harriman any more; I had fallen for him. I had allowed myself to picture a life with him, a fun and loving future that included Yankee games in the Bronx and co-ed softball leagues in Central Park and dinners at Wo Hop. There were afternoon trysts in the House of Emotional Tics, Harriman sneaking out of the squad room to sweep me off my feet. There were long drives to the New Jersey shore in the Camaro, listening to Bruce Springsteen cranked all the way up. There were sunset cruises around Manhattan on the Circle line, arm in arm on the main deck. There were walks along the East River, kissing like crazy under the 59th Street Bridge. There were poker nights and comedy clubs and muscle car shows. There was monogamy, there was intimacy, and, finally, there was love.

It was unfolding for us just that way. Harriman and I were on that road, going it together, taking our relationship as it came, but nurturing it also. We had a good thing, and we both knew it. One time, after we made love, we were lying on our sides, turned to each other, our faces two inches apart, and he said, "I don't like a whole lot of people."

"Are you saying you like me?" I said, kissing him.

"I'm saying I don't fall for people very often," he said.

"So you're saying you're falling for me?" I said. "Why don't you just say that, if that's what you mean? Why do you have to say it as a negative that means a positive? Why can't you just say the positive? Why do you have to be indirect about your feelings for me? You're very direct about everything else. I think you should be—"

He kissed me to make me stop talking, and said, "I'm falling for you, Kate."

Thinking of that moment in Interview 8, how long ago it

seemed, how far away, my arraignment with Morrison in minutes, my life about to vanish in the shadows along with any hope of finding my way back to that moment again, brought forth the unbearable sadness I'd been holding at bay. Tears filled my eyes and fell down my face.

It was hard for Harriman to see me like that. But it was harder for me.

"I'm sorry," I said. "I never meant for this to happen."

"What can I do?" he said. "What do you want me to do?"

"I want you to answer a question," I said, holding back the breakdown that was coming round the corner.

"Anything," he said.

"How did you know it was Charleston?" I said.

He cocked his head as if he didn't understand the question. "What?" he said.

"You said Terry told you there was no ex-wife in Charleston."

"Who?"

"Terry Kramer. Smithtown. Ron Powell's half-sister. On Sunday, sitting outside on the steps, after I cried in the cab, you said she told you Powell didn't have an ex-wife in Charleston. But Terry didn't know about Naomi, the ex-wife in Charleston. She couldn't have told you that. So how did you know?"

I felt him trying to let go of my hands, an unconscious loosening of his grip. I held tight, tears still falling.

"I...I guess..."

"Stony told you," I said. "No one knew about Naomi but Stony and me, because I was Naomi. You spoke to him before he was murdered. That's how you knew. I threatened to blow the whistle on him, and he panicked and called you. He didn't know you, and he *still* called you. How is that possible?"

His body tensed in a defensive way. I could see it in his face, the line of his jaw, the narrowing of his eyes. I could feel it in his hands.

"Because he did know you, that's how," I said. "He fixed Ron Powell's autopsy for a part of the payout. You killed Powell for millions of dollars, then you paid Stony to fake the report."

He pulled his hands away and laid them flat on the table. He was seconds from standing and leaving me to die in jail. I couldn't let him go.

"When Stony panicked, you killed him to shut him up, and then you tried to kill me. When that didn't work, you bought off Gary Wong to frame me. It was you, Harriman. You killed my father..."

I looked into his eyes, trying to connect with the part of him that cared for me. It had to be there. Somewhere inside him, he really had fallen for me. I had to find that feeling in him. That's where the truth was hiding.

He stared at me, tears flowing down my cheeks and dripping onto the conference table, my heart broken in a hundred jagged pieces, and then he shook his head and said, "I didn't kill anyone."

"You're lying," I said, struggling to get the words out. "When we were making love, you were thinking about slipping a leather cord around my neck—"

"No," he said.

"—then strapping me in chair and shooting me in the eyes."

He stood and moved to the door. I stood too.

"I loved you," I said. "Didn't you know that? Couldn't you feel it? How could you do that to me? After everything we said to each other, after everything we did together..."

"It wasn't me," he said, reaching for the door handle.

"Then who was it? Tell me the truth. Don't leave me like this."

The room spun. I was nauseous. I wept and wept. He froze at the door, holding the handle. He stared into the door, as if he could look through it somehow, as if he could see the life waiting for him on the other side. I could feel his heart pulling one way and his head pulling another.

"Please, Harriman," I said. "Please..."

He moved his hand away from the door and turned to me.

"They were professional hits," he said. "Powell, your father, Stone, you. They were corporate kills."

I looked at him, trying to compose myself, trying to make sense of it. "Corporate kills?"

"I tried to stop you," he said, taking a step toward me. "I tried everything to stop you. But you wouldn't stop. You kept pushing."

"So you hired a corporate killer?" I said. "How could you?"

"I couldn't," he said. He was maybe ten feet away and yet he might as well have been on the other side of the Hudson River. "I didn't."

We held each other's eyes across the room. It was the truth.

"It was Russell, wasn't it?" I said.

The answer was there, right there. If he would only just say it, then I would know.

"You owe me," I said.

He glared at me, right through me.

"Tell me the truth," I said, "before they throw away the key."

"Yes," he said. "It was Olivia."

"And Powell? And Stone?"

"Yes."

"And you knew?"

He took a breath to steady himself, and so did I.

"She contacted him, made the deal, I don't know how, she wouldn't tell me, or couldn't tell me, top floor of the corporate chain, way above my head," he said. "I got a prepaid cell phone delivered by messenger. There was a voicemail already on it. I followed the instructions, put the pieces in place, and then burned the phone. I never met him. Never spoke to him. Never saw him. It could be anyone."

"And my father? It was like that for Jimmy?" I said through my tears.

He took two steps toward me. "It's so much money," he said, shaking his head, absolving himself before my eyes. "You have no idea how much money it is, how easy it was."

He held my eyes, waiting for me to forgive him or to at least understand him. Forgive him? Probably never. But understand him? Understand why? Yes, I knew the answer to that now. He was seduced by the life (by the *things*) money gave him—the nights on the town, the tailored suits, the expensive watch, the classic Camaro. The cash in his pocket was what mattered most. I sat in my chair, stunned. There was one question left, and I thought I knew the answer to that one too.

"Are you sleeping with her?" I said.

He came all the way to the table, leaned over it to be closer to me, and said with frustration, as if it were my fault somehow, "You never stop."

Of course he was. "Did she know you were sleeping with me? Falling for me?"

He stood up straight, done with me now, his voice registering pity. It was ugly and disgusting. "She didn't care," he said. "She knew it would end like this." He looked at me and softened his stance. It was over now. "I'm sorry that you're going to jail."

"I'm sorry that one of us is," I said, and the door opened, and Lew Logan walked in with two uniformed officers.

Harriman's hand went to his gun.

"Bad idea, Mike," Logan said.

Harriman stared at Logan and the officers, and his hand fell away. He turned to me, and I showed him the wire that had been taped to the inside of my sundress. His mouth opened, but he said nothing.

The officers handcuffed him and led him from the room. "Detective Mike Harriman, you're under arrest for conspiracy to commit murder," one of the officers said. "You have the right to remain silent. You have the right to speak to an attorney. If you can't afford..." And then they were gone.

Logan watched them go and then smiled at me in a way that said I was still in the top ten percent of all the fuck ups in this big, fucked-up city but that he was proud of me at the same time. Jimmy smiled at me just like that almost every day.

"You're off my shit list, McCall. Just so you know," Logan said.

"Good," I said, "then you're off mine."

He laughed and turned to leave but stopped, looked back at me, and said, "Maybe you really are an actor." Then he walked out and shut the door.

"Not maybe," I said, wiping away the tears.

65

THIRD-RANKED RUMBA IN
KANSAS CITY

STEPHANIE GARNER WAS AS EXCITED AS SHE COULD BE. HERE SHE was, an elementary school teacher from Ellettsville, Indiana, on a year-long, New York City sabbatical, writing a book about what kids really mean when they say things they don't really mean, taking a taxi downtown to a big-time ballroom dancing competition in an off-off-off-off Broadway theater in the City That Never Sleeps, and she could barely stand it.

Her new boyfriend was sitting beside her. He worked in construction and was big and strong and smart and handsome. He was a champion ballroom dancer sidelined by a seriously bad back, which, sadly, prohibited him from working as well, maybe even forever. He owned a spectacular apartment on the West Side, shot a mean game of pool, despite his injury, and was kind to his grandmother, who he took care of and lived with.

He looked especially sexy today: black Giorgio Armani dress slacks, black Bruno Magli dress loafers, a black and gold Dolce and Gabbana silk shirt that he wore untucked, a gold Gucci watch, a gold pinky ring, and a gold bracelet. His breath, as usual, was uncommonly fresh. His teeth were exceptionally white. If not for his medieval back brace, which made *her* back hurt just by looking at it and was the reason he couldn't dance with her in the Ballroom Bash, everything would be perfect. Instead, it was so close to perfect that she couldn't stop beaming. She reached out and took his hand.

Or I did, anyway.

Ken Curry and I held hands all the way to the D-Cup, smiling and laughing, talking about tangos from competitions gone by. As surreal as that was for me, it paled in comparison to what was waiting when we opened the third-floor elevator doors.

While I was under arrest for the murder of Arnold Stone, surviving The Tombs, and proving my innocence at Harriman's expense, Dennis and Posey and Roger and Chloe and the rest of the Schmidt and Parker Players, with help from several sister off-off-off-off Broadway theater companies, had transformed the D-Cup into a sensuous slice of ballroom heaven.

The stage was cleared of all things *Blood Song and Dance*. Sultry blue and red par lights gave the loft a seductive, Latin vibe, ideal, I thought, for the fiery couple in the middle of a killer mambo, dancing their way to gold and glory. A banner, stretched above their heads from one end of the stage to the other, read: *The Big Apple Ballroom Bash.*

Bands of red silk hung from the rafters, swaying in the breeze of the ceiling fans, turning too slowly to cool the crowd, which got hotter with each samba, rumba, and cha cha. Candles in glass bowls, set on cocktail tables that ringed the perimeter of the room, added a passionate glow to the décor. Steamy music pumped out of the D-Cup sound system, bass thumping through the sub-woofers, causing the contestants to move their feet and shake their booty in every corner of the loft.

The place was packed with dancers dressed to the nines in provocative ballroom attire—the mandatory dress code. Most every seat in the D-Cup was taken, and many more people hugged the walls, waiting their turns to take the stage and impress the judges, who sat behind a table on a raised platform that was situated in the center of the third row of seats.

Dennis, Posey, and Posey's sister, Suzanne the seamstress, were the judges. Posey and Suzanne wore matching, screaming-crimson, skin-tight dresses and sat on either side of Dennis, looking like round, red bookends. Dennis wore a red bow tie and tails, with a top hat, a cane, and a bushy white mustache. He looked like Mr. Monopoly.

A registration area was close to the elevator. A cash bar was open for business at the back of the theater. At the last rehearsal, before I was arrested, I had bitten the bartender's neck as he'd waited for a midnight train to nowhere.

"Oh wow," I said.

"Nice," Curry said.

He was cool as a pool on the outside, but his face was flushed with excitement; his eyes were focused, alert, and alive. He was in his element. He drank in the room, the crowd, the judges, and, especially, the dancers on the stage.

I took his arm and said, "I have to sign in and find Norman."

He let me lead him at a snail's pace, if the snail was having a particularly slow day, to the registration desk. A Schmidt and Parker Players actor and aesthetician named Connie Haskell, a woman I had acted with, been naked in front of (while changing costumes together back stage), drank beers with, laughed, cried, and complained about life with, a woman who had removed hair from my upper lip, smiled at me from her post behind the registration desk without a clue of a trace of recognition.

"Hi," Connie said. "Welcome to The Big Apple Ballroom Bash. I'm Connie. Would you like to register? There are cash prizes in ten categories, including a grand prize of a thousand dollars for "Best in The Big Apple.""

"I'm already registered," I said. "I'm Stephanie Garner. I'm dancing with Norman Neville."

"Hi Stephanie," Connie said, looking at Curry. "You're Norman?"

"Nope," he said. "And I'm not dancing. I hurt my back."

Connie made a sad face. "I'm sorry." Then she continued to search for Stephanie's name. When she found it, she made another sad face. "There's a note by your name, Stephanie. Norman called, said he got stuck in Stamford, and won't be able to make it."

"Oh no," I said, showing as much disappointment as possible.

"I can put you on the singles list. Plenty of people find partners that way," Connie said.

"Is there anyone else on it?" I said.

She flipped pages, found the singles list, and said, "Um, no, not exactly. You'd be the first."

I nodded, sighed, looked around the room, and said, "I really had my hopes up."

"What do you want to do?" Curry said, still drawn to the dancers on stage.

"I want to go home," I said.

"You sure?" he said. "We could get a drink, watch for a while. Maybe someone else will show up for singles. You could dance with them."

"I don't think so. Norman and I practiced for weeks. We were—"

"You see, Court. It's like I said. They'll let anybody dance in this town," Roger said, walking up to us like the boss of bosses, martini in hand.

Curry narrowed his eyes ever so slightly. "Do I know you?" he said.

"Bill Calloway," Roger said.

"Courtney Shaver," Chloe said.

"Third-ranked rumba in Kansas City," Roger said.

"Missouri," Chloe said. "The Show Me State."

"We know *you*," Roger said. "That's what counts."

"You're Ken Curry," Chloe said.

"Big-shot, New York, ballroom hero," Ken said. "Beast of the East, are we right? Of course we're right."

"We're always right," Chloe said, also holding a martini. She and Roger clinked glasses. She wore a little black ballroom competition dress that was low cut in the front and non-existent in the back and pretty black Bloch Sienna, open-toe ballroom shoes with an ankle strap and a wedge glide heel. She looked stunning.

"I'm surprised you don't remember us," Roger said. He was dapper as hell, wearing dark gray silk from head to toe, including a scarf that hung loosely around his neck and a gray derby.

"Let's take a walk down memory lane, shall we, Ken?" Chloe said.

"Newport Ballroom Festival," Roger said. "We're sitting pretty in third place until you take the lead with a lindy and leave us in limbo."

"Boston Ballroom Blitz," Chloe said. "Our samba is super, but your polka is perfect and poisons our prospects."

"Atlantic City Tango Tussle," Roger said.

"Chesapeake Cha Cha Championship," Chloe said.

"DC Dance Dazzler," Roger said.

"Every time we come east, you win, we lose," Chloe said.

"It's a bad habit, Ken," Roger said. "And, in Kansas City, we break bad habits like Elvis breaks hearts."

"What does that even mean?" Curry said.

"It means the buck stops here," Roger said. "It means The Big Apple Ballroom Bash is the end of the line. It means that Courtney and I have been dancing our tails off and are ready, willing, and able to kick your can down the road."

"You and Look-what-the-cat-dragged-in," Chloe said, gesturing at me.

They were getting under his skin. The truth is they were getting under *my* skin. As crazy an actor as Chloe had become, she was perfectly cast as Courtney Shaver, the arrogant sexpot of the third-ranked rumba in Kansas City, beautiful to look at, migraine-inducing to listen to.

"Whoever you are, you're really rude," I said, letting my Ellettsville indignation shine through.

For a New York minute, Curry's back stiffened beneath the brace as if he was going to punch Roger in the jaw. "If my back wasn't busted, I'd mess you up right here."

"Your back? You got a bad back?" Roger said, noticing the brace and then turning to Courtney. "Look at little Kenny Curry with his bad back."

"You're not dancing in the Bash?" Chloe said to Curry.

"He'd dance if he could, but he can't," I said, coming to Curry's defense.

"He knows the winds are changing," Chloe said. "He's scared of us."

"That's a shame," Roger said, getting right up in Curry's face, literally nose to nose. Though Roger wasn't as thick or wide as Curry, he was still a pretty big guy and years of lugging cases of frozen shrimp around Staten Island had made him stronger than he looked. Still, in a fight, Curry would snap him in half. Roger knew that, which made his tough-ballroom-dancing-guy performance all the more impressive.

"A crying shame," Chloe said. "We so wanted to crush you."

"I guess there's some consolation knowing he's going to sit here and watch us win," Roger said to Chloe. "Unable to stop the stampede that is the third-ranked rumba in KC."

"Like trying to hold back the tide with a teaspoon," Chloe said, and they clinked glasses again.

"We'll wave from the winner's circle, Ken," Roger said.

"*Hasta luego*, ugly duckling," Chloe said to me.

And then they walked away toward the bar, smug and unbearable.

"Assholes," Curry said. "Everyone wants a piece of me. You still want to go?"

"No way. I'm staying," I said with Midwestern defiance. "Whoever signs up for singles is dancing with me, and I'm going to win. And if I don't win, I'm at least going to beat them."

"You think you can?" Curry said.

"I know I can," I said. "I took lessons at the Arthur Murray in Bloomington."

I glared at Roger and Chloe as they freshened their martinis, but, out of the corner of my eye, I saw Curry looking at me. I think it was right then that he decided he was going to fall hard for me.

"Okay, we'll stay," he said. "Let's see who signs up."

66

THIS IS BOB

We sat in the third row, to the right of the judges' platform, at the very end, so Curry could ease into the aisle seat and keep his legs stretched to relieve the pressure on, tension in, and tightening of his back, which was nothing compared to the pressure, tension, and tightening in my head. The fate of the Rwandan triplets was in the balance. We would never have another chance like this. The Big Apple Ballroom Bash was a one-time performance, the sting of a lifetime.

I had hoped that Curry, distracted by the D-Cup ballroom atmosphere, would take a swing at Roger, who, cast as Bill Calloway, was trying to provoke the Ballroom Beast of the East with jabs and footwork without going for a knockout. Curry, I had explained while outlining the plan at the end of the last *Blood Song and Dance* rehearsal, was too smart for any kind of let's-take-this-shit-outside-and-settle-it-like-men macho affront. He would sense something in the air, and his back would lock up worse than ever. No, it had to be a more carefully crafted assault on his Achilles heel if he was going to forget himself and knock Roger's block off (like Dolores had done).

Round one at the registration table had gone to Curry, who

kept his cool despite the arrogance, belligerence, and pomposity of the third-ranked rumba in Kansas City. But the bell was about to ring for round two. And round two was for all the marbles.

Judge Mr. Monopoly announced contestants in groups of four couples at a time. The dancers made their way through the crowd to the backstage entrance and took their turns on stage from the wings, dancing for dollars, for pride, and for joy. As tango followed meringue, followed mambo, followed jitterbug, Curry coached me, pointing out whatever bad form, bad timing, bad rhythm, bad feet, bad hair, bad manners, bad moves, bad makeup, or bad breath offended his ballroom perfectionist nature, honed and hardened over a lifetime of instruction, practice, and success under the watchful eyes of Grandma Dolores.

"This guy is a turd," Curry said about a suave-looking gentleman waltzing like Matilda. "He's counting steps. Look at him. Look at his lips. Look at his eyes. He's watching his feet while he counts. Total turd. The thing about competitive ballroom is you can't compete up there. You have no competition. You already won the thing, that's how you dance. It's a celebration of your talent, of your style. There's no one else in the world that can move like you, swing like you, jive like you. There's no one else in the world that loves to dance as much as you do, no one else as graceful as you are. That's how you dance. Look at him; his partner is even worse than he—"

"Excuse me, Ms. Garner," Connie said, standing at the end of the aisle next to Curry. "Someone signed up for singles."

Next to Connie was a man I had never seen before. He was six inches shorter than me, very thin, very bald, very soft, and very bland. "Bob," he said. "Alexander. Nice to meet you."

"Nice to meet you too," I said.

"Is it Bob or Alexander?" Curry said.

"Bob Alexander," Bob said. "Two first names."

"I hate that," Curry said to me.

"So would you like to dance with me, Stephanie? It is Stephanie, right?" Bob said, looking at both Connie and me.

I looked at Curry, who sighed with pain (emotional, not physical), then fixed my eyes on the bland little man with two first names and said, "Only if you want to win, Bob. Because I really want to win." I smiled and laughed, but I also meant it.

"Winning is fine, if that's what you want. Are you a good dancer?" Bob said.

"I'm good, but tonight I'm going to be great," I said, wrapping my arm around Curry's arm. "What about you?"

"I'm okay," Bob said.

"But tonight you're going to be great, right?" I said.

"If I count my steps," Bob said.

"Oh Christ," Curry said under his breath.

"Excuse me," Bob said.

"I said, 'Oh goody,'" Curry said.

"Well, I'll let you and Bob get to know each other," Connie said to me, and she flittered back to the registration table, acting pleased as pie that she could hook up two single souls at the Bash.

"Can I squeeze past you...what did you say your name was?" Bob said to Curry.

"I didn't say," Curry said, shifting his weight and making a federal production out of allowing Bob to get past him.

I slid down a seat so Bob could sit between us. Curry rolled his eyes at me, and I rolled my eyes back at him—just like any other boyfriend and girlfriend would do.

"Are you very tall?" Bob said to me. "Because I'm not. My father was five foot eight, but my mother was four foot eleven. I resemble her as far as my height is concerned. In a lot of other ways, though, I'm like my father, who was—"

"I'm taller than you, Bob," I said. "But that's fine."

Actually, it was awesome. A stroke of casting genius by

Dennis, who had not only chosen an actor I had never met and who had never met me—to make our first connection a genuine surprise and lend instant authenticity to our ad lib conversation—but had chosen an actor who was utterly wrong for me and, at the same time, the polar opposite of Curry, someone who, by his physical presence alone, would be a burr in Curry's ass for the rest of the Bash. The fact that he had two first names was just good luck.

"I think we should tango like them," Bob said, taking his seat and gesturing at the couple on stage. "If winning is what you want, a tango is our best bet to look sexy and Latin."

Bob looked like he had been dipped in milk before putting on his vintage, burgundy Nehru jacket with the matching burgundy pants and shoes. There was nothing he could do to make himself look sexy. Bob looking Latin was a preposterous thought.

Curry glanced at me over Bob's head and made a face that said: *Please shoot me, or at least shoot him.*

"Did someone say sexy and Latin?" Chloe said, taking the seat directly in front of Bob.

"Because that's what we are," said Roger, sitting on the aisle, right in front of Curry.

"Hello, duckling," Chloe said to me while gesturing at Bob. "Who's this little piece of milquetoast?"

"This is Bob. He's dancing with me today," I said.

"Bob Alexander," Bob said. "Two first names."

"I *hate* that," Curry said.

"Sweet," Chloe said to Bob and me. "Nothing sexier or more Latin than a milquetoast ballroom dancer and his ugly duckling partner."

"Prepare to get stomped," Roger said, dismissing us before turning to Curry. "Could've been you, Ken."

"Should've been you," Chloe said.

"Except you got a bad back because you let yourself go. What do you weigh, like two-sixty, two-eighty?" Roger said.

"Don't you have any pride?" Chloe said. "Lay off the Ding Dongs."

"You can't dance like a pro when you're fat as a pig," Roger said.

"Oink, oink," Chloe said.

"It's a good thing you got a bad back. You would've embarrassed yourself up there," Roger said.

"Saves us the trouble of doing it for you," Chloe said.

They laughed and clinked their martini glasses.

Curry was fuming. I could see it on his face, in his eyes. Any moment he would leap forward, grab Roger *and* Chloe, and throw them across the theater at the same time.

"You're not the Beast of the East I came to kill," Roger said. "You're a bloated has-been."

"His back's so bad, he can't even say anything," Chloe said.

"The road to 'Best in the Big Apple' just opened wide for the third-ranked rumba in Kansas City," Roger said.

"All systems go," Chloe said.

"We're going to take your title, fat man," Roger said to Curry.

"Watkins-Harris, Greenburg-Hayes, Garner-Alexander, Shaver-Calloway," Dennis called out over the PA system.

From different sides of the D-Cup, Watkins-Harris and Greenburg-Hayes moved to the backstage door. Seductive samba music filled the loft. All around us, couples danced, judges judged, and the Ballroom Bash was as real as if it were real.

Roger stood up, leaned over the seat toward Curry. "That's it? This is what you got?" he said.

Curry glared at him and then slowly stood up, face to face with Roger. *This is it*, I thought, *I've got him.*

"I'm out of here," Curry said, and he walked slowly, painfully away.

"Uh oh," Chloe said.

"Not good," Bob said.

"I had him on the ropes," Roger said.

"Did he leave?" I said.

"I don't know," Chloe said. "I lost him in the crowd."

"Me too," I said.

"He knows," Bob said.

"We're screwed," Roger said.

"The triplets are screwed worse," Chloe said.

"Now what?" Bob said. "Do we dance?"

"What's the point?" Roger said.

"Why bother?" Chloe said.

As I staggered to my corner and sank on my stool, punched out, breathing hard, cut man swabbing me with Vaseline, spitting bloody water into a rusted pail, those very same questions were bouncing around my brain. Round two, in which Curry was hit with body blows and head shots, punched, prodded, and provoked to defend his ballroom pride, was a bust, and that was the round I was banking on. Roger was right. We'd had him on the ropes, but he had bobbed and weaved and slipped away.

Were we screwed? In all likelihood, yes. If Curry was gone, then when he got back to the Upper West Side and Dolores heard about what went down in the D-Cup, she would recognize it as a sting, and that would be that—end of story.

I considered throwing in the white towel, but two voices in my head wouldn't let me quit. First Raul, "You answer the bell until you can't answer the bell," and then my father, "Keep swinging, Katie. The fight's not over until you stop fighting." I heard the bell for round three and stood up.

"We dance," I said, "because the show must go on."

They looked at each other, actors all, and said as one, "The show must go on."

67

TANGO PARADISO

Watkins and Harris, young, attractive, and talented actors from another theater company, performed a terrific jitterbug. Obviously, they had taken several years of ballroom training, possibly even together, as part of their acting education. They were light on their feet and easy on the eyes. Curiously, he had a lion's mane of auburn hair straight out of a shampoo commercial, and she had a shocking-white, Marine Corps buzz cut that was sexy as hell. He wore a tuxedo, and she wore a sheer ballroom gown that left nothing to the imagination. The music ended, the crowd applauded, the judges conferred, and Greenburg-Hayes was called to the stage.

Eleanor Greenburg and Jerry Hayes were founding members of the Schmidt and Parker Players. Longtime friends of Dennis and Posey, they were in their seventies and often played the parents of the lead actors, or the wise and worldly professor, or the kindly physician, or the tough-love judge, or the knowing neighbor that turns out to be the confidant that paves the way for the protagonist to complete their character arc. Eleanor, for instance, played my mother in *Mississippi Boppin'*, and Carl played the old mechanic who had been at the gas station forever. In *Blood Song and Dance*, Eleanor played a nightclub singer who had lost her voice, become a bartender, and dispensed advice and martinis in equal proportion, and Jerry played the Grand Central Station security officer with a heart of gold. Like everyone else in the play, their blood flowed in buckets by the end.

They had been married fifty years and had been waltzing even longer. They were wonderful together, smiling into each other's eyes, holding hands, and dancing with joy and love and an impressive amount of talent. I never thought waltzes had lyrics, but Jerry sang to Eleanor throughout their dance. When the music ended, the crowd cheered with genuine passion. Greenburg and Hayes were acting, like everyone else in the D-Cup, but their waltz was no act. The Bash was a lie, but everyone knew true love when they saw it.

The crowd settled, and Judge Monopoly leaned into the microphone. "Garner-Alexander," he said.

Roger and Chloe stood next to Bob and me. Bob was five two in his dancing shoes. I was five nine in mine. "Time to tango," I said.

Then a thick forearm came between us, accompanied by a voice that said, "I'll take it from here, pal."

It was Curry. None of us had to act the moment. We were all taken by surprise. To a dancer, we believed Curry had vacated the D-Cup, and yet here he was, physically moving Bob out of the way as if Bob were a Chihuahua, which he kind of was.

"It's Bob. Bob Alexander. Two first names," Bob said as Curry swept him aside.

Curry bent down into Bob's face and said, "*I hate that.* Get a real goddamn name, why don't you?" Then he put his arm around my waist and turned to Roger and Chloe.

"Listen carefully, losers. In your whole life, you will never dance like I dance. You got no style. You got no taste. You got no class. You got nothing. From this moment on, I will make it my business to find you at every competition from here to Missouri so you will never win anything ever again. Now get the hell out of my way, and watch me kick your Kansas City asses."

He moved me away from Roger and Chloe and Bob, onto the dance floor and into the spotlight. We stood center stage, all eyes upon us.

"They'll wait for my signal before they start the music," Curry said. "It's a tango?"

"Yes," I said.

"Follow my lead, and dance like you own the place. Don't think about the steps, just move like you're having the best time in the world. Trust me, Stephanie. I got you covered. Okay?"

"Okay," I said. "Where did you go?"

"Bathroom. Took off my brace."

He put his arm around me, and I put my arm around him. No brace.

"You were gone a long time," I said. "I thought you left me here."

"Never," he said. "I looked around to see if I knew anyone or if anyone knew me. I don't like people talking about me when I make a surprise appearance."

"What about—"

"They're from Missouri. They'll be gone tomorrow. It's a crowd full of strangers."

I nodded and said the truest thing I had ever said to him, something so earnest, sincere, and well-meaning from my heart that I thought it might be one of my finest moments as an actor ever. "I understand."

"You ready?" he said.

"You don't have to do this."

"I'm the king."

"Ready," I said.

He smiled at me and then nodded at Dennis, Posey, and Suzanne. The music started, and he took me to Tango Paradiso.

"Dude's light on his feet," Rodriguez had said. "Twinkle-toes," Collins had said. "Nimble motherfucker," Talley had said. They hadn't done him justice. The man could dance like the devil. He was phenomenal, the best ballroom dancer anyone in the D-Cup had ever seen. His energy was beautiful to behold. His confidence was astounding. He moved me around the stage with impossible strength and grace. It was nothing for me to dance like I owned the place. He made me look like I had been dancing the tango with him for years instead of minutes, and he did it with awesome style and ease, like he was born to do it. I never felt sexier in my life.

He held my eyes as the music carried us forward. And I held his eyes too, partly because I had no choice—his performance and persona compelled me to—and partly so he wouldn't see the video camera hidden beneath the judges' table, recording his every brilliant step.

68

YOU'RE TOO DAMN CRAZY TO BE FULL OF SHIT

And then it was Friday. I had to be at the D-Cup at four to prepare for the premier of *Blood Song and Dance*, which should have given me all day to run my lines and focus on Farina LeBleu, but I had a morning meeting on the books with Lew Logan at the Thirteenth and another one in the early afternoon with Barkowski and Shavelson, so reconnecting with my inner vampire had to wait.

A uniformed officer named Ortiz escorted me to the third floor, and the homicide receptionist, a pretty brunette I didn't remember, gestured toward the middle of the room, where Logan sat behind his desk, banging away on his Royal, and said, "That's Detective Logan right there."

"I know," I said to the brunette. "He arrested me on Tuesday."

I crossed the floor to Logan, who didn't even look up from his typewriter.

"Sit," he said, pointing his chin at Harriman's desk.

I looked at the desk and froze. My entire romance with Harriman passed before my eyes, and I thought, *What the hell is wrong with me?* I had a history of demonstrating poor judgment in men, sure, but Harriman was a new low. This time, I had fallen for a man who conspired to have me strangled by a corporate killer. It would take me decades to unravel the reasons for my inability to find a normal, loving, monogamous man.

I must have stood there a long time because Logan said, "I meant today."

"I didn't love him, but I was thinking about it," I said.

Logan looked up at me, then at Harriman's desk, then back at me. He narrowed his eyes until what I was feeling clicked into place for him, and then he said, "Get over it. He would have let you rot forever. You had some good times. Maybe they were real, maybe they weren't. You'll never know, and it don't much matter. In the end, he isn't worth a pint of piss. And you are."

"Thanks, I think," I said.

"No problem. Now take a seat and start writing," he said, sliding a yellow pad and pen across his desk onto Harriman's desk. "Names, numbers, times, dates, everything that happened from the minute you found out about your father's death to the minute you turned the tables on Mike. Don't leave anything out. If we're going to put that insurance bitch behind bars, I need to know the truth. All of it."

I nodded and sat in Harriman's chair. Reliving the Monument case, putting it on paper, was harder than I thought it would be. I hadn't expected the rush of emotions hidden in the words, waiting to ambush me. Writing about my relationship with Harriman, being interviewed at the Thirteenth that first time, accepting a date with my vampire teeth still in, holding hands in Wo Hop while I cried in my honey crispy chicken, kissing in the shadow of St. John the Gigantic, and making love in my apartment (I didn't write that down, but I couldn't stop thinking about it), made my head hurt and my heart ache. I experienced the five stages of grief, moving from denial into anger, into bargaining, into depression, and, finally, into acceptance without getting out of Harriman's chair, without making a sound, without looking up.

Remembering the leather strap around my neck at Stony's, on my knees, about to die, made it hard to breathe all over again. I had to take a break, get a glass of water, stretch my legs, and recover my composure. I wrote until my hand cramped, then I wrote some more. An hour and a half later, I was done. Logan was still typing.

"You're either writing the great American novel, or you have no idea how to type," I said.

"All work and no play makes Jack a dull boy," he said.

"Good movie," I said.

"Redrum," he said.

I slid the yellow pad, now filled with sixteen pages of handwritten notes, back across the desk to Logan, who stopped typing, lifted the pad, and scanned my report.

"Did Harriman flip on Russell?" I said.

"Sure. His lawyer told him he had to cooperate or go to jail for the next twenty-five years. He's going to lose a decade no matter what he does."

"Does Russell know who killed my father?" I said.

"Doubt it. The guy's a ghost. Nobody knows him. Smoke and mirrors until he shoots somebody's eyes out."

"If nobody knows him, how do they find him? How do they pay him? Russell hired him four times. She has to know that much."

"You think?"

"You didn't ask her?"

"She's out of the country on business."

"Where?"

"They don't know. They're working on finding out. They'll get back to us."

"Sure they will."

We sat there for a bit, the homicide squad room buzzing around us, Logan reading my account of the last five weeks. He finished page sixteen, put the yellow pad down, looked at me with what I thought might be the very beginnings of respect, and said, "I'll get her. I don't stop. We got that in common, you and me."

He smiled when he said that. Not with his mouth, but with his voice. Jimmy did that too.

It wasn't the first time that Logan had reminded me of my father. It had happened as recently as Tuesday, when I was in the holding cell, realized it was Time To Tell The Truth, and asked Shavelson to get me Logan. The detective listened through the bars while I explained how I knew Harriman was tied to Russell and that the two of them were tied to the ten-mil insurance scam and the murders that went with it, and then he shook his head just exactly the way Jimmy used to do when I told him something he had no business believing but believed anyway. Then he said, "You're too damn crazy to be full of shit." After that, he arranged for the wire in Interview 8, and here we were.

"So the ghost who murdered my father?" I said.

"Still out there."

"Somebody has to find him, Logan."

"Somebody will. But not you. You got lucky this time, McCall. You could be behind bars or dead or both. I don't want you running around like Charlie Bronson on some kind of personal manhunt vendetta. Tracking a professional corporate killer is dangerous, even for a trained PI, which you are not."

"No, I'm an actor."

"Exactly my point. So right now you're going to look into my eyes and swear to your mother Mary that you are all done investigating any damn thing in New York. Those very words would work for me."

"I am all done investigating any damn thing in New York."

"Good," he said. Then he resumed typing only God knew what.

69

HAPPY BIRTHDAY, TED

THE FIRST THING I NOTICED UPON ENTERING SHAVELSON'S Broadway office was that the Kodiak had been moved from the inner sanctum to the waiting room. Thick chains were wrapped around the bear's mid-section and were secured by two heavy-duty padlocks to a massive metal pipe that was part of the building. It took up half the room in such a way that visitors no longer had anywhere to sit—the couch was behind the grizzly, which was posed for the rest of time in attack position. "Thanks," I felt sure people said to the bear, "I'll stand."

The second thing I noticed was Shavelson searching for something in a file cabinet a bit to the side and just behind the Kodiak. He had a lit cigarette in his mouth and a Johnnie Walker Black on the rocks in his left hand. He glanced at me, drank some Johnnie, and said, "My soon-to-be ex-wife's getting the houseboat in Nyack, the condo on Amsterdam, and most every other goddamn thing that has my name on it. But she's not getting my bear. The bear stays with me."

"At least you've got your priorities straight," I said, thinking, *Give her the grizzly; keep the condo.*

"Barkowski's in my office," he said, finding the file he was looking for. "I hope it's good news, because he's about to tank."

I hadn't told Shavelson or Barkowski anything about the Big Apple Ballroom Bash. I'd simply said I had news to share.

"Let's get this over with," Shavelson said. "It's his birthday, and he looks like a shot pair of shoes."

We left the bear behind and went into the office. Shavelson was right, the contractor looked like death warmed over, like he had aged ten years in the last five weeks. There were dark circles under his eyes, and his skin looked dull and lifeless. The corners of his mouth were turned down in a permanent frown. His shoulders sagged under a weight he could no longer carry. He held his hat in his hands like a lost little boy. I felt terrible for him.

"Turn the screen so we can all watch," I said to Shavelson, gesturing at the computer on his desk, "and put this in." I handed him a DVD we'd burned after the Bash.

Shavelson turned the screen so the three of us could see it and loaded the disc into the drive. He clicked around for a moment and then hit play.

I looked at Barkowski and said, "Happy Birthday, Ted."

The video began with Eleanor Greenburg and Carl Hayes at the end of their glorious waltz. The picture was clear and nicely lit. I could see the love in Eleanor's eyes as Carl danced her around the D-Cup stage.

"What the hell is this?" Shavelson said.

"A waltz," I said.

Barkowski sighed, heavy and cheerless, filled with longing for the days that he and Saint Denise had been so carefree, so light on their feet and in their hearts.

Eleanor and Carl left the stage to impassioned applause, and Stephanie Garner stepped into the spotlight with Ken Curry.

Barkowski sat up. Shavelson leaned toward the screen. They may or may not have recognized me, but they sure as shit knew it was Curry.

"What the hell?" Shavelson said.

"That's him," Barkowski said.

"Watch," I said.

Curry and I spoke softly—you couldn't hear us on the DVD —about following his lead, about moving like I was having the best time in my life, about him going to the bathroom to remove his brace, about him not liking people talking about him when he made a surprise appearance, about him being the king. Then he nodded at the judges, the music started, and we began to tango.

Curry moved with both precision and abandon, with strength and confidence and surprising grace, his broad, powerful back twisting and turning across the stage without pause or pain. The music swelled, and he led me deeper and deeper into the dance, literally lifting me—sweeping me—off my feet and gently returning me to the floor as if I were a grade-school girl instead of his *femme fatale* from Ellettsville, Indiana.

"Son of a bitch," Shavelson said. "You did it."

Barkowski made a sound that could have been "Oh my God," but there were no recognizable consonants.

The dance ended, the crowd applauded, Curry took a deep bow that would have been impossible if his back were in the brace, and we sat there in silence. Finally, in the smallest whisper, Barkowski said, "Again."

Shavelson clicked play, and we watched Curry tango his way into serious trouble once more. We watched it two more times after that, and then Shavelson ejected the DVD, held it up in the air, and said, "I'm going to shove this disc so far up Bajaria's ass that the court can watch it in his eyeballs."

"We've got Curry," I said to Shavelson, "but what about Dolores?"

"She'll say she knew nothing, pretend to be confused and surprised and maybe even disappointed," Shavelson said. "She'll act old and senile and get off without a slap on the wrist. Probably bake cookies for him to take to prison. Tell everyone he's going to summer camp."

"And the asshole doctor?" Barkowski said.

"He's in the quicksand," Shavelson said, "and going down fast. Medical malpractice, interstate fraud, there's a dozen crimes I can tie him to. He's losing his license at least, maybe doing five to ten on top of that. Some kind of huge fine to boot."

"What he needs is for someone to hit him in the face," Barkowski said, "break his fucking nose."

"Done and done," I said. "He walked right into it. Best punch of my life."

Barkowski looked at me, right into my eyes, laughed a little laugh that was just like a nod of approval, and said, "How much do I owe you?"

"Nine days," I said. "Eighteen hundred."

He pulled his checkbook from his pocket, lifted a pen off Shavelson's desk, and wrote me a check.

"Your father would be proud," Shavelson said to me. "You got your own style, but you're a chip off the block, a real PI."

"No, I'm not," I said. "I'm an actor."

"Here you go," Barkowski said, handing me the check.

I looked at it, blinked a few times, and then looked up. "That's ten times what you owe me, Ted. There's an extra zero."

"You earned it," Barkowski said, and he stood.

"But—" I said.

"You saved us, Kate. Me, Denise, the kids, you saved us. An extra zero's the least I can do." Then he nodded at Shavelson and walked out of the office into the rest of his life.

I stood when he was gone. "Well, I guess that's it. Thanks for everything, Shavelson. Don't call me, I'll call you." I started for the door.

"I got expenses, McCall. Phone, mail, cab, copies...client pays," Shavelson said.

Without turning around I said, "I'm not your client."

As I passed the Kodiak, he said loud enough for me to hear, "That's what Jimmy used to say."

70

LONG LIVE THE THEATER

IT WAS FOUR FIFTEEN BY THE TIME I GOT TO THE D-CUP. THERE was no evidence whatsoever of Thursday's Ballroom Bash. The theater was pure vampire.

The cast was dressing, applying makeup, and securing the plastic spouts that would soon spew copious amounts of fake blood across the stage. I put my fangs in place, did my face and hair, squeezed into my first costume—black, skin-tight pants, an even tighter, black, low-cut top, and a long, flowing, blood-red cape to match my blood-red pumps and my blood-red lips —imagined myself a soul-singing vampire with a Grand Central day job, positioned myself behind the curtain, took a deep breath as the lights came up, and sang my first lines, "My life has been one long blood song and dance, This is the story of my one true romance, Of deception, rejection, of darkness and light, I'll drink the blood of the City tonight."

Posey was at the piano, accompanied by a drummer, a guitarist, a bass player, and an electric keyboard guy whose digital instrument made sounds sampled from the New York Philharmonic. The band was orchestral, symphonic, and huge.

The D-Cup was packed. The Schmidt and Parker Players

had corralled family, invited friends, and filled the house. They had read the program and so knew that the first act was about romance and that the second act was about revenge, but no one, I suspect, fully understood or was in any way prepared for the bizarre and bloody theatrical experience that followed.

I moved across the stage, my red cape swirling and twirling around me, the band backing me, lifting me, sounding like my old *Procol Harum Live with the Edmonton Symphony Orchestra* album, my voice rising above the band, filling the loft with lyrics that were ridiculous, and I had two thoughts.

The first was this: If this play made any sense, we could take it to off-off Broadway at least. But the play was nonsense, meaning it was without sense, meaning it made no sense, and so as entertaining as it was, as filled with romance, intrigue, violence, song and dance, and gallons upon gallons of water-soluble, red fluid, it was also a head-scratcher—as in: What the hell just happened? Wait a minute, come again?—and so was destined to play out its run in off-off-off-off obscurity.

My second thought was: I don't care.

I was in heaven. I was fused with each dance, each song, each line of improbable dialogue, each outrageous plot twist, each bite of a New York neck. I was one with the play, with the audience, with the universe. The very act of singing and dancing and being Farina LeBleu was life to me, not merely the reason for living it, though that too, but my life itself, the breath of it, the heartbeat.

The particulars of it all—Chloe's Southern twang that sounded suspiciously Scottish, the New-York-City-Blood-Bank volume of ruby plasma that was spilled in one hundred and seven minutes, the scene where Farina and Mariah catch rays on a tar beach (forgetting that *even in the play* sunlight disinte-grates vampires) and talk about sex until Farina falls asleep while Mariah rubs suntan lotion on Farina's back and sings "A

Fang Affair"—were irrelevant. I was acting. I was living. I was alive.

In the end, "Railroad Street" brought the house down. The audience had a terrific time and adored the cast for pouring their hearts into the play. It was another ludicrous triumph for the Schmidt and Parker Players.

Long live the theater.

After the ovation—there was standing and cheering as the cast took their bows, many of them soaked, stained, and still leaking crimson liquid gelatin—the audience stayed to congratulate the players, who'd filtered into the theater from backstage.

A crowd of friends was waiting for me when I emerged. They surrounded me, told me how much fun they'd had, how wonderful I sang and danced, how convincing a heartsick, bloodthirsty, nightclub-crooning vampire I had been, and how fabulous I looked in my dominatrix get-up.

With one hand, I protested their rave reviews—enough, enough, thank you, enough. With the other, I egged them on— more, please, more and more and more. I glowed in their adulation. It was the very same glow I'd had when Jimmy told me how proud he was at the end of *Bye Bye Birdie* in seventh grade. That part of the theater never changes. And never gets old.

When my friends dispersed, I saw Matthew and Nettling Nina sitting in the second row, Nina on the aisle, in case, I assumed, she got nauseous and had to make a quick getaway. My son had made it clear that a vampiric display of sex and violence posing as art would be like sticking hot needles in her eyes, yet he had dragged her here to support me anyway. What a good kid he was. I sat in the first row, facing them.

"Congratulations, Mom. That was really something. I'm not sure what, but it was fun, at least for me. And you were great."

"Thank you, Matthew," I said. "What did you think, Nina?"

"If you could have seen what I saw," she said, smiling. "Don't get me going."

"Don't worry," I said, smiling back. "I'm not listening."

We drilled each other with our eyes, and Matthew said, "Give me a minute, baby. I'll be right there." He gently nudged her out of her seat and toward the elevator.

As she stood and walked away, she said in her snarkiest, most academic voice, "It was theater reinvented. Somewhere there are Greeks rolling over in their graves."

"Probably in Greece," I said, matching her snark for snark.

Then she was out of earshot. I turned to Matthew and said, "Did you really like it?"

"Yes, Mom, it was fun. But it was also hard to follow, and there were oceans of blood. I mean really a lot. I'm talking about crazy blood."

"It was hot up there, and I was singing and dancing and killing half the neighborhood. I got very thirsty."

We both laughed, and then I shrugged and said, "It's off-off-off-off Broadway. We make up for our shortcomings by bleeding profusely."

"I know. Here," he said, handing me a business card. "This is my real estate broker friend who needs an office manager. He still wants you to call him."

"Matthew—"

"You're not going to walk dogs for the rest of your life, and you're not going to make any money doing this, as extraordinarily talented as you are, I mean," he said.

"Nicely put, counselor," I said.

"Thank you. And we talked about your private investigator days being over, now that you're out of jail and cleared of murder, you remember?"

"I remember."

"So you'll call him?"

I looked at the card. Why the heck not? Office managing

had to be better than dog walking. Maybe I would get my license and broker a few deals myself. Maybe it was time for a change. Logan was right. I could easily have been in jail or dead or both (or both?) as a PI. Maybe Matthew was right too. Maybe everybody was right, and I was wrong. It wouldn't be the first time. "Yes, okay, I'll call him," I said.

He nodded and smiled and said, "Great. Okay, then, I should go." He stood and started toward the elevator where Exasperating Nina was waiting. I went with him.

"It's been five weeks," he said as we crossed the theater.

"To the day," I said.

"It's hard for me to remember his voice. I wish I had recorded him saying, I don't care, anything, reading the phone book. Just the sound of his voice is all I want. I can't believe I'll never hear it again. I'll be in my office, lost in a case, and I'll think that thought, and I'll be wrecked for an hour."

"Only an hour?" I said, and we both smiled sadly.

"How do you keep going," he said, "when all you want to do is stop the world and get off?"

"I close my eyes and listen carefully, and I hear him telling me to quit crying and take care of business. Jimmy wouldn't want us to stop the world and get off. He'd want us to keep fighting. I want to make him proud. That's what keeps me going."

We arrived at the elevator. Aggravating Nina was inside with some other people I didn't know. One of them, an older gentleman, said to me, "I enjoyed the play. I just wish I knew what it was about."

"Me too," I said.

Matthew got on the elevator, turned to me as the door slid shut, and said, "No more investigating anything ever. That's in the past. Your future is around the corner. A door is going to open and all you have to do is walk through it."

The elevator left the D-Cup, and I thought, *Future, here I come.*

71

THREE HUNDRED DOLLARS A DAY
PLUS EXPENSES

M‌Y FUTURE HAD TO WAIT UNTIL S‌ATURDAY MORNING BECAUSE Chloe, Roger, me, and half a dozen other Schmidt and Parker Players, all of whom I had murdered on stage a few hours earlier and all of whom had danced at the Bash the night before that, went out for cheap Mexican food and Tecate in cans, ended up drinking and laughing until five fifteen in the morning, and then, as the sun came up, went for breakfast at the Hercules Diner (of all places). I didn't get back to the House of Emotional Tics until eight thirty. Al and Fu were in the lobby when I arrived.

Al had just returned from a night of dipping donuts in hot oil and then covering them with powdered sugar. He was dusted white from head to toe, giving his deep-set, red, red eyes a voodoo-zombie glow. Fu was using a power tool on my door. Al was hassling him about the busted toilet. He directed his unhappiness at me as I entered.

"Look who finally blew in with the wind," Al said. "In T-minus ten minutes, I'm moving fifteen thousand Spaldeens to a sporting-goods guy in Thailand, if I can get them from this idiot in England for five hundred file cabinets that I'm getting from a friend in Philadelphia in exchange for a truckload of snow shovels I'm shipping from Sheboygan. At the end of that rainbow is a pot of gold for yours truly, but before I can get to it, I have to take a leak, which I'll now be taking out the window because this pig-headed Chinese handyman won't fix my freaking flusher. As I piss on passersby, try to imagine the sheer size of the lawsuit that's going to hit Dai Ying where it hurts the most."

"Fu you," Fu said.

"Fu you too," Al said.

"Good morning, Al," I said. "Yes, the show went great. Thanks for asking. Sell-out crowd. Standing ovation. What's happening here?"

"Towing cars to the pound, selling weed to the world, another day in paradise," Charlie said, coming down the stairs in his official, tow-truck uniform—blue work pants, blue work shirt, heavy black shoes, and a here-I-am-don't-run-me-over, orange safety vest (as if the vest would magically deter someone from intentionally running over a NYC parking employee towing cars to auto jail). He looked stoned, although he always did.

"Forget what's happening here," LaTanya said, rounding the corner from the basement stairwell, carrying a plastic basket of folded laundry. "Where you at with the case?"

"Harriman's going to jail—"

"No shit, Sherlock," LaTanya said, stopping in front of me. She wore an Incredible Hulk T-shirt, baggy, green sweatpants, and her ridiculous bunny-rabbit slippers—meant to look like real rabbits on her feet—that she always wore when she did her laundry. "When it comes to men, McCall, you got to listen to LaTanya."

"Next time," I said as she started for the stairs, passing Charlie, who went to his mailbox to grab the newspaper. I wondered if taking relationship advice from a woman who had once been married for three hours was a good idea, but I let it go and said, "And Russell left the country, so they didn't arrest her yet."

"What about Jimmy's killer?" LaTanya said. "Po-lice get him?"

"No," I said. "Logan says he's a ghost in the City somewhere. Invisible until he kills someone else. They're not looking for him. They don't know where to look."

"And you're good with that?" Al said with one part derision and one part disgust.

"What does that mean?" I said.

"It means you're a PI, and you should jack this fucker," Charlie said, folding the paper under his arm and heading for the door.

"I'm an actor," I said. "And soon I'm going to be a commercial real estate office manager."

"Since when?" Al said.

"Since my son gave me the phone number of a broker who wants me to manage his office," I said.

"Real estate?" LaTanya said, starting up the stairs. "You lost your mind?"

"What kind of job is that for a PI?" Charlie said.

"I'm not a PI," I said.

"If Jimmy's killer still out there," LaTanya said, disappearing around the corner on the second-floor landing, "you should be."

"Don't you want to burn that bastard?" Charlie said. "We do." Then he was out the door.

"We?" I said out loud to no one.

"You dragged us into it for nothing," Al said. "That's so weak, McCall. Weak as water." He walked across the lobby and up the stairs to his broken toilet and Gatorade bottles of urine.

I watched him go, turned to Fu, and realized what he was

doing with the power tool—screwing the brass plate, the one I inherited from Jimmy, the one that read: *McCall & Company, Private Investigations*, to my door.

"What are you doing?" I said, unlocking my door.

"What you doing?" Fu said.

I was about to say "Facing my future" when the front door opened, and Edie and Ray walked in with a thirty-year-old, stunningly beautiful, young woman.

"There you are," Edie said to me. "Raymond and I were coming back from the market, and this young woman pulled up in front of the building looking for you. We brought her in with us. What was your name again, sweetheart?"

"Brooke Barrington," the woman said.

"She's driving a four-hundred-thousand-dollar Rolls Royce Phantom. Anyhow, her chauffeur is," Ray said.

He was carrying a canvas grocery bag filled with food from the Korean market around the corner. He was wearing a sky-blue cowboy shirt with frills on the front and back, red-and-green-striped Bermuda shorts, and orange Crocs with black knee socks. He had a purple ski hat on his head. The hat had a bright-yellow pompom on top. What in the world he was thinking when he put his clothes on was one question that always came to mind with Ray. Another was: Where are the men with white suits and big butterfly nets? Edie was wearing what looked like a wedding gown. These were their outfits for an early-morning jaunt to the market. To her credit, Ms. Barrington kept a straight face.

"It's not the name of the car, Raymond." Edie said as they started up the stairs. "It's what's under the hood that counts."

"I got something under the hood that counts, I'll tell you what," Ray said, following her to the second floor.

Edie said something back to him, but they were at the top of the stairs, and I couldn't hear it, thank God.

"You're Kate McCall?" Brooke said to me.

"Yes," I said.

"Shavelson said I should speak to you about my case."

"Excuse me?"

"Mel Shavelson said I should talk to you. Someone has stolen my identity."

"You're kidding?"

"She's pretending to be me all over the city."

"I mean you're kidding that Shavelson told you to talk to me."

"Excuse me?"

She was dressed casually at first glance. A closer look, however, redefined the meaning of casually dressed: four-thousand-dollar APO jeans, with solid silver rivets and silk-lined pockets, a two-thousand-dollar Giorgio Armani plain-black cashmere T-shirt, silver Manolo Blahnik flats for a thousand bucks, a fifteen-thousand-dollar diamond tennis bracelet on her right wrist, and a forty-five-thousand-dollar Breitling eighteen karat rose gold diamond watch on her left wrist. Her perfectly beautiful face was worth more than all of it combined —soft features, smooth skin, full lips, jade-green eyes, long, luminous black hair. She was young, she was polished, she was gorgeous, she was rich, and she was in the lobby of the House of Emotional Tics looking for a PI, looking for me.

I glanced at the brass plate and then at Fu. He held my eyes for a second and somehow, in his mystical mind, knew exactly what I was thinking and opened my door. I simply had to walk through it to face my future.

I turned to Brooke Barrington and said, "Three hundred dollars a day plus expenses."

"That's fine," Brooke said. "Whatever it takes to find out who's doing this to me, that's what I want you to do."

"Come into my office," I said, "and we'll get the ball rolling."

I moved aside, and she walked into my apartment.

I looked at Fu, he looked at me, and I followed Brooke in and shut the door. It turned out I *was* a PI.

But I was also an actor.

THANK YOU

I hope you had as much fun reading *Workman's Complication* as I had writing it because I had a blast. If you did, it would be fabulous if you could help other mystery lovers find the book by leaving a review and sharing the laughs.

Honest reviews of my books help introduce them to new readers. I would be deeply grateful if you could find a few minutes to post a positive review about *Workman's Complication* or any of the Kate McCall Crime Capers. It only takes a minute to leave an upbeat word or two. Thanks again.

KEEP THE LAUGHS COMING!

Get Swollen Identity, the Second Kate McCall Crime Caper, and keep the laughs coming!

Kate McCall hopes she can balance her passion and her PI practice. Struggling to keep both on stage, the way-off-Broadway performer finds herself in the deep end of a billionaire's allegedly stolen identity. But her role as a sleuth takes center stage when a crime scene replicates her father's unsolved murder. Can Kate shine a spotlight on the killer before she loses her part for good?

HOLD ON TO YOUR HAT!

Get Emboozlement, the third Kate McCall Crime Caper, and hold on to your hat!

Kate McCall dazzles audiences on stage by night but by day she searches for her father's killer. She seems to gain ground until the man who pulled the trigger sends texts that prove he's one step ahead. While investigating the murderous messages, she takes on an embezzlement case from a handsome sports bar owner who might just be her top suspect. If she can't close both cases, Kate's next intermission could be permanent. Will Kate's latest song and dance deliver justice or a fatal review?

FASTEN YOUR SEAT BELT!

Get Gottiguard, the Fourth and Final Kate McCall Crime Caper, and fasten your seat belt!

Kate McCall is determined to make sure it's curtains for her father's killer. But her first priority is playing bodyguard to the bad-boy standup comic who hired her to protect him while he tries to prove he's innocent of murder. That is until the real culprit takes a shot at her client just as her dad's assassin sends her a clue to his next victim. Will Kate have the last laugh and nail two murderers, or is she about to suffer a fatal punchline?

ALSO BY RICH LEDER

ROMANTIC SHADES OF FUNNY

Juggler, Porn Star, Monkey Wrench

DARKER SHADES OF FUNNY

Let There Be Linda

Cooking for Cannibals

Extraterrestrial Noir

KATE MCCALL CRIME CAPERS

Workman's Complication

Swollen Identity

Emboozlement

Gottiguard

ACKNOWLEDGMENTS

Great thanks to the awesome Lulu and our children, David, Eric, and Kate, who have withstood the high and low tides of life with a writer and given me nothing in return but love and joy and the courage to press on.

For my dad, Bob, who told the best stories ever. And for my mom, Barbara, whose lifelong love affair with reading and writing inspires me to this day.

ABOUT THE AUTHOR

Rich Leder's screen credits include 19 television films for CBS, Lifetime, and Hallmark and feature films for Lionsgate Entertainment, Paramount Pictures, Tri-Star Pictures, and Left Bank Films. He has published eight novels through Laugh Riot Press.

He has been the lead singer in a Detroit rock band, a restaurateur, a Little League coach, an indie film director, a literacy tutor, a magazine editor, a screenwriting coach, a commercial real estate agent, a wedding guru, and a visiting artist for the University of North Carolina Film Studies Department, among other things, all of which, it turns out, was grist for the mill.

Contact Rich through his website: www.richleder.com

www.ingramcontent.com/pod-product-compliance
Lightning Source LLC
Chambersburg PA
CBHW020643120726

47906CB00001B/93